Feels Like Destiny

KIMBERLY R. VARGAS

To Jaime,
Thank you for reminding me to rise anyway.

MORE STORIES BY KIMBERLY R. VARGAS

You'll want to read these next:

The Dance

Fallin' for the Fame

For exclusive content and updates, visit:

www.kimberlyrvargas.com

AUTHOR'S NOTE

Thanks so much for choosing to read *Feels Like Destiny*. This story has been in my heart for quite some time and bringing her to life was not easy. But finally, she's here. And I couldn't be prouder.

I didn't write *Feels Like Destiny* because I wanted to write about Broadway. I wrote it because I've known what it feels like to look like I'm *almost* there.

Almost chosen. Almost ready. Almost enough.

Yana walks into rooms where she technically qualifies but still feels like she's trespassing. She looks the part. She sounds the part. She can do the work. And yet there's this quiet voice asking, *Do you really belong here?*

That voice can be loud.

This story is for the woman who keeps showing up anyway. For the one who practices in private. For the one who works when no one's watching. Who wonders if her big moment will ever arrive and keeps preparing as if it will.

Yana's journey isn't about pretending to be someone else. It's about realizing she never had to. And maybe that's the part that matters most.

Thank you for spending time with her. I hope something in these pages reminds you that destiny doesn't always announce itself with applause. Sometimes it whispers, *Keep going.* 🖤

With all my heart,
Kimberly R. Vargas

CONTENT NOTE

Feels Like Destiny explores ambition, image, identity, and high-pressure performance environments. While this is a romance with no on-page sex, it contains emotionally intense themes and moments of danger.

This novel includes references to:
- Housing insecurity
- Attempted physical assault / homicide
- Paralysis / PTSD responses
- Emotional abuse / manipulation
- Power imbalance in professional settings
- Mention of drug abuse
- Grief

Reader discretion is advised.

1

My lifelong dream has become a damn nightmare.

Sweat, perfume, and desperation mix in the air, thick enough to chew, as I lean on the ballet barre, unwrapping a strawberry Pop-Tart. The piano plays a peppy version of Aretha Franklin's "I Say a Little Prayer," extras tapping and twirling at the center of the rehearsal studio.

"This is it," I told my cousin Laura ten months ago, unloading from her SUV at the airport. *"First, regional theater, then Broadway!"*

Bryant told me this was the big one. I'm still waiting for it to feel like a win.

Gnawing on my snack, I gaze out the floor-to-ceiling windows at the bustling Broadway street below. Cabs lean on their horns while tourists clog the sidewalk. Steam curls up from a manhole. Even the sky looks tired, stuck between gray and grayer.

I used to think New York would feel electric. Turns out, it's just loud.

I glance across the room and spot Adrien—Puerto Rican dancer, honey-bronze skin, dark curls that probably cost more in product than my rent—propped against a speaker on the opposite end of the studio, eyelids droopy. Looking like he's posing for a "Hot Dancers of Broadway" calendar.

We clock each other, and he gives me that lazy, half-awake

smirk that says, *We both know you're bored enough to ruin your life right now.*

Clearly, a flirt like me. But harmless. Like a shot of tequila before you text somebody you shouldn't.

Unfortunately for him, I'm taken.

I return my attention to the hot dog cart and delivery bike drivers outside, being sure to toss him a grin as I do.

Back in the day, flirting my way through rehearsals was my favorite pastime. Honey, cast crushes were simply part of the package: sweat, show tunes, and somebody else's boyfriend. But after Bryant, I decided to calm down.

We were at a recital for Maddie—Laura's daughter—when we met. He called me magnetic, and I believed him. Said if I made it to New York, he'd make sure every door opened. So I packed my bags and didn't look back.

But the only thing he's opened so far is his mouth to tell me I need to "work harder" and "act like" I belong here.

Please. I'm great. They just need to catch up.

Across the street, a woman in a bright red coat stops to take a selfie in front of a billboard for *The Lion King*. The same one I auditioned for three times and never booked.

I gaze at the red, white, and blue sprinkles on my Pop-Tart, remembering how independent I felt hopping on the plane to New York, sure that I'd finally got my big break.

Guess the punchline's on me.

"Ooh, Pop-Tarts," a petite blonde coos, resting against the barre beside me. "You're so lucky. There's no way I could eat that and get away with it."

I shrug. "Genetics."

It's true. I got my mama's thin frame, no matter how reckless I get with sugar, but the wild curls and the mouth? That's all my daddy. The two of us used to turn every dinner into open mic night while Mama and my brother, FJ—the more serious of us four—tried hard not to laugh. They always caved.

Back home, it was easy to crack jokes. Easy to be light. In this city, I gotta go looking for it.

Meanwhile, Miss Sunshine is gaping at me like I've sprouted antlers. "Oh. My. Gosh. Has anyone ever told you you look just like Alexia Hyrd?"

"Sure," I say.

A dark-skinned woman about as tall as a basketball player joins us, elbowing the blonde at my side. "Girl, can you feel the tension today?"

"Right?" the blonde whispers back. "I'm just waiting for this rehearsal to turn into an episode of *The Apprentice*. 'You're fired! You're fired!'" The two giggle at the thick Queens accent she puts on.

"What are y'all talking about?" I ask, following their line of sight. They're focused on the cast members gathered around the piano.

"The MD," says the tall one, nodding toward the music director.

The man behind the piano looks like he hasn't smiled since the Clinton era, small-framed glasses low, his hickory brown bald head glistening like he and a bottle of baby oil had a very productive morning. He's leaning toward one of the singers now, expression grave and patient, giving what appears to be a thorough TED Talk on how not to suck.

"Ten bucks says she walks out crying," says the blonde. She and the basketball player shake on it.

"Oh my god," the tall one says, blinking at me. "You look just like Alexia Hyrd."

"That's what I said," the little one chirps. "Do you follow her on social media? She hasn't posted in like, four days."

But I'm still keyed in on the MD.

"Y'all really think Mr. NPR over there is that cutthroat?" In his simple black sweater and jeans, the man doesn't seem too threatening.

"Please." The tall one sucks her teeth. "Everybody in this

room knows when Langston Washington shows up, heads are gonna roll."

Our director made some big announcement when the guy entered the room, but I was honestly too bored to care. Mr. Washington returns to playing the piano and the castmates start belting it out again, shoulders back, chins high, all of them standing a little taller.

"The most prolific young MD on Broadway," the blonde adds. "Plays piano, guitar, trumpet, *and* flute. Hollywood royalty. Went to Juilliard."

I roll my eyes. Somebody's got a fan club.

"Honey, you do so much as look at him sideways and you may as well kiss your entire career goodbye," the tall one concludes.

I don't know. He gives off the vibe of someone who alphabetizes his sock drawer to me.

He shakes his head with a frown and tells the group to take it from the top.

I mean, I suppose he's cute in that "I-grade-papers-for-fun" kinda way. But if boring had a ringtone, it'd probably be his voice saying "again."

"I heard he once got a girl fired from *The Wiz* for adding too much vibrato whenever she dropped an octave," says Blondie, twisting a golden strand around her finger. "Only thirty-five, but the man holds the future of every Broadway actor in his hands."

I scoff. "He's not gonna hold mine."

The two women stare at me as if I just declared my plan to scale the Eiffel Tower, and I snort.

"Somebody oughtta give Mr. Washington a wedgie. Then maybe they can loosen that giant stick up his butt!"

I'm returning to my snack when I notice every eye in the room on me. Somewhere along the way, the music stopped, and everyone seems to have heard my little comment, including the music director himself. I rub my temples.

Why does this crap always happen to me?

The MD stares at me a beat too long. For a split second, his composure slips, something raw flashing there before he pulls it back into place.

"As I said," Mr. Washington says, being sure to project his voice. "We're going to give this number a break and shift focus to 'Respect.' Backup trio for 'Respect,' let's go."

I toss my gossiping companions a crooked smirk. "That's me."

"Good luck," says Goldilocks.

The Amazon model shakes her head. "You're gonna need it, honey."

With a huff, I shuffle over to the piano. Certain Adrien's watching, I plaster on my most gorgeous smile. Mr. Washington runs a hand down his scalp.

"The irony," he mutters.

A freckled redhead and a short Latina with blunt bangs slide in beside me at the piano. They're way more interested in clocking who's whispering with who than looking up at the MD.

Mr. Washington's gaze is firm on the musical score. "Names, please."

"Ariana."

"Winter."

"And I'm Jayana Gardner." I toss Adrien a wink to ensure he remembers, but Mr. Washington frowns.

"Ja-Whatta?"

"Just... Yana's fine."

Mr. Washington scratches his nose, peering at me over his glasses. "Do you plan to hold on to your pastry the entire rehearsal, Mizz Yah-Nah?"

"Oh. Of course not." I scarf down what's left and shove the wrapper in my pocket. One of the girls passes along a copy of the score as I swallow and nod to the director. But he focuses on his fancy Omega watch.

"We've got two weeks till previews, ladies. Let's make it count." Placing his fingers on the keys, he begins to play.

I'll give it to him. The man's got hands. He doesn't just play the piano, he handles it. Coaxes it. Like he already knows what it's gonna give before it does. Every note slides out smooth and sure, like the instrument's been waiting on him specifically. Guess that Juilliard tuition didn't go to waste.

I get the girls to join me in bobbing our shoulders to the cadence as we open with the usual shoops. But the MD abruptly stops.

"No. No." He flicks a hand in the air as if a fly is buzzing round his head. "This is vocal practice, not choreography. Focus on your breathing, not your sass. Let's start again."

He returns to tickling the keys as I smirk at the other girls.

"*Sass*," I whisper.

All of us bite back laughter. The man's jaw hardens like steel as he continues to play.

Somebody hand this guy a margarita and a therapist. Stat!

Frankly, I don't know what everyone's so terrified of. The guy's as intimidating as a rubber knife. Probably just needs to get laid.

It isn't until we get to repeating *re-re-re-respect* that he starts barking.

"Stay on key, please."

"Too sharp, Mizz Yah-Nah."

"Now you're too flat."

"Slow down, Mizz Yah-Nah. This isn't a race!"

All the while, Adrien is over there, chuckling at my pain.

I should've believed the other ladies when they said this director would be a splinter in my ass. He's only picking on me 'cause I clowned him in front of everybody. But what can I say? I call 'em like I see 'em.

The man abruptly stops again. "Mizz Yah-Nah."

"Yes, Mizz-ter Washington?"

People choke back chuckles at my imitation of his snooty voice with just a hint of British flair. He looks at me like I just cost him money.

I didn't mean to mock him. He just makes it so... easy.

But his glare slices clean through me.

"Mizz Yah-Nah. This is a serious Broadway production with dozens of investors' dollars on the line. Not some comedy gig. But if you're looking to work elsewhere, the Apollo is holding auditions next month."

Some of my cast members groan, others cover their mouths to keep from laughing.

The stare-down he's giving is all I need to understand the phrase, *You'll never work in this town again.*

I toss back my curls, standing up straight. "I'm sorry, sir. Won't happen again."

Removing his glasses, he rubs at his eyes, a long exhale wheezing from his nose. "Now, as I was saying, Mizz Yah-Nah, this is a backup role." He replaces his glasses, pinning me with a tired glare. "Do you understand the concept of backup?"

I pause. I thought I did.

"Tone it down. Pack it in. Got it?"

Alright, Director. Message received, loud and disrespectful.

The studio's so quiet, you could hear an ant fart.

I nod, and we start again.

But I ain't come all the way out here to be no damn background hum. I'm supposed to be the main event. And if anybody in this room knew good talent when they saw it, they'd recognize that.

It's an insult, really. So I gotta let loose when I can. 'Cause if I don't, I just might cry. And crying in full glam just feels wasteful.

It isn't long before he's back at it.

"You sound like you're still chewing... From the diaphragm, Mizz Yah-Nah. No one wants to hear your best impression of SpongeBob."

I half expect him to creak when he turns. *Someone please WD-40 this man's soul.*

Brooklyn Ali—the star of our production who'll be playing Aretha—softly sings the lead as she strolls by in her "Queen of

Soul" tee and box braids. I slip her a high-five. You never know when a friendly nod could open doors.

But out of the corner of my eye, the cute little thing goes down with a clatter.

Everyone gasps. The music halts. Brooklyn's sprawled across the wooden floor in a crumpled mess.

The stage director, Felipe, rushes to her side. "Brooklyn! Are you alright?"

Brooklyn groans as she attempts to sit up. "Ah... I just... slipped." She sucks a sharp breath through her teeth. "My arm. Oh! That hurts like a mother!"

Felipe turns to an assistant. "Get stage management."

The assistant rushes off as everyone looks on at poor Brooklyn's condition. I guess her understudy's about to get her big break. But Felipe is fixing the room with a hard stare.

"We're only two weeks away from previews! How did this happen?"

Everyone's silent as another stagehand picks a silver wrapper up off the floor near Brooklyn's feet.

Wait.

It couldn't be. 'Cause I slipped it in my pocket.

Except I forgot. My dance skirt doesn't have any pockets.

My lips press together as Mr. Washington's attention fixes on me. The room goes heavy. Quiet. Like the air itself is holding its breath.

This is it. This is all he needs to shut me down.

Instead, he scratches his head, sighs like I'm the migraine he didn't ask for... and looks away.

Relief hits fast.

Unfortunately for me, everyone else is staring. Pointing. Like they've already solved the mystery.

2

I can't believe they fired me. They seriously fired me, over a Pop-Tart wrapper. As soon as I grab a sandwich, I'm calling my union rep. I won't let them get away with this.

The hall outside my apartment smells like somebody's deep-fried disappointment. Old takeout, mop water, and stale perfume. Random bags of trash lining the wall.

"Ugh. I gotta move," I mutter, unlocking the door.

I moved in with Gracie and Evelyn when I first arrived in New York last year. I never thought I'd be sharing a two-bedroom walk-up in Hell's Kitchen at thirty, but you can't beat the location. And New York ain't cheap. Besides, Bryant insisted it was a smart move.

Gracie's chilling on the sofa, likely scrolling through a copy of *Backstage* magazine on her tablet as I enter, her signature wide-brimmed fedora on her head like she's about to head out. But I know she's not. Homegirl's always selfie-ready. Can't go thirty minutes without snapping one for the 'Gram. She eyes me with little interest as I shut the door.

"You're back early."

"Yeah, there was a... situation," I say, scratching my head. Plopping my tote by the door, I head for the kitchen, but Evelyn appears in the entryway.

"Yana, glad to see you're back so soon." Evelyn leans against the door frame, blocking my way with her solid build and that no-nonsense posture you only see in mall cops and middle managers. "We need to talk."

I take a step back as Evelyn strolls into the living room and sinks into the couch, her thick legs crossed at the ankles. Gracie adjusts her hat like she's in a damn photoshoot.

Suddenly, it's like I'm standing before a panel of judges at an audition.

"Okay. What's up?"

Sliding her tablet on the coffee table, Gracie sits back, arms crossing to mirror Evelyn.

Gracie's been acting since before she could spell it, all community theater and toothpaste commercials. But lately she moves like she's fresh off a Tony win. We both went out for the same part—*Ella: A Neo-Soul Musical.* She got the callback. I didn't. She landed understudy, and now the lead's out sick. Ever since her mama crowned her the next Meryl, she's been chasing the spotlight. And she'd be just the type to shove someone off a ladder to get it.

"You haven't paid the rent," she says.

My gaze shifts between them. "Sure, I did. Just a few weeks ago."

"That was for last month," says Evelyn, tossing her lengthy hair behind her shoulders. "You haven't paid this month."

"And this is the third time you've missed," Gracie adds with a frigid smile.

She's loving this.

"Listen," I say, "things have been tight. I've had a couple gigs here and there, but I'm not exactly rolling in dough this minute."

"Yet you seem to have no trouble grabbing food on the street every day," says Evelyn.

"And aren't those boots new?" Gracie adds.

All of us examine the suede knee-high boots I'm sporting.

"It's winter." I shrug.

Evelyn points toward the door. "Your things are in the hall."

Wait, they're kicking me out?

I peer into my tiny bedroom, and my mouth falls open. It's cleared of everything but the bed frame and mattress. "Those garbage bags I passed on the way in? I figured that was nothing but trash."

"It is." Gracie stands and saunters toward her and Evelyn's room. "Good luck, Yana."

"Bitch..." I've got a mind to call her a few more colorful names, but she shuts the bedroom door before I can.

I can't believe this.

Evelyn sits silent, watching me like some sort of security guard, as if I've been dismissed.

I suck my teeth and turn to go. "Y'all's body wash stinks anyway. Bye."

I'm sure to slam the door behind me as I leave.

Everything I own has been stuffed into three dark garbage bags. No playbills. No posters. Not a single trophy. Not that I ever had one.

The plastic pulls thin when I lift it, the handles biting into my palm. For a second, I picture it splitting open right here on the floor, my whole life spilling out for strangers to step over.

It's fine. We're fine.

This city sucks. But I know one person who cares.

I glance at my phone. Bryant should be home soon. I grab my things and head for the subway.

———

"Yana." Bryant's handsome cocoa-brown face looks pleasantly surprised to see me, that easy, practiced smile already in place. But I'm too worn out to smother his cheeks with kisses right now.

I stomp inside his penthouse, dropping my bags, and kicking off my boots. The warmth of his Persian wool carpet caresses my toes.

Bryant's lived on the Upper West Side for two years now.

Just far enough from the noise to call it peace, but close enough to brag he's still "in the scene." His penthouse sits high above the street, catching the river light. Floor-to-ceiling windows, marble counters, one of those showers with more buttons than a spaceship. Everything in his place looks intentional—expensive without trying too hard. I used to come over and just spin in circles, pretending I was auditioning for a life upgrade.

I told him I was down with living together. I could handle racing across town for gigs—wasn't like I'd never done it. But he insisted I stay closer to Broadway if I wanted to get to rehearsals on time. Which is how I ended up sharing a fridge with a demon.

"Ugh! Honey, today has been trash. This stupid MD—who could *not* get my name right—was giving me hell, and Brooklyn walked by, and—it wasn't my fault she didn't watch where she was going! But Felipe was pissed and didn't even hear me out. And then Evelyn—and that *Gracie!*" I growl in frustration as I head over to the open-space kitchen. "If I just had *five minutes* with homegirl in a dark alley— It smells good in here. What you cooking?"

"Carbonara," he says, slowly shutting the door.

"Mmm. Sounds good to me!" It's a little early for dinner, but I could eat. I grab the corkscrew and a bottle of red wine from the counter, then pop it open. Pour myself a generous serving in the nearest wine glass.

Bryant's staring at my garbage bags in the corner as I chug. "What's all this?"

I toss back what's left of my drink and pour another glass with a pant. "My stuff."

Bryant turns to me, brows drawn tight. "Stuff?"

"Yep. That's everything. Can you believe Gracie and Evelyn had the *nerve* to evict me? I mean, who do they think they are? I bet you Evelyn just wanted a room of her own. That girl's feet are so big she could play center for the Knicks. She probably drooped them off the top bunk and hit Gracie in the face all the time."

"Wait. Wait." Bryant raises a hand. "You got evicted?"

"It's messed up, right?"

He stares at me. "Why?"

"Well, they gave me some nonsense about not keeping up with the rent. But I told them, I just paid last month. And even though I'm a little behind this month, it doesn't mean I won't pay them next month. I'm not a bum!"

Bryant steeples his palms together and presses them to his lips. "Yana... That's not how rent works. It's not—"

"I mean, I know! But—they weren't hearing me out!"

He drags his palm down his face and checks his watch. "So, what are you gonna do now?"

I know that look. He's already doing the math.

He doesn't like to rush things. Says timing matters. But if I lean in, keep it soft, remind him what we have, maybe he'll meet me halfway.

Besides, I wanna be closer to the one who believes in me more than anyone else.

"I mean... I *could* go to a motel." I cross the living room with a wicked smirk, wrap my arms around his neck with the bat of my lashes. "But then again, I *do* know a very handsome casting director I've been seeing for a year."

"Has it been that long?"

"Almost. And he is *so* sweet that I just know he'd be willing to help me out." I press a kiss to his jaw, but he frowns.

"You mean like, money?"

I scoff, shoving his shoulder. "I mean, a warm bed, silly." Slipping my arms back around his shoulders, I coo, "And perhaps a warm body too."

But he steps back. "Look, Yana... This whole thing with us... It's not..."

He runs a hand over his mouth like he's erasing a sentence before it finishes forming.

And just like that, I know exactly what he's about to say.

I've seen this posture before. The soft preface. The careful tone. The way men stretch out bad news like they're doing you a favor.

"I—I mean, it's been cool. But I thought we were just having fun, and..."

Fun?

That's when I see it. The stammering. The distance. The way he won't quite look at me. Frowns like this was always the deal. As if my choice to move to New York was as simple as cashing in a coupon at Applebee's.

My heart cracks in two, and my vision goes red. I bob my head, backing away.

"Guess I'm just everybody's problem today."

Bryant rolls his eyes as I slip my boots back on. "Come on, Yana. You had to know this was nothing serious. You haven't even met my parents."

"Your parents live in Minnesota!"

"And I've gone to visit them twice this past year. Don't you think I would've asked you along? You've never even spoken to my mom on FaceTime."

"You left the room whenever she called. I figured she was camera-shy!" I storm back over to the kitchen counter and snatch a fresh-baked roll off the cookie sheet. "I can't believe this is happening to me. Again." I snag the roll with my teeth as I grab my bags, eyes burning.

But a petite woman's waiting in the hall when I open the door, a cheese platter in her hand. She's gorgeous. With glossy hair, pearl earrings, and a fancy wool coat.

The perfect fit for Bryant. A much better fit.

The woman's gaze only flits over my shoulder once before I put two and two together. I whip my head around and glare at Bryant as he sighs.

"Yana, this is Cassidy. My new... friend."

And that's when it hits me. The soft jazz playing. The dining table set for two. Bryant's wearing one of my favorite sweaters.

The pasta was always meant to be for more than one. But that didn't include me.

"Wow," I say.

Chick stands there with her little platter, all innocence.

Of course this is how today ends. I almost laugh. Because if I don't, something uglier might crawl out.

My shoulders square on instinct.

I flip Little Miss Cassidy's tray as I go.

3

Ms. Doyle's soft, motherly face tightens on the screen.
"Well," she says after a beat, voice gentle but resolved, "I suppose we always knew this day would come. Though I doubt Hayden will be nearly as heartbroken as I am."

I manage a nod, adjusting my laptop on the café table so she can't see my hands curl. "Of course. He's moving on to bigger things."

She exhales, relieved and sad all at once. "You've been wonderful for him, Yana. Truly. But with what's coming up... we're going to need to focus on the show."

Focus. Busy. Temporary. All the same word.

"I'll get him," she says, already standing.

The screen goes blank, and I drum my fingers against my knees, scanning the café. One of those half-empty Midtown spots with hokey music and outlets that barely work. Not where I imagined getting cut loose, but at least the coffee's cheap and the Wi-Fi's free.

Thanks to everyone turning on me, I've been living out of a motel for a week, counting dollars like they might magically multiply. Anything I couldn't carry on my back I sold or tossed. Turns out dreams don't have great resale value.

Coaching gigs were supposed to keep me afloat, but between rehearsals and last-minute auditions, I couldn't keep enough clients to make it worth the hustle. Hayden's the only student I've got left. And now...

Ms. Doyle pops back on-screen with Hayden tucked beside her.

"Yana!" His round, brown face fills the frame, smiling so wide it could light up Times Square. He waves like we're at a concert instead of on a Zoom call. Down syndrome's never slowed him down for a second.

"Hayden! What's up, baby?"

"I got the part!" he blurts. "I'm gonna be on *Home Room!*"

My eyes flick to Ms. Doyle, glowing with pride. *Home Room* is a hit sitcom about teachers and students surviving one ridiculous school year at a time. He auditioned for a mid-sized role in its fifth season.

"Hayden," I breathe, "that's huge."

Huge enough to make triple what I earn. Or used to earn.

"Proud of you baby. For real."

"All that hard work paid off," Ms. Doyle adds, dabbing at her eyes.

"Filming starts next month," Hayden says, bouncing. "Will you come help me?"

Ms. Doyle inhales, then turns to him, voice soft but steady as she tells him the news.

My throat closes. But if years on stage have taught me nothing else, it's to keep smiling.

Hayden looks between us, processing. "Like... for a little while?"

"For now," his mom says. "But when you're ready, we'll pick it back up."

Her voice has that careful shine parents use when they don't plan on returning. The promise hangs there, light and easy. I know better than to grab hold of it.

But Hayden's smile comes back, just as bright.

"I'm gonna make you proud, Yana," he says. "You'll see."

My throat burns, but I don't crack. "That's my boy. You hit me up the second you're on set, okay?"

I close my laptop before the tears can fall and swipe them away fast. I don't expect my phone to light up next month.

I really am so proud of that kid. He's gonna take the world by storm.

Hmmph. That's the same thing Bryant said to me the first time we shared a bed, when I asked him if he really thought it'd be worth me moving to New York.

"*These curls,*" he whispered, playing in my hair, "*that brilliant smile. You're gonna take the world by storm.*"

Guess the high had him just as delusional as me.

I take the tiniest sip of the coffee I've been milking for the past two hours, ignoring the watchful attention of the baristas at the counter. My laptop's dying, and if this coffee gets any colder, I might join it.

Living the damn dream.

I guess I'll check out a few more casting calls then grab a hot dog or something on the way back to the motel.

Man, I'm hungry.

Unfortunately, my union rep informed me that there's no getting my part back in the *Aretha* musical because my termination had "just cause." I was a "threat to others' safety" or whatever. Ridiculous.

I'm recentering with a few breathing exercises when my cousin Laura calls.

"Hey, girl, hey!" I answer.

But besides her five-month-old, Kyngston, gurgling in the background, I don't hear a thing.

"You're not eating," she says. "What's wrong?"

"Huh?"

"You're always munching on something." She pauses again. "What's going on? Did something happen?"

"Wha—?" I scoff, reaching for my cup. "I ate a little while ago. I'm just finishing up my coffee now."

I take a dramatic slurp just to prove my point, drawing several lingering gazes.

"Uh-huh." Laura sounds doubtful. "How's everything? I wasn't sure if you had rehearsal today."

Shoot! She's right. Lucky for me, it's Friday and nearing five o'clock. "Got out like an hour ago. Girl, this show is about to be *everything.* Mmkay?"

"Really?" There's a clatter, followed by Kyng's little giggle. Homegirl's always multitasking like a superhero. "You seemed pretty disappointed last time we talked. Said you couldn't believe they chose some TikTok Aretha wannabe over you for the lead."

"Well, I mean... That's old news." Especially since a lawsuit's probably on my ass like I owe child support. The one good thing about not having an address is no one can forward their medical bills to you. "How about y'all? How's Roman?"

She sucks her teeth. "Roman's fine."

"Don't I know it."

My cousin busts out laughing, but I'm not kidding. Roman started out as Laura's physical trainer when she was trying to get her groove back. Chiseled, brooding, the kinda fine that makes you wanna drop a dumbbell on purpose. One cha-cha later, they were inseparable.

And that baby they made together is cute enough to be on a Gerber jar.

"Speaking of, I know we just got back from Miami Beach, but the two of us are planning our next trip, and we're thinking about dropping in to see you on Broadway this spring. What do you think?"

I nearly choke on my own saliva. I pound on my chest with a cough.

"You alright?" she asks.

"Mmhmm." I attempt another sip of my coffee, but I'm all out. "I just, well... New York is so expensive though. Y'all really wanna waste your money coming out here?"

"It wouldn't be a waste," she says. "I want to hang with you.

Plus, Griffin's talking about taking Maddie and Eli to Jamaica for a week. I don't want to sit around the house stressing about it."

Griffin. Laura's good for nothing-but-a-check ex. Since their divorce a year ago, he's finally learned to stop being a constant pain in my cousin's ass—mostly by keeping his distance. Nowadays, instead of crying about his sorry behind, she's teaching dance at the rec with Roman, her husband-slash-partner-slash-saint, and they're supposed to open their own studio this fall. Between choreography, diapers, and dance moms, I doubt she's got any more time to stroke her ex's fragile ego.

Her life's full now.

I pick at the coffee cup's cardboard sleeve. My stomach's growling, my pride's throbbing, and I'm praying she can't hear either through the phone.

"Give me a few weeks. I'll let you know what I'm doing."

"Cool." Kyng squeals as Laura pops what's got to be a baby bottle cap. Bet she's juggling him on one hip while hunting for a pacifier. But she stops. "You sure you're doing alright?"

"Mmhmm. Everything's fine."

"'Cause if you need anything—"

"I'm fine, girl. Fine!"

She already knows what "not fine" looks like on me. I'm not giving her a sequel.

I drag my nail along the coffee cup's sleeve, shredding it slow. Losing the job was one thing. That I could hustle around. But this? The math ain't mathin'.

Frankly, I don't even know where I'm sleeping tonight.

"Okay," she relents. "I'll talk to you later."

I hang up before she can ask again.

Normally, I'd be happy to accept my cousin's help. But I don't need her worrying about me. She wants me to make it out here just as much as I do. I can't kill the dream for her now. Besides, all I need is one big break.

Nearby, a kid that looks barely old enough to get into a bar is pretending to scrub tables as he stares my way.

"'Sup?" I ask, just to give him a reason to be less awkward.

"Anyone ever tell you you look like Alexia Hyrd?"

I nod and roll my eyes.

Too bad I'm not. Just a nobody.

I better get back to stalking the casting boards. I open my laptop and pull up my bookmarks, but my phone rings again.

Why does everybody start checking in the second you start slipping? I swear, the universe sent out a group text.

But my heart softens the second I see who's calling on FaceTime.

"*Heyyyy* Daddy."

"There's my Songbird! You out there taking New York captive?" Daddy grins, his caramel-brown skin glowing against a plain white tee, salt-and-pepper curls cropped close to his head. Silver eyes not quite shining like usual, but just like me, he's got a right to a long day.

"Please. They're already fighting over what to name my boulevard."

"Just make sure they spell it right on Google Maps!"

His raspy laugh brightens my day as I join him. Can't nobody riff off a joke like my daddy. We used to drive Mama and FJ crazy with our back-and-forths on road trips. It's only been worse since he had to go on disability from his job at the Ford factory and has way too much time to watch TV.

"How y'all doing?" I ask.

Daddy's gaze shifts, and he takes a sober swallow.

Okay. Why does this suddenly feel like a parent-teacher conference?

"Actually, Songbird, that's what I was calling to ask you." Daddy releases a lengthy sigh through his nose. "Your mama and me been worried."

"Worried... why?" I sit up fast, my pulse drumming like I just missed the high note in front of a full house.

There's no way they could know what's going on. Could they?

Daddy shifts, clears his throat as he reaches for something on the side table. He presents a creased letter, the words

DELINQUENT ACCOUNT — FINAL NOTICE

stamped in bold red font across the top.

Pain throbs behind my eyelids as they slide shut. *Shit.*

Before I flew out, I begged Daddy to co-sign my relocation loan. Twenty grand to get my dreams off the ground. Promised him he'd never hear from the lender again. But...

He only did it 'cause he believed in me. Said if Broadway called, I better answer. I swore I'd stay on top of payments. Then rent and reality showed up.

I also may or may not have blown a little—dressing to kill at auditions and sampling the best cuisine the Big Apple had to offer.

"Now... now don't panic," says Daddy. "I talked it over with 'em. We're gonna get all this sorted out—"

"No. Absolutely not," I say. "Daddy, you're not paying a dime."

He flashes that crooked smirk he always gave Mama when I'd make a mess or get in over my head, and he was trying to cover my ass.

My mouth falls open. "Daddy, you did not!"

"Just the last two payments," he says. "I thought it'd be easier but... your mama just got laid off."

I couldn't have heard him right.

Mama's been in that classroom longer than I've been chasing stage lights. Longer than FJ's been living and breathing music.

"But Mama loves teaching," I say. "She loves her math students as much as she loves me and FJ."

Daddy glances over his shoulder. Mama's likely close by in the kitchen.

"I know," he says. "But they're consolidating schools again. Seniority doesn't mean much when they start closing buildings."

Poor Mama. She devoted three decades of her life to them kids only to be tossed aside like she didn't raise half that damn math department.

I could fold myself up and slide under this table right about now. Me and my stupid snack cravings.

"How's she doing?" I ask, guilt crawling up my throat.

Daddy bobs his head, but he's not making eye contact.

"She's doing alright," he says. "Just a few more years till we can tap into that pension."

"And in the meantime?"

Daddy lifts a shoulder, the crooked grin holding steady on his face. "In the meantime, we're trying to take care of you."

I pinch the bridge of my nose, wondering if this week could get any worse. "Daddy, I'm grown. Y'all ain't gotta take care of me no more."

He eyes the letter and quirks a brow at me. "This collection company says otherwise. They've already tacked on another three thousand in fees, Songbird. And we're struggling to keep up with the mortgage as it is."

So this is the dream, huh? Daddy still trying to bail me out while I chase glitter? All this sacrifice, all this hustle... For what? A handful of callbacks and a lifetime of debt?

"We've even considered downsizing," he says.

"Daddy, no! Y'all been paying off that house since I was in high school."

"Yeah." He sighs. "A thirty-year mortgage seems like a good idea before you're on disability."

Daddy threw his back out five years ago. I figured things were tight, but not quite that tight.

"We'd refinance, but... if we don't make these payments, they're threatening to put a lien on the house," says Daddy.

"The house? Whose house?"

His chuckle pierces my heart. Then softly he says, "Our house."

It's like I'm twelve again. Lying in bed helpless while he and Mama whisper about bills.

"I'mma handle this, Daddy. Okay?"

He sounds doubtful. "You sure that latest gig will cover it?"

"Yeah, Daddy. Just give me a couple weeks. Y'all focus on the house."

I say it like I believe it. Because I have to.

"Oh! I think that's my agent calling now. Gotta go. Love you!" I hang up before he can hear my voice crack.

Alright, so it's bad. It's really, really bad. But I'll be fine. We'll be fine. Might have to fill out a couple job applications though.

The awkward kid's still staring as he wipes the tables down.

"Y'all hiring?" I ask.

"You can fill out an application online." He shrugs, returning to the much more intriguing task of scrubbing cream cheese off the table.

Another day, another disappointment. Add it to the reel.

I'm not even sure I can afford a motel tonight.

I sit longer than I mean to, staring at nothing while the café hums around me. A chair scrapes. Someone laughs too loud. The espresso machine hisses like it's mad. Everyone's life keeps moving, while mine unravels at a corner table in Midtown.

I tell myself not to panic. Panic never helped anybody book a role. Or keep a roof over their head. Or stop their parents from making sacrifices they shouldn't have to make. I press my palms flat against my thighs, grounding myself the way my therapist taught me a decade ago.

In through the nose. Slow. Count to four. Hold.

Out through the mouth, longer than the inhale. Again.

All I need is one thing to go right. One decent audition. One callback that turns into something solid. I don't need saving. I just need a little traction.

I reach for my coffee out of habit, then remember it's gone. Of course it is.

I'm considering packing up to head out and see if I can

charm my way into one more night at the motel when I spot a familiar smirk at the counter. Adrien.

Great. Just what I need: temptation with perfect eyebrows.

His stare lingers long enough to make me forget the difference between broke and flattered.

The second he's paid for his venti something-or-other, he joins me at my table.

"Hey, Pop-Tart."

"Hurtful."

He laughs, propping one of his designer boots on his knee, the leather creasing just enough to prove they're expensive. His hair looks great, and his cashmere scarf cannot be cheap. I keep meaning to ask if he's ever modeled. Or if he's just naturally insufferable.

"How ya been?" he asks, checking out my sweater like he's got x-ray vision.

"Good. Just out here chasing the dream." I doubt he believes me, but he nods anyway. "How's rehearsal going without me?"

"Boring," he says, eyeing me over the lip of his cup. "Not a whole lot of pretty things to look at, ya know?" His grin spreads slow before he takes another sip.

Goodness. He's thirsty.

"Got another gig yet?" he asks.

"My agent's on it." I take out my phone, pretending to check messages. Truthfully, I fired my agent when I started dating Bryant. But Adrien doesn't need to know that.

"It's so messed up how Felipe cut you over Brooklyn's accident. She should've watched where she was going."

"That's what I said." I throw up my hand and we slap fives.

Somewhere, Aretha's ghost is shaking her head.

But my laugh fades when his eyes lock on mine, all heat and intensity. He's been giving me that look since the first casting call. The one that says, *You first.*

Once, I almost took him up on it. Back when I thought

loyalty to my man meant something. Now it just feels like a punchline.

Adrien's thumb circles the lid of his coffee cup like he's got nowhere else to be. His eyes drift, unhurried, down the slope of my neckline and back again. He doesn't need words. His slow blink says it all: *We both know how this ends.*

The air between us settles into something warm and inevitable, an ease that asks for nothing deeper than chemistry and a dim room.

And damn if I don't feel how simple that would be.

"Some of the cast is linking up at The Harlem Lounge tonight." His gaze lingers a beat longer than polite. "Wanna be my date?"

4

If I were being completely honest with myself, I'd admit that I can't afford my new minidress or the fly leather boots I'm sporting as I round the corner toward The Harlem Lounge. My credit card's gasping for air. Daddy just showed me a red-letter notice with his name on it, and Mama's out of work. I should be stacking every dollar. I should be wiring something home instead of swiping what little I've got left.

But this ain't about fun. It's about staying afloat. Already sold everything I can't fit into my bag.

You don't survive this city by looking like you're drowning. You show up polished. You stay visible. You remind people you exist before they forget you ever did.

As soon as I'm steady again, every extra dime is going back to Detroit. Every single one.

Tonight's about positioning and networking. Building momentum. That's what I tell myself as the music spills out onto the sidewalk. Because a night with Adrien certainly sounds better than curling up on a bench.

He's waiting just outside the entrance when I arrive, his dark hair flowing to his shoulders. The top few buttons of his silk shirt are undone, as if he were in L.A. and not New York at the end of a frigid February.

His gaze lifts from his phone, and that dangerous grin elongates as I approach. "Sexy."

"You like?" I open my coat to give him a better view of the minidress I'm rocking.

"Very much." He presses a kiss to my cheek and gives me a twirl. "Let's go have some fun."

The Harlem Lounge smells like Hennessy and hope. The kinda place where people come to be seen but act like they stumbled in by accident. A live band's tearing through "Chain of Fools," and the walls practically vibrate. Spotlights flicker across velvet booths where Broadway dancers and broke dreamers blend like smoke.

Adrien keeps his hand at the small of my back as he reintroduces me to some of the cast. Most of them seem cordial enough, but I catch a few whispering as we part ways. Probably reminding each other that I'm the girl who took out "Aretha."

But the past is the past. And I'm on a mission.

I need a warm bed tonight, and Adrien's got one. I don't even wanna think about what could happen if he doesn't take me home.

So I lean in. Run my fingers through his hair as we chat over drinks, let them graze his scalp like I'm just being playful. When he grins, I reach for the smile I use at auditions. The glossy one. The easy one. The one that says, *I can fit wherever you need me.*

He slips an arm around my waist, palm grazing the sway above my ass. "Aren't you glad you came, Pop-Tart?"

I shoot him a glare, but his lips hover so close to mine I can barely hold it. "You gon' stop calling me that."

"You sure?" He pulls me closer, mouth near my ear. "'Cause I like my dessert warm, sweet, and saying my name."

My jaw drops at his wicked smirk and I shove his shoulder. *Sounds like I'm in for one hell of a night.*

Our attention shifts toward the entrance as applause ripples through the room. Brooklyn steps inside, waving with her good arm like she's accepting an award. Cameras lift. Phones flash. People sit up straight. And my stomach drops.

If she sees me, there's no telling how she spins it. It doesn't take much. One comment in the right ear and I'm the reckless girl who left a wrapper on the floor and cost a lead her arm. Intent won't matter. It never does. In this business, the loudest version wins. Truth is optional.

She drifts closer to the dance floor. And if I'm not careful, I'm sure a lawsuit isn't far behind.

I shift Adrien's body slightly, angling us away before she has a clear line of sight.

"Shall we dance?" I ask.

His lips curl slow. "If you lead, I'll follow."

The lights dim to amber, and the band slips into a neo-soul groove. Just enough funk to make your shoulders roll. Adrien slides in behind me, one hand tracing my hip, the other finding my waist as we start to sway. It's slow, easy, hypnotic. I close my eyes and lean into the warmth of it.

So he's no director. I doubt Adrien's knocking down doors for anyone but himself. But right now, he's here. And he wants me. No questions or games. Just the promise of a reckless good time.

I toss back what's left of my drink and let myself feel every second. Not to mention the slow drag of his mouth near my ear, like he's daring me to misbehave.

"Excuse me—OMG—hi!"

I crack one eye open.

A guy's standing way too close, phone already in hand, his friend hovering behind him like he's filming backup content.

"Can I get a selfie?" the guy blurts. "I love you!"

"Uh..." I blink. "Sure."

I've got no idea how he knows who I am. Maybe one of my old productions?

Adrien exhales behind me, hands dropping from my waist. "I'm grabbing a drink," he murmurs, disappointment threaded through his voice. Lips pursed, he peels off toward the bar, leaving me to whimper inside.

"It's my birthday," says the fan, pulling up his camera app.

"Best day *ever*! I mean, this one time I met Ariana Grande—she was out to lunch with Guy Fieri, and I'm like, 'I didn't even know they were friends!'"

I bob my head as he goes on and on, his camera guy recording the entire thing. The part of me that knows how to stand under lights takes over on instinct. Smile locked. Chin angled. Doesn't matter that I don't have a show to plug. Doesn't matter that I'm technically unemployed. If someone thinks I'm somebody, I can't afford to correct them.

Meanwhile, Brooklyn's drifting dangerously close to the dance floor. Adrien's at the bar, flashing that wicked smile at other female castmates as they pass. I track both of them without moving my eyes too much. I can't lose him. I can't let her see me. And I definitely can't look like I'm begging for either.

I need to make this quick before I end up sleeping on the subway.

"Uh-huh." I smile. "You ready?"

"Honey, I was born ready," says the fan.

And for no reason at all, Brooklyn glances my way. Then does a double take. *Shit.*

Finally, the fan slides in for a quick side hug, snapping the photo like it's a time-sensitive mission, and I'm grateful for his stride.

"Thank you!" he says, already bouncing on his toes. "You're way nicer than I expected."

Before I can ask what that means, he's gone, dragging his friend with him like the moment's already expired.

Whatever.

Darting through the crowd, I make a beeline back to Adrien just as he tips back a shot of something amber. He wipes his mouth with the back of his hand, grin easy and unbothered.

"Wanna head out?" he says.

"Thought you'd never ask."

————

I couldn't tell you what Adrien's apartment looks like. We fell inside the door making out and found our way to his room without taking a breath.

His scent is pure trouble. Something expensive that clings like whiskey on lips. His body crowds mine, solid and demanding, and his hands roam like permission's already been granted.

My breath stutters when he pulls me back against him, every inch of him telling me exactly what he wants. There's nothing gentle about it.

After the week I've had, gentle can go to hell.

Adrien's laugh vibrates against my throat as my dress slips off my shoulder. "Knew you'd be down," he murmurs between kisses.

"Is that right?" I breathe.

He grins, drunk on lust. "You just give off that energy. Like... the kind of girl who knows how to have fun. Drive a man wild all night."

"Hmmph." My laugh is brittle. *Fun.*

Bryant said the same. All starch and ambition by day, calling me over to take the edge off at night. I was the intermission. Never the show. Adrien likely won't be any different. I have a talent for landing these kinda roles.

Adrien groans the second my zipper gives, presses sweltering kisses down my spine. He squeezes my hips like he's bracing for impact. Mutters a prayer against my ass. "Oh, I'm gonna have *such a good time* with you."

I giggle, thinking about all the filthy options and swallowing my pride at the same time. 'Cause at the end of the day, no matter how good this will be, it's just for tonight. And then I'll be back to where I started: homeless, jobless, and alone.

My dress falls to my waist, and Adrien turns me back to him. He rakes his tongue across his lips as his heated eyes take in the dip of my bra, the soft swell of my cleavage fighting to stay behind satin. I've never been shy about what God gave me up top, but the hunger in his stare makes me wonder if I should be.

"Try not to fall too hard," I say.

He returns my smirk with one of his own. "Simple and sexy. Just my type."

Simple?

He yanks me into his arms and starts on what's sure to be a hickey, but the word sinks into my gut like he socked me.

Simple. Like a snack at the convenience store?

His teeth graze my skin, hands burning hot as they trace my torso. But all I can think about is that word.

Simple.

It's the kinda compliment you give a girl you don't plan on calling later. Then again, I knew the assignment.

But sometimes I catch my reflection in their eyes, and I look thin. Like a sketch instead of a person. Like something you can fold up and tuck away once you're done.

And I'm so damn tired of making it easy.

"I can't do this," I say.

Adrien's face falls as I tug my dress back on.

"Wait, what are you—What just happened?"

"This isn't me." I zip my dress. "I don't... I mean, I *have*. But this isn't..."

The man looks like I just kicked his puppy instead of his libido.

"What I mean is, I don't... do this just to do it."

And I don't wanna sleep with men for shelter.

I grab my coat and move toward the door.

"Okay, Yana..." Adrien steps in my way with his hands raised, like I'm some psych ward patient on the loose. "Chill... You're gorgeous."

"Just not gorgeous enough to take seriously, huh?"

He blinks at me.

I shake my head and continue on my way.

But it's cold out. I think it might even be snowing. The wind from the hall chills my shoulders as I turn back.

"Look. Can I just crash here tonight?"

The words scrape my tongue as they tumble out. But really, what choice do I have? My pride's already shot to hell. Maybe he'll take pity. Maybe someone still will.

The air between us freezes, my words dangling like icicles, fragile and humiliating.

By the way he frowns at me, you'd think I cursed in church. "You're kidding, right?"

I nod, backing away. "Break a leg, Adrien."

———

TINY SNOWFLAKES SNAG IN MY CURLS AS I MAKE MY WAY down the frosty steps, the winter wind biting at my cheeks like it's got a bone to pick.

Triflin' ass.

Bet he'd be more than willing to share his pillow if I'd given him some.

Adrien's place is in Harlem, one of those narrow brownstones with chipped paint and a front stoop that probably doubles as a hangout spot come summer. A block removed from the noise. Just enough separation to feel intentional.

Even on a Friday night, the street's nearly silent.

Streetlights cast long, crooked shadows across the snow. Somewhere far off, a siren wails and fades. I draw in a breath that doesn't quite reach the bottom of my lungs.

The cold hits different when you've got nowhere to land. Heavier. Meaner. Like it knows.

I pause at the end of the stoop, suddenly dizzy, the world tilting in a way that makes my stomach lurch.

No address and no plan. Just streets and time and cold.

Not again.

Hunger curls low in my gut, gnawing like it's been waiting its turn. I swallow, but it doesn't help. My body remembers this feeling. The counting of blocks. The praying for warmth. The quiet terror of realizing you can't just *walk it off*.

I scan the street, heart thudding too fast, like if I stop moving the cold might seep in and refuse to leave.

Tucking my chin into my coat, I make a right at the sidewalk. Or should I go left? I'm not even sure which way the nearest shelter is. Let alone the cutoff time.

The wind numbs my fingers as I tap my phone screen, trying to pull up the closest spot.

I slow, listening. The crunch of boots on ice snaps my head around.

But instead of Adrien chasing after me with a bleeding heart, I find Langston Washington—Mr. Can't-Crack-a-Smile himself—standing near a stoop with a bag of trash in hand, gaping at me like I just crashed his Sunday Service in a mini.

Of all people.

He's bundled in a navy puffer jacket and gray winter cap, glasses slipping down his nose like they're just as tired as he looks.

Abruptly, he turns away and tosses his bag in the nearby dumpster.

"It's okay, Mr. Washington," I call across the snowy sidewalk, my words puffing white in the air. "You can say hi."

He turns back toward the stoop, hands in his pockets, staring at the sidewalk like it personally betrayed him. "Do you need help?"

Something in my chest eases, whether I want it to or not. I hate that I notice.

There's no denying how pathetic I must look, but I'll be damned if I let him see it. I tug my coat tighter. "Help? What makes you think I need help?"

He studies me for a beat, his brow lifting a fraction. "You seem to be struggling to figure out which way to go."

I press my lips together, wave my hand in the sting of the cold. "I was just trying to decide where to wait for my Uber."

He doesn't argue. Just gazes at the OPEN bodega sign flickering up the street.

But that somehow makes it worse.

"Didn't know you lived in Harlem," I add.

He points a thumb toward the brownstone next door. "Didn't know you and my neighbor were... friends."

I glance back at the apartment with a breathy chuckle. "Just dropped by to check out his junk. I mean, not his *junk*, but... you know... He's got a nice album collection."

Another awkward silence stretches between us. And Mr. Washington looks like he's waiting.

I cross my arms, squinting down the street.

"How far away is your place?" he asks.

"Twenty minutes or so." I lift my shoulder, hoping he'll buy the lie.

Question is, why do I feel the need to lie? Guess dignity dies hard.

"And your ride?"

"Hmm? Oh!" I look at my blank phone screen. "'Bout five."

I glance away, shivering in the cold, but I can still feel his gaze boring into me. Turning my back, I pray he'll just go. I don't need the entire theater community knowing about my pathetic situation by Monday.

For a second, I think he might be gone. Then he softly clears his throat.

"You can wait in here if you want."

I snort internally. Sounds like the sorta thing directors say right before desperate hopefuls end up on the casting couch.

Then again, I gotta remember who I'm dealing with. Mr. Washington looks like he schedules intimacy in fifteen-minute increments.

I shake my head. "I'm good."

"It's freezing," he says. "And you're not wearing gloves."

I hesitate, pride and survival locked in a staring contest. Survival clocks pride upside the head.

———

MR. WASHINGTON'S PLACE IS WARM LIKE MY GRANDMA'S AND twice as neat. Fluffy white carpet and shiny displays. But not so expensive that you feel like you can't sit down. The inside stretches long. An overstuffed couch to the left, open kitchen to the right, trumpet on a stand and piano at the back bay window. A jazz musician's dream.

My shoulders loosen on their own. I don't remember telling them they could.

"Boots off," he says. "Please."

No point fighting it. I've had enough drama for one week. Boots come off, and I step farther inside, curiosity getting the better of me. I trail my fingers along rows of jazz vinyl, then freeze at a glass case full of Emmys and Grammys. "No Tony, huh?"

His glare burns into my back as I check out all the framed playbills on the wall.

"Wow," I whisper.

A bright yellow bird is perched in a cage near the bookshelves.

"Ooh! A parrot. Polly wanna cracker?"

"He's a cockatiel. And he doesn't speak," says Mr. Washington. "Please stop touching things."

It's no wonder the place is so spotless. I doubt this bruh *ever* has company.

He pulls off his boots and hat. "Tea?"

"*Tea?*" My mouth goes dry just thinking about it. "You got anything else? Coffee? Cocoa?"

"I have tea," he says.

A lengthy sigh eases from my nose. "Sure—"

But any other words jumble in my head as he pads toward the

kitchen. He's stripped down to a plain black shirt, the fabric pulling across his pecs, bold as hell.

Well, damn. I ain't know he was packing all that under his Urkel sweater.

He moves through the kitchen, filling the stainless steel kettle, lighting his fancy stove, thumbing through a spinning rack of assorted herbal tea blends. My intrigue spirals as I take a seat on the sofa, wondering things like:

How is a man with trophies, money, and a brownstone still so miserable? And does he practice being this uptight, or is it a natural talent? Because no one is born clenching that hard. Granted, those are quite the sculpted cheeks to clench. Man must do a hundred squats daily and double on Sundays. Never would've known if he was still on that piano bench.

I'm enjoying the view when my stomach reminds me, I'm still in need of a hot meal.

"You got any food?"

"Of course I've got food," he says, not bothering to turn around.

I bite my lip to keep from saying something I'll regret in the morning. But at this rate, I don't know when I'm gonna see a fridge again. Swallowing my pride, I ask, "Can I have some?"

He grabs a biscotti from above the fridge and passes it my way without missing a beat.

Cheapskate.

I'm too hungry to turn it down, so I accept.

"Is there anything else you'd like?" His voice is dripping with sarcasm as he grabs a kitchen towel and starts scrubbing the counter like he spilled something when he definitely did not.

"I'd like to know who left that stick up your ass," I mutter, unwrapping the dry treat.

He turns back. "Excuse me?"

"I'm good, Mr. Washington." I take a giant crunch.

"Langston's fine." He pulls teacups and saucers from the cabinet. "And please try to avoid leaving any crumbs, Yah-Nah. I'd rather not vacuum before morning."

There he goes, saying my name wrong. Again. I chew hard.

My silence draws his attention, and he stops.

"Is something wrong?" He glances back but doesn't bother to make eye contact.

"That's not how you pronounce my name." I shrug. "It's not all drawn out like that. It's simple. Just... Yana. Or Jayana if that's easier. But not... *that*. That's not it."

He doesn't move, just stares at the door like it might clarify. "Why didn't you just say so?"

I open and shut my mouth. I honestly don't know.

He tilts his head side to side as he pours water over a steel filter into each cup. "Jay-Yah-nuh..." he says, rolling the name around in his mouth. "Jay-Yuh-nuh? Jayana... Jayana."

I don't even know why a man this bad at hospitality would invite me inside. Maybe he's lonely? Or maybe this is just what he does before poisoning his victims...

I eye the cup warily as he passes it into my hand, but I'm too hungry to not take my chances. "Thank you," I mutter before downing a burning gulp.

He starts toward the sofa, hesitates. Then grabs a dining chair and slides it to the opposite side of the coffee table instead.

Guess I've got cooties.

I'd call him out, but I'm a little less hungry and the space is plenty warm. Let him be weird. I focus on my tea as he struggles to decide whether to cross his legs or not. He decides not.

"So... Jay... Yana, where do you live?" he asks.

My throat tightens as I run a list of lies through my head. "Hell's Kitchen," I say, settling on what's closest to the truth.

His brows rise as he sips. Like he isn't judging me when we both know he is.

"Hmm," he says, setting his cup on his saucer. "Common for a lot of performers."

"Unfortunately." At least, that used to be the case. "How long you been staying here?" I ask, anxious to pivot the spotlight back to him.

"A good while," he says.

Quite the conversationalist.

We sip in tandem for a few quiet seconds, neither of us meeting the other's eyes.

It crosses my mind what I'd be doing if I'd made a different choice at Adrien's or even paid the rent on time. Either way, enjoying myself. And at the end of the night, at least I'd know I'd have a warm bed to sleep in.

Abruptly, Langston sets aside his tea and jogs up the lengthy hall. It's only got two doors: one on the left, and another at the end. Similar to Adrien's from what I can tell, but more spacious.

He disappears into the door on the left.

"You got a big bedroom?" I call out.

"Not your business," he answers.

"Of course... What's it matter when you're sleeping alone anyway."

He returns and passes me the blanket, casual as hell. As if he didn't hear me.

Asshole.

"Thanks," I mutter, accepting the blanket and draping it over my knees.

There's a smug gleam in his eye as he sits, and something in me bristles at how sure he looks. But damn if it isn't captivating.

"Your ride?" he asks, breaking the spell.

"Right." I check my blank screen again. "Damn it! He must've gotten lost."

I haven't got a clue where I'm headed next, but I could stand to nurse this warm tea a bit longer. I give my best dramatic sigh.

"I'll have to try for another. And *you... Jhamar...* will be getting *one* star," I say, stabbing the black screen with my finger. "And a crappy review!" I scowl.

But when I look up, Langston's staring at me, lips parted. Like he had something to say and I cut him off.

"What is it?"

He quickly looks away. "I was going to say, it's... unfortunate what happened to you at the *Aretha* rehearsal. For the record, I told Felipe it was... unfair."

Something soft stirs low in my ribs. It warms my heart that he bothered, let alone even remembered me.

"You're damn right it was unfair," I say, lifting my chin. "I should've been leading that show."

When he doesn't give me so much as a blink, I break into my personal rendition of Aretha's "Respect," the version I used to belt into my hairbrush every night before bed.

But the guy hasn't got a funny bone. Just watches, like I'm an exhibit he's trying to understand.

"Have you landed a new gig?" he asks, taking another sip.

I softly shake my head. I really shouldn't lie, but I can't help it.

"My agent's on it, though," I add, trying to shield myself from the taunts he's clearly holding back. But instead of throwing an easy jab, he nods.

"With your looks, it shouldn't take long."

The words catch in my lungs. I'm not sure whether to thank him or tell him to go to hell. There's no leer in it. Just an obser-vation, stated like a fact.

His gaze slowly meets mine. "Anyone ever tell you you look just like—"

"Goodness. *Yes!*" I wave my hand, exhausted. "All the time."

He releases a light breath that sounds almost like a chuckle. And for the slightest moment, a hint of a smile inches into his cheek.

A really sexy one.

But it quickly vanishes. Gone before I can fully enjoy it.

I don't know why that annoys me more than if he'd never smiled at all.

Langston stands with a yawn, the faintest hint of his woodsy cologne lingering. "I'm heading to bed."

"Bed?" I frown as he crosses to the kitchen. "It's ten o'clock on a Friday night, party animal."

He places his dishes in the sink and turns for the hall. "Lock the door on your way out, please." He flips off the light—leaving me in the dark—then slips into the bedroom, shutting the door behind him.

I exhale, long and slow, staring at the teacup in my hands. I truly appreciate his kindness, regardless of how much of an ass he's been.

But what do I do now? Leaving means facing the fact that there's no next stop waiting for me. Just more night and whatever pride I've got left.

Instead of sitting in it, I pull up social media and start scrolling.

I WAKE WITH THE SUN IN MY FACE AND IMMEDIATELY CLOCK two things. One, I am not where I expected to be. And two, this place looks even better in daylight. The rays of the morning sun spill across the counters, bouncing off stainless steel and clean lines like it's proud of itself. Even the little bird is up, perched and staring out the window like it pays rent.

Damn. I must've knocked out.

I start to sit up, already rehearsing my quiet exit, when I notice the pillow tucked under my head.

He didn't make me leave.

That fact settles somewhere soft and uncomfortable in my gut. It matters more than I want it to. And somehow, that almost makes it worse. I kinda wish he'd told me to go. At least then I wouldn't be wondering if he knows I don't have anywhere else to be.

My cheeks heat as I grab my coat and bag, suddenly very aware of how long I've overstayed. At least I won't have to see him again. Truly. This is cleaner.

But. Bathroom first.

The place is eerily quiet, like one of those newly renovated brownstones with walls thick enough to keep secrets. I pad down the hall, boots in hand, trying not to make a sound.

But his bedroom door's cracked open. Just a sliver.

Do I peek? Of course I do.

Langston's sprawled across the bed, glasses gone, scowl too. Face relaxed like a tyrannical toddler who finally lost the fight. Whatever had him wound up last night ain't there now.

I linger half a second too long.

Ew. Yana. He's a nerd.

I tear myself away and duck into the bathroom, handling my business like a professional ghost. Wash hands. Don't snoop. Leave no trace.

Except something feels off.

I glance at the sink. Two toothbrushes.

Weird. But with a man this anal, I wouldn't be shocked if he had a system.

I open the medicine cabinet, curiosity piqued. Tylenol. Benadryl. Floss. Normal. Too normal. I crouch and peek under the sink.

Tampons.

I straighten so fast I almost knock myself out.

Why would he have...

Nope. Absolutely not. Whatever this is, it is not my business. For once in my life, I am choosing peace.

I ease out of the bathroom and move down the hall, careful with each step.

I don't know what I've stumbled into, but I ain't about to stick around long enough to find out. I refuse to be the extra in somebody else's mess.

5

"Hey, girl! I didn't know you were staying here, too!"

The blonde, linen-blazer-wearing woman frowns as I give her a light hug at the hotel elevator.

"How you been?" I maintain full eye contact as her face shuffles through all the emotes: confusion, panic, phony genuine surprise.

"I'm good," she says. "And... you?"

"Girl, life has been *life-ing*, okay?" I release a dramatic huff, falling in step beside her as we head for the breakfast area. All-you-can-eat continental. "But this conference was simply one I could not miss. You know?"

Homegirl nods, knowing full-well she hasn't got a clue what I'm talking about.

"Anyway, let me get a bite before I have to rush off. Session one's about to be *so* dope. Good seeing you, girl!"

She's still trying to conceal her stupor as we part at the coffee station, but she'll be alright. Daddy ain't pay for fourteen years of acting lessons for me to not put 'em to good use.

I jump in line and grab myself a plate. The omelets smell *amazing*.

Lying ain't cute. Neither is starving. And this certainly beats a soup line.

My phone buzzes as I take my place like I belong here.

It's Gracie.

Your junk mail is cluttering my coffee table.
Come get it.

All this rudeness is really so unnecessary.

Shoot. Battery's at 3 percent. I should've charged my phone at Langston's.

I roll my eyes and tuck it away. I won't even waste my energy on a response.

Then again, mail ain't the only thing I left.

Returning my plate to its stack, I grab myself a biscuit, and head for the subway.

———

"It's open!" calls Gracie when I knock.

"So we're not even bothering to open the door now?" I ask stepping inside. "Is that how we're doing it?"

She's set up at a vanity in _my_ old bedroom, wrapped in her silk robe, rollers in her hair. Today's project? Attempting to curl her lashes while lining up a selfie.

"I don't have time for this," she says, struggling to keep her eye open as she presses the curler shut. "Your mail is on the table."

I glance from her to the stack of envelopes. Likely just bills. Maybe a few late notices. Nothing useful. But I know exactly where I could shove 'em.

Lucky for her, the ache in my stomach is loud.

"Cool," I say, heading for the kitchen.

Everything's pretty much the same since I left. Counters packed with takeout containers and mismatched dishes. A full trash bag slumped against the doorframe. Bread's on top of the fridge.

Gracie races in as I reach for it, her rollers bobbing like angry little satellites. "Excuse me... _Excuse me?_ What are you doing?"

"I'm taking what's mine."

I haven't eaten since yesterday afternoon. Not really. Tea and a biscuit don't count. Pride definitely doesn't. I go to open the fridge, but she jumps in my way.

"Besides disappointment, there's nothing left for you here," she says.

"Wanna bet? I paid for groceries too." I bump her out the way with my hip. "I'm making a sandwich."

"Like hell you are."

She grabs at my arm, but I yank out of reach. I pull the turkey, lettuce, cheese, and mustard.

"Yana!" Her octave could rival Mariah Carey's. "You're not touching my kitchen!"

"*Your* kitchen?" I huff as I push past her to the counter. "Girl, please. You think you're the queen of New York just because you got your little understudy position. Ain't nobody checking for you."

I rip off a couple lettuce leaves before she snatches the head back.

"At least I could *land* an understudy position," she says. "You couldn't hold a sustained belt octave if there was a gun to your head."

"Cute. Very cute."

I grab the mustard and she attempts to pull it from my grasp. She forgets I'm much stronger than her. Mustard goes flying through the air and lands smack dab in the middle of her rollers. "Ooh. That color looks good on you."

She scowls like a pissed-off pug as I dress the bread.

"Take your mail and go," she mutters.

"After I eat."

"Give me back the turkey!"

"Stop hovering like a fruit fly and I will! When I'm done."

Her arms flail as she tries with everything in her to keep me from applying the deli meat to my sandwich.

"Yana—give me... *Ugh!*" Her face is tomato red.

"Gracie... I'm eating this sandwich."

"Over my dead body!"

"Don't tempt me."

"What in the entire hell is going on in here?" Evelyn stands in the doorway, gaping at the bread and cheese scattered everywhere.

"She broke in!" Gracie yells, jabbing a thumb at me.

"I was invited," I say, taking a bite.

Evelyn groans. "Why is there mustard on the ceiling?"

"She's stealing food!" Gracie flails again, nearly slipping on mustard. "Look at her!"

"It's a sandwich. Not the crown jewels," I say.

"Yana," Evelyn drags a hand down her face. "You can't just waltz in here and raid the kitchen."

"I wasn't raiding. I was... assembling." I hold the sandwich up high where Gracie can't reach.

"She was feral!" she yells.

"You're being dramatic," I say.

"Enough!" Evelyn tosses her keys on the table with a sharp, exhausted huff. "Yana, take your mail... and your sandwich, and go."

"No problem."

Gracie's mouth drops open like she's been shot. "Evelyn!"

"Just... chill, Gracie," says Evelyn. "You look unhinged."

Worth it.

I grab my mail and head straight for the door.

Swear I've never had a better sandwich in my life. It's no continental breakfast, but I can live on pettiness and victory for now. Next time, I'm making ramen.

Traffic hums and horns layer over each other as I move down West 45th, scarf tucked high against the cold. I pull out my phone to check the time, but I'm greeted with a black screen.

"Of course." I tip my head back toward the winter sky. "A little break would be nice."

The café up ahead glows warm and inviting, promising Wi-Fi, an outlet, something small and steady in the middle of this day. I veer toward it, already thinking about charging cables, and maybe a hot drink if I can scrape up a few dollars.

I'm mere steps from the corner when tires shriek behind me, urgent and restless. I turn just as a black Sprinter van jerks toward the curb, too close to be anything accidental.

"What the—"

I step back and my boots skid on ice, my balance slipping just as the van stops inches from my knees. The side door rips open before I can recover, and a thick man in black sweats and dark sunglasses jumps out like this has been rehearsed.

Cold sinks deep in my bones, and something I buried years ago snaps awake.

"Oh, hell naw."

I pivot to run, but his arm locks around my ribs before I get two strides in, crushing my elbows against my sides. It's not a grab. It's a clamp. I drive my heel down hard and he grunts, and when I throw my head back it connects with something solid. His jaw maybe.

Good.

I twist, turning into him the way I remember, trying to break the hold instead of fighting straight back. For a second I almost slip free, my shoulder sliding loose enough to taste air.

But his palm slams over my mouth and something chemical and wrong floods my nose. I jerk my face away and bite down, hard enough that he drops a couple f-bombs. His grip falters, giving me a second to suck in air.

"Fire!" I scream. "Fire! Fire!"

The city keeps moving. A horn blares. Footsteps pass. Someone laughs down the block.

Oh God.

A second man appears behind me, grabbing my shoulders and shoving me forward as the first one tightens his hold. I kick backward and connect with something soft, a shin or a thigh, I don't know. I claw at fabric, at skin, at whatever I can reach.

"Hold her—"

There's a quick sting high on my leg, sharp enough to make me flinch before I understand what just happened.

"What—"

It burns fast and shallow, and I lash out again, but my aim is off this time. My balance shifts like the pavement isn't where I think it is, and my heart pounds so hard it makes everything feel distant.

Stay up.

I swing again and my arm feels slower than my thoughts, my knees wobbling even though I'm still fighting. The strength drains out of me in uneven waves, like my body is unplugging piece by piece while my mind is still screaming.

No. Not like this.

They lift me and my boots scrape uselessly against the ground as I try to hook a heel on the curb or grab the van door or anything that will anchor me. My muscles won't answer the way they did a second ago.

Mama told me to carry mace. I didn't.

The van door slams and the world tips sideways, the ceiling blurring above me while I try to focus on something solid. A screw in the panel. A scratch in the paint.

Count.

One. Two—

The numbers slip before I can finish them, and everything folds in at the edges until there's nothing left to hold on to.

THE FIRST TIME MY EYES OPEN, IT'S DARK.

The second time, it's fuzzy. But a sliver of light is glowing beneath a door.

The third time, my vision finally clears.

I'm sitting in a dark room in a cold folding chair. The smell hits before my brain catches up: sweat, burnt coffee, desperation, hope.

A rehearsal studio?

"Thank God." A man releases a shaky breath. "I thought I was gonna have to call 911 or something. And *that* would've been a mess to explain."

"Wait..." I wave a hand, trying to clear the fog. "Where am I? Who... Why?"

"Should we give her water?" the man asks.

"That would likely cause vomiting," says another voice. A much more familiar voice. "Didn't you research any of this?"

"This is an *emergency*, Langston. You think I had time to research in the middle of an *emergency?*"

"L-Langston?" I blink twice as he appears in my vision, leaning against a piano.

He wheezes a lengthy sigh through his nose.

"Langston... What's happening? Have I... Have I been kidnapped?"

"Technically, abducted," says the other man from behind me.

"Either way, a bit dramatic," says Langston. "But that's just Julian's style."

"Julian?" *Why does that name sound familiar?*

"Julian Frazier," says the man stepping in front of me with half a spin. He extends a lanky hand, lips curling into a boyish, theatrical smile. "Broadway director, writer, and occasional producer." He's tall in that narrow, artsy way, hair trimmed low, scarf draped like it's got its own agent. Giving Black Willy Wonka with better lighting.

Julian Frazier. The director of Ella? The Neo-Soul Musical?

His fingers are cold as we shake hands.

"I remember you," I say. "I auditioned for your musical last year. You cast my roommate instead. And she's awful."

His grin falters, but he quickly replaces it. "Well, you know the biz. Not that your submission didn't make a *significant* impression." He looks at Langston who glowers right back.

"You know, Julian, I knew you were no scholar," says

Langston. "But this is, without question, the most idiotic deci-sion you've ever made."

"You were the one that said we should track her down!" shouts Julian.

"Yes! But not like this!" Langston shouts back.

"What was I supposed to do?" Julian whines. "I couldn't get through by phone."

I look from one to the other like I'm watching a low-budget courtroom drama. Langston's in stern director mode now, voice clipped and exact, like somebody just missed their cue. It doesn't match the gentleman who let me in from the cold last night. Or the one who left a pillow under my head and walked away without waking me.

Guess we're back to factory settings.

"Can somebody please tell me what's going on?"

Langston pinches the bridge of his nose. "After I... ran into you last night, I sent Julian a text. But by morning, you were gone—"

"So, I pulled your audition," says Julian.

"Then had her abducted," Langston says dryly.

"I sent a van and requested privacy," Julian snaps. "How could I know they'd be so abrasive about it?"

Langston steps closer, scanning me head to toe. "Did you hit your head?"

I lift a shoulder, thrown that he'd even ask.

"She could've been seriously hurt," Langston says.

The way he searches my face, like I'm glass and he's checking for cracks, makes my shoulders square without thinking.

He turns back to Julian, voice flat. "No one's touching her again."

"You look *just* like her," says Julian, steepling his hands at his nose.

"She *resembles* her," Langston says, returning to his perch. His eyes soberly drift back to me. "And we've been shut down for a week."

"Shut down?"

"The preview," says Julian. "We thought we'd get by with the understudy. But that was a *big* mistake."

"The audience hates her," adds Langston.

"And considering my wife's got blonde hair and blue eyes, social media's pissed that I'd throw in a... less-melanated understudy," says Julian, pressing his hands to his narrow waist. "Pretty sure my Black card's been revoked."

"So we're asking for your help," says Langston.

I'm still stuck on *van. Abducted. Shut down.* "What's happening again?"

Julian grabs a chair and slides it across the floor, piercing my headache with the screech. I wince as he straddles it backwards, Slater-style.

"Jayana... I need you to be Ella. And I'll pay you top dollar to do it."

My stomach turns as I register what he's saying.

Is he offering me the lead in his play?

Julian sits back, not blinking, desperation etched all over his face. Even Langston seems to be holding his breath.

This is it. The windfall I've been waiting for. Exactly what I need to help Daddy. To get a roof over my head. To eat.

But the question gnaws at my belly like a subway rat.

"Why me?"

Julian grins as if it couldn't be more obvious. "Because... you're her."

"She's not her," says Langston, voice edged with anger.

Julian raises a hand with a tut. "I know. I know. I'm just saying, she's a dead ringer."

Langston rolls his eyes, jaw clenching.

I look between them, slowly. "A dead ringer for... Alexia Hyrd?"

Julian's beaming as he nods. "She's been missing for three weeks. But you..." He gently cradles my face. "*You* are the one I've been looking for, Jayana. The answer to *all* my prayers."

I look to Langston in a panic. "Missing?"

"Look," says Julian, "investors are threatening to shut us down, permanently, if we don't get Alexia back or someone damn close to her... You're our only hope."

Langston scoffs. "She can't just *play* Alexia, Julian. She's a person."

"And right now," Julian shoots back, "she's a missing person. Which means the show dies unless we act."

It takes a minute to digest what they're asking. "Wait. Not just an understudy? You want me to... *be* Alexia Hyrd?"

Both of them nod once, as if terrified to say it out loud.

"Naw..." I lean back, shaking my head. "Naw. That's crazy."

"Just for thirty days!" says Julian. "Thirty days. You help us keep the investors calm until we find Alexia... And then you can go on to do whatever great things you wanna do on Broadway. This could be *great* for your career."

"Assuming the deception doesn't backfire," adds Langston.

"Who says they ever have to know?" Julian tosses him a frown, then resets as he turns back to me. "Yana... I could see it in your audition. That hunger. That *fire*. This is your big break, sweetheart. The moment you've been waiting for your *entire* life."

I swallow, slow, my knee bouncing on its own.

Thirty days. Sheets that aren't borrowed. Money that lands on time.

It sounds almost reasonable when he says it.

Julian steps closer, in no hurry at all.

"What do you say we flirt with destiny?"

6

They pull me into a small composer's room, crammed with a piano and whiteboard. A rolling TV cart sulks in the corner, hooked up to an ancient laptop. Sheet music and half-drunk coffee cups everywhere.

Langston ushers me into another hard-backed chair as Julian wipes the board clean.

I glance at my dead phone in my palm. Basically a paperweight.

Langston's hand closes around it before I can react. He doesn't ask. Just plugs it in behind the cart.

"You'll have something in twenty," he says, making sure it's charging.

I watch him slide onto the piano bench like he didn't just do me a big one.

"Next preview's in three days," says Julian, reaching for a marker.

"Three days?" I frown.

"Time's running out," says Langston. "We've got to get someone up on that stage before rumors turn into refunds."

I swallow hard. "No pressure, huh?"

He blinks at me without even a hint of a smile.

"Step one: we've got a simple goal." Julian scribbles the words ALEXIA HYRD across the top of the board in bold red letters and taps it with a marker. "Be. Her."

"No," Langston cuts in. "Pulling off Ella is all that matters. We don't need all the theatrics."

"Have you *seen* social media? *Read* the reviews?" Julian squints. "Without Alexia, there *is no* Ella."

"She just needs to nail the show," says Langston. "Pop up late. Leave early."

"Without selfies or interviews?"

Langston's jaw works once.

Julian pins a photocopy to the board. And my breath stalls.

Same cheekbones. Same mouth. Even the eyes—gray, not brown—staring back at me like they know something I don't.

It's like looking at the upgraded version while I've been chilling on the clearance rack.

"To sell this illusion," Julian says, "you become her. Fully step into her life. The cast and crew *can't* know Alexia is still gone. The investors *must not* see you break character. If anyone senses something's wrong, the show goes under."

Right. If this crashes, it's not just me going down.

I glance at Langston for some sort of reassurance, but he's busy glaring at the piano keys like they socked him.

"This..." Julian taps Alexia's photo hard with his marker. "*This* is the role of a lifetime. And only *you* can pull it off, Jayana. Or should I say..."

His smile stretches like taffy.

"*Alexia.*"

I nod, hoping some of his confidence rubs off on me. "Where do we start?"

With the clap of his hands, Julian pulls the TV cart into the center of the room. "We need you studying the star constantly. Onstage footage, backstage footage, social media, interviews."

He taps a button on the laptop, and an image of Alexia comes to life.

She's in a music studio, her razor-sharp bob draped over one eye. I'd think it was me in a wig if I didn't know any better. She laughs melodiously, tossing back her head.

"Well, I can't spend every week in Cabo," she says. *"Even a diva's gotta work."*

Her smile beams bright as she and the interviewer laugh.

"My teeth ain't ever been that white," I mutter.

I look to Langston for confirmation, 'cause we both know this is gonna be a stretch.

Instead, he's watching me. Not the screen. Me.

Still. Focused. Like he's adjusting the equation.

Is this why he was staring last night? The resemblance between me and her?

Something flickers in his face before he drops his eyes to the piano.

"Don't worry about the small differences," says Julian. "Nothing hair and makeup can't fix. Do you hear the articulation? The laugh?"

"I do," I say. "It's more of a *ha-ha-ha*, instead of a *heh!*"

Julian winces. "Exactly. More of the first one. Please."

We go over how she laughs, how she talks—even how she sneezes—for what seems like hours. In between, Julian drills me.

"Birthday?"

"June 14th."

"Hit songs?"

"Heat Wave, Fever, and... *Unbreak."*

Julian and Langston groan.

"No, no, no," says Julian.

"It's *Unbreakable,*" says Langston.

"Potato, Puh-tah-toh," I say.

Julian shakes his head. "Again."

An hour later, we're rehearsing movement. Not for the show, but for her.

"It's sort of like this," says Langston, awkwardly strutting with a hand on his hip. His shoulders dip side to side as he attempts the cringiest sashay I've ever seen.

"No, really, it's more like this," says Julian, passing in front of me like a runway model.

Both of them nod in agreement.

They review every detail: how she stands, how she tilts her head, holds the mic, greets fans.

"No. No. No." Julian wags his head with a frown. "Ella's innocent and sweet like that. Alexia's more of a... bitch."

Langston frowns.

"It's true!" says Julian.

They make me mimic her social media clips.

"That's no way to treat a celebrity," I say, rolling my eyes like Alexia.

Julian shakes his head. "That's no way to *treat* a celebrity," he says, emphasizing the intonation. "Treat. *Treat.* Watch again." He replays the clip.

It's obnoxious. It's painful. But necessary.

I gotta nail this thing. If I don't, I don't know how I eat. Or where I sleep. And apparently, I take everyone else down with me.

We're going over food allergies during lunch when both Julian and Langston stop.

"What?" I ask, cheeks stuffed with sushi, my fork still loaded with rice.

"Alexia... never ate like that," Langston says slowly.

I shrug, still chewing. "I'm hungry."

I realize I may have overdone it when they call in wardrobe.

The petite Hispanic woman gasps when she sees me. "Alexia?"

"She's not feeling well," says Julian, cutting me off. "No questions, please."

She nods and gets to work. Taping, wrapping, shoving wigs on my head. I grunt like I'm being punished. She's pinning everything tight as hell.

"Just a few minor adjustments," says Julian, waving his hand. "Couldn't exactly work out while she was away."

I fight the urge to faint.

The second she's gone, Julian shoves a giant binder in my arms. "You've got 48 hours to memorize your lines."

Because of course I do.

He pats my shoulder with a reassuring nod. "You've got this."

He means it. I can tell. It's so casual it almost makes me forget what this is. Almost.

The thought needles at me until I can't ignore it anymore. "Then why didn't you call me back in the first place?"

He draws the word out, repeating my question. "Why?"

I nod. "If you thought I could do it, why didn't you let me audition?"

He glances at Langston, who's flipping through sheet music at the piano, and the two exchange some sort of silent argument. Not even subtle. Julian lifts a shoulder looking back at me.

"Someone didn't think you had the pipes."

The room goes smaller around the words.

I glare at Langston, but he's scowling at the ceiling like there's a sewage leak.

Julian checks his phone and grabs my free hand. "Hairdresser's here."

I keep my gaze pinned on Langston as Julian drags me out the door. "Hurtful!"

———

Julian's hairdresser has me locked into a chair like I'm about to undergo a psych evaluation, her bangles knocking softly against each other as she reaches for another section.

Flat-iron heat hovers too close to my scalp, spray hangs thick in the air, pins clicking like tiny warnings while I crack open the binder on my lap and start skimming like my life depends on it. Which, apparently, it does.

Ella: A Neo-Soul Musical is basically Cinderella, if Cinderella lived in a Brooklyn brownstone and spent her days fixing boilers and mopping stairs while her stepmother ran the building like a petty little kingdom.

I scan the script like it's brand new, though I auditioned months ago. But I'd been distracted then. Focused on the wrong things. Like Bryant.

Ella's daddy used to own the place, used to write songs, too. Then he died, and she got demoted from daughter to maintenance girl, paid pennies to keep everyone else comfortable. The stepsisters call her "Elly" to her face when they want favors, but behind her back it's "Elephant." Because of her ears. *Cute.*

I squint at the page as the hairdresser pulls a section of hair taut, laying my part with surgical precision. She smooths my edges into careful curves, as intentional as her own.

"You're doing... a lot," I mutter, eyeing my reflection.

"I'm doing Alexia," she says, gold nose ring flashing as she tilts her head to check the symmetry.

Julian definitely had her sign something. Probably an NDA. And still, I'm grateful for five whole minutes of not pretending.

"I'm Nia," she offers quietly.

"Yana," I say with a nod.

No smile. No extra. But it feels like a door cracking open.

I turn another page and sigh. "Julian really went in on this one. Said, 'Let's emotionally ruin a woman and call it art.'"

The softest chuckle whispers from Nia's nose as her comb stills for a beat.

"The concept was all Langston," she says carefully. "He wanted it grounded. Real struggle. Voice over polish."

My brows rise in the mirror. "This fairytale was Langston's idea?"

Her mouth twitches, almost a smile. "Julian just put dialogue on it."

She resumes working, smoothing my hair back like she's done it a hundred times before. Like she's done this version of me before.

The binder feels heavier in my lap as I nod, eyes drifting back to the page.

Ella fixing boilers.

Ella being dismissed.

Ella humming to herself until someone finally listens.

Langston came up with this?

The man who controls everything down to a half-beat? Since when does he write about girls who get overlooked?

Doesn't add up.

Still, the pages don't lie.

———

WE DON'T EVEN ATTEMPT THE FIRST SONG UNTIL AFTER choreography, which will need to be heavily revised if I'm ever gonna keep up. Julian was giving the choreographer some weak excuse about me being dehydrated when I left, so hopefully they'll have some new moves for me when I return.

And apparently, I'm taking piano lessons now, since Alexia played keyboard and Ella does too. Langston said I didn't need the whole song, just the first half of Ella's opening number. Enough to look like I knew what I was doing. Enough to sell it.

I did my best. But Langston slid in at the keys and waved me off, saying my voice mattered more right now.

Seeming to note my tunnel vision, he passes me a lukewarm bottle of water. "Do you need five?"

"I'm good," I say, wrists aching as I twist the cap off.

He watches a beat longer than necessary before turning to note his sheet music.

"Let's take it from the top."

We're back in the composer's room, the air stale with sweat and coffee, sheet music scattered like casualties across the floor. I take a lengthy gulp of my warm bottled water and nod.

Langston's fingers move across the keys with an ease that

doesn't beg for attention. It just takes it. The sound changes under his hands, and the room adjusts around him.

"Now draw the breath lower," he says over the melody. "All the way down."

Following his instructions, I let it out:

"I was born from shadows...
but I don't live there no more."

Julian enters quietly, bobbing his head as I sing.

"They said 'Know your place, stay in the wings'
Tried to dim my voice, cut off my wings
But silence never fit my name..."

Julian winces as my voice cracks.

"Push through, Jayana," says Langston. "This isn't open mic night."

I pull in a breath that scrapes on the way down. Try singing softer. Try belting harder. But Langston shakes his head.

"No. No." He slams his fingers on the keys, piercing the air with a dissonant chord. "Enough! This isn't going to work, Julian. I told you!"

Julian flinches, hands raised like he's trying to slow a car wreck.

"She's not her!" Langston yells. "She's never going to be her!"

The words hit like a verdict. *She's not her.* Translation: *not good enough. Not worth the gamble.* Just a warm body filling space until the real thing returns.

Julian catches the way my lip trembles and sharply turns back to Langston. "Yana, could you step out and give us a moment, please?"

I do so, refusing to look at Langston as I go. He doesn't have to be such an ass about it. I know I'm not perfect, but I'm trying. Damn.

Langston must've forgotten sound still travels into the hall because he's not bothering to lower his voice. "I'm serious! We need to just cut our losses now."

Julian's much calmer. "I know. And I hear you... But it's just her first day—"

"I don't care if it's her first day!"

"*Shhh*. Calm down..."

I close my eyes as I rest my head against the cold brick wall. With this prick judging auditions, it's no wonder I didn't get the part. But I'm here. And he said it himself. They need me. Whether he believes it or not, I can be Ella. I can be Alexia Hyrd.

I practice a few of her runs until Julian waves me back in. Langston's still behind the piano, simmering, but silent.

"I've gotta take this call real quick," says Julian, glancing at his phone. "But we're gonna keep it going. Yana? Chin high, breathe deep, *be* her. Langston? Don't scare her off." He dances out the door and shuts us in silence.

Nothing follows.

I guess I could apologize. But for what? Being me?

"Again. From the top," says Langston, more to his sheet music than to me. Without another word, he starts playing.

I shut my eyes and let the melody carry me, let the sweet tone spark my senses, soak in its grace.

"I was born from shadows...
but I don't live there no more."

I try not to think about how thin the line is between break-through and bust. I didn't move to New York to be background. I didn't grind through auditions and callbacks just to almost make it. If I can't hold this, I go back to being the understudy of my own life.

"Relax," Langston mutters.

I fill my lungs and keep going.

"They said 'Know your place, stay in the wings'
Tried to dim my voice, cut off my wings..."

"Relax," he says again.

I can do this. He doesn't believe I can. That's exactly why I have to.

"But silence never fit my name.
I was made to rise, not stay the—"

He stops playing. "I *said* relax!"

"How is anyone supposed to relax with you being so damn uptight?" I shout back.

He goes still, brow furrowed behind his glasses, lips pursed. Then he stands and strides toward me. I stumble back, ready to jab him in both eyes, Three Stooges style.

He gives me a once-over and huffs. "Calm down. I'm not going to hurt you." Then he presses a hand against my ribs without asking.

His touch lingers, firm but careful, and my pulse jumps.

A tense breath slips out of me. "Am I gonna have to report you to the union, Director?"

"I'm trying to keep you from passing out. Now sing."

I swallow and pick it up at the bridge.

"Ohh — don't tell me who I'm meant to be.
I write my own destiny.
I found the power in every scar
You don't need a crown to be a..."

As I climb toward the high octave, he presses harder.
"Out... Out. Out!"

And somehow, the note comes. Not perfect, but stronger. Like it's been hiding in my gut all along. Langston's eyes meet mine, and I can't help smiling.

"That's her!" Julian says as he bursts back in, giving his own personal round of applause. "That's it! That's it! Yana, you might just save this musical after all!"

Langston retreats to the piano like nothing just happened.

My body still hums from what I just did, from the way they looked at me like I wasn't a risk for once. I lift my chin, fresh energy rising under my skin. "What's next?"

"Next, we rest," says Julian. "Head home and get some sleep. I'll see you at ten tomorrow."

But I don't know where I'm sleeping. I can't exactly go back to Gracie with my tail between my legs.

Langston presses his hands in his pockets and tilts his head toward the door. "Get your things."

I frown. "Where are we going?"

Julian scratches his nose as Langston exhales deep. "Alexia lived... with me."

7

Not gonna lie, riding in a private car with Langston instead of dozens of sketchy strangers on the subway wasn't half bad. The driver kept sneaking glances at me in the mirror, holding them too long, like he was trying to reconcile what he saw with what he heard. I get it. The hair. The makeup. The silhouette. Close enough to confuse people. Close enough to make them question what they think they know. Langston told him not to ask questions, and the man nodded like that explained everything.

I kick off my boots the second we step inside the brownstone, the silence wrapping around me like it did last night. Warm. Intentional. A quiet that costs money. The floor's still spotless. Air still smells like tea and clean wood. Nothing out of place, like the house expects order and gets it.

Alexia lived here. Slept here. Probably stood in this entryway after rehearsals, humming to herself, keys still in hand. And now I'm the one dropping my boots by the door like the switch was nothing.

I've got my reservations about this whole setup. About him. About how easy it is to slide back into a house that isn't mine. Still, standing here in my socks, surrounded by peace I didn't have to fight for is... nice. Beats wrestling Gracie for a sandwich.

"What you got to eat?" I ask, pulling open the fridge. *Prepped greens? Mason jars of fruit?* "Kale and quinoa? Langston, you ain't got no Hot Pockets? No *wine?*"

Spotting the bottles of alkaline water lined up on the counter, I pout.

"Settle down," he says, shutting the fridge. "I'll warm something up."

I scoff, dropping onto the couch. "At this rate, I'm gonna fit into Alexia's costumes no problem." I lean back, draping an arm over my face. "At least staying here, I've got one place I don't have to *be* her."

"Don't get too comfortable," says Langston, pulling leftovers from the fridge. "If it were up to me, you wouldn't have to *be* her at all. Hot Pockets? *Pop-Tarts?* With a diet like that, it's no wonder you can't hit her octave."

Little does he know, I've barely eaten a thing.

I sit up and lean my elbows on my knees. "So what would you recommend I eat, Mr. Washington?"

"Nothing fried. Nothing processed. Dairy, alcohol, and carbonation are definite no's."

"So you're starving me?"

He huffs as he pops some grilled chicken in the microwave. "Lean protein and steamed vegetables. Warm food that won't inflame your vocal cords. *Not* cold. If you drink anything besides room-temperature water, I'd recommend ginger tea. Honey. If you must."

"That sounds nasty."

"Your voice is an instrument, Jayana. Stop treating it like a garbage disposal."

Thank God this is only for thirty days. Another month of this, and I'll be nothing but bones and attitude. If I don't pass out first.

Langston plates the rest of the food as the microwave beeps. "Lights are out at 10. Be up by 7. Keep showers to fifteen minutes or less, please."

"Anything else? Curfew bracelets? Room inspections?"

He tosses me a glare before returning to whatever master-piece he's making. "No touching the piano. It's a Hamburg Stein-way, and yes, it's older than you. No slamming doors. And absolutely *no* turning the heat past 72."

"Got it." I whip out my phone and pull up the Notes app. "How do you spell Steinway?"

I scowl when he doesn't break stride.

"Isn't it exhausting being a prick all the time?"

"Isn't it exhausting being a clown all the time?"

Stick-in-the-mud.

Crossing the living room, he sets the plates on the coffee table. "Any other questions?" He grabs silverware from the dining area before I can answer, complete with a rolled cloth napkin.

The chicken looks bland and the vegetables look limp. "Got any hot sauce?"

"We don't do spice," he says, pulling his dining chair across from me. "Inflames the larynx and constricts the pharyngeal muscles."

"*Constricts?*" I snort, taking my first bite. "I've seen skinny jeans looser than you."

He frowns. "Excuse me?"

I have to fight my smile. Getting a rise out of him feels too damn good.

"Relax, Mr. Washington. I mean... if you can."

His jaw rolls as he sets the plate on his lap and digs in. Not even a hint of a smirk.

If I ever wondered what it'd be like to live with Bert on *Sesame Street*, I think this would be it. Why is he like this? And what the hell did Alexia Hyrd see in him that possessed her to move in?

"I can have the driver swing by your place tomorrow if you want to get more of your things," he says.

Panic shoots through me. "Eh. Don't worry about it," I say too quickly. "Let the roommates wonder where I'm at."

Something flickers across his face. Gone almost as soon as I notice it.

With Alexia still missing, that couldn't have sounded more insensitive.

"I mean..." I release a breathless laugh, already scrambling. "I didn't mean it like that. It's not the same."

He doesn't respond. Just drops his gaze back to his plate, face hard, attention closed.

Based on the temperature shift alone, he couldn't care less what I meant.

We chew in silence, and the quiet stretches in a way that makes my skin itch. I stab a piece of squash and pretend I'm fascinated by the steam rising off it.

I could keep lying. I could let him think I've got some over-priced Midtown shoebox waiting on me, roommates and rent and a bed that belongs to me. But he's feeding me. Housing me. Sticking his neck out for me. And I can't keep throwing blows with Gracie every time a check comes in.

If I'm gonna sleep in his house, I at least owe him the truth.

"I don't actually *have* a place."

The words sit between us.

He doesn't move at first. Then he sets his fork down. "For how long?"

His voice is steady. Controlled.

"Just a week or so." I wave it off like it's nothing. "Stayed at a motel."

Like I wasn't counting every dollar. Like I wasn't triple-locking the door. Like I didn't almost sleep with his next-door neighbor just to eat and have somewhere warm to land.

"How long were you planning to stay there?" he asks.

I shrug, keeping my eyes on my plate. "Until something hit."

I glance up and regret it. Langston sits still in a way that isn't cold this time. He looks me over like I just told him I've been in a car accident and he's checking for bruises.

"You were alone?" he asks.

The question lands softer than I expect.

"I've handled worse," I say automatically.

His expression doesn't change. "How were you planning to manage auditions like that?" he asks. "Travel. Rest. Food."

Practical. That's where he lives.

"I was managing," I say, even though I just told myself I'd stop lying.

He studies me for another second, and this time I don't look away. Something shifts behind his eyes. Quieter than irritation. Like he's recalculating, and I can't stand not knowing the math.

"Why'd you do it anyway?" I ask.

"Do what?"

"Remind Julian about my audition."

He thinks for a beat. "Desperate times."

Of course.

"The girls at the *Aretha* production were terrified of you," I say.

He chews slowly, like he's thinking. "Based on your... boisterous comments, *you* didn't seem too terrified."

He's got a point. Then again, maybe if I'd been a little less of a clown, I wouldn't be over here selling my soul for a gig.

Rather than toss a weak comeback, I shovel some squash in my mouth. Not half bad for my third meal in two days.

Langston dabs his lips with a napkin, eyeing me. "I don't always... have a stick up my butt."

I swallow my chuckle. One, because him saying *butt* is the funniest thing I've heard all day. Two, because both of us know he's lying.

Just the same, he continues his attempt to persuade me. "That day at the Aretha rehearsal, I was... irritated. I was doing a favor for a colleague who's *never* respected my work, on a production that honestly, wasn't very creative, and to top it off, the talent was... subpar."

He winces at his own words.

For a second he looks less villain and more human. Maybe even a little tired.

"Thanks." I nod, not withholding my sarcasm.

"What I mean is..." He waves a hand. "I had a lot on my mind. I would've preferred to focus on... other things."

Something clicks for me. "Alexia had already gone missing by then. Hadn't she?"

He bobs his head, focusing on his plate.

That wasn't an answer. That was a dodge.

And just like that, all the questions return. *Where is she? Why did she go? Did something bad happen? What if whoever wanted her gone doesn't care which face is onstage?*

"Were you the last to see her?" I ask.

He chews like the question caught in his teeth. "I don't know," he says softly.

His face gives me nothing.

I think about the tampons and the two toothbrushes. He ain't got bunkbeds, and I highly doubt he had a Grammy award-winning celebrity sleeping on his couch.

I'm two seconds away from confirming what I already know when he abruptly stands and puts his chair away. I stare at him as he grabs his plate and moves toward the bedroom.

"Where are you going?"

He doesn't answer. Just shuts the door behind him.

But I've got questions. What the ID channel is going on around here?

"Hey! You making me sleep on this sofa again?"

The bedroom door opens just long enough for a pillow to sail through the air. I catch it against my chest.

"Rude."

The latch clicks shut like he means it.

I stare at the door longer than I mean to, the quiet stretching thin. He thinks I'm stupid—or maybe he thinks I won't notice what he didn't say. Either way, I know this much: he knows something. And sooner or later, I'm gonna find out what it is.

———

I WAKE THE NEXT MORNING UNDER ANOTHER SCRATCHY blanket, but at least I'm not cold.

"Count your blessings, Songbird." That's what Daddy always told me.

I sit up and crack my neck. "Langston! Ain't no way in hell I'm sleeping on this sofa for the next thirty days!"

But there's no response. Just the bird on its perch, staring me down like I missed something.

Asshole.

I'm about to call Daddy when I spot a stack of fluffy towels on the table. "Shoot, I could've slept on these." There's an expensive-looking toothbrush too.

Guess the jerk has manners after all.

Just beside the display is a yellow Post-it note:

> At the gym.
> Car will be around at 9.
> ~Langston
> P.S. Hydrate. Eat the berries.

Isn't that just like him? Bossing me around from blocks away.

I find the small bowl of berries on the kitchen counter along-side a protein bar and bottle of alkaline water.

"Count your blessings, Songbird," I repeat to myself.

Grabbing a berry, I head for the bathroom.

This shower's about to be twenty minutes. Minimum.

8

Langston's knee bounces as the car pulls around to the Majestic Theatre's entrance Tuesday morning. It's not a cute bounce. It's a stress bounce. The kind that says, despite his guidelines, he hasn't slept, hasn't eaten, and he's definitely rehearsed the worst-case scenario in four different keys.

He looks exhausted. Not that I can't relate. I spent the past forty-eight hours in a bootcamp with him and Julian, and I'm still struggling to remember my opening lines. Hair and makeup arriving at the crack of dawn didn't help either.

"Now remember," Langston says, picking at invisible lint on his slacks, "you only respond to Alexia... or Lex. That's what I used to call her."

I'd tease him about it, but my stomach's doing gymnastics. What if I slip up and act like myself? What if I literally slip and end up all over TMZ? There's no version of this where my mama's proud.

"In fact, just... don't speak to anyone besides me or Julian," Langston adds. "Nod, shake your head. And no eye contact. Okay?"

I bob my head with a swallow. I still haven't mastered this silence thing. My face wasn't built for quiet.

Langston checks his phone as it chimes. "Julian says, 'You're gonna knock 'em dead.'"

"Heh," is all I manage, brushing my brand-new Alexia bangs

aside. Typically, I'd never let my hair hang in my face like this, but this is Alexia's world, and I've gotta play the part. Especially if I wanna stay off the street and help my family. I can't think straight without food in my belly, and those showers at Langston's have been magical.

Here goes nothing.

Langston jumps out and opens my door before the driver can. He grabs my hand with a squeeze as I step out in my Alexia-style black wool coat and thigh-high leather boots. The warmth of his touch settles me in a way I don't wanna clock. Something soft stirs inside me anyway.

Langston's been... kind the past couple days. Steadier than I expected. Almost careful. I keep waiting for the other shoe to drop, but so far all I've gotten is the shoe holding the door open like a gentleman.

His throat works as we cross the threshold, a quick visible swallow. "Just... remember who you're supposed to be."

I nod like I'm not terrified, and we go in.

THE HALLWAY BACKSTAGE IS DIM AND NARROW, LIT BY BUZZING work lights and scuffed exit signs. Black curtains line the walls, and cables snake along the floor like booby traps. The double doors swing open into the rehearsal space bordered with mirrors, taped floor markings, and the faint echo of music bouncing off the rafters.

Cast and crew mill around, stretching, chatting, dancing through counts, pushing racks of costumes and half-built props. My gut flips. Too many faces. Too many people to lie to. Dozens of men, women, and...

Gracie.

I spin so fast I almost smack into Langston. I press into his chest like he's a human panic button. "It's Gracie."

He frowns like he didn't hear me. "Hmm?"

"*Gracie*," I hiss. "My old roommate. She's gonna know it's me!"

My heart pounds like it's trying to escape first. In all the urgency to become Alexia, I forgot this was Gracie's production too. She knows my walk. My voice when I'm nervous. The way I tuck my chin when I'm bracing for a lie. If she clocks me, this whole thing collapses. Not just tonight. *Everything.*

"We gave you the cast list," Langston whispers. "Why didn't you say anything?"

I could kick myself. It had photos *and* notes about the crew. "I didn't exactly get around to checking it out."

Langston's face goes full disappointed principal.

"I was slightly busy," I say. "You know. *Identity theft.*"

He shushes me. "Compose yourself."

No sympathy or softness. Just that crisp conductor tone that makes you feel like you're a trumpet coming in early. He turns me back around like I'm a misbehaving chair.

Gracie's over by the piano, arm extended, taking a selfie. That familiar sucking on lemons expression is plastered on her face. But she's not staring. At least not yet. Maybe she's still stewing over those trash reviews? Or maybe she's already putting the pieces together, and I'm about to find out how long she plans to make me sweat.

Everyone else slowly grinds to a halt as they spot me at the door. Watching, whispering, gasping. The whole room rearranges around me like I'm a live grenade.

I smile big and bright, just like Alexia.

"Is that…?" someone whispers.

"She looks different," says another.

"You owe me twenty bucks," another hisses.

A loud clap echoes from behind me, and I jolt like I've been caught stealing. Julian marches into the room in a charcoal sweater and pressed trousers, a dramatic red scarf around his neck.

"Yes! Our star is back," Julian declares. "I'm sure you've missed her just as much as I have."

Someone attempts to start a slow clap from the edge of the room. It dies after two beats, dozens of question marks sitting on everyone's faces.

"Where'd you go?" someone calls.

"Are the rumors true?" asks another.

Across the room, Gracie finally lowers her phone. Her mouth sets as she barely glances my way. I'm sure this wasn't the version of rehearsal she planned for. She exhales through her nose and straightens her shoulders, seeming too ticked to take a closer look.

Julian clears his throat. "I'm sure all your questions will be answered in due time."

Questions? It ain't like I got answers!

I shoot a look at Langston, but he rubs my shoulder like, *Breathe, don't combust.*

"Now that... Alexia's returned, the show can go on," Julian says. "Full dress and tech rehearsal today, and as you all saw in the company chat, previews continue tonight! Let's go. No time to waste!"

Just like that, everyone returns to their milling, though a few lingering eyes stick to me like lint.

"Hope she lasts this time," someone mutters.

"She looks tired," another adds. "Poor thing."

Poor thing is right. If I make it through today without passing out, I deserve a medal and a nap.

Langston's arm stays around my shoulder, firm enough that I don't drift, close enough that I feel it. "Just stay quiet," he whispers.

I bite my tongue to keep from screaming.

Langston's ushering me toward my dressing room, his hand light but insistent at my elbow, when a body slams into mine.

Arms wrap around me. Tight. Too tight. My cheek is pressed into someone's shoulder before I can react.

"We're so happy you're back," a voice breathes, already wavering. "Like... so happy."

Okay. Personal space?

The hug goes on. And on. I pat her back once, then twice.

Finally, the person pulls back enough to look at me. Freckles, low pigtails, clipboard tucked tight like it's part of her spine. Her focus doesn't waver. "I cried," she announces. "I'm not crying now. That was earlier. Different crying." Her eyes shine anyway.

Langston adjusts his glasses. "How's it going... Kai?"

Kai. Who's Kai?

"Awesome. We start in ten," she says quickly, gaze flicking over me, sharp. Attentive in a way that makes my skin itch. "You still like your mirror angled stage right, yeah? I know you hate the overheads."

Somebody call craft services. I think we're outta espresso.

Langston scratches his nose, glancing up the hall. "Really, Kai? Shouldn't an SM already know these things?"

SM. Right. Stage manager.

I shoot him a grateful look before nodding back at Kai like I've been following along this entire time. She tilts her head, studying me with alarming focus.

"Anyway." She smiles, wide and bright. "Welcome home." She squeezes my arm once, then disappears down the hall.

———

ONE WARDROBE CHANGE AND A HEADACHE LATER, I'M TRYING to make my way to the stage, but I think I take a wrong turn. Instead of slipping through the stage entrance, I drift into the front of the auditorium and stop the moment I realize where I am.

The Majestic Theatre.

Plush red seats spill upward in elegant rows, empty and expectant. Gold detailing gleams beneath the house lights, catching where it can. The ceiling stretches high above me, ornate and grand, like it was built to hold breath and sound and dreams.

My feet slow on their own, like my body's paying respect before my brain can remember we're technically committing fraud.

Awe rises anyway. Despite the lies, the borrowed name, the fact that I don't belong here as myself.

Daddy brought me here to see *The Lion King* on Broadway when I was ten. Ever since, I've been dreaming of getting up on this stage. And finally, I'm here. Not quite in the way I'd expected, but here just the same.

Hope's a dangerous thing. And this place is full of it.

"Isn't she a beauty?" Julian asks, wrapping an arm around my shoulders.

I nod, wishing I could call Daddy and show him right now, but Julian insisted we leave our phones backstage during dress rehearsal.

Julian levels his eyes with mine, a loose grin on his lips. "This is it... Lex. The moment we've all been waiting for. You ready?"

I'd scream loud enough for all of Times Square to hear if I could. Instead, I hold my peace like Langston told me, and bob my head, resolute.

It's time to work.

———

THE OPENING SCENE SETS ELLA'S WORLD IN MOTION. CITY residents hustle by in the Bronx. Extras chatter. Music swells.

I wring my hands behind the flats, running my opening lines on a loop. My pulse races as I mouth the words, just to be sure they're still there. The timing's off. Everything's off.

"How's it going?"

I startle at the whisper brushing my shoulder.

Langston. His nose is mere inches from mine, and for a second my brain does something stupid and personal, like notice the heat of him. Then I remember we're in a theater surrounded by a hundred people and his ass is on the line.

"It's okay to speak," he whispers. "It's just us."

I swallow, relaxing. "I figured you'd be in the pit."

"Assistant conductor's taking over. I'm with you today and tonight."

I study him, trying to place why that registers like comfort. I'm not supposed to be comforted. I'm supposed to be convincing. Still, a part of me softens.

"I'm nervous as hell," I confess in a harsh whisper.

"Not an option," he says. "Lex had enough confidence to fill this entire theater. Rehearsal studios included. If they see you shaking, they'll know something's up."

"Thanks for the pep talk."

I swallow as the woman playing my stepmother interacts onstage. Her skin is the color of warm honey under the lights, hair pressed smooth and swept back from her face, cheekbones sharp enough to command attention without asking for it.

"Who's that?" I ask.

"That is Charlotte Harrington," Langston says, eyeing her over his glasses. "Been in the Theater District for over a decade. Gigs in Hollywood even longer."

"For real?" I whisper, watching her move like the stage is her living room. She doesn't seem a day over thirty by the looks of it. Can't believe I've never heard of her before. "If that's the case, I can't imagine what my stepsisters will..."

My words catch in my throat as a young Black woman with a burgundy wig marches in from stage left, Gracie on her heels.

I stumble back into Langston.

"Whoa, whoa, whoa..." he says softly. "What's going on?"

He searches my face like he's checking for signs of life. And for half a second, it feels like he actually gives a damn.

I swallow, glancing back at Gracie as she delivers the line.

"Honestly, she's hopeless," she says, dramatically throwing up her arms.

"I thought you said Gracie was an understudy," I whisper harshly.

Realization dawns on Langston's face. "She was but... when she's not, she fills in as Anna. Ella's stepsister."

"Thanks for the heads-up, Langston."

"No problem."

"How am I supposed to convince the chick I just wrestled for a sandwich two days ago that I'm a Grammy Award-winning singer and headlining actress, Mr. Washington? Can you tell me that?" I hiss.

Langston frowns as he stares at the catwalks overhead. "You wrestled her for a sandwich?"

"Not the point," I mutter, even though it absolutely is the point.

I swallow hard as Charlotte, Gracie, and whoever my other stepsister is break into a song about how hard it is to find "good help."

"Listen, it's no different from what we went over," Langston whispers. "Chin high, shoulders back... A bitch."

"You make it sound so easy."

"For some of us, it is."

He's got a point. I don't even wanna think about what sex might've been like if he and Alexia were actually hooking up.

"Settle down. You don't need to perform."

"Nobody asked for your notes."

The number ends onstage, and the phone rings again.

"Yes. I know. I know! We're handling it," Charlotte says, hanging up. "Ella... Ella!"

I'm still frowning at the thought of Langston and Alexia growling at each other in bed when he turns me toward the entrance.

"That's your cue!"

He thrusts me on stage into the spotlight.

I freeze, knees crooked, blinking from the glare.

What do I do? What do I say?

"Line?"

No one answers. Then an arm wraps around mine and pulls me into a space where I can see.

"Ella, 3A's calling again. No heat," Charlotte says...or, my stepmother, I guess. "I thought you fixed that furnace."

I take in the set like I'm scanning a crime scene. Worn sofa. Low coffee table. A small dining set tucked in the corner. Stairs climb up to an open bedroom that barely counts as a room at all.

My Black stepsister glares at me like she's ready to pounce. Gracie shifts in her leather skirt, hip cocked like she's posing between lines. I pray the hot lights keep her from looking too close.

"Well?" Charlotte asks, prompting me.

Shit. Shit. Shit. What was I supposed to say?

"Uh..."

"I did, ma'am. I can check it again," Langston murmurs from the dark.

"I did, ma'am," I say, promising myself I'm gonna kiss him for that later. "I can check it again!"

"You'd move faster if your father were still around," Charlotte says. She and the stepsisters drop their heads dramatically and cross themselves.

"God rest his soul," they say in chorus.

The tension unfurls in my chest as Charlotte prattles on, pulling me around onstage.

"There's trash in the hall," says the Black stepsister.

"And the faucet's leaking in 4C," Gracie adds.

I nod, eyes cast low.

Move when they move. Breathe when they breathe. Don't look anybody in the eye too long.

And just like that, I'm back in rhythm, reciting my lines, hitting my marks. Just as Alexia would. It ain't easy, but I've got this. This is what I was born to do.

Then comes the song.

Ella's opening number isn't flashy. It's small. Intimate. Just her in a bedroom with a beat-up keyboard by the window, singing low like she doesn't expect anyone to answer back.

It only works if you believe her, and that's the problem. Everyone in this room is listening for proof. Not just of the note, but of whether they still buy it. Whether she deserves to step back into the spotlight like she never left. Langston needs this to work. The cast needs this to work. Even Alexia, wherever she is, would expect me to step in and see it through.

When I open my mouth, the room narrows. The chatter fades. It's just the melody and the air in my lungs.

Support. Space. Don't push.

I pull the breath the way Langston drilled into me and let the first lines sit easy, soft but steady. A few heads lift. The orchestra hums beneath me.

Then the climb comes. The note sitting right at the edge of her range. The one that makes the song ache instead of float.

I reach for it.

The pitch runs sharp before I can catch it, my voice splintering just enough to reveal the strain.

The crack is slight. But in a quiet number like this, slight carries.

A violin drags half a fraction behind me before correcting. Someone in the ensemble inhales too fast from the wings. I feel the shift without looking up, that ripple of bodies bracing.

Downstage left, I can feel Langston go still, eyes locked in, measuring.

Heat floods my face. I don't look at anyone, but the tension creeps into my shoulders.

My throat feels raw, like they can see straight through it now. I know they heard it. I know they're marking it down somewhere in their heads. One flaw. One pause. One more reason to question whether I belong on this stage.

The song keeps moving, so I do too. I reset my breath mid-phrase and let the next line fall lower and cleaner. But the damage is already done.

The spell changes. I remember the lights. The bodies. The borrowed name. I remember exactly where I am. But I've gotta keep going. This could be my only shot. And if I don't pull this off, all of us could be out of a job.

By the time I meet my fairy godmother—Stella Miller, according to Langston—I'm in my element again. She glides onstage bathed in warm light, thick silver curls framing her face, skin deep brown and luminous, body solid and grounded in the way only Broadway-fit women in their sixties are. A crisp cardigan, clean sneakers.

"You okay, baby?" she asks, resting a hand on my shoulder as I complete Ella's latest task—mopping the lobby floor.

"I'm fine," I say, tossing back a lopsided grin.

But Fairy Godmother just stares at me.

What is it? Did I get that wrong?

I glance down at the X taped beneath my feet. I didn't miss my mark this time.

The theater goes quiet as we wait for her to respond.

"Stella?" Julian calls from the front row. "Need a line?"

With a quick glance at Julian, she picks it back up. "Hmmph. That's not what fine looks like."

Stella presses her lips together, then nods like she's made a decision.

And finally, we can move on.

The rest of the scene goes smoothly. I settle into the rhythm, balancing Ella's sweetness with Alexia's polish. Pretty soon, we're wrapping up Stella's number, a sultry, jazz-soaked tune reminiscent of Lena Horne's performance in *The Wiz*. It's called "Dreams Don't Ask for Permission."

Langston and I slap fives as I run offstage. My chest feels too full. This is the life I've been auditioning for since childhood. And somehow, Langston's had my back through it all.

He awkwardly turns away as the costumer helps me quick-change.

What a sweetheart.

Though I'm sure he'd be happy to look if I were his precious Alexia.

"Excellent job, everyone!" Julian calls from the front row as we return to the wings. "Lex, you're looking beautiful. Gracie, remember your marks, please. Noah, you're up!"

"Noah?"

Langston meets my frown with a nod.

"Your prince."

9

Noah Rivera is the definition of Prince Charming. Brown hair falling where it wants. A smile that knows exactly when it's being watched. Tall, broad-shouldered, built in that unfair way that says doors have always opened for him. Probably not the only thing.

My goodness.

He steps onstage in his blazer and polished boots, gaze locked on me like I'm the only thing he can see. He meets me center stage, wraps me in his arms, and doesn't let go.

"I'm so glad you're okay," he whispers, his breath soft against my neck. My spine softens as he holds me close, his cologne a smooth, barely sweet scent. Like warmth and soap and skin, teasing me into forgetting where I am.

"Noah?" Julian calls from his seat. "Is there something you're informing Ms. Hyrd of that you'd like to share with the rest of the cast?"

With one last gentle squeeze, Noah backs away. "Just... relieved our star is back," he says.

A few whistles and howls echo through the auditorium, but his eyes never leave mine as he presses a kiss to the back of my hand.

Oh. He is bold.

"Watch out, Langston!" a voice teases from the wings.

A goofy laugh escapes me, and I clap my mouth shut.

Typically, between runs, my cackle wouldn't be a big deal. Maybe endearing even. But in a role like this, I can't forget I've *always* gotta be on.

Julian scratches the back of his head, eyes flicking between us like he already regrets letting this go on. Langston holds his place in the wings, seeming completely unbothered, which is either impressive or deeply annoying. I still can't tell.

"Alright, alright," Julian calls. "Save it for the spotlight, Noah. Places, everyone!"

Noah lets go slowly, like he doesn't want to, then takes his place across the stage. I step on my mark, the back of my hand still tingling, as he holds me in his gaze like a finish line.

Not Noah. Prince Santiago.

The Prince Santiago. The R&B star who vanished from Brooklyn years ago and resurfaced with a microphone and a headline, promising one girl a shot at everything. A blind audition. Masks. No faces. Just voice and chemistry. The winner gets a duet on his album. He sings on hers. A career wrapped up in a fairytale.

And Ella? Ella's been in love with him forever. From afar. From the radio. From dreams she never let herself say out loud. Ella just sang for him at the audition and he's done for. Just followed her out to the street, breaking every rule.

That's where we're at now.

"Okay... Ella," Julian tosses me a grin as he steps toward the stage. "Remember what just happened between you. Prince feels it too. I need both of you to dig deep. Let's recapture that magic we had just before previews."

Right. If only I'd been here when that spark happened.

I take a deep breath as the orchestra strikes gentle, romcom sweet chords, and we pick it up at Noah's line.

"Do you believe in miracles?"

The question lands too close to home.

For a split second, I'm not acting. I'm in my old apartment

with overdue notices and a daddy who still believes I'm destined for something bigger.

Noah's eyes don't waver.

"I do," I say in return.

He closes the distance between us, like it belongs to him. Like I'm the thing he's been walking toward all day. His blazer shifts as he moves, the fabric catching light, and for half a beat my attention snags where it shouldn't. On the clean line of him, the quiet confidence, the way he carries his charm like it's a birthright.

"Some people say miracles are just coincidences in disguise."

"Maybe that's just how fairytales sneak up on you," I say, and the line hits different coming out of my mouth. It feels aimed at him and not the scene. Like part of me meant it.

Right on cue, he swings around the light pole with a smile, then freezes when he sees me.

A real pause. Like something about me caught him off script. His focus drops, quick, then returns to my face like he's collecting details he didn't expect to want.

"You're hard to catch," he says, easy, amused.

My pulse skips, which is deeply inconvenient, 'cause this isn't the show. This is rehearsal. This is pretending. I'm already in trouble and he hasn't even touched me.

"I'm not supposed to stay."

I turn, but he closes his fingers around my hand, firm enough to steady me, careful enough to feel practiced.

"Then don't," he says, gaze steady on mine. "Just... wait."

In his mouth, the phrase feels intentional. Like he knows exactly how to make someone hover on the edge of a decision.

"Line?"

"Maybe just a moment," Kai murmurs from the wings.

"Maybe just a moment," I repeat, softer this time, and it comes out like a confession instead of a cue.

His hand stays wrapped around mine, thumb in the wrong place for professional. Not really crossing a line. Just enough to make my attention catch and hold. I can feel his pulse in his grip, steady and slow.

My heartbeat is loud. My skin is too awake. And I hate that I'm standing here acting like I've got time to want anything.

A guitar comes in low and steady, and for a second I almost forget what that means.

This is the song.

His hand stays where it is as he begins to sing, eyes fixed on mine, the space between us suddenly tight in a way I don't wanna name. Because naming it makes it real and I'm already juggling enough lies.

> *"I used to dream with my eyes wide shut*
> *Hiding from the light, sayin' love's too much*
> *But then you came like a melody so true*
> *And I knew... I knew it was you."*

The cue hits and I go for the chorus before I can overthink it.

> *"No one but you*
> *Can reach this heart the way you do*
> *No fairytales, no sweet disguise*
> *Just truth inside your eyes..."*

My voice wobbles for half a beat, then settles into something usable.

Close enough.

I'm distracted by his hand longer than I should be, by how easy it feels, how natural it is to stand here with him like I belong. Like this is what I wanted before life started punching me in the face. When I glance up, his expression shifts, open, like he didn't see this coming either.

We turn on the next beat, and I catch Langston in the wings watching. He looks relaxed enough, arms folded, weight settled.

But his eyes are sharp, tracking every move like he's listening for something off key.

I hesitate a fraction, thrown by the weight of it, and I miss the mark and come down squarely on Noah's foot.

"*Sorry!*" I hiss.

"It's alright." He chuckles softly.

The music dies down. Everybody's staring.

Julian's watching too. "Lex... that was your cue."

"Sorry! I mean..." I clear my throat.

Right. Not supposed to be speaking.

My gaze snaps to Langston in the wings. He doesn't move much, just a subtle shake of his head as he gestures for me to turn back around.

Noah clocks it all.

Julian glances at the cast and crew. "I know you've been saving your voice. We'll pick back up on your verse, Lex."

I nod, and the guitar comes back in.

Come on, girl. You got this.

I close my eyes with a deep breath as the lyrics come back to me.

> *"They said a girl like me should play it small*
> *But love, you saw the fire through it all..."*

Noah smiles as I sing, and I almost lose the beat entirely. But when he takes my hand again and spins me, my feet cooperate for once. I don't trip. I don't hesitate. I actually hit the landing.

His attention stays on me like the room isn't full of people. And for one stupid second, I think, *Oh.*

Which is dangerous, because *oh* is how you get ideas.

We sing in harmony as we move through the bridge, but once again my voice cracks on the octave. My nerves spike and I look to Langston, but Noah steps in my view.

"Don't let him get to you," Noah whispers. "Just keep going."

Don't let him get to me?

"Show must go on," Julian sings over the music. "Don't forget your choreography..."

Choreography. Right.

Noah launches into the routine I must've rehearsed with the choreographer a hundred times over the weekend. His body remembers. Mine absolutely does not.

Backup dancers flood in from both sides, moving like they got the memo I somehow missed. Either they're early, or I'm late, or we're all wrong and Broadway's about to find out in real time.

Someone trips as I scramble to hit what I think is my mark, and suddenly the music screeches to a stop.

Behind me, the stage turns into a mess of bodies and curses, feet clipped, arms tangled, somebody definitely on the floor. Even Noah winces, one hand braced on his knee like he caught the worst of it.

I stand frozen, wondering if this is how careers end. Not with a bang, but with jazz hands and regret.

Langston heads backstage, rubbing his temples, as Julian steeples his fingers at his lips. The quiet that follows feels heavier than the music ever did.

"Um, why don't we take fifteen, everyone?" Julian collapses in his seat as the cast attempts to recover. "Can someone get me some aspirin? *Please?*"

"She's losing it," someone whispers as I head offstage.

"She just needs rest," another says.

"She's spiraling. Again," someone adds.

Again?

I find Langston at the end of a hall backstage, staring out the window like he's trying to intimidate the universe.

"Langston, I'm—"

He lifts a hand, stopping me. "No need. I didn't expect much different."

Right.

I start to step back, but his fingers catch mine. The touch is brief, corrective. My lungs forget their job anyway. He lets go the second he remembers people are watching.

"You're overthinking everything," he says, voice low. "You keep reacting instead of committing."

"I *was* committing," I snap. "Nobody told me Noah was gonna be... Noah."

He shushes me, glancing around. "You're sounding too much like yourself," he mutters.

"Guess that's exactly the problem."

Langston blinks, bored. "It definitely isn't him."

"Excuse me?"

"You're chasing him. Chasing the room. You can't do that. You've gotta stay planted."

"So what, you want me to stand there like a mannequin?"

"I want you to be consistent," he says. "This isn't about how you feel in the moment. It's about control."

"Funny. Coming from you."

He exhales slow. "Tonight's preview is on the line. Stop improvising. Stop reacting. Do the work that's on the page."

"Well, sorry I'm human—"

"You don't get to be human out there," he says, blunt as hell. "You get to be right."

"Langston!"

Julian's voice cuts down the hall.

"Coming!" His hands settle on my shoulders, grounding me. "Don't chase the moment. Hold it. Deal?"

Got it. Focus.

He takes off to put out the next fire.

There he goes being decent.

I press my hands over my costume, steadying what he just unsettled.

Okay, girl. We got this. All you gotta do is be Alexia. Just like Julian said. Be. Her.

I'm turning to go find an empty rehearsal room where I can

review my steps when someone grabs my wrist and pulls me side-ways into the nearest door.

"Noah?" I blink as his face comes into focus in the dim studio, sunlight barely leaking through the heavy drapes.

"Babe, that was genius," he says, grinning. "I been trying to get a minute alone with you all day."

Babe?

"I never would've pulled a stunt like that just to buy us a fifteen." His eyes dance over my face as he steps toward me. "But that's just how brilliant you are."

He closes the distance, but I back away.

This feels like more than flirting.

"Noah, I... I wasn't—"

He doesn't let me finish. His arms wrap around me, pulling me in like this is muscle memory. Like this is where he expects me to be.

"I've missed you like crazy," he murmurs. "Every day. You know I'm sorry for everything, right?"

Sorry? My pulse spikes. *Sorry for what, exactly?*

He's looking at my mouth now, waiting. Like there's a script I'm supposed to follow. Like this is supposed to be a *thing*, and not some harmless backstage tension.

Shit. They were together.

Together together.

I slip out of his grasp and move toward the window, trying to buy myself time.

Okay, Yana. Think. Fast.

"Of course you're sorry," I say carefully. "Now."

He exhales, relief softening his shoulders like that was the right answer. But my mind's racing. *Sorry* could mean a thousand things. Sorry for lying to her. Hurting her. Pushing her off a bridge.

He moves closer again, but I maintain the distance. His face falls, all wounded sincerity.

"Lexy... baby. You've gotta believe me. I never meant for

things to go this way. I just—" In one swift move, he's got me backed into a corner, his hand closing around mine. "I'm gonna make this right," he says quietly. "Just meet me at lunch. In our secret spot."

Secret spot?

If they had a secret spot, then they had secrets. Time alone. Conversations no one else heard. Arguments that never made it past the walls.

I force a small, careful smile. "You mean... the first place we—"

"Of course not," he laughs too quickly.

"You mean..." I let the words trail off, heart hammering, hoping he'll fill in the blank for me.

A slow smile spreads across his lips.

And suddenly the question isn't whether Noah knows something. It's what he *did*.

Or what he's been covering up since Alexia disappeared.

10

"It's like she had a lobotomy," one of the cast members jokes as she washes her hands.

"Please," says the other. "I saw you stumbling all over yourself in the block party number!"

They laugh as they exit the bathroom.

I flush and step out of the stall. Wash my hands. Stare at my reflection like I'm supposed to know which of us is real.

In the mirror, I look the part. Hair flat ironed. Glitter on my cheeks. Alexia's perfectly arched brow staring back at me like she knows something I don't. But I can't afford to linger on it. At least not now.

I draw my eyes shut as I dry my hands, willing my stomach to stop doing gymnastics.

One more hour until I get answers. Until I finally understand what the hell I just waltzed into.

I step out of the bathroom and head up the hall.

"Alexia... Lex!"

Oh, right. That's me.

Julian waves me over from his office.

"Go ahead and shut the door, please."

He looks beyond stressed as I do.

Papers everywhere. A half-drunk coffee sweating on a stack of schedules. His phone buzzing on the desk like it's possessed. He drags a hand down his scalp with a long exhale.

"How ya feeling?"

I glance at the phone. At the coffee. At the way his knee won't stop bouncing. Then I lift a shoulder.

"I'm good."

"Good?" He stops short and stares at me like I just said the theater's on fire. "Good how?"

"I mean... aiight," I say.

His eye twitches. Just once.

"*Aiight? Aiight* doesn't calm investors," he says. "*Aiight* doesn't sell tickets. *Aiight* does not justify a seven-figure budget."

The phone buzzes again. He sends it to voicemail without looking, then presses both palms to his eyes like he's trying to keep his brains from spilling out on the desk.

"I'm... doing my best," I say.

"I know," he says quickly. Then, quieter, sharper, "But listen to me... Yana."

He says my name in a whisper. Like it's contraband. His eyes flick to the door.

"This isn't some workshop. This is *Broadway*." He points vaguely at the ceiling, the walls, the city beyond them. "There are unions. Contracts. Press. People who would love nothing more than to see this production implode."

I give him a crooked smile. "No pressure."

He doesn't smile back.

"Do. You. Understand?" he says, planting his hands on the desk.

He's cracking.

I take a small step back. "Yes, sir."

But I *do* understand. If I mess this up, it's not just me who falls. Julian knows it, too. It's in the way he's staring at me like he's trying to decide whether I'm a miracle or a mistake.

Then just as abruptly, he composes himself and slaps the baseball cap back on.

"Good. Now let's get back to work."

NOAH'S CHARMING SMILE NEVER WAVERS AS WE WALK through the finale.

Ella's stepmother sends her off to "check the furnace" just as Prince Santiago shows up looking for his R&B queen. Then she locks Ella in the basement like that's a totally normal response to romance.

But Prince hears her singing. Of course he does. Because destiny. And acoustics. He finds her almost immediately. And then they sing together.

It's the same duet Noah and I sang earlier, just bigger now. Louder. Sweeping. All the feelings laid out where the audience can't miss them. A number designed to make people believe in love again. Or at least text their ex before the lights come up.

And it ends the way fairytales always do.

With a kiss that's supposed to feel inevitable. Earned. All-consuming.

Noah's gaze is locked on mine as he sings from his chest, belting out declarations of love.

I hate that I understand it. The jacket's tailored, the arms are *ridiculous*, the hair's doing that slow romantic sway like it's auditioning for a shampoo commercial.

Yeah. I get how Alexia got caught up.

But attraction ain't an alibi. And last I checked, being beautiful never kept anybody out of handcuffs.

Okay. This is it.

I take a deep breath and push from my diaphragm like Langston taught me, pacing myself as I sing. There's a glimmer in Noah's eye as we hold the final note together, and he moves closer.

Bet he's been aching to do this all day.

I tell myself this is part of the show. Part of Prince Santiago finally finding his girl.

Still, something pulls low in my ribs as he closes the space between us, like my body knows before my brain does that this is about to get complicated.

I glance toward the wings. Toward Langston. Isn't somebody supposed to call cut? Julian? Anybody? But no one does.

Noah's breath is warm as he leans in... and then his mouth opens against mine.

Okay. Stage kisses are usually nothing. A suggestion. Closed-mouth. All angles and timing and pretending. The last one I did in college tasted like mint gum and panic.

But Alexia consented to *this*?

It's soft. Confident. Unrushed. Like he knows exactly where to put his hands and how long to linger. Like he's done this plenty of times before and wanted to do it again. My brain scrambles to catch up.

This ain't for me. Not really.

It's for Alexia. For the woman he's been imagining this moment with. For the version of her he's been holding onto. The thought knocks the air out of me even as his arms tighten, even as the kiss deepens and the room seems to tilt.

"And... cut!" Julian finally calls.

But Noah's not stopping.

The applause hits first. Cheers. Whoops. Somebody whistles.

"I said, cut," Julian snaps. "Noah, let Alexia breathe, please."

Noah finally pulls back, smiling like a kid who stole an extra cookie and plans to do it again. His eyes stay locked on mine, searching. Expectant.

My lips tingle. My head spins.

Well, damn.

"He's been waiting for that one!" somebody calls out, laughing.

From the wings, I catch Langston's profile. His jaw is tight. Shoulders squared. Not angry really. Just... measured. Like he's already filing this away as something he doesn't like and doesn't intend to talk about.

"Let's just wrap with the final number," Julian says, sounding exhausted. "Please."

Noah slaps fives with one of the fellas as he finally backs away, grinning at me like he's just delivered the perfect birthday gift.

Whatever was going on between him and Alexia didn't end when she disappeared. And I need to figure out what it was before I'm standing in her place for more than just the show.

———

JUDGING BY THE WAY THE STAGE CLEARS WHEN KAI CALLS FOR us to take lunch, everybody's starving as much as me. But I've got a meeting to catch.

I make my way through the hallway traffic and slip into an old supply closet.

Noah's waiting inside, surrounded by bleach bottles and mopping buckets, holding a single prop rose like we're in a romcom.

I managed to get him to cough up the details earlier as we took a little walk down memory lane. Apparently, this is where the two of them shared their first kiss, during a heated fifteen.

Votive candles flicker on crates. Takeout containers crowd a shelf. A picnic blanket's spread across the floor with NOAH + A scrawled on masking tape.

What the actual...?

He strides over and passes the velvet rose into my hand with a straight face, as if we're auditioning for cheesiest promposal of the year.

A snort slips out of me, and I slap a hand over my mouth.

"Baby..." Noah's grin falters. "That's a new one."

I clear my throat, waving my hand. "You just... surprised me," I say in my softest Alexia voice. "That's all."

He nods, fully convinced. "Here. Have a seat."

He guides me to the blanket. Beneath it is a foam exercise mat. Bless him.

"Now, I know how bad you said Kung Pao was for your voice last time," he says, reaching for the takeout containers on the shelf, "so I went with the ginger chicken."

Last time?

He flashes that dimple I'm sure makes audiences melt. "I hope you like it."

With the way Langston's been starving me lately, that pint could be full of crickets, and I'd still try it. I snatch it up and dig in.

Oh, thank the Great Wall of China.

I throw back my head in relief.

But the cool sensation of Noah's mouth on my neck makes me jolt back.

"Hey! Hey!"

For a second I think he's moving way too fast. Then I remember. Noah's used to this with Alexia.

Right. Alexia.

"I mean," I soften my voice, forcing calm, "can I eat first... babe?"

Noah pauses, then bobs his head. "You're right. You are absolutely right. I just... got carried away."

I flash a crooked smile and take another bite of ginger chicken.

"In fact," he says, reaching behind his back, "I meant to give you this first."

He presents a little white napkin with the word *sorry* scribbled across it.

Glad to see the Sharpie didn't go to waste.

"Thanks, babe." I dab my mouth gently.

He moves closer again, forgetting the boundary I set five seconds ago.

"Listen, Lexy, I get it," he says. "I can be impatient."

"You think so?" I ask, leaning back and praying for peace.

"I know so," he says. "I shouldn't have rushed you, *negrita*."

Nuh-what now?

"I wanted more, but you weren't ready. I pushed and pushed... until I pushed you right back into his arms."

Langston? Or somebody else?

"You must've been spiraling, baby." His hands settle on my shoulders as he searches my eyes. "I figured you took off to rehab or something. Where'd you go?"

He looks genuinely concerned.

So he didn't engineer her absence? He wanted her back all along?

Noah sighs. "Doesn't matter. I should've known something was wrong. Especially after the way he treated you in that last rehearsal."

I chew slow. "You mean... Langston?"

He nods. "You deserve better, baby. I've always told you that."

The shape of it starts making sense. I keep chewing, then swallow and set my container aside. If I don't slow down and think, I'm gonna say something that gets me murdered or exposed. Or both. New York's efficient like that.

"I know you're right... babe." The word still feels strange in my mouth. Borrowed. "I was just having second thoughts. About him. About us. It was... a lot."

I bob my head the way Alexia always does, that small deliberate nod I've been practicing in the mirror.

"And then I got sick and... well. You know."

Noah studies me for a beat, like he's deciding whether to believe it. Then his expression softens into relief. Want.

He leans in, slow. Just close enough that I feel the warmth of him, the quiet expectation in the space between us, like he's waiting for me to stop pretending I'm not part of this.

I should say something. Create distance. But we already did this once. Why not?

His lips meet mine with an ease that feels practiced and

personal, like they've been here time and time again. And not just for rehearsal. His hands settle at my waist, cocky and greedy. His pinky tickles the top of my waistband like they're old friends.

I mean, I'd be down if this wasn't way above my pay grade.

Up the hall, somebody starts running scales, followed by Kai's sharp claps. "Break means break!"

Okay. I need to refocus, and fast. Getting swept up has a cost and I cannot afford another one.

I scoot back, heart thudding. "Babe, I totally forgot, Julian asked to meet in his office to go over a few notes. I'm already running late."

His handsome face crumples as I grab my takeout and stand.

"Thanks." I duck out before I can change my mind.

Goodness. What a guy. A sexy, horny, and maybe a little pathetic guy. But certainly no psycho. Good taste in Chinese, though.

I'm thinking I'll finish lunch in the mezzanine when Langston blocks my path.

My stomach drops like I just missed a step.

"Where were you?" he asks, brow creasing.

The supply closet flashes in my mind. Noah's hands. His mouth. The way I let it happen because it wasn't me he was kissing. Or so I told myself.

Langston's expression hardens, waiting, and guilt hits me right in the chest.

That mingled with all the thoughts Noah placed in my heart just now. Thoughts about Langston getting to her. Thoughts about him pushing her away. If there was more, what did he do?

Then again, what if he didn't? What if he didn't know anything? Just like he probably didn't know what Alexia had been up to behind his back. If he knew what I just let happen, it wouldn't just piss him off. It would gut him.

"Just..." I resist the urge to glance back at the supply closet. "Around."

He frowns at the takeout in my hand. "Tell me that isn't spicy."

"It's not. Promise."

Question is... did he know how spicy things were getting between his little girlfriend and Prince Charming?

He studies the small pint, then nods. "Listen, I wanted to... apologize."

I freeze. That looked painful for him.

"I know I was a little... harsh," he says. "And I wanted to say, you're good. This final run was good. Don't worry about tonight."

Sure, I could see his crazy pushing someone away. I've seen how hard he pushes. How narrow his vision gets. But I've also watched him choose tenderness when he didn't have to. That doesn't fit the villain Noah's sketching.

I school my face, but my smile slips out anyway. "Thanks, Langston."

He nods once, eyes flicking down the hall like he's checking for witnesses. Then he steps closer. Close enough that I can smell him. Woodsy and spicy and sweet. Like he's the type of man who knows his cologne costs too much and wears it anyway.

Before I can flinch, his arms come around me. It's brief. Careful. Like he means it, but doesn't wanna admit how much.

His lips brush my cheek. Warm. Gone almost as soon as they land.

Oh. My. Gosh.

"Don't freak out," he whispers. "You know the peanut gallery's watching."

Right. I'm Alexia. And she and Langston were together... too.

Damn, this is messy.

I nod, checking out the small clusters of cast and crew pretending not to glance our way.

Quickly, I peck his cheek in return. His five o'clock shadow isn't too prickly, and the cologne is nice. Really nice.

He pulls back, gaze lingering like a warning. "Don't get too used to this."

"Of course not," I say.

I don't even watch his ass when he walks away. Except for when I do.

11

Break a leg tonight. You know we're all rooting for you! Laura sent the message twenty minutes ago, but honestly, I don't feel up to responding. She knows tonight's my first preview. She just doesn't know I'm at the top of the bill as someone else.

I owe Daddy a call, too, and I keep dodging it like he ain't gonna hear the guilt in my hello.

Curtain call for previews is in three hours, and everybody went home to eat and recharge. Everybody besides me. Or should I say, Alexia.

Langston and Julian insisted I stay to review my blocking and go over some lines.

"*You can eat later*," Langston said.

He doesn't understand my metabolism. He's lucky I'm not calling my union rep.

They keep getting on me for slouching. I keep forgetting not to cackle. And my eyes are burning like somebody sprinkled sand in them just for fun. I sigh, looking out at the empty theater from the mezzanine, the seats all velvet and promise and judgment.

Just like the brochures.

"Looks like you and I had the same idea."

It's Stella. Ella's fairy godmother. Silver curls pulled back into a loose knot, lipstick still perfect, holding a bottle of gin in her hand like it knows her better than most people do.

"Almost," I say, eyeing the liquor. "Is pre-gaming Broadway a thing now?"

"Honey, I've been in this business for forty years," she says. "They gave up firing me decades ago."

We slap fives as she takes a seat beside me, and something in me softens, almost against my will.

"First show jitters?"

I open my mouth to answer, then remember who I'm supposed to be. "This isn't—"

"It is," she says. "And both of us know it."

My gut does a full nosedive.

"How'd you—"

"Please, child." She waves me off. "I knew from the moment I stepped onstage. You're an imposter. Her doppelgänger. Julian's pathetic excuse for a last resort."

"Pathetic?"

She smirks. "Effective, though."

I don't know whether to be offended or impressed.

"What's your real name, anyway?" She lifts a hand at my dropped jaw. "On second thought, don't answer that. I'd rather not be an accessory to the ruse."

I blink, then the corner of my mouth lifts. I love her already.

"Was I that bad?" It comes out softer than I planned.

"Child, listen..."

She tosses back a swig of her drink like she's got nothing but time.

"I understudied twelve years before anyone let me near center," she says. "Chorus. Swings. Replacements. Watched girls half as ready walk into their moment 'cause they believed they belonged there. Took me a minute to learn that part."

She eyes me sideways.

"This is your first time carrying, hmm?"

I gaze down at the dormant set in the shadows. "On such a grand stage? Yeah."

She nods, like she just stamped a form in her head.

"Here's the trick. You can't treat this like borrowed space. If you want 'em to believe you're Ella, you've gotta believe it first. Take up the room. Own the air. *Be* Ella."

I stare at her, the idea settling low and quiet. Not a solution, exactly. More like a door cracking open where I didn't know there was one.

She grins. "Besides. Nobody ever rooted for the girl who stumbled into the spotlight."

A laugh slips out of me, and suddenly, my chest doesn't feel so crowded.

Stella raises her bottle in salute.

———

I carry Stella's wisdom in my chest, like a note I don't wanna forget, as I wait backstage for my entrance.

Be Ella.

My eyes drift shut as I inhale deep and exhale long, reminding myself not only to be Ella, but like Julian said, Alexia too. The woman the audience came to see. The star they've been whispering about all week. That part is still the weirdest, because they're not whispering about me. Not really. They're whispering about somebody else's face that I'm wearing like a mask.

Just minutes ago, I was swarmed backstage, everything buzzing with pre-preview chaos. Nervous laughter. Warm-ups bleeding into one another. Hands squeezing shoulders a second too long like we're all trying to borrow bravery from whoever has extra.

Julian gathered us close in the rehearsal room, everybody linking arms as he gassed us up. Then he started this chant that everyone but me seemed to have memorized. But I quickly caught on:

One show. One heart. One family.

It's the kinda thing that seeps into your bones and steadies you before you can talk yourself out of it.

Langston caught me right after, already halfway back into his professional armor.

"Knock 'em dead tonight," he muttered. *"And there just might be dessert in your future."*

Dessert.

I let the thought of my much-deserved treat settle my nerves, indulgent and sweet and waiting on the other side of the curtain.

No stress. No stress. No stress.

You are a professional actress, Yana. This should be as simple as breathing. People do that all the time.

I jump when a stagehand slaps me lightly on the back.

"Break a leg," he whispers as he passes.

"Thanks," I murmur, heart pounding like he just tested a live wire.

The orchestra hums just beyond the stage, strings tuning, brass murmuring to life. Langston's down in the pit, baton poised, I'm sure. I guess he and Julian decided he should conduct after all.

Which leaves me... on my own.

No biggie. Just a thousand critical faces and a handful of investors waiting to see if Alexia screws this up.

The hum tightens, purpose replacing chaos.

The downbeat lands, and the show begins.

Outside the apartment, the city moves. Neighbors drift through the block, singing about double shifts and late trains, bills that don't wait, and dreams that have to. There's no time for wanting more. Just get through the day. Keep it pushing.

The music carries us inside.

Mrs. Hale, Ella's stepmother, is already on the phone, voice all customer service sweet as she fields complaints about broken heat and unhappy tenants. The moment she hangs up, the smile vanishes.

"I swear, these people act like winter snuck up on us," she says, Brooklyn accent thick. "And that apartment smells like cat piss. Far as I know, she don't even own a cat."

The audience chuckles, warm and soft, and I feel it in my bones like a little permission slip.

The stepsisters, Anna and Draya, played by Gracie and... Regan, according to Langston, burst in from school, loud and dramatic, griping about classes and careers they haven't earned yet. Fashion design, apparently. Big dreams. Zero talent.

The lights warm my face as I peek through the set, watching Gracie fling her designer bag onto the couch like it's lucky she chose it.

"Really," she scoffs, "if this building falls apart, it won't be my fault."

She was born for this role. She should be thanking me for stepping in as Ella, honestly. Some girls have to reach for mean. She just exhales it.

Mrs. Hale shuts down the stepsisters bickering with one look, the music swelling under her lecture about money, responsibility, and buildings that don't run themselves. Their opening number kicks into full gear.

I swear I can feel Langston glancing my way from the pit as he conducts, likely struggling to stay locked in. I know he's holding his breath, praying I won't crash and burn.

But I can do this. For him. For Daddy. For everybody.

Even Gracie's pale ass.

The number ends with Mrs. Hale and the stepsisters frozen in a final pose, and right on cue, the phone starts ringing again.

"Ugh! That lousy furnace," my stepmother snaps.

Here comes my cue.

I smooth my hands over my costume and nod to myself. If I don't collect my nerves, I'm gonna start shaking and never stop.

It's time to shine, baby.

"Ella!" she calls sharply. "Ella! Where are you?"

I step onto the stage, into the glowing lights. "Yes, ma'am?"

She and my "stepsisters" turn toward me, their gazes sharp and expectant as light applause ripples through the theater. Julian warned us this might happen. But my knees still threaten to give out.

All these people excited to see me. Or... *her.* But right now, I *am* her.

The applause fades, the house settles, and my stepmother waves a dismissive hand. "Ella, 3A's calling again. No heat. I thought you fixed that furnace."

"I did, ma'am. I can check it again!" I turn to leave right on cue.

"You'd move faster if your father were still around," says Charlotte.

She and the stepsisters dramatically cross themselves like before. "God rest his soul."

The audience barely chuckles as Charlotte takes me by the arm.

"There's trash in the hall," says Regan.

Gracie's line is next.

But she doesn't speak. Just blinks. Once. Slow. Assessing.

It's the same look Stella gave me earlier. That brief unsettling pause right before recognition. Right before...

What if she knows? What if I slipped somewhere I didn't even feel?

I hold still, forcing my face into neutral, willing my body not to betray me.

Don't rush. Don't overcorrect. Don't give her anything.

Gracie's gaze lingers a heartbeat longer. Then she rolls her eyes like she's bored.

"And the faucet's leaking in 4C," she says with the flit of her hand.

Maybe she forgot her line?

I meet their stares, just like we rehearsed. But this time, I don't freeze.

"On it," I say, voice clear, strong, carrying all the way to the back row.

I turn to go again, but my stepmother stops me with a pointed glance. "And, Ella. Make sure you don't come back reeking of smoke this time. I won't have my house smelling like some factory."

A beat. "Yes, ma'am."

As I exit stage left, the crowd offering charmed applause, I feel Langston's eyes on me like a current. My solo is coming. The one that can't be faked or rushed or hidden behind choreography. Just me and the stage.

Ella's bedroom glows soft and blue, lit by a single lamp and the spill of moonlight through the window. The room feels smaller than it did before, quieter. Intimate.

I sit at the keyboard her father left behind, fingers resting on worn keys that have been loved hard. There's supposed to be a history in them. Calluses. Grief. Hope pressed down and played out one note at a time.

The orchestra hushes. I strike the opening chord, gentle and deliberate, letting it ring. The spotlight rests on me. I breathe deep.

"Mmm... yeah..."

The words come easily at first. Muscle memory. Truth.

"I was born from shadows...
but I don't live there no more..."

The audience leans in. I can feel it. The way a room shifts when people stop watching and start listening.

Verse one carries me forward.

"Tried to dim my voice, cut off my wings..."

My voice settles into the melody like it's always belonged there, like Alexia's vocal cords have taken the wheel.

And then... my mind blanks.

Damn it.

Just one line. Gone. Slipped clean out of reach.

My heart stutters, but the piano keeps moving under my fingers, steady as a heartbeat. I let out a soft, sad chuckle, like the moment is simply part of the story.

A murmur ripples through the audience, but I can't be sure if it's concern or connection.

Hopefully connection.

I find my way back into the lyric, sliding in on the next phrase like I meant to do it all along.

"Even broken dreams still leave a mark
And I wear mine like a work of art..."

My pulse settles as the chorus rises, and the orchestra joins in.

"I will shine through the dark...
Turn my pain into light..."

The sound swells. Strings rise around me, the piano holding underneath as my voice rides the top. Still, fear flickers at the back of my mind.

Don't crack. Not on the final note.

Alexia's signature note. The one the critics wait for. The one that makes or breaks the room.

I make it through verse two, the part where my voice usually wants to show off. I keep it steady. Then the choir comes in on the bridge, full and warm, filling the space behind me and carrying me through.

"Ohh—don't tell me who I'm meant to be..."

My hands shake just a little as the final chorus builds.

I feel it coming. That spot. That note. The one Alexia always nails. The one Langston drilled into me until my throat burned. If I reach for it the same way, I'm gonna lose it.

There's no room to borrow here. No space to hide in somebody else's voice.

Take up the room.

So I stay.

I pull back just enough, bend the note, let it turn where my voice wants to go instead of where it's supposed to land. It isn't planned or brave. Just me, trying to survive.

The riff slips out. The sound opens.

And applause crashes in waves, loud and sudden and alive. Cheers. Whistles. Feet stomping. I have to fight to stay in character, to keep Ella grounded in her story when every cell in my body wants to laugh and cry and lift off the bench.

The rest of the production flies.

Scene after scene unfolds clean. Noah plays it straight, no extra heat, no lingering kiss. Just story. Just truth. We hit the final number, voices braided together, lights blazing.

And then it's over.

The curtain falls. Then rises again. We take our bows.

When I step forward, the applause swells just a little louder. Warmer. Like they're clapping for more than the performance. Like they're clapping for the fight it took to get here.

My throat goes thick.

Then Julian appears with a thick bundle of roses. He presses a kiss to both my cheeks as he passes them over.

"Thank you," he murmurs, before turning to take his own bow.

My chest aches in the best way.

This moment is bigger than me. Bigger than ego or fear or

ambition. It feels good to help something live. To be a part of it... even if I don't belong to it.

Then, just as we rehearsed, the entire cast turns toward the pit, gesturing as one.

Langston stands as if caught off guard, lifting a hand in a half-wave. He looks almost embarrassed. Almost. His lips make the tiniest twitch, humble and proud at the same time.

Man, he's cute.

The applause rolls on.

My first time out front in a preview. And I didn't break.

———

THE HALLWAY'S A BLUR OF MOVEMENT AND NOISE ONCE I STEP offstage.

Rolling carts clatter past with costume racks and prop bins. Somebody whoops from behind me. Somebody else squeezes my hand, then keeps moving like we're all riding the same current.

"You killed it, Lex," says Kai, breathless.

I laugh softly in response, because I've never known how to hold joy quietly. My whole body still feels like it's vibrating. Adrenaline. Relief. Something bigger I don't have a name for yet.

Then I see him. Langston.

He's charging down the hall toward me, long strides, jaw set, eyes locked on mine. The crowd parts around him without him slowing down.

Here it comes.

I missed some marks. I rushed some lines. I dropped a whole damn lyric. I straighten instinctively, hands flying up like I can brace myself for impact.

"Hey," I start, words tumbling out too fast. "I know that I—"

He reaches me and pulls me into his arms, like he doesn't wanna give himself time to overthink it. His lips brush my forehead, warm, steady, and for a split second it feels less like a kiss and more like a blessing.

"I think you may have just saved this show," he whispers.

All that breath I've been hoarding since the curtain went up spills out of me in one shaky release, like my body finally got the memo that I'm not about to die.

He pulls back just enough to look at me, and his eyes are bright. Lit up. Fired. Not Langston in charge. But maybe actually... impressed.

He flicks a glance down the hall, like we're not standing in a building still buzzing from the crowd. "How about we go grab some dessert?"

———

THE ICE CREAM SHOP IS WARM AND NOISY AND STILL AWAKE. Sugar hangs in the air, the neon sign humming softly as people drift in and out. It feels like a place that doesn't care who you are, only that you showed up.

I step to the counter and reach for a sample spoon.

"Ah-ah." Langston's hand comes down gently on my wrist. "No dairy tonight, superstar. Your cords will hate you tomorrow."

I pull my hand back and fold my arms. "Then why bring me to an ice cream shop?"

"Because they have sorbets." He scans the menu like he's conducting a symphony, then taps the glass. "Lemon, raspberry, or mango. And a cup of lukewarm water. You need to hydrate between bites."

I order mango with a pout.

Add it to the list of things I'm not allowed to enjoy.

We slide into a cracked vinyl booth by the window. The city glows outside, taxis streaking past, people rushing by with places to be and stories I'll never know.

I take my first bite.

Oh. Okay. That's actually incredible.

I sigh, eyes fluttering shut for half a second. "I gotta say... it's nice to finally get a little recognition from y'all." I scoop another bite. "I think I've worked harder this week than I have since I moved to New York."

Langston eats his sorbet like it's oatmeal. Completely unimpressed. "And yet, you still missed a lyric. And an octave."

"And no one cared but you! Sir, give me a little credit." I snap over my head. "As hard as you and Julian been working me, I *still* showed up and did the damn thing. Mmkay?"

He pauses. Just long enough to be intimidating. "An arrogant actress is a difficult actress."

"Where'd you pull that from? *Lame Men's Almanac 1995*?"

We eat in silence for a beat, and I let myself feel the booth beneath me, the cold sweet on my tongue, the fact that I'm not onstage anymore. No spotlight. No cue.

"I suppose," he says slowly, "your improvisation could've been worse. Guess maybe there's some soul in that diaphragm after all."

I press a hand to my chest dramatically. "You know what a soul is?"

Of course he doesn't laugh.

"Looks like them voice lessons my daddy put me through are finally paying off," I say.

A smile tugs at my lips, my gaze resting on my sorbet.

"First time we went to see *Disney on Ice*, I told him I wanted to be Princess Jasmine. He signed me up for classes the next week." My eyes burn before I can stop them. "Been calling me Songbird ever since."

Langston quietly nudges the cup of water closer.

I sniff and take a sip. "Anyway, now that I'm finally making some dollars, maybe I can start paying him back."

"Paying him back?" Langston's brow furrows.

I open my mouth. Close it. "I used a relocation service to move out here. Kinda got in over my head. Told Daddy I'd catch up on my own, but he insisted."

Langston frowns deeper. "Those services can run into the tens of thousands. Didn't you know before you signed?"

"I mean... yeah." I shrug. "But I had a dream."

"This is New York City, Yana," he says quietly. "Everyone's got a dream."

"And finally," I say, meeting his gaze, "I'm realizing mine."

He stares at me like he's trying to solve a puzzle that refuses to fit.

"Can I just enjoy my skinny ice cream, please?"

He exhales through his nose and leans back. "Fine."

I tilt my head. "So. Was Broadway always your dream?"

He thinks. Really thinks. "I honestly can't say it ever was. More the logical conclusion to a well-thought-out plan."

"You make it sound like a blueprint for a strip mall."

"It really could've been." He sips his water. "Private education. Prestigious schools in L.A. Four years at Juilliard. Another at Columbia. Etcetera, etcetera."

"Obviously," I say. "I take it your parents were loaded?"

Langston watches me over his cup like he's weighing how much truth I can carry.

"Not were. *Are*. Spencer and Cree Washington. You may have heard of them."

My mouth falls open. "*The* Spencer and Cree Washington? No wonder they said you're Hollywood royalty!"

"How could I ever forget?"

The words sit heavier than he probably means. Not defensive. Just... exposed.

I lean back in the booth, clocking the way his mouth tightens, like he already regrets saying it. Meanwhile, I'm thankful to Alexia—wherever she is—that I'm not out here rocking scuffed boots with a cracked sole.

"Hmmph." I fall silent. "Guess that silver spoon really is a thing."

"Don't get me wrong," he says evenly. "I worked my ass off to get where I am. But I won't pretend the runway wasn't already built."

"Sure."

Our plastic spoons scrape against the paper cups as a horn blares outside. Someone laughs too loud. The register whirs and spits out another receipt. Normal noise filling the space where my thoughts start crowding in. But I won't follow them. Won't turn this into some sorta comparison I lose before I start.

Still, I feel it. The pull. The way being here with him feels easy in a way that makes me itch. Honestly, that part scares me more than the difference ever could.

He clears his throat. "You and your dad seem close."

"We are."

"Same with your mom?"

"Oh, Mommy? We're good. But my brother is her homey. She taught middle school. Now he's teaching music at Michigan."

"Excellent."

"Don't get any bright ideas. He's way cooler than you."

Langston doesn't even blink.

"Anyway," I add, needing to fill the quiet, "I'm much more like my daddy. Keeping it loose, making people laugh."

"That is so interesting," he says flatly.

I purse my lips, studying him. "Which of your parents are you closest to?"

"Neither. Never have been."

"Oh."

The silence stretches. Thick. Awkward.

"Any siblings?"

"A brother. Younger. I was the oldest."

Another awkward beat.

"What's his—"

"So how will you be able to afford moving out anytime soon if this… debt of yours is priority?"

I tilt my head, thrown by the pivot. "I haven't gotten that far."

Langston stares at me. "How much do you owe exactly?"

I shrug. "I'll have to ask Daddy later."

He presses his fingers to the bridge of his nose, exhales like he's trying not to say the wrong thing.

"Yana," he says, quieter now. "That's the kind of math that matters."

I frown. "So what you trying to say?"

"I'm saying you can't afford to float on maybes."

Oop. That stings worse than if he'd raised his voice.

"Hey!" I lean forward, heat spreading through me. "Don't you judge me, Lord Farquaad. You've got no idea what I've been through, okay?"

His gaze falls to my lips as I lick my spoon, then quickly flicks away.

"So let me get this straight," he says. "You come out to New York on a whim—"

"Not a whim. A promise. From my boyfriend. A casting director."

"A casting director? Who?"

"Bryant Taylor."

His brows lift. "*You* dated Bryant Taylor?"

"Why is that so hard to believe?"

"Anyway," he continues, voice sharpening, "you come out to New York on a wish and a prayer that your casting director boyfriend—who doesn't bother to help you relocate, by the way—will find you the job opportunity of your dreams? No plan? No backup? Not even a reliable credit card. Just... love and vibes?"

I shrug, spoon hovering midair. "I mean, we weren't exactly in love, but... Yes. I was single, he was fine. The way we met was serendipity. It just felt like... destiny."

Langston frowns. "Destiny?"

"Yes!" I lean in, lowering my voice like I'm sharing a secret with the universe. "Can't you feel that buzz in the air? I'm telling you, something big is about to happen. I can just *feel* it!"

He blinks. "And where was this... serendipitous meeting?"

"A dance recital for my cousin's daughter."

Langston runs a hand down his face, slow and tired. "And why haven't you been staying with Bryant?"

I suck my teeth. "We broke up. Well, not really. I went to his place, and would you believe that man was hooking up with some chick behind my back? I mean, you should've seen her with her camel jacket and pearl earrings—"

"Yana, Yana." Langston waves a hand, stopping me. Levels his eyes with mine. "You're deep in debt. You've got no home." His voice lowers as he scans the room. "The man you moved here for cheated on you. You call *that* destiny?"

I think for a second. "Yes."

He throws his head back. "You are some kind of optimist."

"I mean, look where I am now!" I gesture vaguely around us. "Look at what happened just tonight."

I shrug.

"Ain't you got any dreams?"

Langston stares at me like I'm speaking Swahili, and he never took lessons.

But something shifts behind him.

It's subtle at first. A girl at the counter goes still, staring at her phone a little too hard. Then another screen lights up. Then another. Heads tilt. Brows lift. A girl gasps hard, and suddenly three people are looking at their phones and then at me and then back at their phones again. My stomach dips. That kind of attention's got a temperature.

"What's going on?" I instinctively reach up. "Is there something in my hair?"

Langston pulls out his phone. His face drops as he stares at the screen.

Two young girls approach our table, eyes wide.

"Ms. Hyrd, can we take a selfie?" one asks.

I look to Langston, then back to them. "Uh, sure."

I smile like Alexia as they snap the photo. Langston leans back, watching.

"After that clip, we're *definitely* getting tickets!"

"What clip?" I ask.

One of the girls tilts her phone toward me, screen glowing too bright. And there I am, under the lights, mouth open mid-note, not hiding behind a thing. I watch myself sing like it's happening to someone else, like the girl on the screen knows something I don't yet.

The shop hums around us, but all I can hear is that sound. Mine.

"Thanks, guys." I wave goodbye as they head off, struggling to keep my composure. When I sit back down, my grin breaks free. "You see that?"

Langston stares back, eating crow.

"I need to call my cousin," I say, bubbling with glee. "I need to call my daddy!"

"And tell them what?" Langston lowers his voice. "You went viral pretending to be someone else?"

I lift my chin. "Destiny."

I cackle loud, and Langston shushes me.

12

The house is quiet when I step out of the shower, steam still clinging to my skin. For once, I'm not rushing. No early call. No rehearsal before rehearsal. No Langston pacing the hallway like a disappointed ballet instructor.

I'm still smiling. Last night didn't fall apart. I didn't fall apart. That little riff of mine is still making rounds online. My first preview, and I went viral.

Not as Alexia. As me.

I should call Daddy as soon as I get dressed. He's probably already seen it.

Of course I'll have to explain the little name mix-up. I blow out some air and towel off slow. Who knew dreams came with so many disclaimers?

I wrap the towel around my hair instead of my body because the bathroom's warm and I forgot to bring in my clothes. But it's fine. Langston's out.

I step into the hall and let the heat from the shower follow me, padding toward the living room like I own the place. The hardwood is cool under my feet, and for once, I'm not bracing for critique.

No Alexia voice or posture correction. Just me.

I stretch my arms over my head, rolling my shoulders loose as I cross into the living room... and freeze.

Langston stands in the kitchen in gray sweats, one AirPod still in, holding a mug. Mid-chew.

We stare at each other.

His eyes widen just slightly before they lock somewhere above my left shoulder with military precision.

I look down. *Oh. Oh!*

I'm completely naked. Full, unfiltered, first-thing-in-the-morning naked!

A sound leaves my throat that is not dignified. "You were supposed to be at the gym!"

"I don't go *every* day," he says, still staring aggressively at the ceiling. "I just took a jog around the block."

My brain short-circuits and my hands fly in opposite directions, which helps absolutely no one.

Shoulders rigid, he turns his back to me as I grab throw pillows from the sofa and slap them against my chest and nether regions. I'm not fully confident of the coverage.

Langston takes a very deliberate sip of whatever's in his mug.

"I apologize," he says, far too calm. "I'll give you a moment."

I bolt for the bathroom like the building's on fire.

This is why people wear robes.

"*Have you Hyrd?*" Julian reads aloud, already laughing. "*Broadway's R&B Star Is Back!*" He looks at me across the desk like he just struck gold.

The fluorescent office lights catch his grin as he scrolls on his phone. The man's energy is infectious, especially when he thinks he's right.

"*A triumphant return,*" he reads boldly. "*A thrilling revival.*"

I can't help the smile tugging at my mouth as I glance at Langston. He sits beside me like this is a briefing, not good news, back straight, hands planted firm on his thighs, fingers spread like he needs the contact. His face gives nothing, but his eyes keep moving. Phone to me. Me to Julian. Except when they brush past me, they move a little too fast.

Probably replaying the image of my boobs on a loop and disciplining himself for it.

Julian keeps going. "*Alexia Hyrd returns with poise, power.*" He pauses, dramatic. "*And a voice. That fills. The room.*" He claps once, sharp and ecstatic. "I told you, Langston. This girl is it!"

Langston's mouth tightens into that same thin line he wears when he's swallowing opinions for the sake of professionalism. "We've still got a lot of show to do."

"But aren't rave reviews a good thing?" I ask. "Especially this early on?"

"I wouldn't exactly call them rave reviews."

Julian waves him off like a gnat. "Don't be a killjoy. She had a job and she did it."

"Almost," says Langston.

I snap my head around. "Almost?"

But he refuses to look at me.

"Either way," says Julian, trying to ease the tension, "the audience loved it. Social media loved it. And the investors?" His smile turns sly. "They're loving it too."

My smile deepens, pride swelling, like maybe I'm not just a walking liability in a wig. Despite the human metronome sitting at my side.

"Not too much chit-chat between sets today." Julian points at me. "We've gotta save that voice for tonight."

I nod, still riding the moment. I've been allowed to speak to the castmates more recently, so long as I keep it light.

"If previews hold," he continues, "we're talking extensions. Touring interest. Maybe awards conversations by spring."

"Previews aren't promises," Langston says, voice even enough to drain the shine from the room.

Julian exhales, the patience in his face wearing thin. "Langston, come on. Let us enjoy it."

"Enjoy it after opening," he says, worrying his bottom lip like he's drafting a score in real time.

The room goes so quiet it's as if the air itself turns to look at him. Julian and I stare too.

I tell myself to let it pass. But I don't.

"Is it really that hard," I say, voice low, "to believe in me?"

For the first time all morning, I hold Langston's gaze, and something in him recalculates. The look lingers a beat before he swallows and eases back, returning to his default setting: suppressed.

"Alright," Julian says with another clap. "Enough philosophizing. We've got a show to run."

He tucks his phone away.

"We'll keep today light. No full-out runs before half hour. Mark it where you need to. Save it for tonight." He points between us. "Langston, I want the pit locked. Same tempos as last night. No experimenting."

"Already planned."

Julian turns back to me. "Hydrate. Rest. You know the drill."

I nod, still buzzing, like my whole body's humming in a key I didn't know I had. I can already picture Daddy's face when he says he always knew.

"If tonight looks anything like yesterday," says Julian, "we're in good shape."

The last word hasn't even settled when a knock cuts through it.

Gracie steps in and her eyes go straight to me. Not him. Me. Something flickers there and stays. Like she's tasting something bitter and deciding to swallow it anyway. My spine straightens.

"Julian," she says, eyes still on me. "Can I speak with you for a moment?"

"Of course," he says, oblivious.

Langston and I step into the hall, the door clicking shut behind us.

"She knows," I whisper as we head toward the studio.

Langston's brows pull together. "What do you mean?"

"*She knows*," I repeat, harsher. "You see the way she looked at me just now? That wasn't a vibe. That was a *look*."

"Lower your voice," he says, eyes fixed straight ahead. "There's no sense working yourself up over something that hasn't happened. And even if she *had* something, Julian would already know."

It almost makes sense. Except since that sideways assessment onstage, I've been counting every beat, every breath, wondering what she sees when she looks at me. Alexia? A risk? The truth? Still, I roll my shoulders back and act like it doesn't crawl under my skin.

"You've got a point," I mutter.

He gives a small nod, but his attention stays forward.

I sigh through my nose. "You can look at me, you know. I'm fully clothed now."

Something in him shifts, more human than flustered. "That's not—"

He stops himself, then releases a slow breath.

"I'm aware." His mouth twitches a hint. "And a professional."

"Mmhmm. You know you like what you saw."

Alexia might share my face, but she ain't got all my curves.

He huffs sharp, dragging a hand down his face. But I can't be sure if it's a scoff or him trying not to laugh.

The air loosens, just enough.

"And besides," he continues, tone steadier now, "if she's learned anything from this experience, it's that she's expendable."

I stop short, thrown by the bluntness of it.

Langston shrugs like he's just doing the math. "All of us are. That's why the work matters."

And he's not wrong. Gracie fought like hell for this role. I heard her going over lines at 2 a.m. Saw the way she lived on lettuce to fit the costumes. And still, even after her moment in the spotlight, she was... expendable. Regardless of looks, talent, network.

What's stopping the same from happening to me?

So that's where I place my focus. Not on Gracie's side-eyes or what she may or may not think she knows. But on the next note, the next line, the next thing I can control before my brain tries to run off and make a horror movie out of nothing.

Rehearsals settle into a rhythm after that. The days blur, but in a good way—costume fittings, press photos, notes that get smaller instead of bigger. I learn how to move like it comes naturally, how to let the music carry me instead of fighting it. My body remembers the blocking. My hands find the keyboard without hesitation. I don't brace anymore. I trust the work.

Langston becomes a constant in the quiet spaces. A nod across the room when something clicks. A dry comment that makes me laugh when the tension breaks. We talk music, then the small in between things—our past shows, the late nights, the way the room changes once an audience breathes back. He stops circling me like a problem to be solved and starts treating me like a collaborator. And that shift messes with me more than I wanna admit. Somewhere along the way, it stops feeling like I'm borrowing Alexia's life. It starts to feel like I'm building something of my own inside it.

And when it comes to previews, the show already feels lived in. The applause comes fast, warm, real. People say Alexia's name like it's settled again, like the world's righted itself. I take my bows without flinching, and it almost feels like... I'm not pretending anymore.

———

I TWIRL ONCE AS I STEP INTO LANGSTON'S APARTMENT. HE shuts the door behind us, letting the quiet settle.

"Man," I say, grinning as I take it all in again, "I don't know how Alexia ever walked away from this."

The words feel harmless until I look at him.

Langston hovers near the door, keys still in hand, expression frozen in a way I'm starting to recognize. Not ticked. Guarded. Like something just shifted under his feet and he's deciding whether to look down.

I've been filling in for almost two weeks now. Two full weeks of rehearsals, previews, press buzz, standing in her light.

And still no word. No sightings. No answers.

"Langston, I didn't mean to—"

"Forget it." He lifts a hand, already turning away as he drops his keys on the side table. "Out of sight, out of mind."

He mutters it, but I hear it anyway.

He heads to the sink, washes his hands like he needs the water to reset him, then opens the fridge and pulls out vegetables, lining them up with quiet precision.

The domestic normalcy of it almost throws me.

Like this is a man who knows how to make space for himself when things get complicated, and I'm just standing here in the doorway like the complication with legs.

I rest my scarf on the suitcase he insisted I needed last week, then wander into the kitchen, leaning my palms against the counter.

"So," I say casually, like I'm not walking into something tender, "how'd y'all end up together anyway? You never told me."

He doesn't look at me. Just starts chopping.

"Didn't feel like my story to tell."

I tilt my head. "Why not?"

The knife keeps moving, rhythmic and controlled.

"Because when it comes to Lex," he says, "she's the star. Onstage and off." He pauses, then adds quietly, "The rest of us are just footnotes."

Hmmph. From the sounds of it, Alexia didn't just treat him like a footnote. She treated him like a placeholder. Dipping with Noah every chance she got, like loyalty's a costume you hang up between scenes. And making this gig that much harder for me.

I told Noah I needed time to think a week ago. Bought myself some space. I still don't know what I'm supposed to do with the truth. And I'm not ready to watch Langston's face change when he finds out.

I lean back against the counter, arms crossing over my chest. "Okay. So, what would *your* footnote say?"

The chopping stops. Langston tips his head back, staring at the ceiling like he's searching for stars.

"*He fell for her,*" he says. "*Twice.*"

Something in his voice tightens.

"*And boy, did he fall.*"

He goes back to chopping, but the rhythm is slower now.

"Twice?" I ask.

He nods, jaw flexing, clearly hoping I'll let it go.

Instead, I wait.

Eventually, he exhales, seeming annoyed he said anything at all.

"Six years ago, before Broadway, I was a vocal arranger," he says. "Reworked melodies. Shaped phrasing. They brought me in for her sophomore album."

I watch him as he talks, the way memory settles into his shoulders.

"I expected a diva," he continues, "and she delivered. Showed up late. Barefoot. Rewriting songs on the fly and daring me to keep up."

She sounds impossible. And unforgettable.

A corner of his mouth lifts.

"We argued for twenty minutes about keys and range and how many times a voice can be pushed before it gives out."

He pauses, knife hovering.

"She laughed," he says softly. "Said I was the first man in the room who didn't flinch."

There's a hitch in his voice when he says it, but I won't point it out.

"And I was drawn to her light," he says, careful.

When he says her name, something settles over his face, softer than nostalgia, heavier than pride. It's the look of a man who once staked his whole future on somebody.

I hesitate, then ask, "So... y'all started hooking up?"

He frowns. "It wasn't like that."

I already know, but I ask anyway.

"Then what was it?"

"She was my first."

I pause. "Your *first?*"

"Not sexually," he says, glancing at me before looking back down. "My first love. I didn't really date... before her."

I school my expression, but my mind races.

No wonder he was hooked.

He isn't confessing so much as confirming what I already get. And the steadiness of it does something to me. I find myself studying him, thinking how different it must be to have someone choose you and keep choosing you, flaws and all. I've been desired. I don't know that I've ever been that deeply known.

I keep my voice gentle, even when my brain wants to sprint. "Why'd y'all break up?"

"She loved the spotlight. I didn't." He sets down the knife. "We hid it at first. My idea. Lex used to say women need to be loved out loud. That it gives them life."

I never really thought about it like that. But I suppose she had a point.

"Six months later, she does a track with Malik Saint."

"The rapper?"

He nods. "Rumors start. Her team leans into it. Says it's good PR." His voice slows. "One day, she texts me that it's not working anymore. That was the last I heard from her for five years."

"That's brutal," I say.

"I noticed," he says, dry but not dismissive.

He pulls a pot from under the counter.

"Then I created *Ella*. Partnered with Julian. Got the funding. Opened auditions. Everything was fine until... you showed up."

I point at myself, genuinely thrown. "Me?"

He nods once. "Julian pinned you as Alexia immediately. We knew you weren't, but he didn't care."

Something in me stills. I imagine a different version of the moment. One where I walked into that audition as myself. Where the applause was for me, and not somebody else. The thought catches in my throat on the way down.

"So why didn't you call me? Oh, right. I didn't have the pipes." I smack his shoulder. "Jerk."

But he doesn't react, even a little.

"That's not exactly true," he says, more quietly. "When I saw you, for a minute, I thought you were her."

I almost roll my eyes. Never had this problem in Detroit.

But my pulse slows as he looks at me.

"Same striking eyes. Same radiant smile."

Heat rises, and I've gotta swallow it back. Compliments from him don't exactly land neutral.

He pulls his gaze away, focusing on the floor. "The bitterness was still there. It was going to be an immediate no."

So it wasn't about my talent? He was just in his feelings? That stings in a way I don't wanna unpack.

"And when I realized that wasn't the case," he says. "I knew you'd be a perfect fit. But... I didn't exactly want reminders of my first heartbreak staring me in the face every day. So, I lied."

Just like that, the picture sharpens. Every rehearsal. Every cue. Every note shaped around a woman who disappeared... while I walk in each day wearing her face, her voice, her role. A ghost he can't avoid. A memory that sings back at him whether he wants it to or not.

My stomach dips at the reality of it all.

I was almost collateral damage in a story that wasn't mine.

"I handled that wrong," he says, looking at me now. "I shouldn't have let my history bleed into your audition."

It's not a full-out apology. But I see the sincerity in his eyes. And though I'm sure I'll find a way to make him pay for this later, I appreciate the acknowledgement.

"Perfect fit, huh?"

He nods, quietly holding my gaze. He doesn't rush to fill the space. Doesn't soften it either. And slowly, gently, something shifts between us. The room feels closer than it did a second ago.

I don't trust myself in moments like this. The ones where the air changes and nobody names it.

So, I do what I do best. I step into his space with a grin. Close enough to be annoying. Close enough to make a point.

We lock eyes and stay there. Neither of us blinking first. Neither of us backing down. No scolding or warning. Just a stubborn pause that stretches longer than it should.

His cologne settles in my lungs, spicy and sweet. And suddenly I'm very aware of the steady rise and fall of his chest, measured and calm, like this isn't affecting him at all.

Except... it is.

I see it in the slope of his jaw, when his throat works through a slow swallow. The slightest flicker crosses his eyes. Not irritation. Amusement, maybe?

That's what stops me. For half a second, it feels like he's enjoying this. Like he's curious how far I'll go.

My smile falters, just a hair.

Is he—

His lips twitch, like he almost grinned back and caught himself mid-thought.

"Would you stop," he says, low.

I take a reluctant step back, wondering what's gotten into me. Knowing this ain't the time to chase it.

"When Julian went behind my back and got Lex to sign anyway," he continues, "she and I reconciled. It was inevitable, really. Public this time. I never stood a chance."

"And now she's gone," I say.

He nods, eyes dark. "I think about her every day."

Of course he does.

Silence stretches between us, thick with what neither of us says. It settles deeper than I expect. Not just that he misses her, but that he carries it without apology.

"Have the cops got any leads?" I ask. "What about Malik? What if—"

He chuckles softly. "You need to cut back on the true crime."

"But it's been—what?—a month since she disappeared?" I shrug. "You know these cases have an expiration date—"

"Between us, I'm the only one who should be worried." He fills the pot with water, glancing at me. "*You* need to worry about hitting her octave."

Dodging, again. Like critique is safer than conversation.

I blow a raspberry. "You heard the fans. My spin is good enough."

"Her *true* fans want her octave," he says. "Not yours."

A scoff slips out. "Maybe I don't wanna do her octave."

"You think you can?"

I lift a shoulder.

He wipes his hands on a towel and gestures toward the piano. "Sit."

I comply.

The lamp casts warm light over the sheet music as he sets it in place.

"Refrain," he says, firm. "Just before the octave."

My fingers hover above the keys. Confidence should be automatic by now, but it's not. Part of me wants to play it off with a joke and run. The other part—the stubborn part—plants my hands and decides we're doing this anyway.

I play. Clean. Careful. Quietly determined. I take the breath and sing, focusing my voice as it builds.

When the octave comes, my throat constricts and the note strains, thin at the edges. So I stop, eyes closing, because I don't wanna see his face decide what I already know.

"Your fingers are fighting your breath," he says.

I glance back at him. "What does that even mean?"

"Lex doesn't belt on top of the chord," he explains. "She lets the chord invite her."

He steps behind me, close enough that I feel the heat of him without him touching me. His woodsy, spicy scent slips in with my next inhale, and for half a second my breath forgets what it's supposed to do.

"If your hands strike too hard," he murmurs near my ear, "your throat compensates. Play it again."

I do. But my shoulders creep up as the octave approaches.

"Stop."

His fingers settle over mine, and my breath trips like it forgot the count.

Oh. That's... unfortunate.

What's worse is that it doesn't feel foreign anymore. Startling, yes. Distracting, absolutely. But not unfamiliar in the way it should be. I'm already getting used to the weight of his hands guiding mine, the quiet confidence of it.

Outside of that brief, messy makeout with Noah—and whatever you wanna call the stage blocking—I haven't been touched like this in a long time. Not with intention.

I tell myself it's just muscle memory. Just coaching. Just proximity doing what proximity does. But my hormones are already voting, and they are wildly unhelpful.

"You feel that?" he says softly. "That tension starts here."

He adjusts my wrists, careful and exact, like this is purely technical. Like my pulse isn't hopping around like it's late for something. Like my brain isn't screaming *focus, focus, focus* while also filing this moment under *do not think about later*.

"Let the piano carry you halfway."

I try as I start again. I really do. But then his chest grazes my back, warm and solid, and suddenly I'm very aware of how close we are. Of how easy it would be to lean. Of how bad an idea that would be.

"Drop your shoulders."

His hand presses between my shoulder blades, and a shiver runs through me. Traitor.

Get it together, Yana. This is not that. This is technique. This is posture. This is...

"Don't stop," he murmurs. "We're almost there."

I whimper inside.

"You don't need armor for this note." His hand slides to my stomach, firm and steady. "Ah-ah. Keep it strong."

I try again. Fail.

"I'm sorry—"

"No apologies."

We meet eyes in the piano's reflection.

"We keep going." He presses my torso lightly. "Breathe into here."

I do. Low. Quiet.

He stays there a moment. Longer than necessary it seems. Then his fingers return to mine.

"I've got your hands," he says. "Speak the octave."

"Star," I say.

He stills. "Again."

"Star," I say, louder, clearer.

His breath warms my ear. "That's the placement. Now sing it. Smaller than you think."

I try. It wavers.

"*Shhh.*" His hand steadies me. "Again. Trust yourself."

Air gathers in my lungs like it's got somewhere to be. Langston's hands stay over mine, not gripping, guiding. The pressure is light, but it changes everything. It makes me aware of every note I press, every inhale I take. He plays the lead-in again, soft enough to be a suggestion.

"Breathe," he murmurs.

The word threads through me. I pull the air low, deeper than panic, deeper than pride. The chord opens under my hands—

inviting, like he said—and for a second the piano feels like it's carrying me instead of daring me to fall.

I sing.

The octave approaches and I don't brace this time. I let the breath settle lower, let the note build where it wants instead of dragging it there. And when it lifts, it doesn't feel like a test. It feels like something I've lived in long enough to claim.

The note rings out, steady and clear. It lands and holds, completely focused. Hangs in the room like a held gaze.

"Oh," I whisper.

We turn to each other, closer than I realized, mouths inches apart. Langston doesn't move. His hands are still over mine. His warm breath grazes my cheek. Measured. Controlled.

Which makes it worse. 'Cause I'm not sure I am.

The note is still hanging in the air between us, thinner now, settling into the walls.

"It's a start," he says.

13

I'm center stage, still waiting on my cue, while my attention keeps drifting to the pit.

Langston moves like he belongs there, patient and sure. The orchestra follows, no hesitation. Like if they blink wrong the whole thing could crack. Watching him work, I'm kinda starting to get it. What Alexia saw. How she could fall. There's something grounding about him. Something steady in a world that thrives on chaos.

But where is she?

As if he feels me staring, Langston glances up. His eyes catch mine and he does a double take, just a flicker of surprise before it settles. I smile at him, and he nods back, subtle but deliberate.

Something in my gut does a quiet little flip, which is rude. I'm supposed to be focused. I'm supposed to be Alexia. I'm supposed to have my life together and my breath supported and my damn cues on lock.

"Lex... Lex!"

I startle, snapping my attention to the front row.

"Yes?" I say, blinking at Julian.

"You hear what I just said?"

I hesitate, the moment stretching just long enough to give me away.

Great. Caught zoning out like a freshman in Chem.

"She may have been a little distracted," Gracie says smoothly.

A few cast members chuckle. Regan included.

Julian exhales, restless. "We're taking 'Shine Through the Dark' from the top. You're up."

"Got it," I say, already moving.

"Try not to miss your cue," Gracie sings as I jog up the stairs.

I picture shoving her into the pit. Just once. For growth.

After that exchange in Julian's office, I was waiting for her to make a move. But this past week she's mostly been herself. Center of her own universe. Snapping photos. Adjusting angles. Acting like rehearsal is just background for her next post. Every now and then she'll toss a comment my way or let her eyes linger a second too long. That? I can handle.

It's the others that feel different. The sideways glances. The whispers that don't quite die when I look up. Smiles that read polite but careful. Like they're measuring me. Like they're waiting to see if I crack. Or slip. Or prove I don't belong on this stage.

So I keep moving. Smile fixed. Career intact.

Julian stands, script tucked under his arm, and turns to Kai. "Any notes?"

"None from me."

He nods, then looks back at me. "We're only gonna run this once. I want full swoon. Make 'em feel it in the back of the house. You got that?"

"Yes, baby!" I snap over my head without thinking.

Langston's head jerks up from the pit, and my stomach drops.

"I mean—of course, babe," I add quickly, softening my voice with a little laugh.

Julian scratches his scalp as he sits. "Ready when you are, ma'am."

Tossing me one last stern glance, Langston turns back to the orchestra, already murmuring to the strings, tapping the stand. Whatever irritation I earned for slipping out of character just now, he's filed it away for later.

This is rehearsal. The music still matters more.

The auditorium settles into that familiar hush, the one that always comes right before a solo. Not silence exactly. More like attention. Expectation leaning in. Rows of seats waiting to decide if I'm truly worth the light.

I sit at the keyboard and let my hands rest for a beat, resisting the old urge to brace. Langston's voice flickers through my head. *Gentle hands. Loose wrists.* I drop my shoulders, the way he's corrected me every day this week.

The piano opens soft.

I was born from shadows...

And the lyric pulls something loose. Middle school hallways. Laughter trailing behind me until I learned how to make fun of myself first. If I beat them to it, they lost interest. I figured out early which version of me went down easiest.

They said know your place, stay in the wings.

My fingers press a little deeper, still controlled. I think of Bryant, already dressed, already halfway out the door, promising he'd take me next time. I told myself I didn't care, same way I say I'm fine hovering at the edge of dressing room conversations that pause when I walk in. I've learned to sell it.

Halfway through the verse, Langston brings the orchestra in. Just enough to widen the floor beneath me. Strings bloom softly around the piano, and I let the phrasing stretch the way he's been asking. Smaller than I think. Easier than I expect.

The song keeps moving, and so do the memories. My high school boyfriend... Jarel. The way he looked past me, like I was temporary. The way he...

Some hurts don't need words. They show up right before you breathe.

By the final chorus, the choir slips in behind me, low and

steady. Gospel warmth lifts the sound without taking over. I stay grounded at the keyboard, wrists loose, breath even, letting the piano carry me halfway like Langston taught me.

What settles in is quieter than need. Being seen without pushing. Being chosen without pleading. Sitting here, stripped of wigs and tricks, trusting the sound to say: *This is enough.*

As the octave approaches, I don't attack, let it settle in my mouth before I release it. And this time I don't brace. I let it ring.

The sound fills the room, clean and effortless.

Julian's head snaps up.

"Ow-ow!" Noah calls from the wings.

For a beat, the auditorium is silent as I finish the song. Then applause breaks out, starting with Julian, spreading fast. Loud. Real.

I beam, reckless with it, like the space might actually be mine.

"Langston!" Julian points at the pit. "My man. Whatever you're doing, keep it up!"

Langston nods once. His gaze flicks to me before settling back on his score.

And just like that, the lift in my chest tightens.

We take five.

Hands clap my shoulders as I head backstage. Smiles. More compliments than side-eyes this time. The kind meant for Alexia, not me. I take them anyway. This is the deal I made.

In the dressing room, Regan grins at me. "I knew you still had it in you, girl. Welcome back."

"She just needed a little time to warm up," says Stella, with a knowing smirk.

"I don't see why," Gracie adds flatly. She's posted in the corner like an unused set piece. "I nailed that octave in forty-eight hours."

Stella snorts. "How could we forget? We couldn't even take five without hearing you run scales in the hall."

Everyone laughs. Even me. Even though the praise still slides right past who I actually am.

There's a knock at the door.

Kai steps in, holding a massive vase of roses. "Special delivery for Ms. Hyrd."

My jaw drops, and I press a hand to my chest. "No way."

Gracie studies me like she's taking notes. "You act like you're not used to the attention."

My smile holds a beat too long. I fix it.

"I mean—this one's just... big," I say.

"I'm not surprised," says Kai, smoothing the tissue around the stems. "After the way you were locked in today? That last pass gave me chills."

I bow my head, letting out a soft Alexia laugh. "Thanks, Kai."

"*And* there's a card!" she adds.

I pull it free.

I miss you.
~N.

Noah.

Regan leans in. "What's it say? Is it from Langston?"

"Give her space," Stella laughs, tugging her back.

According to Langston, everyone knew about him and Alexia. They weren't too sloppy, but they weren't exactly hiding either. Union folks frowned on it. Directors whispered. Stage managers pretended not to see what they absolutely saw. The sorta thing that's tolerated when there's history involved and both parties are too valuable to push too hard.

Apparently, they weren't the only ones with history.

"Maybe it's a secret admirer," says Kai.

Regan gasps. "*Who?*"

I laugh with them as I close the card, even as something settles heavy in my stomach.

The flowers are beautiful. The note is sweet. But I've been dodging Noah all week for a reason. Ever since the supply closet, something about it has felt wrong. Not just awkward or complicated. *Wrong*. Like I'm standing on the edge of a line and everybody's acting like it's cute to dance there.

I keep thinking about Langston. About the way Alexia did him. Slipping off with Noah like it was nothing. Like loyalty was optional as long as the chemistry worked.

Sure, Noah implied things. Darker things. But that doesn't make betrayal clean.

No matter how fine Noah is, and how perfectly he nails every single stage kiss, some lines aren't meant to blur. And this one? I know exactly where it leads. Especially after the grimy way Bryant did me with Little Miss Cassidy.

The flowers? They're for Alexia. Not me.

"Just know," I say, waving the card high, "he's got great taste."

Everyone laughs.

I freeze when I see Langston in the hall. Just there. Quiet. Watching. I can't tell how long he's been posted up by the door, and that's what makes my stomach flip. If he'd walked in normal, I could've worked with that. This feels like I missed a cue.

My pulse spikes, like I've been caught mid-thought. Mid-wrong.

The roses. The card. Me sitting here cheesing like I ain't got sense. I fix my face quick and slip the card away, start messing with my hair, smoothing, tucking, rearranging strands like I can rearrange what he saw too.

He doesn't say a word. Just lingers long enough for me to go stiff, for explanations to line up and choke each other out before I can grab one.

Then, just like that, he backs away and keeps walking. Already refocusing. Already gone.

Relief rushes through me, and my lungs finally remember how to work. But it only lasts a second.

Because I don't know what he saw.

I'M AT A FOOD TRUCK, COMMITTING A FULL-BLOWN SIN against my vocal cords—a chili cheese dog buried under too much of everything—when my phone buzzes.

I smile before I even answer.

"*Heyyyy*, Daddy."

"There's my Songbird," he says, voice warm and teasing. "You behaving out there or causing a scene?"

I take another bite, grease slick on my fingers, as I start walking. The March air is sharp enough to cut through the steam rising off the sidewalk, gray slush clinging to the curb like it refuses to admit winter's over.

"Little of both."

He laughs. "That's my girl."

The sound loosens something in my chest.

"What's up?" I ask, then hesitate. The last time we talked, things were heavy. "Y'all good?"

"You should know," he says. "That's why I'm calling. To say thank you."

I slow my steps. "For what?"

"For keeping your word. You said you'd take care of that bill, and you did. Just got the email."

I stop dead in the middle of the sidewalk.

People stream past me, brushing shoulders, laughing, living their lives while my ears start ringing.

"They must be paying you big out there on Broadway," he says, affection thick in his voice. "I'm proud of you, Songbird."

I barely hear the rest.

I SLAM THE DOOR BEHIND ME AS I ENTER THE BROWNSTONE.

"Langston!"

He glances over his shoulder, completely unbothered,

spooning bird feed into a dish. "Appreciate the punctuation," he says calmly. "We need to be back at the theater in..."

He checks his watch.

"Thirty."

"I can't believe you," I snap. "Asshole!"

He frowns, finally turning. "I mean, I've heard worse. But can you fill me in on what I've done?"

I stalk over, heart pounding, and shove my phone in his face. I don't need to read it. I know it by heart.

Account closed.
Balance paid in full.
Final payment made by a third party:
L.Washington.

He scans it once, then looks at me. "Right," he says. "You're welcome."

Something in me snaps. I growl as he puts the bird feed away and washes his hands like we're discussing the weather.

"I shared that with you because I was excited," I say, voice on edge. "Not for your frickin' charity."

"I never said that you did," he replies evenly, drying his hands. "Most people would just say thank you."

"I don't want or need your help!"

He looks at me. "Given that you've been sleeping on my sofa for three weeks, I doubt that." There's no edge in his voice. That almost makes it worse.

I collapse on the couch in a huff, emotions tangling so tight I can't tell them apart. My throat burns. Tears push forward and I shove them back down, hard. I hate how much it helps. Hate how fast it steadies me.

Besides Daddy... nobody's ever caught me like that before. And I don't know whether to be furious or relieved.

He stands there like it's nothing, broad shoulders, steady hands, like saving me is just another errand.

It makes my heart do something stupid.

"I'm gonna pay you back," I say, voice thick. "I swear, I will."

He grabs a bottle of alkaline water off the counter and cracks it open. "Tell you what," he says. "Why don't you save that money for when you get your own place?"

I stare at him as he opens the cabinet.

"Fine," I mutter.

It's no different from when he bought me that suitcase. No different from him letting me crash on his couch without ever making it a thing. Something twists in my gut, knowing he's willing to stick his neck out for me and expect nothing in return.

Silence settles between us as he pours two glasses and passes one to me. The bird chirps softly, like it's filling space neither of us wants to claim.

"By the way," he says, before taking a casual sip. "I know you're enjoying socializing at rehearsals. But it isn't wise to get too... cozy with the other castmates."

What?

He meets my gaze and doesn't flinch. Doesn't push either. Just holds it like he's asking something, almost like a plea.

"This is a job," he adds. "The fewer hearts involved when it's over, the better."

The thought hits sideways, incomplete.

What is he getting at?

I search his face for the answer, but he doesn't offer one. Just tosses back his water and sets his glass in the sink.

"Thirty minutes," he says, heading to his room.

14

Langston slides into the car, the leather seat creaking under his weight. I barely have time to lock my phone before the door shuts.

He squints at me. "You good? You look like you've just swallowed a quarter."

I force a laugh that I hope sounds casual. "I'm fine."

So maybe I was looking into Alexia's past against his wishes. That's my business. Still didn't find anything. But I'm getting close.

He doesn't respond. Just shuts the door and studies me like he's deciding whether to push.

My phone burns in my palm like it's about to confess for me. I move first.

"Was just looking up new restaurants, actually. Tomorrow's my first day off in *weeks*," I say, already looping my arm through his, "and you're taking me out."

A frown settles on his face like it's used to living there. But I'm not backing down.

"I'm itching to see what it's like to spend a *real* day in Alexia's shoes."

He blinks. Once. "No."

I do the whole sad-eyed routine, exaggerating just enough to make him sigh internally.

"We need to lay low," he says. "Recuperate."

I groan, throwing my head back against the seat. "Come on, Langston! If I gotta stay in that stuffy apartment one more day, I'll go crazy!"

He shakes his head. Not even a flicker of sympathy.

I turn fully toward him, clasp my hands together like I'm praying to a very particular god. "*Please?* You know I'm like a flower. Without sunshine, I'll wilt and die."

He stares at me. "You're so dramatic."

I don't drop the pose. Bat my lashes. Hold the silence hostage.

I need air.

Finally, he releases a long breath. "Fine. But you *must* stay in character."

I throw my arms around him before he can change his mind. "Thank you! Thank you!"

I'm so happy, I could kiss him right now.

But I won't.

———

I frown as I slide into the booth, the vinyl cold against the backs of my legs. The café is all exposed brick and mismatched chairs, Edison bulbs strung low like they're trying to sell *cozy* instead of *overpriced*. An upscale Panera, basically. Better lighting. Less motivated staff.

"Really?" I say, glancing around. "This is the best we could do?"

Langston slips into the seat across from me, smooth and composed, like he belongs everywhere he goes. "What do you mean? This is one of Lex's favorite spots. The scones are delicious."

I wrinkle my nose. "Why would I ever trust the taste of someone that eats scones?"

I snatch a menu from the corner and flip it open. At least

there's balance. Half pastries and desserts, half soups, salads, and grain bowls pretending they're not trying too hard.

"Ooh! Lemon blueberry cupcakes."

He doesn't look up. "No."

"But it's my favorite."

"Sugar dries your cords," he says, already bored. "Your voice is an instrument. You know this."

"Langston, it's my day off."

He ignores me.

"Coffee?"

"Acid reflux."

I pout. "Are you enjoying this?"

"Immensely."

I drop the menu, convinced this is his sadistic form of torture. It's my day off, and somehow, I'm still being managed like a rehearsal schedule. I don't know why I ever thought he could show me a good time.

Then he reaches over and taps the laminated page with one finger. "Anything on the left-hand side."

Oh, yes.

The server arrives, bright-eyed and unsuspecting, and I order like I've been stranded on an island for weeks. Eggs. Toast. Lightly fried potatoes. A savory thing I can't pronounce. Extra bowl of oatmeal on the side.

Langston's expression hardens, but he says nothing.

He works carefully on his scone while I dig in, barely pausing between bites.

"Slow down," he says.

I ignore him. Just like he ignored me.

"Another one?"

I keep eating.

"Lex..." His voice drops. "Yana."

A couple nearby tables stare, phones subtly angled, curiosity buzzing.

Langston reaches over, trying to yank the fork from my hand mid-bite. But I ain't letting go.

"That's enough," he says.

"But you said I could have anything on the left side of the menu."

"Lex would never eat all this."

"She's eating it today!"

"*Shhh*." He glances over his shoulder as I cackle, mouth full.

"Let me eat!"

By the time he's practically dragging me out of the café, a few people have asked for selfies. Someone calls Alexia's name like we're old friends. Langston's shoulders creep into his ears like he's already over it.

I could get used to this. Probably shouldn't. But I could.

———

THE PARK SITS QUIET IN THAT SAD, FORGOTTEN WAY. BARE trees. Rusted benches. A stretch of cracked pavement pretending it's still useful.

I look back at Langston, unimpressed. "Let me guess. Alexia's favorite."

He nods once.

"If you can't stay in character," he says, "our entire operation could be blown wide open. It's best to avoid crowds right now. Stay low-key."

I get it. Punishment for cutting up at the café.

"You should work for C-SPAN," I say. "You'd have a lot more fun."

He doesn't answer as I spot the lone swing still hanging from the frame. The chains creak when I hop on, metal cold through my coat.

"Push me?"

He frowns. "Lex would never—"

"And I ain't her," I say. "Push."

He glances around, finds no one, then walks over and gives me a tentative shove.

The swing lifts. The breeze hits my face. Cold and clean and freeing. I close my eyes and let the rise and fall take over.

"Higher, Daddy! Higher!"

I know that's gotta irritate the hell out of him.

He presses the small of my back harder, and I fly, laughing before I can stop myself.

"You know, there's a name for your condition," he says. "It's called Peter Pan Syndrome."

"There's a name for yours too. Amusaphobia."

"I believe the word you're looking for is cherophobia. And I don't have it."

"Tell that to the dictionary you read in your downtime."

He just keeps pushing. I can't tell if he's rolling his eyes or smiling.

"What'd Alexia do for fun?" I ask.

"Besides work?" He hesitates. "Old films. Dim jazz clubs. The occasional room service at a hotel. Lex relaxed best when she could disappear—"

He swallows too late. Silence hangs between us.

I see it settle on him, that old grief tightening everything up again. And I know it's only getting harder with each day that passes. But there's still a chance she's okay. This ain't a memorial. We came out to breathe, maybe even enjoy ourselves.

I force a small smile, trying to pull him back. "So she was a sucker for a good snoozefest?"

A soft breath escapes him. Almost a chuckle.

I'll take it.

"What about you?" I ask. "What do you do for fun?"

"I just—"

"Besides work," I say. "Try again."

He thinks.

"Doing things like that... for *fun*... was never really an option for me," he says. "I was trained to work hard. Stay focused. From as young as I can remember. At my school, we played chess for recess."

I soften despite myself. "You poor tortured soul."

"It does sound pretty bad, doesn't it?"

"Yes."

The swing creaks as it settles.

"You always liked swings?" he asks.

"I liked anything that made it easier to breathe."

The words hang heavy. Memories flicker. Kids laughing. Me laughing louder first so it wouldn't hurt as much. Thinking about the way people stare at the floor when he speaks to them. The way smiles fade when he enters a room. The way he is in rehearsals: stern, commanding, glares sharp enough to cut. I wonder if that's what he's doing too, pulling back before anyone can point.

I slow the swing with my feet and hop off.

"You know what's fun?"

He stills. "I'm afraid to ask."

"Letting someone else be in charge for a minute." I walk around and nod toward the swing. "Hop on."

He doesn't move. "You're kidding, right?"

I cross my arms and wait, because this isn't about him grabbing hold of the chains, it's about him loosening his grip on everything else.

After a moment, he sighs and sits, stiff as a statue.

I pull back on the swing.

"Whoa, whoa!" His shoulders shoot up, feet scraping the gravel as his entire body locks stiff.

"Just relax!" I laugh. "I won't drop you!"

I give him a solid push, and he clutches the chains like they might betray him.

"You gotta kick out! Push through the wind with your legs."

"This... is insanity," he says.

"This is *fun*." I shout. "It's worth trying once in a while!"

"I don't..." He looks down as the ground moves farther away. "I don't think I like this."

"Yes, you do," I say. "You just gotta give yourself permission."

"If anyone sees this—"

"No worries," I tell him. "I'm certified in bad ideas."

I give him another push.

———

I didn't wanna wait for the car, so we agreed to take the subway home. Langston says he hates the subway, but he didn't push back much this time. The car rocks beneath us as we sink into plastic seats, shoulder to shoulder. The air smells like metal and brake dust, and something fried from a bag two rows down.

It's loud. Crowded. Alive. And weirdly... I don't hate it.

I watch Langston from the corner of my eye as the train rattles forward. He's loosened since earlier, jacket unbuttoned, gaze unfixed from his phone for once. Chilling with him feels easier now. Existing beside him doesn't feel like work.

When he's like this, he's actually kinda... cute.

But I check myself, remembering the line I can't cross. Alexia.

This isn't my life. He isn't mine to want.

The train slows at the next station, and the sound of a guitar drifts through the car. A man stands near the pole, fingers rough but skilled, playing for a handful of half-interested commuters. A battered case sits open at his feet with barely any cash inside.

He finishes the song and lowers the guitar, shoulders sagging a little. Either taking a break or... giving up.

I know that look. I remember how it feels.

I glance at Langston, and he follows my line of sight before shrugging like it's none of our business.

But then an idea sparks. Sudden. Reckless enough to be brilliant. I lean in, brushing my mouth near his ear as I murmur it low.

Halfway through, he's already shaking his head. Too late. His protest dies somewhere between me grabbing his hand and tugging him to his feet.

In front of the guitarist, I lay it out fast, like I didn't just think this up three seconds ago.

The man slides a wary glance to Langston, who answers it with a sigh before coughing up fifty bucks.

You'd think we handed the guitarist salvation by the way he offers up his instrument like a holy offering.

Langston takes a seat across from me, the guitar settling stiff against his thigh. He adjusts it once. Then again. Tests the strings like he's negotiating terms. He lifts his eyes to mine, cautious, waiting.

"More Than Words," I say.

With another exhale, he starts playing.

I don't know why the strum surprises me. It's clean, steady, unshowy. A confidence that doesn't need to announce itself. Of course, it sounds like him.

I step into the space and sing, letting my voice slide into the pocket he's made, warm and unguarded. I don't copy him or perform for anyone. Just let it be mine. It loosens something in my gut, the way good music always does when you allow yourself to simply *feel*.

Around us, the car shifts. Heads turn. Phones lower. Attention gathers without being asked. The guitarist moves through the aisle with his hat, and money starts dropping in—ones, fives, a ten—each bill dropping like punctuation.

Except for the man seated closest to us. Thick coat. Arms crossed. Face carved into permanent irritation. He doesn't clap... or smile. Just stares straight ahead like joy is a personal inconvenience. Langston's kinda guy.

I take the first verse steady, easing the car into it, letting the melody breathe the way it wants to. When the second verse rolls around, I fall quiet, giving him room.

Langston looks at me like I've set him up.

"Don't be shy!" someone calls.

"Sing!" another voice chimes in.

The chant builds, clapping and laughter rolling through the car. Langston swallows, nods once, and then... he sings.

And everything rearranges.

His voice is rich and smooth, warmer than I expect, held back just enough to make it dangerous. There's restraint there, and choice, and the quiet confidence of someone who knows exactly what he's capable of. It settles into the song like it's always belonged.

I did not know he had it in him.

Applause breaks out mid-verse, and Langston leans into it, claiming the space inch by inch. I fall back in with him without thinking, our voices finding each other easily, instinctively, braiding together as our eyes lock.

For a moment, the train disappears. The crowd fades. There's only sound and breath and the space between us.

We finish together, the last note hanging just long enough to matter before the car erupts.

Cheers. Whistles. Applause that feels earned.

The grump in the thick coat finally exhales. Reaches into his pocket. Drops a single bill into the hat without looking at either of us. Still doesn't clap. But he pays.

I'm already looking at Langston when it ends.

And he's looking back.

For just a second—just barely—he almost... kinda smiles.

And I'm captivated.

15

I give up on the tab with a quiet huff and lock my phone.

Another dead end.

Alexia's old boyfriend was my best guess. The easiest answer. Jealousy. Control. A blowup bad enough to make someone disappear. Men do reckless things when their pride's bruised. But that breadcrumb turned cold fast.

A producer mentioned it earlier like it was nothing, scrolling her phone as we waited for notes from Julian. "He's still in Europe," she'd said casually. "Honeymoon tour. Social media's been updating daily."

Daily.

I checked for myself just now. Photos in Italy. France. Greece. Sunsets. Champagne and smiles.

He couldn't have done it. Which means whoever did... is closer.

The theater hums below me as I slip my phone in my bag, empty seats glowing faintly under work lights. The smell of velvet and old wood settles into my lungs.

Someone moves along the mezzanine.

"Hey, beautiful."

My head snaps up.

Noah.

He leans against the railing, eyes soft. Relief flutters through me. I smile before I remember to be careful.

"Hey."

I expect him to tease or compliment. Pull me into one of those easy backstage moments that make me feel seen.

Instead, he walks over and quietly drops into the seat in front of me. Slouches. Throws his head back, staring up at the ceiling. Lips pursed like he's holding something in.

"What's wrong?" I ask.

He studies my face like he's searching for the version of me he remembers. "You got anything to say to me?"

I still. "Enjoy your day off?"

His face collapses as he sits up straight. "You're joking, right?"

I hesitate, suddenly aware of how isolated this balcony feels.

"Of course I didn't enjoy my day off," he says.

He's got this pout that hits me right in the gut. I feel like a total ass for all the distance I've been putting between us. Never being near him alone. Pivoting when I see him up the hall. I didn't even bother to thank him for the flowers. Like acknowledging them would make this any less complicated.

I lick my lips, searching his face. "Why not?"

He scoffs, gaze drifting out toward the empty floor seats. "Because yesterday I turned thirty-two, and the woman I'm crazy about didn't so much as bother to text me *happy birthday*."

My mouth falls open. "Happy birthday..."

He rolls his eyes like that's the last thing he wants to hear. "I figured you'd surprise me at the party. But you didn't even drop by."

That hits lower than I expect. "There was a party?"

He glares at me. "My surprise party? Everyone was there." His mouth goes thin as he stares at his hands. "Everyone besides you and Langston anyway."

I shake my head, panic creeping in. "Noah... I had no idea—"

"You know, I get that you wanted some time to think," he cuts in. "I only sent the roses to show you how I feel. I didn't know it was crossing a line."

"It wasn't."

Really, whatever line there was to cross, it got worked over long before I got here.

"Sure." He looks at me, hurt naked on his face. "Damn, Lexy. I thought what we had was real."

But what do you say to that when you're standing in someone else's life?

"I'm... sorry?"

He bobs his head slowly, like he's already done arguing with himself.

"I guess I'll give you your... space or whatever."

He's gone before I can think of anything else to say.

And that's the part that sits wrong. Not the distance. The damage.

At the end of the day, he didn't mean to hurt anyone. He misjudged, sure. Crossed *several* panty lines he shouldn't have. But he's still got a heart, bruising in real time.

Langston's voice floats back to me, uninvited.

Don't get too... cozy.

Ugh.

But really, I don't see why he's so concerned. Since apparently, people around here don't like Alexia nearly as much as I thought.

———

I TRY TO KEEP MY FOCUS WHERE IT BELONGS. ON THE LIGHTS. The preview. The rhythm of the scene.

But Noah's sitting right across from me. In character. Close enough to feel. And even through the lines, I can tell he's pulling back. The warmth we used to trade so easily is muted now, wrapped tight behind Prince Santiago's posture. And it stings.

Because I didn't know about the party. Nobody invited me.

And somehow, even while standing center stage, I still feel left out of something everyone else knew to show up for.

"So..." Noah says as Prince, voice smooth, measured. "Why'd you come tonight?"

We've just come back from intermission. In the musical, the blind audition is already in motion. Girls line the length of the stage, masks in place, hands folded, waiting to be dismissed or remembered. No names or faces. Just voices, posture, and whatever courage you can summon under hot lights.

Ella sits on a tall stool, center stage, Prince Santiago across from her, bodyguards flanking each side. His stage manager hovers nearby with impatience written all over his face. Other girls shift their weight, as Prince keeps leaning in like he's forgotten they're waiting.

I swallow and answer as Ella, heart thudding a beat too fast. "Because..." I search for the next line, my mind blanking for half a breath. "I sing. And because... I don't usually let people hear me."

"Why not?"

The question hits wrong. Too close. Too real.

I freeze.

Not Ella. *Me.*

I forgot my line. Shit. I forgot my line!

"Is it nerves, or...?" Noah adds gently after a beat, trying to nudge me along.

But I'm stuck.

What the hell is wrong with me?

This is my twenty-fifth preview. I've said these words a hundred times. And still...

Come on, Yana. Get it together.

I clear my throat, snapping back into place. "Sorry, I'm just so... nervous."

"Don't be," Noah says it kindly. Reassuring. But his eyes don't soften the way they used to. There's distance there now. Something guarded. "You were saying why you don't let people hear you sing."

I force myself to breathe, the words suddenly coming back to me.

"Yes. People decide things fast. Sometimes before I even open my mouth." A beat. The truth slips out before I can stop it. "I got teased a lot growing up. Mostly about my ears."

"They're perfect," he says, finally flashing that charming smile, seeming almost as relieved as me that I recovered.

But I swallow a lump anyway. Because I can feel Langston watching me from the pit. Feel it like heat on the back of my neck.

Afterward, when we pass each other in the hall, his jaw is set, eyes hard. He doesn't even look at me.

"I've got a meeting," he says flatly. "Take the car. I'll meet you at home."

And just like that, the distance widens again. Between me and Noah. Between me and Langston. Between who I am and who I'm pretending to be.

———

I scroll from the couch, thumb moving on autopilot.

No "Alexia bombed" posts. No viral clips tearing her apart. Not that it matters. People don't like Alexia anyway. They like the idea of her. The polish. The illusion.

The front door opens harder than necessary.

Langston strolls in simmering, tosses his keys on the table hard enough to make the wood protest.

"I just spent forty minutes on a call with our lead producer and two frazzled investors. You want to tell me what happened tonight?"

I lift a shoulder. I honestly don't have the bandwidth for another lecture.

"Did you know about the party?"

He frowns. "What party?"

"Noah's surprise party! Everyone was there but you and me."

He pauses, eyes narrowing. "I knew, but wasn't interested in going. What does that have to do—"

"You could've told me!" I stand, heat rushing to my face.

His mouth opens, then closes. "I didn't know you weren't invited."

My shoulders sag. "So apparently, there are people in this cast who don't want Alexia around. Including you. A detail you neglected to mention."

He blinks. "You made it abundantly clear that you wanted to go elsewhere. I figured you'd decided it was a waste of time as well. Besides, we had vocal training to do."

I collapse back on the couch, heart cracking in a way I didn't expect. I can't tell if I wasn't invited because I'm pretending to be Alexia... or because I'm me.

"This is just as bad," I say, voice barely above a whisper. "I'm losing myself trying to be her."

He rolls his eyes and crosses into the kitchen. "You're not losing anything. You said it yourself: This is the opportunity of a lifetime. I suggest you start acting like it before you squander another away."

I glare at him as he opens the fridge. "What's that supposed to mean?"

He slams the door shut, and my shoulders jump on instinct.

The sound ricochets through the apartment.

"*You know how Lex would've spent her day off?*" he shouts. "Writing brilliant lyrics! Or studying the works of her peers!"

Hold up. I don't know who the hell he thinks he's yelling at. It's completely uncalled for... and a little unsettling.

"Reviewing her tapes!" He barks. "Figuring out where she fell flat, where she excelled, and how to top that performance the next time. Then the next, and the next!"

I maintain my gaze, bitter, but steady. "I'm. Not. Her."

"You're damn right you're not."

We stare each other down like unhinged gangstas.

So I flubbed a line? He's outta pocket.

But clapping back won't fix whatever's crawled up his spine. And right now, answers matter more than my pride.

Why does he act like she's gone for good? And why don't people want her around?

"You know, if you'd just listen to me, maybe we could figure this out," I say. "I been thinking. Maybe Gracie had something to do with her disappearance."

His expression flattens, and he heads for the bedroom. "Don't be ridiculous."

"Don't you think she'd want us to look for her? We need to start digging!"

He turns back, eyes sharp. "*You* need to focus on nailing your part before we start losing investors."

That one stops me cold, 'cause I know he ain't talking to me. Early mornings, late nights, vocal rest when I wanted to laugh, missed birthdays, skipped calls home. I've carved pieces off myself to fit inside Alexia's shadow, and somehow it still ain't enough?

He disappears into the bedroom, and it feels way too familiar.

Being dismissed. Being talked over. Being the only one who cares enough to ask questions and still being treated like a liability.

A second later, he reappears in the hall and hurls a pillow at my chest. The bird startles, chirping in protest, as he slams the door shut. Breaking his own damn rule.

Ugh! That's it. I'm sick of this. I'm sick of him!

I stomp up the hall and throw the door open.

And he's halfway through pulling off his shirt.

Oh. Wow.

Langston is... ripped. Broad shoulders. Cut arms.

Scrumptious.

He freezes, shirt bunched in his fist, eyes dark. "Can I help you?"

"I... I..." I force myself back on track. "I'm done with your obnoxious rules and all of your damn abs... I mean, assumptions."

I straighten.

"You and Julian keep acting like you're doing me a favor. But at the end of the day, y'all need me. And I need a place to sleep that won't throw out my back."

He stills. His gaze drops, then lifts again, face neutral as hell. Like he's already recalibrated. "So... what? You want to leave?"

I hesitate.

Because it isn't always like this. There are some parts I *do* like. The luxurious showers. The late-night vocal sessions. His cooking, which is better than he lets on. And yeah... I'm not hating the current view.

But not hating something is no excuse to accept just anything.

I lift a shoulder. "Maybe I do."

He just stands there. Shirtless. Silent.

If he wants me to stay, he's not saying it.

I nod, turn, and pull the door behind me.

I've got a paycheck. I can get a motel.

But his hand comes down over mine, stopping the door. "Wait."

I pause, and we lock eyes.

He exhales, chest rising and falling like he's fighting with himself, then backs into the room. Grabbing a blanket, his phone, his earbuds, he heads for the door.

He stops at the threshold and lifts a finger. "Don't. Touch. Anything."

I smile as he stalks toward the couch.

"So should I put my bra next to your socks or your boxers?"

He groans as I cackle and shut the door.

16

This morning was mine.

I slept hard for the first time since I got here. Langston's bed felt like feathers, and his sheets smelled clean, threaded through with his cologne. The kind that lingers. The kind that follows you into sleep. Which, combined with the shirtless visual he gave me last night, made for interesting dreams.

I woke slow. At ease. A little disoriented in the best way. Ate a real breakfast instead of choking down lukewarm bottled water and anxiety.

Langston was already gone, which meant no tension, rules, or hovering. Just peace.

I warmed up my voice on the ride to the theater, quiet scales under my breath, feeling the sound settle into my body like it actually belonged there.

Today, I'm not apologizing for taking up space.

Previews were supposed to end this week. Instead, they quietly tacked on two more. *Investor nerves*, Julian says. *Momentum. Buzz. A chance to steady the ship.* No one asked if I wanted the extension. They just assumed I'd stay.

When I step into the rehearsal studio, my gaze cuts just once toward Gracie across the room. She's laughing with Regan, loose and easy. No guilt or nerves. Nothing I can grab onto. I log it anyway. 'Cause if someone wanted to look innocent, that's exactly how they'd do it.

A few heads turn, then a few more. The looks feel different than yesterday. Tight. Measuring. Almost pitying, like they already know something I don't.

Kai's near the mirrors, phone clutched in hand, eyes blown wide. I cross the room fast.

"What's going on?"

She swallows. "You might wanna pull up TMZ."

Everything suddenly feels too loud. I retreat to my dressing room, shut the door, unlock my phone.

No.

No, no, no.

Photos. Videos. Alexia everywhere. With Julian. Laughing. Touching. Kissing. Angles that leave nothing to interpretation.

But I didn't. I wouldn't.

What the hell is this, AI?

This is bad. Really bad. And Langston...

My thoughts scatter as I shove my phone in my bag and bolt down the hall. Composer studio, empty. Rehearsal rooms, nothing. I turn for the stage, and the door shuts behind me.

"Looking for me?"

I stop short.

Noah.

Shit.

If I look startled, if I look guilty, he'll clock it. Alexia's already under a microscope. Sneaking around. Lying. Julian. She'd owe Noah an explanation.

So, I smooth my face into something easy. Familiar. "Actually... yeah."

He steps closer. I give ground without meaning to.

"To explain?"

"Mmhmm," I say, steadying myself. "None of this is how it looks."

"You and Julian smashing faces?" he says. "Some sort of CPR I don't know about?"

I force a laugh. Alexia's laugh. "Noah... it was just a PR stunt. We wanted to boost visibility for the show. Get people talking."

He tilts his head. "And Julian's wife was cool with that?"

"She's... open to more than you think?" I say, and it comes out like a question even though I don't want it to.

He doesn't smile. Not even a little. His hand snaps around my wrist. "Damn it, Lexy. I'm sick of all these games!"

"Okay—*ow*. Noah, let go! What the hell?"

He holds my stare like he's daring me to vanish. Then, finally, he releases me.

I rub my wrist, pulse hammering, eyes tracking the door.

"Jeez, Lexy." He drags a hand through his hair. "You just make me so... I can't do this anymore."

I steady my voice. "You mean you want this... thing to be over between us?"

He turns back, eyes sharp. "I mean I want you to be mine. And nobody else's."

Cold slides up my spine. Possession like that doesn't come out of nowhere.

He pulls me in, gentler now. Familiar. Like high school secrets. Stolen kisses.

It would almost be romantic if my instincts weren't screaming.

"It's time, Lexy," he says. "I wanna tell the world."

The certainty in his voice hits harder than his grip. "Tell the world what?"

"That this is it. We're a thing." His voice drops. "That I'm crazy about you."

I search his face for a crack. Doubt. Anything.

I need to find Langston. Now. I need to explain the clips with Julian before this blows any further. And still, I hate myself for the way Noah's eyes soften, for how real his hope feels. He's serious about Alexia, and I'm standing in her skin, breaking his heart anyway.

"Noah, I—"

He kisses me. Slow. Like we've already agreed to something.

No. This is wrong.

The door clicks. I jerk back.

Langston stands there, taking it in. Me. Noah. Too close.

His face shuts down in real time. Then he turns and walks away.

"Langston! Langston, wait!"

His footsteps are clipped and furious, echoing off the narrow corridor like punctuation marks. Final. Unforgiving. He doesn't look back.

"Langston, please," I call, my voice chasing him the way my feet can't.

I cut him off just before the corner, planting myself in his path. He tips his head back and stares at the ceiling like he's counting tiles.

"Listen, I'm sorry. I have no idea what's going on. I just got here and all of this fell into my lap. What happened back there? I didn't mean to. I mean, really, I didn't. *He* did! And apparently, he and Alexia had this whole thing going on for a while, and I was trying to get out of it but didn't know how, and then—well, *you saw.* I didn't wanna make things worse by telling you something I wasn't sure about. And then the TMZ drop hit, which is *way, way* worse, and I just, I feel awful."

Something shutters behind his eyes, and suddenly I'm talking to a wall.

"Yana," he says, too calm, "do you really think your feelings are my top priority right now?"

Something caves inside me.

"Please," he adds. "Get out of my way."

I move.

He storms down the hall... straight into Julian's office.

Oh no.

I sprint after him. He already has Julian by the collar when I bust in.

"Langston, please!" Julian cries. "I never meant—"

"But you did," Langston snaps, grip tightening. "I thought you were my friend."

"I am! It was before I even knew about your history. Before I knew you two were a thing!"

"Langston, please don't!" I shout, but it's like he can't hear me.

Cast and crew clog the doorway, the room holding its breath.

"How could you do some shit like this?" Langston growls. "If I find out you had *anything* to do—"

"I didn't!" Julian yells. "I would never hurt Lex, I swear! It was a mistake. A *stupid, stupid* mistake!"

"I ought to introduce your head to the underside of a piano."

"Langston, I swear it wasn't me!" Julian stammers, gasping. "You know I took Miriam to see *Wicked* that night. There's no way!"

"And somehow," Langston says coldly, "I've still got every right to make you bleed."

"Langston, stop!" My voice cracks.

That does it. He lets go, eyes flicking to the doorway, to the phones, to the audience this has become. He adjusts his sleeves like he didn't just consider breaking a man in half.

"Just forget it," he says. "We've got work to do."

He doesn't look at me when he leaves.

The room holds its breath for a second, then exhales all at once.

I step closer and rest a hand on Julian's shoulder. "Are you okay?"

He nods, already waving it off. With a clap, he quickly pulls himself together.

"You heard him," he says to everyone. "Show must go on."

Sure, I've seen Langston irritated, sharp, controlling even. But that? That was something else. And now I can't unsee it.

People drift out, murmuring, avoiding eye contact. The space empties fast.

Julian and I are left behind, sharing the same tired look. Like neither of us is sure how much just broke, or who's gonna pretend it didn't.

———

THINGS ARE STILL TENSE WHEN WE STEP BACK ON STAGE.

I tell myself to focus. Just get through today. Whatever this mess is with Langston, Noah, Alexia, TMZ... it can wait. The only way out of a scandal is through it. Overshadow it with a performance so undeniable people forget the whispers.

But Noah won't meet my eyes. His face is tight, like he's been crying and hates that I might notice. Gracie's been side-eyeing me since the blowup in Langston's office, her stare crawling up my spine.

Focus.

We reset for the after-audition scene. Prince chasing Ella backstage, desperate to know who she is. Romantic. Urgent. Noah still shows up, still plays his part, even with whatever's churning behind his eyes.

I'll deal with him later. Maybe before we head home. Maybe never.

"Wait! What's your name?"

Noah's voice carries, clear and practiced, even as he keeps his focus anywhere but me.

"I, I can't—"

"Take off the mask," Noah says. "Just—"

He stops. Looks up.

The orchestra cuts off mid-breath.

"Noah?" Julian calls from the front row. "You still with us?"

Something creaks.

I look up just in time to see a stage light swaying above us, the cable snapping loose like a gunshot.

The world narrows. The light drops.

Of all ways, this is how I die?

"Watch out!"

Noah slams into me. Hard.

The air blasts out of my lungs as I hit the floor, my head clipping a set piece on the way down. The stage light crashes where I'd been standing a breath ago. Sparks fly. Metal cracks sharp into wood. The floor trembles beneath us. My stomach drops as people scream, dust billowing up like smoke.

I blink, trying to figure out which way is up, everything else blurs. My ears ring.

Noah touches my face. "I don't know—"

"Get out of my way."

He disappears, and then Langston is beside me.

"Lex! Are you okay?"

"Ugh... Stop calling me that."

"Langston! What's happening?" Julian shouts.

Langston presses a hand to my forehead, cups my chin, panic wide open on his face. "Can somebody get some ice, please!"

"I think someone's trying to kill me," I mumble.

"Yeah, no kidding." He scans the auditorium, furious. "What are you doing? Someone call the medic. Now! Where's that ice?"

I look up at him, dizzy, heart pounding.

Under any other circumstance, I'd swoon. Being held by a man who looks like he might unravel if I blink wrong.

Oh my gosh. I think I've got a crush. And at the worst possible time.

Julian rushes onstage. "Good grief! What happened?"

Everyone just stands around. Watching. Like they're waiting to see if I bleed.

Julian yanks off his cap and drops his head into his hands. Noah stands back, fists clenched, expression tight.

"Enough." Langston scoops me up like I weigh nothing, and everything tilts as he carries me offstage.

MOMENTS LATER, KAI RUSHES INTO MY DRESSING ROOM WITH ice, hands shaking as she passes it over. Cast members hover in the doorway, whispering, as Langston presses the ice gently to my forehead.

"Any update?" he asks.

"It looks like someone removed a safety cable," says Kai.

Langston's gaze locks with mine.

"Are you okay, Alexia?" asks Kai, scanning my face for any signs of damage.

"I will be."

That's a lie. I just don't know how to say the truth yet.

"If there's anything I can do," Kai says softly, "let me know."

Langston swallows once. "Can everyone clear the room so Lex and I can have a moment, please?"

They slip out quietly. Kai shuts the door as she follows.

"Langston, what the hell?" My voice shakes. "I didn't sign up for this shit."

"*Shhh*. I know. I know."

He runs a hand over my hair, pauses. Then gently peels my wig off, the tape releasing with a soft rip.

"Sir."

"Please. I've seen you in a bonnet. Come here." He pulls me into his chest, resting his chin on my head. "You're not alone. You know that, right?"

I look up at him. His eyes are steady. Sincere.

"Any idea who'd try something like this?" he asks. "Anyone been rude to you lately?"

Gracie flashes through my mind. Fast. Then the others. I've been living in side-eyes and half-whispers since the day I stepped into this theater. But that's nothing new.

I shake my head.

He exhales and pulls me closer. "I know it's a lot. And I haven't had my wits about me lately. But I'm really sorry, Yana. I really am."

My chest locks at the sound of my name. I nod into his shirt, breathing him in. The warmth. The strength. The almost-safety.

"Langston... I'm scared." My voice breaks. "What if what happened to Lex happens to me too—"

"*Shhh*," he says softly. "I won't let anything happen to you."

I press my face into his chest, a sob slipping out despite myself. He sounds so sure, and I want, *need*, to believe him.

But he couldn't protect Alexia.

And just now, on that stage? He couldn't protect me either.

17

The show is canceled thanks to the falling stage light—and what could've easily turned into a crime scene if it had landed a few feet to the left.

The cast scatters, shaken and buzzing. But Langston never leaves my side. His hand stays at my back as we exit the dressing room. Then he's holding my hand. And somewhere between the curb and the backseat of the car, his arm slips around my shoulders and doesn't move again. I'm not sure if he realizes he's doing it, but I don't mind.

The car hums as we pull into traffic, rain tapping lightly against the windows while the city slides past in streaks of gold and red. I lean into him, just enough to feel anchored. My breathing slows, syncing with his, and for the first time all day, my body unclenches.

I feel safe here.

The thought surprises me. So does the quiet warmth that comes with it. Maybe he doesn't hate me. Maybe he never really did.

We sit like that for a while, both of us staring out opposite windows, the silence easy instead of awkward. His breathing stays steady. Mine does too. The window fogs faintly beside my shoulder, the seatbelt pressing gently against my arm. I don't shift away. Then he looks at me.

"Maybe you shouldn't be in such a rush to move out."

Aw. He's worried about me. "And keep waking up shaped like a question mark?"

I laugh harder than the joke deserves, mostly because I catch the flicker in his eyes. Amusement, yes, but something else too. Concern.

He doesn't smile, not exactly, but the tension eases. "Maybe we could work something out," he says. "Like we did last night."

"Maybe," I say. "But don't get it twisted. I don't need anyone rescuing me. I'm a grown woman, mmkay?"

"I might believe you," he says calmly, "if you'd survived getting abducted last month."

I scoff and smack his chest, more offended than hurt. "I told you. I was eating a sandwich!"

"Good to know that's all it takes."

His lips twitch. He almost laughs. Almost.

"You're so pleased with yourself, aren't you?" I say with a nudge. "Look at you. You wanna laugh."

He looks back out the window like nothing fazes him. I swear this man could win a staring contest with a brick wall.

"Fine," I say. "Since you wanna be my knight in shining armor, will you settle for being my bodyguard when I go out tonight?"

Just like that, any sign of humor fades, replaced by something more run-down.

"Yana, you just nearly got killed."

"*And?*" I lift my chin. "All the more reason to have a good time while I can. I'm too young and too fine to let some psycho —or tabloid peddler—keep me locked up like some bored-to-tears prisoner."

Langston's gaze drifts down my body before he catches himself and looks away. Mmhmm. That wasn't curiosity. That was a flashback. He's already seen me naked and knows I'm not exaggerating. That's what scares him.

"My place isn't that boring," he says quietly.

I fight the urge to smile. Just barely. "Maybe to you."

He glares at me, and I bat my lashes, hopeful. No reaction. So I pivot.

I clear my throat and launch into my best Whitney Houston impression, belting "I Have Nothing" from *The Bodyguard* like it's a personal mission. I commit fully, dramatic hand gestures and all. The driver shakes his head in the mirror, amused. Langston lets out a low groan and drops his head back against the seat, eyes closing like the sound physically pains him. And somehow, it hits different. That groan. The exposed line of his throat. The way his jaw tightens before he pulls himself back under control.

My voice falters mid-phrase, the song slipping off my tongue. And before I can redirect my thoughts, I'm staring at his mouth. That's when his smile breaks through. Slow. Reluctant. Completely real.

"You're impossible," he says.

"I'll take that as a yes!" Giddy with triumph, I squeeze him tight.

He stiffens for half a second, then relaxes, his arm tightening around me like this isn't new to him.

I grin into his shoulder as the car rolls on.

He's already hooked.

Or maybe it's the other way around.

***

SoHo doesn't care what time it is. It never has. The bass is already thumping when we step inside the bar, neon signs buzzing, the floor tacky with history. I feel alive the second we cross the threshold.

I curled my hair, did my face, and picked a little black dress that made me feel like myself. Unstoppable. And tonight, I am.

Langston doesn't share my enthusiasm. His hand settles at my lower back out of habit, protective even now. But he stills the moment he takes in the room. The crowd. The noise. The lack of control.

"This is no place for a celebrity," he mutters.

I laugh and tug him forward anyway. "Relax. I doubt most of these people even know who I'm supposed to be."

I'm here to let loose. I wanna have fun. And I wanna have fun with *him*.

Hopefully, Alexia won't mind.

At the bar, I order two shots of tequila while Langston scans the room like an underpaid bouncer, eyes tracking exits, shoulders tight.

The shot glasses are cold when the bartender slides them over.

I pass one to Langston and grin. "You must be wearing your briefs tonight."

His face tightens. "I told you to stay out of my things."

My mouth falls open. "I was joking."

That only makes it worse. I cackle as he purses his lips, clearly regretting every decision that brought him here.

"Tighty-whities, Langston? For real?"

He looks like he might combust. But when I lift my glass, he slowly follows suit.

"To a night of bad decisions," I say.

He masks the flash of panic and tosses it back.

"Now, let's dance." I grab his hand before he can rethink it and pull him to the dance floor.

Reggaeton pulses through the room, bodies moving together like it's instinct. I start grooving, hips loose, shoulders rolling. But when I turn, Langston's just standing there, hands shoved in his pockets, stiff as a coat rack.

I lean in his ear. "The goal is to move your body."

"I can't," he says quietly. "I don't..."

Of course he doesn't.

I take his hands and place them where they belong. "School is in session." I drop my hips to the beat. "Come on. I know you feel it. In your spine. In your *chest*. Let your body do what it wants."

He tries. Really tries.

The result is a stiff, awkward bob, like his joints are staging a quiet rebellion. I bite down on a laugh, hand flying to my mouth. But it's too late. He catches it and stills, eyes flicking around like he's just been caught doing something illegal.

"I told you." He starts to bail.

I snag his hand before he can escape. "Ah-ah," I say, mocking his tone as I tug him back. "We're not quitters, sir."

He rolls his eyes but stays.

I lift his arm and spin beneath it, then twist back into him, close enough to feel his breath warm against my cheek. I linger, just a beat longer than necessary, but he doesn't pull away. Instead, his gaze goes dark, unfocused. The tequila's doing its job. Good.

I step closer, guiding his hands back to my hips. "Just follow."

And he does. We sway together, slow and intimate, bodies finding a rhythm that surprises us both. He adjusts once, subtle as a breath, and suddenly we fit. The kinda fit that pulls your focus sharp and low. His presence settles behind me, and my spine warms, attention narrowing until there's only movement and contact and the quiet click of *yes*.

Langston's no Roman, but he's got a little groove in him. By the second song, he's moving without thinking. By the third, he's flush behind me, breath brushing my neck, not backing away when I press into him. Based on what I feel against my behind, he's enjoying himself. And so am I.

I turn to face him, amused and a little stunned. His eyes roam over me, unapologetic now, heat clear in his gaze.

"You doing alright?" I ask, smiling.

He leans in close, voice low. "I have to go to the bathroom."

My cheeks burn as I nod. He disappears into the crowd, and I head back to the bar, already knowing this night is nowhere near over.

We take the subway up to Midtown, the train screeching into the station like it's mad we're still asking it for favors. I grab a pole, the metal cool against my palm, and lean into Langston as ads flicker past the windows. He doesn't push me away.

But he looks at me like I've lost my mind once we arrive at our destination.

"Trust me," I say, already tugging him forward.

I found SPYSCAPE my first month in New York, back when I was killing time between auditions that went nowhere. I was trying to convince myself I was smart enough to survive here even if the business didn't love me yet. I wandered in alone, half by accident, and spent hours reading about codebreakers and double agents, taking personality assessments that told me I was *adaptable* and *observant* and *resilient*. It made me feel clever when everything else made me feel... disposable.

Langston pauses just inside the entrance, already clocking exits and liabilities. His mouth settles into that polite, resigned line he gets when he thinks he's about to endure something instead of enjoy it. I don't explain. Just lace my fingers through his and pull him along.

This place doesn't care who you are. Only how you think. And something about that feels safe. For both of us.

The lighting shifts, and so does he. Langston slows without realizing it, shoulders loosening as he starts reading plaques about Cold War surveillance and intelligence networks like he's forgotten I'm standing beside him. He lingers. Rereads. Frowns at diagrams and timelines, correcting a display under his breath like it personally offended him. When he takes the personality profile, he scoffs at first. Then the results pop up.

Strategic. Hyper-focused. Risk-averse. Motivated by achievement more than joy.

A laugh slips out of me. "That's spot on."

He doesn't comment. Just stares at the screen a beat too long before moving on.

By the time we reach the Spy Ops Challenge, he's fully invested, even though he pretends otherwise. The room is dark, all lasers and pressure plates, beeps and buzzers echoing off the walls.

He looks at me like I've dragged him into a ball pit. "What's this? A play place for kids?"

"This isn't McDonald's," I say, grinning. "It's for us. Now stop being a stick-in-the-mud and put your thinking cap on."

He rolls his eyes as a digital clock flashes above us, counting down our failure in angry red numbers.

It isn't long before he gives in, methodical and focused, mapping the grid with his eyes before he even moves. The red laser lines flicker like they're daring us to misstep.

Seconds blur as we inch forward, stopping, recalibrating like we're solving something bigger than a museum game. He treats every step like a test he's determined to pass, even as the clock dares him to mess up. I grab his arm once when I almost drift too far, stifling a laugh. He freezes me in place with a quiet, urgent warning about my foot placement. I follow his lead, trying not to distract him, trying not to enjoy how commanding he sounds when he's in his element.

We reach the end together, breathless and triumphant, staring at the final set of white buttons like they're the gates of heaven. We hesitate. Overthink. I press one.

"No, no, no!" he shouts. "That's—"

The alarm blares as he stares at me.

"Did we just fail?" I ask.

"We absolutely failed," he says.

Then he laughs. Really laughs. Soft and disbelieving and completely unguarded.

And I love the sound.

———

THE AMERICAN DREAM MALL FEELS UNREAL AFTER SPYSCAPE. Neon lights. Carnival music drifting up through the air. Laughter echoing off polished floors. Langston doesn't fight me anymore. He just follows as I pull him toward the indoor rides, his shoulder brushing mine, steps lighter than they were an hour ago.

We split a paper cone of fried dough dusted in powdered sugar. It's a no-no for him, I can tell, but he doesn't say a word. Just eats it anyway, licking sugar from his thumb and pretending he doesn't enjoy it.

I count it a small victory.

The Ferris wheel creaks softly as it lifts us above the chaos, music and laughter bouncing off a glass dome ceiling, neon lights spinning in dizzy circles below. By the time we reach the top, everything looks smaller. Like the whole world's been zipped up and gift-wrapped just for us. The car sways gently. Suspended.

For a moment, nothing is urgent. We're just here.

Langston lets out a low breath. "This view is incredible."

I turn toward him, fascinated. "You've never been here before?"

"Never had the time," he says. "Hit the ground running the second I got in from L.A. Classes, meetings, studios, rehearsals. Sometimes it's hard to catch a breath."

"And you like it that way, don't you?"

He nods, eyes still fixed on the sprawl below us. "You know, people in Hollywood are no strangers to hustle," he says. "Plenty of folks grinding past sunset. But this place..."

He gestures vaguely at the chaos below.

"It means business. Everyone's got something to do. Somewhere to be. And hell if they're going to let anyone get in their way."

"They'll pound you into the pavement," I add.

"Exactly." He tosses me a half grin.

And it hits me how rare that is. How easily it lands tonight.

I lean back against the seat, shoulder brushing his, thinking about my early days in New York. "I was such a cliché when I got here. Thought Detroit was tough, but I had *no* idea. My cast-mates tried to warn me. 'Broadway's cutthroat.' I didn't listen."

He turns toward me, really listening, not fixing, not interrupting.

"My flight wasn't even two hours," I continue. "And I still knew there was no turning back. Flying over the Statue of Liberty. Watching the ball drop on New Year's Eve. Counting down with Bryant. Kissing him when the confetti fell. I thought that was the moment everything would change."

I meet Langston's gaze as the carnival glows between us.

"But you know what they say about God laughing at our plans."

He doesn't respond, but he hears me.

"And when I sat on that motel bed after losing everything," I say quietly, "lost, confused... alone, I kept asking myself one thing. *What did I do to deserve this?*"

He reaches for my hand, squeezes gently. His thumb settles there, grounding me.

"You didn't deserve that, Yana."

I nod, even if I'm not sure I believe it yet.

"Anyway," I say, forcing a smile. "Thanks."

"For tagging along?" he asks.

"For changing my life," I say.

After a beat, he gives a small, humble nod. "Honestly, I suppose you've got *destiny* to thank for that."

I nudge his knee. "You're becoming a believer!"

"Yeah, yeah." He exhales. "Or at the very least, Alexia could take the credit. If she hadn't..." He trails off.

I wait. Hold his gaze. Give him room.

"Before she vanished," he says, rubbing the back of his neck, "we sort of had a falling out."

My stomach pulls tight.

Falling out.

Two words that sound simple enough to complicate everything.

"We couldn't get on the same page," he continues. "She said she was done and just... left."

He looks past me for a second, eyes closing off, like he's replaying a conversation he wishes he could interrupt.

"Never responded to my apology. Never returned my calls." His jaw flexes like he almost stops himself. "At first, I thought she was just upset. Then she didn't show up for rehearsal. Or preview."

He bows his head, like the weight of it still lives there.

"So you broke up?" I ask.

He nods once. "I figured focusing on the work was better than stressing about where she was," he says. "We had a show to deliver. Investors didn't care how we made it happen. But she never came back. She never..."

He stops himself, his hand tightening around mine.

"And now it turns out she was screwing other men, including my best friend." His expression hardens as he gazes out at nothing. "Makes me wonder if I knew her at all."

It's no wonder he didn't wanna talk about her. He's been carrying this alone. No closure or answers. Just silence where an ending should've been. And now? The scandal. Like the universe decided to kick him while he was already down.

And awful as it makes me feel, the truth settles in too. There's space there. Where she used to be.

"We didn't laugh a lot, but..." He looks at me softly. "I'm finding I kind of enjoy laughing."

The Ferris wheel slows as it reaches the top, the tangle of steel and neon dissolving into soft halos beneath us. Hovering. Weightless. Like the world has decided to give us privacy. Langston shifts closer. Close enough that I feel his breath, warm and steady, brushing my cheek. Close enough that stopping now would take effort. He gives me time. Time to fall back. Time to tell him this is a bad idea.

I don't.

His lips meet mine gently, almost reverently. A quiet, searching kiss, like he's making sure I'm real. Like he's afraid I might disappear if he presses too hard. Then he deepens the kiss, slow and intentional, heat sliding through restraint like a held breath finally released. My knees soften as I lean into him, the spinning lights below blurring into color. Everything else fades.

It feels like midnight. Like watching that ball drop all over again.

———

WE HARDLY SPEAK ON THE RIDE BACK. THERE'S NO POINT. Hands wander. Breaths tangle. The car fills with quiet sounds we don't bother to stop. Every red light feels like an insult, like the city's trying to test our patience.

By the time we reach his building, we're already half unraveled.

The door barely shuts before he's on me, backing me into the wall like he's done waiting.

His mouth finds mine, hungry and sure, like the question's already been answered. I kiss him back, fingers sliding up his arms, feeling muscle flex beneath them. His hands skim my sides, then cup my breasts through the thin fabric of my dress, grip firm and possessive. I gasp into his mouth, the sound swallowed by his tongue.

"Boots off?" I murmur, barely getting the words out.

"Who gives a shit," he says, palms sliding to my ass.

He lifts me like I weigh nothing as I wrap my legs around him, my laugh breaking loose against his mouth. He groans at the sound, low and helpless, like it hits somewhere dangerous.

"If we start," he says, breathless against my lips, "I'm not going to stop."

I pull back just enough to look at him, the heat in his eyes unmistakable. "Then don't."

He carries me down the hall, my laughter fading into something softer, heavier, as the bedroom door shuts behind us.

***

LATER, WE LIE TANGLED IN THE SHEETS, THE ROOM HUSHED IN that way it only gets after something real has happened. The lamp stays on low, casting everything in a warm blur. Outside, the city hums close by, footsteps and distant voices filtering in through the windows, but in here time loosens its grip.

My body feels soft. Unrushed. Like I've finally landed somewhere instead of bracing for impact. Langston's warm beneath me, solid and steady. Arm behind my shoulders, thumb stroking slow at my neck like he knows exactly what it does to me.

There's something about him like this that catches me off guard. The quiet confidence. The way he doesn't fill the space with noise or expectation. He just exists, present in a way that makes my chest feel fuller than it should.

I trace lazy shapes along his skin, appreciating the hills and valleys of his sculpted chest, the way his breathing evens out when I touch him. And okay. I clock the details. The broad shoulders. The strong hands. The fact that when everything came off, there were absolutely no tragic tighty-whities involved. Blessings where blessings are due.

And for the record, there's nothing boring about the way he moves through a room, or through me. I've really gotta stop making assumptions.

He inhales deep and exhales slow. "I want a Tony," he says softly.

I lift my head. "A Tony?"

He nods, eyes fixed on the ceiling, voice unguarded now. "That's my dream."

Something shifts in me at that. Not the ambition. The vulnerability. The way he says it like it matters, like it's been living quietly inside him for a long time.

I smile and press closer, my cheek settling against his chest. "And it's one hell of a dream."

I feel him grin against my hair. Not careful or controlled. Just real. And when he leans down to kiss me, it's slow and unhurried, like the world can afford to wait.

And for once, I let myself believe it might.

18

I wake up blissfully content.

Morning light spills across the bed, warming my legs. The apartment hums quietly around me, distant traffic, pipes settling, the soft sounds of a day already in motion.

My body feels loose and relaxed, the kinda comfortable you don't rush away from unless you're stupid.

Last night was full of many firsts. And seconds. *Hmmph*. And thirds.

For somebody without a ton of experience, Langston is excellent in bed. Confident, more chill than I've ever seen him. And that body? *My gawd.*

I roll over, reaching for him, already considering asking for one more round before we start our day. But his side of the bed is empty. I blink, taking in the room. Sheets rumpled. Pillow barely touched. The door to the hall sits slightly cracked. "Langston?" No answer.

Maybe he's in the shower.

I sink back into the mattress, enjoying the quiet and the fact that I woke up here for a second time. Finally, I slip out of bed, scoop up my clothes, and head for the door.

But I stop short.

Until now, I've respected his wishes and haven't touched a thing. But considering everything I let him touch last night, maybe I've earned a little trust. I pad across the room to his closet and peek inside.

Black tee.

Black tee.

Black tee.

Of course. Man's clearly taking his styling cues from Charlie Brown.

Then I gasp.

A white button-down, tucked all the way in the back.

I slip it on and happily button it up, the fabric settling easily against my skin. Perfect fit, and I swallow the stupid little thrill that comes with it.

I'm starving.

Noting that Langston isn't in the shower either, which is honestly rude, I drift toward the kitchen instead.

The smell hits before I even turn the corner, warm and sweet and unmistakable. A single Styrofoam container waits in the middle of the counter. "He did not," I murmur.

I lift the lid and laugh under my breath. Four perfect triangles of French toast, a side of bacon, syrup. The high fructose kind, no less.

What a sweetheart!

I steal a slice of bacon and start munching, already knowing this is gonna do my voice zero favors tonight. Worth it. A Post-it sits beside the container.

Thanks. ~L

I smile around my bite. There's a P.S. underneath.

Emergency meeting. Juice in fridge. Apology tour today.

"Apology tour?"

The doorbell rings. Then pounding.

I freeze in the middle of the kitchen, bacon in hand, and glance down at Langston's dress shirt swaddling my body. More pounding.

With the lift of my shoulder, I head to the door.

A petite Hispanic woman stands on the stoop, a giant briefcase slung over her shoulder, phone pressed to her ear. She gives me a quick once-over, precise and assessing.

"I'll call you back," she says, before hanging up.

I'm not sure if I'm supposed to know her, so I give my best Alexia grin. "Hi."

"You can cut the crap," she says, barging right past me. "I know who you are."

I shut the door behind her, instinctively straightening my posture. "You... do?"

"Of course." She sets her things down and extends a hand. "Marisol Vélez. Alexia's crisis manager."

"Oh."

We shake, and she drags her palm down her blazer like the touch left residue.

"When they told me someone was stepping in for Alexia, I said no one would ever buy it." She looks me over again. "But given your appearance, I can see why Julian and Langston took their chances. Wouldn't suggest you fill the role *quite* so thoroughly though."

My smile tightens. I cross my arms, suddenly wishing I'd slipped on pants.

"You here for the apology tour?" I ask.

She smiles like she's deciding whether to hug or threaten me. "Honey, I'm here to save your life." Opening her briefcase, she pulls out a tablet and stylus, the screen glowing bright against the counter. "You ever heard that phrase bull in a China shop?"

I nod.

"I'm the one that cleans up the mess."

She waves me over, pulls something up, and places the tablet on the counter.

"Sign here, here, and here."

I skim. *Confidentiality. Restrictions.* What I'm allowed to say. What I'm not. My pulse ticks steady in my ears as the pages scroll. It all blurs, so I go ahead and sign.

"So you're like, Olivia Pope?" I ask.

"Sweetheart, I'm Olivia Pope's worst nightmare in five-inch stilettos. Now—"

The doorbell rings again.

"That's hair and makeup," she says, clapping her hands. She starts toward the door, then looks back at me. "Maybe a shower and some pants before we get started, hmm?"

I grab clothes from my suitcase and rush to the bathroom.

———

WHEN I RETURN, THE APARTMENT'S TRANSFORMED. MIRROR lights. Hair tools. A full studio setup where Langston's kitchen used to be.

RIP, counter space.

Marisol rattles off the itinerary like she's reading a verdict. Two magazine interviews. A podcast. *The Morning Show.* Millions of eyes waiting on the other side of a camera. There's no pause. No space for questions. Not mine.

The stylist doesn't ask who I am. Just pins, smooths, perfects. Another face. Another job.

But this ain't my first rodeo. I barely flinch as muscle memory takes over.

The woman in the mirror looks flawless. Familiar. I look away first.

Something about it nags at me. Not the transformation itself, but the care behind it. The precision. The way everything is being preserved, not erased. That level of attention doesn't happen by accident. If Alexia wasn't coming back, none of this would be necessary.

Which means someone is making room.

If Marisol knows everything there is to know about the real Alexia, maybe she knows where she is now.

"I was hesitant to step into all this," I say, carefully. "But Langston and Julian didn't know what else to do. Everyone was so shaken by Alexia's disappearance."

Marisol keeps typing, eyes on her phone, not seeming all that concerned.

Even if Alexia isn't dead, someone was trying to get rid of her. Someone close. Someone who isn't satisfied with the current results.

"Have you... heard from her?" I ask.

Nothing.

She finishes the message, sets the phone aside, then reaches for her tablet and passes it to me.

"Right. Here are the types of questions to expect and the answers you should give. If they ask about your parents, your health, or where you've been, you are to respond with these answers and these alone."

With pursed lips, I take the tablet as her finger hovers and points.

The words are smooth. Polite. Empty in that specific way meant to satisfy without giving anything real. I can already hear my own voice saying them. Calm. Grateful. Contained. Like a version of me that doesn't exist outside a camera lens.

"Outside of that," Marisol says, eyes still on her phone, "you are to keep your mouth shut and your head down. Got it?"

I nod on instinct, fingers curling into my palm like they always do these days.

Marisol bends slightly, meeting my eyes. "Trust me. All this is for the best."

Over by the bookshelves, the bird lets out a short, restless chirp, probably aggravated by all the commotion.

"Wardrobe should be here any moment," Marisol says, turning toward the window. "So I do hope you can fit into a size six."

She says it like it's a character requirement.

Langston really could've given me more of a heads-up.

At this point, I'd much rather be back in bed, 'cause I am exhausted. Not just tired but worn thin from guessing. From being moved from place to place without ever being filled in. If no one tells me the truth, I have no way of knowing how safe I am. Or what happens when Alexia comes back. *If* she comes back. And then what happens to me? What happens to Langston? What happens to us? And how many of those answers does this woman already have?

"Marisol."

She turns slowly, deliberately, like the pause itself is part of the calculation. Her gaze fixes on me, steady and unblinking, and I try not to flinch.

"Please," I say. "I need to know what I've gotten myself into."

She rolls her eyes, impatience flashing through the polish. "Jayana, what you need to do is focus. Millions of dollars are on the line. Including my own. And I *will not* let you ruin this for me or my client. Do you understand?"

Her client. Sounds like a very much alive client.

I nod, my heart thudding a little harder than I'd like.

"Fewer questions," she says. "More studying. Got it?"

I lift my chin and let her think that's the end of it.

BACKSTAGE AT REHEARSAL, I POST UP IN THE HALL, RUNNING through quiet vocal warmups. Breath controlled. Shoulders held where they belong. Focus is the only thing keeping me upright.

Posters line the walls, curling at the corners like they've been here longer than anyone wants to admit. Faces and titles stare back at me as crew members weave through with headsets and clipboards, all urgency and momentum.

The building feels alive. Too alive.

Every creak above us makes my skin prickle. Every light hum feels louder than it should.

Yesterday a cable snapped and a stage light dropped where my head used to be.

People called it a malfunction. A freak accident. But someone cut that wire.

Marisol's voice echoes in my head. Calm and rehearsed.

I will not let you ruin this for me or my client. Do you understand?

Alexia isn't dead. If she were, the story would be louder. Public. Strategic.

No. She's somewhere.

Which means someone wanted her gone.

Which means someone wanted *me* gone.

I press my palm to my sternum and hum into the vibration, letting it ground me.

Stay focused. Stay normal.

The apology tour this morning was enough theater for one day. Smiling through questions about Julian. Pretending not to see the way Noah keeps staring. Pretending I don't feel the ripple of speculation every time I enter a room.

Footsteps approach.

Before I can turn, arms wrap around me. Tight.

"*Soooo* glad you're okay!"

Kai.

Her hug presses firm and close. As usual, longer than necessary.

My hands hover before I return it, careful, aware of how easily my body tenses now.

"We almost lost you yesterday," she says, pulling back but keeping her hands on my arms like she's checking for fractures.

"I'm fine," I say lightly.

She brushes lint off my shoulder.

"So dramatic," she says. "One second you're center stage, the next you're almost a headline!"

She laughs. I don't.

Kai leans closer, voice dropping. "Is he still mad at you?"

I frown. "Langston?"

She shakes her head slow, concern etched on her face. "Noah."

The name drops heavier than it should.

"What?"

"Oh, come on." She nudges my elbow. "It's *me* you're talking to."

She tilts her head, awaiting all the juicy details.

I didn't think anyone knew.

"I'm not sure," I say carefully.

Maybe she peeked at his note when she delivered the roses?

Her eyes sharpen for a fraction of a second, and finally she falls back.

"Well," she says, patting my arm again, "I'm sure you'll decide who's best for you."

How much has Alexia told her? And why is she bringing up Noah after what happened yesterday?

"So glad you're good," she adds, again. "The show would be dead without you."

Then she's gone, swallowed by the hall traffic.

I feel like I showed up to rehearsal without the script.

Drawing in a slow breath, I start my scales again, quieter this time. I need to get through rehearsal. I need to stay sharp. I need to stop jumping at shadows.

But my body snaps tense when arms slip around my shoulders from behind.

Then the intoxicating scent hits me. Spicy. Sweet.

Langston.

I soften. And that scares me more than the hug ever could.

His voice is low when he speaks, close to my ear. "I saw *The Morning Show*. You did good."

I smile as he presses a light kiss to my temple, letting myself soak in the contact. I hadn't realized how much I'd missed him until this second. The way he feels behind me. Solid. Familiar. The relief of not having to perform.

I turn in his arms, and slap his chiseled abs. The same ones I couldn't stop tasting last night.

"You could've given me a heads-up about the interviews yesterday, sir."

"My fault," he says. "There was a lot going on."

I'd think he meant the murder attempt if it weren't for the heat in his eyes, reminding me of how he looked at me when my bra came off last night.

I slide my hands across his chest, wanting more than this. Wanting him.

"How was your meeting?" I ask.

"Good," he says, but his eyes drift up the hall.

Someone laughs nearby. Crew members pass. The low hum of rehearsal builds.

I step closer, lowering my voice. "How about a private meeting of our own?"

We've still got time. A few minutes. A door that hasn't closed yet. I'd also prefer to not be left alone right now.

He steps back, sudden enough that the space between us feels deliberate.

"Yana," he says quietly, tone shifting professional. "You know we can't."

I pause. "Why not? I'm pretty sure half the cast does."

I lift my arms toward his neck, but he moves out of reach.

"I'm not the rest of the cast," he says. "I'm me."

Something in my smile slips.

"Langston, what's going on?" I ask. "It's not like people know what's up. They expect to see us together."

He blinks, like he's choosing his next step. "I know. Let's just keep things professional today. Alright?"

The shift is subtle, but I feel it anyway. The moment he puts himself back on the other side of the line.

Nearby, the rehearsal doors swing open. The lights dim as people begin filtering inside.

He presses a quick kiss to my cheek and disappears down the hall, leaving me behind.

I stay where I am a second longer than necessary as the hallway noise rushes back in. The ache settles quietly, right where it knows how.

And I hate that I recognize the feeling.

By first fifteen, I cave.

I duck into a quiet stretch of hallway near the stairwell, the kind no one really uses unless they're hiding or catching their breath. I lean against the wall, phone warm. Before I can overthink it, I tap Laura's name.

She answers on the second ring.

"Hey cuz," she says, breathless.

I smile despite myself. Her voice is steady even when she's winded. Always has been. "You on that damn treadmill again, ain't you?"

"You know it!"

Ever since she met Roman, she's been on that contraption a good four days a week minimum. She swears it's the only way she can maintain her weight loss. And honestly, it shows. Confidence looks real cute on her.

Me? I prefer to burn my calories horizontally, long as I've got a good workout partner anyway.

Which is exactly why I'm calling her.

"What's up?" she asks between breaths. "You didn't get fired again, did you?"

I hadn't planned on filling her in. Plenty of paperwork says I shouldn't. But Laura doesn't count, and I struggle to keep things from her. Besides, after falling into this role, ending up on Langston's couch, and nearly getting taken out yesterday, lying feels like too much work.

"I'm good," I still say. "They're just working me hard. You seen TMZ lately?"

She takes a long gulp of water and exhales. "Nah."

"Okay, don't," I say. "And if you do, just know it wasn't me, alright?"

There's a pause.

"O-kay," she says slowly. "You sure you good, cuz?"

I gnaw my lip, glancing up the hall. Kai's pacing with a clipboard, muttering to herself. A few cast members stretch nearby, laughing, running scales. Langston's in Julian's office, the door closed—which is honestly a miracle considering how close Julian came to getting punched this week.

So much drama. So much scandal. I almost got *killed* yesterday. Yet, this is what's sitting heavy in my chest.

"We kissed, girl."

She gasps so loud I hear it over the treadmill. "You and the music director?"

"Yeah," I say. "And then more. A whole lot more."

She goes quiet for a beat. I pace once, then back again, sneaker scuffing the floor.

Then she laughs.

"Girl, you are something else. I should've known you'd hit that."

"I'm pretty good, right?"

We both chuckle, and my chest eases like it's been waiting for permission.

"But," I say, sober now, "I woke up this morning and he wasn't there. Said he had a meeting. Sure. But then I kissed him at work and he pulled back. I'm scared, cuz. What if he does me just like the others?"

The words sit heavy once they're out.

I think about the guys from other casts. The ones who never

asked me on a real date. Never called unless it was late. Before Bryant, commitment wasn't really my thing either. But with Langston, I don't want this to be that. Not after last night. Not just hooking up, but everything before it. The laughs. The talking. The way he held me like I was special.

"I honestly don't know what to say, Yana," Laura says. "From what you told me, he didn't sound like that kind of guy."

"I didn't think he was." I fall back against the wall, rolling my eyes to keep from crying. "Girl, no joke. Last night was amazing. And *hot*. But now he's acting brand new. I've got no clue why."

I'm quiet for a second, wondering why I was stupid enough to believe this time would be any different.

"I'm sorry, girl," Laura says.

"So now it's gonna be weird," I say. "And you know I don't do weird."

She grunts in agreement.

"Hey, didn't you say Roman was tripping just after y'all got together?"

"The first time we kissed?" She chuckles. "Yeah. But not because of me. He just hadn't felt that way in a long time. It freaked him out. Maybe that's all this is with your guy."

My guy.

I huff a quiet laugh. No one's ever been mine. Not even Bryant.

"Listen," she says. "If what you told me is true, he's not the type to hook up on impulse. But as fine as you are, how could he resist you?"

"That's what I said!"

She laughs again, but the baby cries on her monitor.

"Hey, I gotta go," she says. "But keep your head up, okay? This is the opportunity of a lifetime. And I don't care who's into you, don't you let him steal your moment."

I smile, steadier now. "Okay."

"I love you. We'll see you on opening night."

"See you then."

I hang up, phone still warm in my hand, breath finally even again.

I can't do this thing where I spiral. Can't do the thing where I give my heart front row seats to a situation that hasn't even decided what it is yet. Not this time.

Laura's right. This is my moment. My lead role. I didn't claw my way into this chaos just to lose my footing over a man who can't make up his mind.

So I tuck it away. The hope. The fear. All of it.

Heart on pause.

I square my shoulders, slip my phone back in my pocket, and head for my dressing room.

I've got a show to kill.

———

REHEARSAL GOES BETTER THAN IT HAS ANY RIGHT TO. THE show is another hit. Applause crashes down on us, loud and relentless, the music swelling as the curtain rises again. I take my bow, chest lifting, sweat cooling along my collarbone.

No scandal goes viral. No stage light falls. Nobody gets exposed, arrested, or almost murdered.

I make it through the night in one piece.

Afterward, I hang back with some of the cast. Laugh a little too loud. Sip a little too slow. A few glances linger longer than they need to, but that's alright. If I'm gonna be Alexia for now, I need to be the type of actress they wanna get next to. And I plan to enjoy the process. I'm not losing myself in a man again. Not even one I really like.

When I finally get home, Langston's at the sink, sleeves pushed up, washing dishes like this is just another normal night. The fridge hums low. The apartment's quiet in that end of day way.

"'Bout time you got here," he says.

I almost ask if he missed me. Almost. But I don't wanna reach for something and come up empty.

Still, I missed him.

I hop onto the counter and grab the berries, eating a few while I watch him at the sink, trying to read what's written across his shoulders. His silence. The distance. Whether it's about me.

Before I can settle on an answer, he turns and steps into my space, hands warm at my waist. His mouth finds mine, like he's got nowhere to be. The kiss is long. Sweet. Familiar in the way that softens me before I realize it has.

Hmmph.

Then he turns back to the dishes, the faintest twitch at the corner of his mouth. Like today never happened.

Okay, Yana. Don't trip.

"Long day, I know," he says, noticing I've gone quiet. "How'd you feel about this morning? Did Marisol go easy on you?"

I almost laugh. Instead, I shut the thought down.

"She's cool people," I say. Then, slower, "How long's she been working with Alexia?"

He shrugs, still turned away. "At least since that time the music skipped at one of her concerts. So maybe three years ago."

I nod, filing it away. "Have you asked her if she's heard from Alexia?" He doesn't react to me dropping the assumption that she's dead.

Of course he rolls his eyes.

"Can we not do this again tonight? I'm exhausted."

Frustration flares fast. I wanna be able to talk. I want this to feel real. But last night was the only time he didn't keep me at arm's length, and of course it couldn't have been more convenient. If he keeps shutting me out, it hasn't just got the potential to hurt my feelings. It's got the potential to wreck me.

I set the berries aside.

"Langston, we need answers." *I need answers.*

He sighs and turns back to the sink. "The answers will come when they come. Right now, they're not our concern."

"*Our* concern? Or *my* concern?"

I meet his eyes and stay there.

He thinks he can control everything. Not this. Not after Marisol. Not after the realization that Alexia might not even be dead.

He blinks first.

Grabbing a towel, he dries his hands. Then tosses it aside before stepping to me. Without warning, he presses a kiss to my neck. A breath slips free, and I gently push him back.

"Come on." He frowns. "I haven't been able to stop thinking about you since last night."

He leans in again. I back away.

He's trying to distract me. Does he really think I'm that dumb?

"Surprised you're so interested," I say. "You would've thought I was the Grinch with how much distance you were keeping at the theater."

He scoffs, half-amused, then pauses. "You serious?"

I hold his stare and don't look away. I need to know.

Will he disappear this time too?

"Yana, I was just trying to exercise some restraint," he says. "I can't risk the cast and crew seeing me get carried away."

"Carried away?" The words sting more as I repeat them.

So what am I? Some sorta reckless one-night stand?

He steps back, hands on his waist, swallowing.

I realize I'm gripping the edge of the counter when my palms start to throb. I force myself to let go. To breathe.

Stepping closer, he cups my face.

"Yana, I know all this is complicated. I've got just as many questions as you. But this? Us?" He shakes his head, searching my eyes. "There's no doubt."

I know better than to let words undo me like this. But it almost sounds vulnerable. Sincere. Despite myself, I grin.

"None?"

He mirrors me. "Not a single one."

Something inside me gives way. Not all at once. Just enough.

He kisses my forehead. Then my eyelids. My cheeks. My mouth. Slow, like he's proving a point. The tension drains from my shoulders, replaced by something warmer, heavier.

My heartrate climbs. My pulse follows.

His mouth trails lower, lingering at my neck, my shoulders. Heat gathers low, patient and insistent, as he removes his glasses and presses closer. His fingers slide under my skirt, slip beneath the thin lace of my panties. He tugs gently, and a moan escapes my throat without my consent.

Then he drops to his knees and pulls them the rest of the way down.

"Director," I whisper, half warning, half plea.

His eyes never leave mine as he spreads my thighs and presses a kiss to each one, close enough that my breath stutters and my hands clutch at nothing.

———

It isn't long before we're back in his bed, the city glowing faint through the window. Everything slows as we collapse on the pillows, our breathing finding the same rhythm.

He said he couldn't get me off his mind, and tonight, he certainly proved it. If that was him holding back, I'd hate to see what happens when he doesn't.

He pulls me close from behind, arm anchored around my waist. Kisses my shoulder, already half asleep.

I've still got questions. So many. But he said he does too. Maybe he just needs time.

Or space.

I ease myself out of his grasp and cup his cheek. "This was fun," I whisper. "Goodnight." I kiss his sleepy face and slide away.

"Where you going?" he murmurs.

"To the couch to get sleep. Besides, you said you were exhaus—"

He yanks me back into bed and wraps his arm around my waist like I'm not going anywhere.

"Stay," he says, gravelly and soft.

I settle against him, breath leaving me in one long exhale as the sheets warm around us.

My heart does that stupid flutter thing again.

Yeah. I think I will.

19

I'm still warm from Langston's shower, skin loose and humming like I just did something reckless and got away with it. Steam clings to the mirrors, the bathroom smelling like eucalyptus and money, clean enough to make you forget your problems for a minute.

I step into the hall wrapped in a towel, combing my fingers through my damp hair, savoring the memory because I know this is the last pocket of peace before I put Alexia back on.

Another preview. Another night of pretending I've got this under control.

I look up and nearly jump out of my skin. Langston's in the middle of the hall, gym bag slung over his shoulder, eyes locked on me like he expected this.

He's back early. And I was definitely in there for over fifteen minutes.

"Hey," I say.

"Hi," he says.

And then my towel slips and tumbles to the floor, because of course it does. We both look down, then back up at each other. His mouth curves slow, dangerous.

"Get back in there."

I yelp and bolt for the bathroom, my laughter bouncing off the tile as he comes after me.

Several very distracting hours later, we're still laughing when Langston locks the door behind us, keys jingling as he pockets them. The sound barely finishes settling before the cameras explode.

"Alexia! Alexia!"

"Ms. Hyrd, over here!"

My stomach drops so fast my knees almost follow. I freeze and look at Langston, who looks just as caught off guard as he takes in the swarm rushing the stoop.

"Alexia, is it true you're carrying Julian Frazier's child?"

"What do you have to say about the escort rumors?"

Escort?

Langston reacts on instinct, arm firm around my waist, body shifting to block the flashes as he lifts a hand. That's when a familiar voice slices clean through the noise.

"Yana?"

I look up. Adrien stands on his stoop, blinking like he's trying to make sense of a picture that suddenly doesn't match the frame. His brow furrows. Recognition flickers. My heart sinks hard enough to hurt.

If this goes sideways, everything does. The role. The show. Julian. Langston. Me.

Langston slips off his jacket and tucks it over my head, pulling me close. "We've gotta go."

I duck as we move, flashes chasing us all the way to the car, my pulse loud enough to drown out the shouting. He doesn't look away from the paparazzi swarming the curb as we pull off.

"This wasn't a coincidence," he says, voice tight and clipped. "Somebody tipped them off."

The rest of the ride passes in silence, both of us wound tight, lungs working as the city blurs past.

What's going on? Why have they all turned on her? On me?

The theater answers that question. Protesters crowd the

sidewalk, signs bobbing, voices sharp with anger. Police tape flaps uselessly in the breeze. Langston stares out the window like he just swallowed something he can't get down.

Our phones buzz at the same time. Kai.

Company, please use stage door C. Do NOT talk to press.

We pull around, but it doesn't matter. The crowd surges the moment we step out. Security strains to hold the line. Someone throws a shoe. It misses, thank God. Langston pulls his jacket back over my head and hustles us forward, shielding me as best he can.

But I still see the signs when they bob too close.

Fraud!

Liar!

Homewrecker!

They're yelling at Alexia, but my face is the one taking the hit.

"That interview was a joke!"

"I used to be your biggest fan! I hate you now!"

They hate me.

My lungs lose their rhythm, breath skidding too fast as dread creeps up my spine.

"Don't panic," says Langston, arm tightening around me. "Just keep moving. It's gonna be alright."

I nod, praying he's not wrong.

———

INSIDE, REHEARSAL CARRIES ON LIKE NOTHING HAPPENED, because stopping would mean admitting something's off. Julian doesn't say a word, and neither does Langston, but the room doesn't need them to. The whispers fill the space anyway, soft and constant, like static humming just under the music.

Gracie's eyes stay on me, her stare clean and merciless, stripping me down to whatever version of the story she's decided I am. Noah keeps trying to catch my gaze, something unfinished hovering between us, heavy enough to feel even when I look away. Silence presses from one side, judgment from the other, and the space starts to feel too tight, too loud, too close.

By lunch, I can't bring myself to leave the dressing room. I scroll, which is a mistake I already know better than to make. They tear the interview apart. Say my tears looked fake. Say Langston deserves better. Say Julian and I deserve each other.

This is my fault. I should've prepared more. Kept my focus. Sold it harder.

If Alexia ever comes back, she's gonna kill me. If Marisol doesn't beat her to it.

"Alexia... Alexia?"

I blink. Kai stands in the doorway, fingers tight around the clipboard, knuckles pale.

"You okay?"

Oddly enough, I almost forgot who I'm supposed to be.

"Been better," I say, forcing a small grin. "What's up?"

"Production's moving forward," she says quickly. "More security. Tighter press rules." She nods as she says it. Once. Then again. Like she's trying to convince herself.

Sure. Build the walls high enough, and maybe the story won't slip through the cracks.

Kai hesitates, then steps closer. "They forget fast," she murmurs. "But I don't. I've watched you build this from the ground up." Her arms wrap around me, squeezing like she's steadying herself more than me. "You always land on your feet."

I let her hold me. I even lean into it a little, because it feels good having somebody this sure. Somebody who doesn't blink when the headlines turn ugly. Only problem is, she's not wrong about the landing. I do land on my feet. I just don't always know whose they are lately.

Before I can respond, she's gone, clipboard pressed tight to her chest like it's the only thing holding her together.

The show still needs me.

I smooth my hair, square my shoulders, and stand. I need a

snack, and the bag with my protein bars is still in the rehearsal room from warmups. I'm just stepping inside to grab it when I hear the piano.

Noah sits at the bench, pressing the same low, aching note over and over, letting it hang there unresolved. He stops when he sees me.

I can't do this right now.

"Sorry," I say, soft, grabbing my bag and turning. But he's already got his arms wrapped around me before I can step away.

"It's gonna be alright," he whispers. "I'm here for you. Whatever you need."

My eyes drift shut for half a second, like my body's answering on its own. Kai implied the same. Guess it helps to hear it more than I realized. But I've gotta get off this merry-go-round before I make myself sick.

"Noah." I pull back gently, putting space between us. "You're really sweet. I appreciate you. But this. Us. It's gotta end. Right now."

He blinks like he didn't hear me correctly, then shakes his head slow and disbelieving.

"You don't mean that."

"I do," I say, keeping my voice even. "I'm sorry."

"No. No!" He steps back, hands clenching near his temples like he's trying to hold something in.

My breath catches for a beat as the memory of his grip locked around my wrist hits fast and unwelcome.

Alright, girl. Stay calm. Stay smart.

"You're just nervous," he mutters, voice thick. "The media's dragging you. That's all this is. This'll pass, and then we can get back to normal and we—"

I move before he can finish, careful now, reaching for his shoulder instead of his arm.

"Noah." I meet his eyes and don't look away.

If I can't fix everything, I can at least fix this.

I won't do to Langston what Alexia did.

Noah just stares at me, breathing hard, like he's seeing me clearly for the first time. He shoves past me toward the hall, momentum unchecked until Langston fills the doorway and stops him cold.

For a breath they're chest to chest, neither of them moving. Langston doesn't flinch, just holds the frame like it belongs to him, gaze level and patient in a way that makes Noah the one who has to blink first.

Noah mutters something under his breath and pushes past, shoulder brushing shoulder on the way out. Langston doesn't turn to watch him go. The door swings shut behind him as he steps inside.

"How long have you been there?" I ask, the adrenaline still buzzing in my veins.

"Long enough," he says. His eyes move over my face, slow and searching.

"I didn't plan that," I say quickly. "I just... it needed to be done."

"I know." He shifts his weight, sliding his hands in his pockets.

"He didn't take it well," I say.

"No. He wouldn't," he says, softly. "You alright?"

The question feels different this time. And I hate that he's the one asking it.

Because technically, I should be checking on him, apologizing for the mess. I should be explaining why I let that linger, why I didn't shut it down sooner. Even if I walked into a fire already burning. Even if Alexia lit the match. He's the one who's had to stand in the fallout.

"I'm fine," I say, softener now.

He studies my face for a second longer than necessary, like he's deciding whether to push or let me keep my pride. Everything's still unraveling. My heart's still racing.

He extends a hand anyway. "Let's go get some lunch."

LANGSTON TAKES ME TO LUNCH LIKE A MAN WHO KNOWS exactly what kind of morning I've had. The place is tucked off a side street, all white tablecloths and hushed confidence, no cameras popping or voices raised. Just soft restaurant clatter and the low murmur of people important enough not to be impressed. He says it's a favorite for high-profile types.

I'll take it.

My stomach's still doing that tight, nervous thing, but I could eat. Lately, I'm surviving on crumbs of calm wherever I can find them.

His hand settles at the small of my back like it never left as we're led to our table.

"Hey. Hey! Langston. Alexia!"

We stop in unison. The man waving us over is unmistakable. Italian. Open collared dress shirt. Thinning dark hair pulled back into a long ponytail.

Elliott Moretti.

World-renowned film casting director. The best in the business.

My pulse spikes. *Of all people.*

Panic flickers across Langston's face for half a second before he schools it. He knows who this is too. We share a glance, and then I do what actors do best. Smile.

"Elliott Moretti," Langston says, ensuring I keep up.

"So good to see you," I add, slipping seamlessly into Alexia.

And that's when I see him, sitting across from Elliott. Same smooth dark chocolate skin. Same baby face. Same high cheekbones that used to make me forgive things I shouldn't have.

Bryant.

My mouth stays open a beat too long. He stares right back at me, blinking like he's walked into the wrong universe.

Convincing strangers who've only seen you on TV is one thing. Fooling a man who's seen you naked is another.

"Bryant," Elliott says, completely oblivious, "have you met Alexia Hyrd? Everyone's talking about her right now."

For better or worse.

Bryant doesn't look away from me. "As a matter of fact," he says slowly, "I have."

He stands and presses a kiss to the back of my hand, eyes locked on mine.

"It's good to see you again... Alexia."

Langston's likely already done the math.

"Bryant," he says, his grip tightening at my back. "It's been too long."

The two exchange a rigid nod.

"Please," Elliott says, already waving us in. "Sit. We haven't even ordered drinks yet."

I look at Langston, silently screaming. He nods once. So we sit.

Bryant slides in beside Elliott, still staring, while I try to keep my eyes anywhere but him, hands clenched beneath the table as Elliott launches into praise for our show.

"*Rave* reviews," says Elliott. "You keep this up, Langston, and I see a Tony in your future."

Langston ducks his head, bashful. "We'll see."

Under different circumstances, I'd tease him for that, eat it up. But with my ex sitting across from me looking like he swallowed bleach, I'm running out of options.

So I kick Bryant under the table.

He startles, knocking his knee into the booth. I smile sweetly.

"You know," I say, turning to Langston, "I think I'll hit the restroom before we eat."

Langston studies me for a beat, then nods and lets me out. I try to telepathically signal Bryant to follow, but judging by his furrowed brow, he's not picking up what I'm putting down.

I pull up our last message thread as I walk.

Go to hell was the last thing I said.

Yeah. That tracks.

I text him to meet me near the bathroom. My phone buzzes the second I hit send.

You alright?

Not Bryant. Langston.

I'd be better if you weren't sitting across from my ex right now I type back.

But the screen goes blank. No response.

I pace near the restrooms, nerves screaming.

What the hell am I gonna do?

Thankfully, before long Bryant appears, collar undone, eyes darting once down the hall before locking onto me.

"Yana," he says under his breath. "You wanna tell me what the hell is going on?"

"I know this looks bad," I blurt. I don't have time for finesse.

"Yeah," he says, giving me a scan from my razor-sharp bob to my stiletto boots. "Really bad."

"But you gotta believe me. I wouldn't be doing this if they didn't need my help."

"They?" His hands slide in his pockets.

"Langston. Julian. The whole cast."

He studies my face. "Where's Alexia?"

"I honestly don't know."

His mouth flattens into a thin line, skepticism written plain across his face. He's never been quick to take my side, especially if it meant getting his hands dirty.

"Bryant, please," I say, clasping my hands together. "Don't blow my cover. If you do, everyone loses their job. Including me." I hate that I'm asking him for anything, but I don't have another move.

He's got the nerve to hesitate. Suddenly, ethical as ever. *Damn him.*

Bryant rubs the back of his neck like *he's* the one who's got something to lose here and not me.

At my wit's end, I point a finger in his face.

"You owe me." For the promises he never kept. And for breaking my heart. Especially knowing how much coming out here meant to me.

His shoulders square, then slump, like he's bracing for a decision he doesn't wanna make.

"This is a terrible idea," he says. "A really, really terrible idea."

He glances toward the booth, then back at me.

"But if Langston Washington and Julian Frazier are in on it, I hope they know what they're doing."

Langston and Elliott are clinking glasses when I slide back into the booth, Bryant close behind. Under the table Langston's hand settles on my knee, gives one firm squeeze like he's steadying both of us, and I force my body to follow his lead.

Thirty minutes. Tops. I can survive that.

"Lex," Langston says smoothly, "Elliott was just telling me about his latest film project."

I glance at Bryant, who's stone-faced as he reaches for his water. But Elliott is none the wiser.

"Really?" I ask, feigning interest.

"You're gonna love it," Elliott says. "Mood lighting. Lengthy gazes. Soft jazz club solos."

I chuckle like Alexia. "Sounds like a dream."

"It will be," he says. "And I want you to star."

I freeze. "Me?"

"Who else?" He gestures at my face. "That look. Those pipes. People will line up around the block."

My heart leaps. Then crashes. 'Cause I ain't that girl. And with the exception of Elliott, everyone at this table knows it.

"He's right, Lex," Langston says, slipping his arm around my shoulders like it's the most natural thing in the world. "Sounds like the part was written for you."

I look at him, and he gives me a heart-stopping grin before pressing a light kiss to my lips. Bryant chokes on his water.

Langston's looser than usual. Less director, more man. Like he's got nothing to prove. Or maybe everything.

I can't tell if he's just putting on an act for Bryant or if he truly believes in me. He holds my gaze steady. Like he's already decided something and isn't in a hurry to explain it.

And right now, that's enough.

I nod at Elliott, voice even. "Have your people call my people."

20

I sit in the mezzanine the next afternoon, legs tucked beneath me, phone glowing too bright against the dim theater. I tell myself I'm just checking the show's Instagram, killing time. That's a lie. The comments are coming in too fast to read, so I scroll and scroll, watching the pile build like it's got a heartbeat.

She's acting so weird.

When did Alexia get this obnoxious?

Was she always like this?

I miss the old Lex.

My stomach tightens. A week ago they loved me, and that's the part that burns going down. How easily it flips. How quickly people turn once they decide you've disappointed them, like grace was never part of the deal. I've worked too hard and given up too much for strangers to talk about me like I'm... expendable.

Then I see it.

That's not Alexia.

My heart stutters. I tap the comment immediately, pulse roaring in my ears. The profile loads slow, dragging it out like it knows I'm scared of what I'll find. And when it finally opens, it's nothing. A sock account. One post. No followers. No picture.

I go back, fingers shaking, trying to find the comment again, but it's gone, buried under new ones stacking too fast for me to keep up.

My phone buzzes again. And again.

"Uh-oh."

I jump so hard I nearly drop it.

Stella plops into the seat beside me, peering over her sunglasses like she owns the mezzanine and the air in it. "I know a panic scroll when I see one."

I lock my phone and exhale. "Show page."

She hums, satisfied. "Let me guess. You've discovered the joy of public opinion."

I unlock the screen again and show her the evidence. "Have you seen some of this stuff? I mean, just disrespectful. I don't know how Alexia did it."

Stella barely reacts. She leans back, crosses her legs. "Honestly, honey? That shit should be part of the job description. In this business, for every die-hard fan, you've got three people who want you dead."

I swallow and tuck my phone away, recalling how I nearly got taken out by a stage light last week, the way my whole body still remembers that sharp metal crack. But the crew triple-checked every rig after that. Security's tighter now. Cameras everywhere. Still... metal falls fast.

And I thought I had it bad before.

"I'm glad we've got a few days off," I say. "I'm gonna need it."

It's Easter weekend, one more week of previews when we get back, then the show goes live. I just hope people still show up, that there'll be butts in seats to watch me carry this thing and not just curiosity.

"*Now* you're starting to sound like Lex," Stella says.

I glance at her because she's not wrong. Between the media, the temperamental fly systems, the so-called fans foaming outside the theater, yeah, I get it now. I get why Alexia might've wanted to disappear.

"And add to that the pressure Langston had her under every day?" Stella continues, rolling her wrist like she's flipping through memories. "I honestly was the least surprised when she didn't show up for rehearsal."

I still. "Pressure?"

She waves a hand like it's obvious. "Oh, yeah. 'Too sharp, Lex,'" she says, dropping her voice into a manly baritone. "'No. That's flat. Again.' The way they'd scream at each other behind closed doors. You could hear it up the hall."

The words press heavy against my lungs. I've seen that side of him—the fixation, the control. The way he locks onto a detail and won't let it go, like it's not art unless it hurts a little. It's not far-fetched at all.

"Did you know," I ask slowly, "about Julian?"

Stella snorts. "Honey. Julian. Noah. Filipe too."

I nearly choke. "Filipe? The director?"

She shrugs like she's discussing the weather. "No shame. Lex was a free bird. But Langston?" Her mouth tightens. "He never learned the difference between love and passion."

My mind flicks to that yellow bird in his apartment, quiet and contained, caged in pretty light like it was supposed to feel romantic instead of wrong.

Fish are meant to swim. Birds are meant to fly.

But Langston would never hurt anyone. Would he?

"There was a huge blowup," Stella goes on. "Last day we saw her. That little tiff you witnessed between him and Julian the other day? Nothing compared to this."

My spine straightens. "What happened?"

Stella glances at the rows behind us like she's checking for eavesdroppers. "We're doing a key run-through," she says, voice low. "Twenty-four hours before previews. She's center stage, belting like always, and her voice just... gives."

My jaw falls open.

"Not a crack," Stella says. "A *full* collapse. Vocal folds. The whole thing."

I clap a hand over my mouth.

I think about the octave I've been chasing every night, the

way Alexia sits higher than my comfort zone, how I have to place it just right or feel that burn bloom behind my sternum, the tears that creep up my throat when I'm supposed to sound fearless while half the internet wants me gone. But it's never been that bad.

"Langston stops the band," says Stella. "Julian's panicking. The room goes dead quiet."

"What did she do?" I ask, though my throat's already tightening around the answer.

"She ran," Stella says. "Locked herself in her dressing room. Both of 'em in there for a *long* time. When she didn't show the next day, honey, I knew it was over."

I stare out at the empty theater, lights low, seats waiting.

Langston never told me any of this. As close as we've gotten, there's still so much he won't touch.

I've toyed with the idea that Alexia's disappearance could've been voluntary. But hearing this story, I realize it's a very strong possibility. What if she just... left?

"Don't get me wrong," Stella adds. "If the man were born a decade earlier, I'd give him a whirl. But charmer or not, he knows more than he's letting on."

I'm still sitting with that when Kai pops up beside us, bright and bubbly. "There you two are," she says, a little too loud. "Is this where all the cool people hang out?"

I manage a small laugh. Stella just blinks at her.

Kai's holding a small white card and a pen, already uncapped. "I'm collecting autographs," she says. "Figured you'd wanna sign before the party."

I frown. "There's another party?"

"Of course," Kai says, eyes flicking between us. "Julian's surprise party. Didn't you hear?"

Langston throws his head back like he's pleading with the ceiling for patience. "You know, I used to enjoy my days off," he says, voice tired and a little dramatic. "Maybe sketch a melody. Read a decent book. Why's it always got to be a *thing* with you?"

We're in my dressing room, preview minutes away, vanity lights humming warm and steady, turning everything gold. I tug my knit cap into place, smooth the straps of my overalls, adjust the small details that turn rags into intention. Modern-day Cinderella with a mic pack.

"You can do whatever you want," I say, giving myself one last look. "I'm going."

Langston's behind me, watching through the mirror like he's trying to read the thought right off my face. His jaw flexes once. "You really think I'm letting you strut around the city after dark like some random nobody?"

I meet his eyes in the reflection. "You're not *letting* me do anything. I'm a grown-ass woman, and if I wanna go to a party after dark, that's my business."

"I mean, I respect that," he says, flustered. "It's just—"
Silence drops between us, heavy.

I keep getting ready anyway because I refuse to fold. I don't even know why I wasn't invited. I just know I'm done swallowing disrespect and calling it part of the gig, not like this. Whatever power comes with this face, I'm done pretending it isn't mine.

But Langston pouts like a whole child. Nothing like the orders-barking monster Stella described just hours ago. And I know he ain't about to start thinking he can control me.

"I'll make you dinner," he says, face softening into something almost ridiculous. "Maybe even rub your feet?"

He pauses when I don't react, shoulders slumping a little.

"Let's just stay in," he adds, quieter now. "Please?"

It's too cute. Annoyingly cute. The kinda cute that almost makes you forget you're guarded and mad.

Almost.

I slip the rag into my pocket and head for the door, then stop and press a kiss to his cheek.

"You can come along or not."

———

OF COURSE HE COMES.

The lounge hits me the second we step inside, that charged nightlife energy that makes you stand a little taller without realizing why. Low lighting. Velvet booths. String lights overhead. Soft enough to feel romantic, bright enough to remind you you're being watched. Music thumps through the floor, bass steady in my ribs, and everyone's dressed like it's a fun night out, just elevated. Clean lines, shiny fabrics, designer perfume, and money in the air. A surprise party for a famous theater director, and it looks the part.

Langston stays close as we move through the crowd, his hand finding its resident spot at the small of my back. Protective, possessive, maybe both.

He leans in, top button of his black dress shirt undone because I told him to—and I'm still shocked he listened.

"Second we yell surprise," he murmurs, "I'm out."

I almost smile. Ever since he nearly took off the director's head for sleeping with Alexia, both Langston and Julian have been all business. Cordial in rehearsals. Quiet in meetings. But the friendship they used to wear so easily feels cracked now. And I hate that Alexia's ghost keeps showing up between them like a third body in every room.

Speaking of unwanted company...

Gracie.

She's at the bar, taking her two millionth selfie, and when she clocks me in the background, she doesn't bother hiding it. As usual, she turns, lips pursed, squinting like she's been waiting to catch me breathing wrong.

Even wearing Alexia's face, she still looks at me the way she always has, like I was born by mistake.

From what Kai told me, Gracie threw this whole thing together.

Which explains a lot.

I make a beeline for her. Langston hurries to keep up, hand firm at my back, like he's steering me without wanting it noticed.

Gracie's dressed to the nines in a sleek gunmetal dress, confident and bold. It clings without begging—alley cat bite with highbrow polish. Regan's attached to her hip as usual. Noah's with them too, and the second he and Langston clock each other, the air tightens, an icy glare passing between them like a blade.

Alexia didn't leave baggage. She left an unclaimed terminal.

"Oh my God, Lex!" Kai materializes at my side, fingers latching around my forearm before I can move. "You look unreal. I mean, *unreal*. Like always!"

"Yes!" Regan adds, eyes dragging over the black silk hugging my hips. "Lex, that dress is *everything*."

I give her the signature Alexia grin. "Thank you!"

Noah bobs his head, looking me over like he's trying to decide how mad he's allowed to be, but he says nothing.

It's still awkward between us, even after I tried to let him down easy. But I don't have time to care. Besides, I'm sure Alexia put him through worse.

Kai's gaze trails down the length of my dress like she's cataloging fabric, cut, skin. "I wish I could rock a dress like that." She tugs her oversized cardigan higher on her freckled shoulders. "You still drink green smoothies every morning, yeah?"

This is not the conversation I'm having.

I wave to the bartender and order a couple shots for me and Langston. He hangs back, hands in his pockets, scanning the room like he'd rather be getting a root canal. The man loosens up just fine between the sheets. Anywhere else? It's gonna take alcohol. Maybe then we can have some fun.

But first.

I turn to Gracie, who's nursing her drink and pretending she can't see me. "Heard my invite got lost in the mail."

Langston reaches for my hand, a quiet warning, but I gently tug free. Regan and Kai glance between us like they're watching tennis.

Cool as a cucumber, Gracie lets her gaze drift over the crowd instead of meeting mine. "Figured you wouldn't need one," she says lightly. "As close as you and Julian are."

Regan's mouth drops open. She turns to Kai like, *Did she really just say that*, while Noah lifts his drink and swallows whatever opinion he's got.

Langston cuts Gracie a look sharp enough to draw blood, then schools his face as the bartender slides our shots across on a napkin.

I pass one to Langston. We clink, and I tip mine back, the liquid flaring hot.

Kai's eyes glint. "Tequila?"

I shrug. "Why not?"

Despite Langston's glare, I wave for another. I'm gonna need it tonight.

Gracie tilts her head, voice light, almost curious. "Didn't you say you were laying off after that drunken rant you posted last fall?"

The bartender sets down two more shots. Conversation nearby thins, attention sliding our way.

My smile holds even as my stomach tightens.

"I mean, sure. Everything in moderation. You know?"

I offer another shot to Langston, but he turns it down. Guess I'll take his too. I raise the third, but Langston takes it from me before it reaches my lips.

"Yes," he says, low and pointed. "Moderation. Let's practice that, hmm?"

I glower as he sets it aside. Then his arm slips around my shoulders, pulling me in. I hate how much it soothes me.

Gracie watches the PDA, eyes narrowing just a hair.

"Y'all are so sweet," says Kai. "I've always been Team Langston."

I hold Kai's gaze just long enough for her to take a small step back. I'm in over my head as it is. The last thing I need is her, in all her loveliness, spotlighting Alexia's love triangles, trapezoids, or whatever the hell else.

"You know what," she says, too bright. "I'm gonna go make sure we have enough candles for the cake."

Gracie's still studying us as Kai disappears into the crowd.

"It's so brave of you to address the rumors about you and Julian head on."

For half a second, I can't tell if that's support or shade. I choose not to care.

"I didn't want it to spiral," I say, shoulders loosening a notch.

Gracie sighs and looks to Noah and Regan. "I could never. I hate putting my business in the street."

"Yeah." I nod. "Sometimes silence protects everyone."

Gracie smirks slow. "You used to say staying quiet was worse than being disliked."

Regan chokes back a chuckle. Even Noah winces. Heat climbs up my neck.

This bitch...

I'm about to put Gracie in her place when Kai rushes back over, breathless and giddy.

"He's coming! He's coming! Everybody duck!"

The music dips but doesn't die, laughter rippling as people crouch and giggle like it's cute.

"This is so obnoxious," Langston says, loud as hell.

Someone shushes him. I'd laugh if I wasn't already irritated.

He leans close, voice softer now. "You alright?"

"I will be," I mutter.

Julian walks in and the room erupts. *"Surprise!"*

He's thrilled, grinning wide, cheeks flushed. His wife's at his side, gorgeous and polished, looking like she belongs at a fancy fundraiser. Sleek dress. Perfect hair. Bright smile for the crowd.

They kiss, and everyone claps.

Gracie looks at me and mockingly pouts. "Stay strong," she whispers.

I picture punching her in the face so vividly my hand twitches.

Langston's grip tightens like he clocked it too.

Julian starts a speech, hands waving, voice loud and warm, a charisma that fills space whether you want it to or not.

"I just gotta say," he tells the room, "this cast is everything. You all carry this show on your backs and make it look easy."

People cheer. Glasses clink. Somebody whistles.

"And Alexia," he says, turning to me, "regardless of what anyone says, thank you. For coming back. For showing up. For reminding us what this show is supposed to be."

A swell moves through the room like everyone's been holding their breath for it. I smile because that's what's expected, because that's what Alexia does. But something's shifted, subtle, like the floor moved and nobody warned me.

Somebody clears their throat. Silent glances are exchanged.

Standing between the man praising me and the man holding me, I can't tell where I end and Alexia begins.

"Yeah," Gracie shouts, "she's always been *so* principled."

Groans and chuckles ripple through the room. A few people laugh too loud. A few don't laugh at all.

Since Julian said the name, Langston hasn't looked my way once, his silence doing more than any glare could.

Julian smirks like he's on a celebrity roast and can't afford to look bothered. His wife, on the other hand, freezes, the color draining from her face. Because even though Julian had no clue Alexia was seeing Langston when they hooked up, it doesn't change the fact that he was married.

Langston says nothing.

That's when I know I've had it.

I mingle. Wish Julian a happy birthday. Have the most awkward, cordial exchange of my life with his wife, and share an intentional glance with Stella.

Then Gracie heads to the bathroom.

I follow.

The bathroom is brighter and colder, tile and mirrors and that sharp clean smell of soap covering perfume and liquor. I'm waiting by the sink, arms crossed, when the toilet flushes and Gracie steps out of the stall.

She scoffs, gives me a once-over, then walks to the sink like she owns the place.

Why is she acting like this? Doesn't she know Alexia could ruin her with one phone call? Or does she simply not care?

I keep my voice calm, bold like Alexia's. "I'm gonna say this and I'm only gonna say this once. You knock it off with your snooty little comments or you're gonna regret it."

Gracie watches me in the mirror as she washes her hands.

"*Snooty?*" She huffs a laugh. "Alexia would never say that."

My mask slips for half a second, just long enough for my pulse to spike.

Gracie rips paper towel from the dispenser, dries her hands slowly, then steps into my space, close enough that I catch her perfume, expensive and biting.

"You really think I don't know who you are," she murmurs, "Yana?"

My heart drops so hard I swear my stomach shifts.

She chuckles like she's enjoying a private joke. "That's some kind of poker face," she says. "The poor posture? That ridiculous cackle?"

She tosses the paper towel over my shoulder into the trash without looking.

"I clocked your pathetic imitation on opening night, sweetheart."

My ears ring. My heart pounds so loud it feels like it's bouncing off the tile.

I straighten my spine, steady my voice. "Why haven't you snitched?"

Gracie lifts a shoulder and checks her makeup in the mirror. "Tried," she says. "Went straight to Julian, not realizing he was in on it."

She tosses me a glare in the mirror, hard and bitter.

"But he doesn't play fair. Had me sign an airtight NDA. Keep my mouth shut or I'm replaced before curtain."

My pulse won't slow. Every sound feels too loud. Every second too long.

She knows. And the only reason this hasn't blown up yet has nothing to do with mercy.

Gracie scowls at my reflection. "I've been watching you tank the show ever since."

"Please." I scoff, more confidently than I feel. "You've seen the reviews. Those people love me."

Gracie turns, amused. "They love who you're supposed to be."

I don't speak. I don't breathe. She holds my gaze like she's daring me to blink first.

"No," I say, softer but firm. "I went viral for singing like me. Being me."

"Under Alexia Hyrd's name?" Gracie lets out a little laugh. "You must not have read the comments."

My stomach twists.

"I'm not worried though," she adds, fixing her hair one last time. "Alexia thought she'd be around forever too. And, well. We see how that went."

Her smirk slides into place.

What does she mean? Does she know what happened to Alexia?

Did she have something to do with it?

Gracie walks to the door, stops when she grips the handle. "Keep your head up," she says with a glance. "Never know when a stage light might fall."

Then she's gone.

And I'm left alone, staring at my own reflection like I don't recognize my face anymore.

Laughter spills over me as I step back into the lounge, loud and careless and completely undeserved.

"Lex!"

Kai's voice slices through everything.

She's suddenly in front of me, hands fluttering, energy dialed up to eleven. "Can you believe tonight? I mean, the press, the buzz, the way Julian teared up. He's right, you know. The show would be nothing without you."

I blink at her, trying to reassemble my pulse.

Her eyes scan my face like she's scanning for cracks. "You okay?" she asks. Then gasps. "Is it Gracie? I swear, I don't know what is up with her tonight. Probably jealous. I mean, when she stepped in while you were gone, it couldn't have been more of a nightmare..."

Her voice keeps going, words piling on top of each other.

I barely hear them.

All I can see is Gracie's smirk in the mirror.

You really think I don't know who you are... Yana?

Kai's still talking.

"I mean, it's not my fault craft services doesn't carry sugar-free balsamic vinaigrette," she continues. "I'm an SM, not her PA. I mean, maybe for *you* I'd make an exception, but—"

I step back just enough to breathe.

"Kai?" I don't raise my voice. I don't need to. "It's enough."

She freezes, mouth open.

"Oh. Yeah. Of course."

Her eyes linger on my face a beat before she finally steps aside.

I've gotta talk to Langston.

But he's in a giant circle beside Julian like nothing in the world could be wrong. Most of the cast is here. Gracie too, back in place like she never left.

Langston's bobbing his head, mildly amused, while Julian tells a story, gesturing loose, already a little too drunk.

"Y'all don't understand," Julian says, laughing. "We were trying to build this thing from scratch. And Langston was *such* a control freak, he kept changing song lyrics every two days. I must've revised the first act twelve times!"

People laugh. Langston gives the smallest grin like he's trying not to.

When I step beside him, his arm slides back around me automatically. Then he does a double take. He feels it, the tension in my shoulders, the way my body's too stiff.

I need to tell him. I need to tell him right now. That she knows. She's known for a while. And I could be in more danger than we thought.

Gracie watches me with taunting eyes.

"And when *that one* entered the scene," Julian says, lifting his glass toward me, "we knew we *really* had something."

Langston goes rigid as Julian's gaze lingers on me a beat too long.

Goodness. As drunk as Julian is, he might slip up and spill the beans before Gracie ever gets the chance.

I give Julian a warm grin anyway, quick and polished. Awkward glances bounce around the circle.

Julian's wife nudges him hard enough to mean *stop*, and he shrugs.

"Just saying," he tells her.

The silence that follows is thick and clumsy like no one's quite sure whose move is next.

No one, except Gracie.

"Yes," she says, taking a slow sip of her drink. "She's so talented. You must share what you do behind closed doors, Alexia."

A few laughs pop up, then more. Once it starts, the rest follow, relieved to have instructions.

I used to beat them to it. Laugh first. Say something sharper.

Turn it into a joke before it turned into me. But Alexia doesn't do that. She can't.

Gracie doesn't need to smile. She's already got the room.

Langston's still frozen beside me, shoulders set, mouth tight. I wanna tell him, right now, wanna lean in and whisper, *She knows. At any moment, everything could fall apart.*

But Gracie's watching, waiting for me to slip, to overcorrect, to remind everyone I'm playing a role I don't get to fumble.

And the worst part isn't her. It's him. The way I know if I say the wrong thing, if I flinch, if I even crack a little, Langston will feel it. He'll know I let it get messy. That this is all my fault.

So I don't move. I don't explain or apologize.

Smile easy. Shoulders loose.

Stay Alexia.

But Langston's voice cuts clean through the noise.

"If we wanted sideline commentary, we would've asked someone who mattered."

Hands fly over mouths. A hush ripples out. I'm trying not to laugh myself.

Langston holds Gracie's gaze across the circle until she returns her attention to her drink, cheeks flushed.

I look at Langston, words clogging my throat, just as Julian forces a laugh.

"Hey, hey. Langston. It's all in fun."

"Yeah," Langston says, refusing to take his eyes off Gracie, "and at whose expense?"

Gracie lifts her drink like she's done with the conversation, pivots, and lets the crowd absorb her.

But Julian's less amused.

"Langston, chill."

"Chill?" He finally looks at Julian. "You're in no position to lecture anyone on restraint."

A few uneasy laughs mix with gasps around the circle. "Damn," someone breathes.

"Hey!" Julian's face shifts, uncharacteristically angry. "If you've got a problem, your stiff ass can get the fuck out!"

The bass keeps thumping low, but every voice drops out. Even the bartender pauses mid-pour.

Langston blinks at Julian, something ticking behind his eyes. His jaw locks, fists curling slow at his sides like he's measuring distance.

I've seen that look before, the one that comes right before he stops caring about consequences. For one sickening beat, I recall how easily his hand closed around Julian's collar the other day, the quiet certainty in his voice when he told Julian exactly where he planned to shove his head. Like it wasn't a threat, just logistics.

Everyone feels it, the shift, the danger.

And suddenly this isn't about jokes or drinks or Gracie anymore. It's about whether Langston's about to make good on the man he warned us he could be.

But then Langston turns and leaves without a word.

Even drunk, Julian tosses me an apologetic look like he knows he went too far but doesn't know how to fix it.

I hesitate, aware of every pair of eyes clocking my reaction.

I go after Langston anyway.

Outside, the air burns cold, streetlights flaring against the sidewalk. Langston's stomping like he's trying to outrun his own anger.

I think about what he just did, how he stuck up for me, how he was willing to look like an idiot in front of everybody. For me.

It's sweet. It's real. Deep down, I know it. If no one else respects me, Langston does.

I jog to catch up with him and wrap myself around his arm. He slows, tension melting from his shoulders like he can't hold it up anymore.

"I'm sorry," he says, shaking his head. "I know you wanted to have a good time. Sometimes he just makes me so—"

"*Shhh,*" I whisper.

I slide my hand down, find his, lace our fingers. Warm. Steady.

"This," I tell him quietly, "is all I need tonight."

21

"Hold up. Hold up!"

I pull the slice from my teeth, the cheese stretching out in a glossy, dramatic ribbon before it finally snaps.

The pizzeria's loud in that classic New York way, all clatter and chatter and a bell over the door that never gets a break. The air smells like browned crust and garlic and oregano and something fried that's got no business smelling this good at midnight.

Langston blinks at me like I'm eight years old and unsupervised. Then he raises his slice, takes a bite, and stretches his string of cheese twice as long.

"Oh-ho!" I laugh, pointing my slice at him. "You've had that one in your back pocket, I see!"

"I'm a man of many talents." His mouth twitches. Barely. Like a crack in marble.

I'll take it.

Since we didn't stay at the party long enough to eat, we decided to grab a couple slices on the way home. With no previews for the weekend, Langston's willing to let it slide, which means I'm taking full advantage and demolishing every greasy slice this paper plate can hold.

The city feels different tonight. Softer. More like we're settling in before the house goes dark, and less like we're sprinting toward an opening-night cliff. Considering he just nearly pulverized his best friend for the second time this month, I'm glad I could convince Langston to go anywhere else at all.

"Certainly didn't see that one coming," I say around a chew, "especially after you asked the cashier for a fork and knife."

Langston looks back at the kid behind the counter like he's personally offended by his youth. "They really should carry them. This is the city, and germs are everywhere."

He's wiping his fingers between bites with flimsy napkins like they're surgical towels. He's gone through at least six already. But he's eating with his hands. Growth.

"Let me guess. No Friday pizza nights with the fam?"

He shakes his head once, like he's describing the weather, not his childhood. "My parents were the type to spend their Friday nights out rubbing elbows with the right people. My brother and I usually spent the evening with a nanny. Balanced dinner at six. In bed by eight."

I give him my most tender look of pity. "That's... devastating."

"Only had it a couple times at Juilliard. Few more with Lex."

The way he says her name still does something strange to the air, like it gets colder for half a second. He plops the slice back on his plate and snatches another napkin, frowning at the grease as he wipes it off his fingers like it betrayed him.

And all I can think about is what Stella told me. The screaming. The way the walls carried it. The idea of Langston's voice raised at Lex the way it was raised at Gracie tonight. I swallow a bite that suddenly tastes less fun.

"Surprised you let her choose the menu."

He holds the silence, then scoffs it away. "Lex wasn't really the type to ask permission. It was one of our strongest areas of contention."

Hmmph. I suppose that tracks. The man's not exactly built for spontaneity.

"So there were *multiple* areas of contention?" I lean in a little, playing with it, smiling like it's just curiosity and not the way my stomach's been knotting for days. "Think you'll ever tell me what that final argument was about?"

He lifts the slice back to his mouth and glares at it like it insulted his bloodline. "I think... you should stop digging."

The words fall soft. The meaning hits bone. That wasn't a request.

I'll let it go. For now. Because after tonight, I know exactly what it feels like to sit on information that could blow everything apart. To weigh the damage before you open your mouth. To decide whether the truth is survivable.

Gracie's face flashes in my mind. That smile. That warning. One wrong move and this whole thing goes down.

The show. The deal. Me.

And beneath that, something older cinches in my chest. A reflex I didn't choose. The reflex you pick up young when being honest threatens your safety, not because you were wrong, but because you were vulnerable. When silence felt safer than being seen, abandoned, disposable.

Some truths don't ruin you because they're ugly. They ruin you for what it costs to say them out loud.

So instead, I take another bite and swallow it down.

———

Outside, the night's got teeth. Streetlights spaced too far apart, shadows collecting where they shouldn't. Wind sneaks under our coats and camps out, cold and annoying. The city's loud in the distance, but this block feels off. Too quiet.

Langston keeps hold of my hand like letting go ain't an option. Then he stops short and I almost walk into him, our fingers locking tighter like something just clicked.

He glances around, swallowing hard. "It's getting dark. Maybe we should call the car around to pick us up."

I tug him forward, rolling my eyes like I'm not secretly

clocking the dark corners too. "We'll be fine, scaredy cat. Besides, we both could stand to blow off some steam."

We turn the corner, the noise thinning behind us, and I try to settle back into the night. Into us. Langston makes a low sound in the back of his throat.

"Does seem like it's working," he says. Then quieter, almost to himself, "Was kind of starting to miss you."

I slow and look at him. "Miss me?"

He nods, eyes forward. "I mean, I know being *her* is part of the deal, but... tonight you were even less *you* than usual."

The thought goes down wrong, almost medicinal. I swallow it anyway, like a pill I don't wanna taste, blow it off with a shrug and a breathy laugh. "That Gracie just... grates on my nerves sometimes."

He hums like he agrees. Doesn't push.

But the truth taps at the back of my skull, because he's right. I haven't felt like myself lately. Not fully. And that scares me more than Gracie ever could.

Langston shakes his head, mouth tense as his grip firms around my hand. "She was out of line," he says. "Completely. I don't care what she thought you—or Alexia—did."

The space behind my ribs narrows. I don't fill him in. Can't.

"She doesn't get to talk to you like that," he continues. "Nobody does. Doesn't matter who you are."

He says it simply, like it's always been true. The relief is quiet but it's there, that rare feeling of being seen without being examined, of being given grace without having to ask.

Grateful, I hook my arm through his and press in close. Tilt my head, all sweetness and suggestion.

"So..." I flutter my lashes, trying to coax him back into the light. "How should we spend the rest of our first night off? Wrapped up in a blanket in front of the TV? Or in the bed wrapped up in sheets?"

He meets my gaze with a dark smile, full, ravenous, the sort that makes my pulse thrum. I laugh into the night air, breath puffing white.

Then a shape peels away from the shadows. Hoodie low. Face half-gone. Steel glints in his hand.

My breath hiccups. My feet root. Langston freezes beside me so fast it's like somebody unplugged him.

The man points the blade at Langston, then me, his hand trembling with the kinda desperation that burns through reason.

I know that look, the edge of it, the point where dignity no longer matters. Considering what I almost did to Gracie for a sandwich, I've gotta wonder how much worse it gets when hunger's got a weapon.

"Give me all your money!"

Oh God. Oh God. I don't even have cash!

My mind tries to sprint in every direction at once. My pulse thunders in my ears. My fingers go numb.

Langston blinks at the man but doesn't move or speak.

The mugger shifts his grip on the knife, rolling his shoulders like this is already taking longer than he planned. "You deaf or somethin'?"

And that's when he lunges. He yanks me into his chest. And suddenly the blade's against my neck, cold and real, pressed just enough to make the threat sink into my skin.

I was wrong before. This is it. This is how I die.

And my brain, because it's cruel, decides now is the time to wonder if they'll bury me as myself or Alexia. Will my parents even be notified?

The man's breath hits my ear, heavy and hungry, his grip tight across my collarbone, pinning me like I'm nothing.

"Wallet," he snaps at Langston. "Phone. Watch. Now!"

Langston still doesn't move. He's barely breathing, eyes locked on the blade like he can't compute.

"Come on... come on!" the man yells, voice cracking, the blade pressing harder.

My heart rate spikes so hard my vision blurs at the edges.

I can't wait for Langston to unfreeze. If I do, we might both die right here on this dark, stupid block with pizza grease still on our fingers.

I force myself to inhale, slow, like I'm surrendering. I let my shoulders soften, let my weight settle just enough to make him adjust his grip. Then I move.

Fast.

I stomp my heel down hard on his foot. He yelps, the blade wobbling for half a breath, pressure easing just enough. I throw my elbow back into his ribs, sharp and mean, then duck low and twist out of his arm on instinct. Hooking his wrist with both hands, I wrench it down and away from my throat, forcing the blade toward the ground.

He stumbles, off balance. That's all I need.

I drive my knee hard into his crotch, feel his body give with a grunt, then shove him with everything I've got.

He goes down groaning, the blade clattering away like it's embarrassed for him. For a second, he tries to scramble, but he's winded and twisted up, one arm curled tight to his middle.

I don't wait for round two.

I grab Langston's hand so hard it almost hurts. "Let's get out of here!"

My lungs burn as we run. My boots slap the pavement. The night air slices cold into my throat.

Langston breathes ragged, finally moving like he's alive.

I don't look back. Just keep pulling him forward. 'Cause if I stop now, I might collapse right in the street.

LANGSTON PRESSES THE WASHCLOTH TO MY NECK, RIGHT where the blade kissed skin, his touch soft and deliberate like he's afraid the wrong pressure might send me spiraling.

The bathroom smells like soap and eucalyptus, steam still

floating from the shower he rushed me into. The scent hits and lingers, curls low in my chest. It's wrong in my nose.

Too close to the calm I had while showering alone before everything cracked open.

Too close to the moment he pulled me back inside, hands sure, mouth hot against my ear. My back pressed against the cool tile while water traced every line of us. The way the world narrowed to skin and breath and the quiet urgency in his touch. The way he made me feel safe. Before the world decided to punish us for it.

My heart's finally slowing, but my body hasn't caught up. Everything still feels buzzy. Overexposed.

"I'll give your makeup girl a call in the morning," he says quietly. "She'll show you how to cover this properly while it heals."

I'm on the bathroom counter, bare feet swinging just above the tile, staring at the ceiling like it might have answers. My voice comes out rough. "At least it wasn't my face. This is prime real estate."

A soft sound leaves him, not quite a laugh, more like air through his nose.

"And what beautiful real estate it is."

That makes me look at him. I mean sure, he implied I had a radiant smile, and my eyes were "striking." But he hasn't spoken to me with that kind of certainty since the first night I slept on his couch. Back when he sat across from me quietly sipping tea, so sure I'd land on my feet.

And look at me now.

He doesn't soften it with humor or take it back. He studies my face like he means it, like he's seeing me, not the role or the risk wrapped around my name.

He turns to the sink, rinses the cloth, and presses the warmth to my neck again, careful and steady.

You'd never guess he was petrified ten minutes ago. On the

street, he looked frozen solid. Here, he's all control again. It makes my chest ache in a way I don't fully understand.

"Where'd you learn to defend yourself like that?" he asks.

"A self-defense class," I say. "In high school."

When I finally went back.

His brow creases just slightly. "Were the streets of Detroit that bad?"

"Chicago," I correct.

He stills completely, the washcloth lowering an inch. His eyes lift to my face, searching, recalibrating, Detroit peeling away. He doesn't ask, just looks at me, waiting for the part of the story that doesn't match the map he's been carrying.

I really don't wanna go there. That version of me feels far away and way too close all at once. But I can't expect him to open doors he's locked tight if I won't crack one of my own. I sigh and roll my eyes, buying myself a second.

"I lived on the streets for a bit. When I was younger." I keep my tone light, but my fingers curl against the counter. "I was sixteen. Young and dumb. Met an older guy online... Jarel."

I whisper his name, because it burns my throat to say it. Langston leans in close, like he's willing to hold it for me.

"He made me feel special. Like I mattered." I swallow. "I was in love. Or at least what passes for it at that age."

I don't say how I skipped school or how I lied to my parents, just the shape of it.

"He needed money. Said it was temporary. Said we should run away and start a life together. I believed him." I let out a breath that feels older than it should. "We stopped at a train station in Chicago. It was late, and he told me to rest. But when I woke up... he was gone. So was my phone. My parents' money. Everything."

For a second, I'm back on cold concrete, knees pulled tight to my chest. The stink of piss and old grease, my stomach clawing at itself so hard it feels like it might fold inward. Men pacing too close. Addicts arguing with nobody. Fear louder than common sense. The constant math of *Where can I sit? Who can I trust? How fast do I need to run?*

I force myself back the way my therapist taught me.

In through the nose. Slow. Count to four. Hold.

Out through the mouth, longer than the inhale. Again.

Tile under my feet. Solid counter beneath my palms. Warm light overhead. Langston right in front of me, alive and breathing and real.

I'm not there anymore. I'm here. *Safe.*

My chest settles. My hands unclench. The memory loosens its grip just enough for words to form.

"I spent a week out there before I finally called my daddy. Only number I had memorized." I take another breath. "After that... I asked him to sign me up for lessons. I never wanted to feel that helpless again."

Langston doesn't say anything right away. His jaw flexes once, like he's filing the information somewhere careful. He keeps the cloth in his hand, thumb still, eyes steady on me. After a moment, he lets out a quiet, almost disbelieving chuckle.

"Why didn't you use those skills when Julian had you abducted?"

"I tried but..." I lift a shoulder. "Didn't see 'em coming."

That earns another small breath of amusement, but it doesn't linger. Something's still sitting heavy behind his eyes.

If I don't say it now, I never will.

"Seems like you been carrying something too."

He gives nothing at first. Just a long breath pulled through his nose, held, then released. Finally, he sets the cloth aside.

"I used to avoid parties," he says. "Still do. My brother didn't."

He's talking about his brother. He *never* talks about his brother.

I let the silence do its thing.

"Everyone loved him," he continues, studying his hands.

"Levi walked into a room, and it bent toward him. Teachers. Investors. Girls... My parents."

A pause. Smaller now.

"I learned early how to stay out of the way."

That's when it hits me. Not the accolades or the confidence everyone sees now, but what it must've been like before that. Growing up in the shadow of someone who never had to fight for the spotlight. I wouldn't have guessed it, not from him. And suddenly, it's not just his story anymore.

"Everything came easy to him," Langston says softly. "He wore his success like armor. Jewelry. Confidence. Attention. Full ride to USC."

I nod slowly, because I know that armor all too well. I've lived my entire life just outside it. Watching other people be understood, guarded, picked, while I learned how to try harder, how to wait my turn.

For the first time, I don't just hear what he's saying. I know exactly where he's been.

"He visited me once, at Juilliard. Begged me to come out. I refused." His gaze drifts to the sink, somewhere distant in time. "They said someone pulled a gun on him. Took his watch... He didn't walk away."

My hand flies to my mouth. It's no wonder he froze.

I hop off the counter and wrap my arms around him before he can brace for it. He locks up for half a second, then exhales into me, shoulders finally dropping. I kiss his cheek, then the other.

"Langston," I whisper. "I am so, so sorry."

"No, I should be," he says quietly. "I should've been there for you. I should've been there for him. I should've been there for —" His voice cracks as he presses his face into the crook of my neck.

His breath stutters once, then again, the sorta sound you don't make unless something inside finally gives way.

I hold him while it happens. Don't rush him or fill the space. Just stay.

Eventually, he pulls back enough to breathe, eyes red, jaw tight, like he's embarrassed by the evidence of it. Like grief is something he should've learned to manage better by now. I don't comment on Alexia. I don't have to. The shape of her is all over this moment anyway, in the pauses, in the words he can't say.

"Guess this is what happens when you actually say things out loud," I murmur, trying for light but not flippant. "Cathartic. Mildly horrifying. Ten outta ten, would recommend."

He huffs despite himself. Doesn't smile, but it's close.

"Maybe we should do this more often," I add. "Might keep us from strangling coworkers."

He looks at me then, serious, searching.

But a part of me isn't joking. I think we both learned how to survive by staying quiet. Just in different ways.

Now the truth presses hard against my ribs. This thing with Gracie, the ticking clock. The way holding it is already starting to feel heavier than whatever happens if I let it go.

What good is protecting the peace if it's already cracking?

I draw a breath. Open my mouth.

"How would you feel," he says, "about coming with me to L.A.?"

22

Walking through the airport with Langston feels surreal. People keep looking at me, double takes, whispered names, phones lifting too slow to be subtle. I try to play it cool, but my chest keeps buzzing with the novelty of it all.

This is what Alexia's life looks like. Priority lanes. First-class tickets. Strangers smiling at you like you've blessed them simply for existing.

A girl about my age jogs up beside us, breathless. "Oh my gosh. Hi. I'm so sorry, but can we take a picture?"

I give her a practiced smile. "Of course."

She snaps it, squints at her screen, then frowns. "Ugh. It's a little blurry. Can we do another?"

I nod, already shifting back into place.

But Langston waves a hand and gently pulls me away.

"We've got a flight to catch. Have a good one!"

I glance back at the fan, appalled, as he ushers me toward our gate. "Langston, that was rude!"

"She'll be fine," he says. "One blurry photo is more than enough for clout."

We're supposed to be on a weekend getaway, but he's frowning at his phone, scrolling through our flight information like it's a lifeline.

"And *you* need to learn it's okay to say no."

"You kidding me? You see all these fans?" I gesture at all the folks pointing and whispering, pretending not to stare. "I haven't had this many people interested in my whereabouts in my entire life."

"It wears off fast." He pulls me into line as they call first class. "Also, have we forgotten that someone just tried to kill you last week?"

"But let's be real. What are the chances danger booked first class?"

Langston rolls his eyes, typing something into his phone. "Let's just agree to no outlandish stunts this weekend, hmm? This is your chance to take a breather. Not get your star on the Walk of Fame."

I grin wide and hug his arm, soaking in the moment whether he's ready or not. "But we *can* agree that I'll have that star one day, right?"

His glare melts, softening into something quiet and warm. He presses a kiss to my forehead. "Without a doubt."

———

First class is obscene. Wide leather seats. Endless legroom. Soft lighting that makes everything feel expensive and unreal.

I laugh too loud as I drop into my seat, stretching like I just hit the lottery for breathing.

Langston's voice is a harsh whisper as he pulls me back. "Would you calm down... *Lex?*"

Right. My bad.

I settle into the window seat, releasing a happy sigh as the cushion molds around me.

"So what's on the itinerary, *babe?*" I say it the way Alexia would. "Hit a couple nightclubs? Link with some of your old Hollywood pals?"

"None of that," he says, adjusting the air overhead. "I've got to get home and look over the score before our final week of rehearsals. We'll be back by Sunday."

"But I want you to take me dancing," I say, adding a small pout for effect. "I packed the perfect dress and everything!"

"*Shhh*." He peers at the passengers around us. "I'm sorry to hear that, but maybe next time."

A promise that costs him nothing.

I focus on what's sure to be an incredible hotel suite instead. "Room service?"

He shifts in his seat, holding my gaze. "We're... staying at my parents'."

I pull back so hard the seatbelt tugs. "Langston, what the hell?"

"I just figured it would be a good weekend for you to see where I come from," he says, scratching his arm like he can erase the sentence. "And with everything that's been going on, it wouldn't hurt for us to get away for a bit."

"You didn't think to tell me I was walking into your *parents'* house?" My voice drops, sharp and contained. "You couldn't have mentioned that *before* I packed my lacy red G-string?"

His mouth drops open as he glances around. "The lacy red?"

I nod, and he pouts hard.

"Listen," he says, trying to recalibrate. "My mom called twice, insisting I fly in for the holiday. I originally wasn't going to come, but... I didn't feel like having that argument from New York."

A hot, sick drop settles in my gut.

"And here I was, thinking this was a real date." I glance out at the tarmac, at the little workers moving like ants under the wing, suddenly aware I have nothing. No classy outfit. No mental prep. No rehearsed introduction.

While it's sweet that he wants to introduce me to his parents, I ain't exactly the kinda girl you bring home to Mama.

"I should've told you sooner," he admits. "I just didn't want you to back out."

I look at him. Is he really that desperate to share what we have with his family?

"But also..." He reaches for my hand, warm and steady. "I kind of wanted you all to myself for the weekend."

I should stand my ground. He doesn't deserve my smile.

But his mouth hovers close, close enough that I feel the choice in it. I give in, letting his lips find mine in a soft kiss.

And for just a little while, I choose to let it go.

———

BY THE TIME THE CAR CURVES UP THE LONG, WINDING DRIVE, I've talked myself down from a full spiral.

The house comes into view slowly, like it's showing off. Tall. Wide. Stone and glass and money stacked on top of more money. Gates glide open without a sound. Hedges clipped so precisely they don't look real.

I smooth my palms over my travel sweats as we climb the front steps and immediately regret it. If only I could've gone to a hotel. Showered. Changed. Thrown on something dramatic. But here I am, smelling like airplane air and stress, trying to convince myself that my smile can do the heavy lifting.

I glance at Langston, waiting for the moment he squeezes my hand and murmurs something reassuring like, *They're going to love you.*

Instead, he shoves his hands in his pockets and stares down at the marble-paved porch like it's his therapist.

I study his profile as we wait in silence, the tight line of his jaw. If I didn't know any better, I'd think he was nervous too.

Before I can ask, the massive front doors swing open.

And there she is.

Cree Washington in the flesh, long jet-black hair cascading over her shoulders, cocoa-brown skin glowing under the porch lights like she's been professionally lit her entire life.

Which, to be fair, she has.

I've seen her movies. I've cried over her romcoms. But up close, it hits different.

Standing beside her is Spencer Washington. Taller than I expected, dignified, silver threading his beard. He's traded the baseball cap I've seen in interviews for a blazer and glasses, looking more professor than powerhouse director.

I paste on my best smile.

Langston steps forward first, kissing each of their cheeks. Then he gestures toward me.

"Mom, Dad... Alexia Hyrd."

My stomach drops straight through the floor.

Alexia?

I barely manage to keep my face from betraying me before Cree pulls me into the warmest hug imaginable. She smells like literal roses. Fresh, expensive roses. The kind you don't buy at the grocery store.

"Thrilled to finally have you," she says warmly. "I figured you'd be a string bean based on those magazine shoots, but you're filling out nicely."

She shoots Langston a playful look.

"Anything you want to share with us, dear?"

For half a second, panic flashes through me. *Does she think I'm pregnant?*

Langston gives his mother a dry nod. "Not particularly."

Something icy flickers in Cree's eyes before her smile snaps right back in place.

But I'm still stuck on the introductions.

Alexia?

Spencer pulls me into a hug of his own, squeezes my shoulders like he's assessing furniture. "She *is* a little thicker than expected, huh?"

Cree chuckles.

"That's enough," says Langston, the same way he does when the orchestra's goofing off. His hand closes around mine and firmly tugs me away.

I've never been self-conscious about my body. Not really. But standing here under their collective gaze, I suddenly feel inspected.

Langston's grip tightens, strong and protective. But honestly, it's too late.

He already tossed me in the ring.

———

We're ushered into a sitting room that looks like it belongs in a museum, neutral tones, sculptural furniture no one actually sits on, everything perfectly placed.

Cree gestures toward a curved sofa. "Please, make yourselves comfortable."

I perch on the edge of the sofa, knees together, posture locked. I get the distinct sense that if I lean back too hard, an alarm might go off.

Across from us, Spencer sinks into an armchair like it's molded to him, legs crossed, one hand draped over the armrest.

A server materializes at his shoulder with a tray of crystal glasses and begins pouring before anyone speaks. A ribbon of pale gold catches the light, like even the pour has been choreographed.

I don't remember ordering anything. I don't remember being offered a choice.

"Travel okay?" Cree asks, swirling her drink. "The flight in can be exhausting."

"It was fine," I say. "Quiet, actually."

Langston nods once. "Smooth."

That's it. Just the word, dropped neatly into the space between us.

Cree smiles, satisfied. "Good."

The server disappears. The silence lingers, deliberate now. Like the pause before the first question in an interview.

Langston lifts his glass and studies it, turning it slightly as if checking for imperfections. Meanwhile, Cree studies me over the rim of her flute, expression pleasant but alert, like she's clocking details for later.

"So," she says lightly, "the rumors."

There it is.

Spencer exhales, almost amused. "Julian has always been… indulgent."

I glance at Langston. A small invitation.

Step in. Say something.

He doesn't move. His eyes stay fixed on the glass in his hand, his face carefully blank.

Something tightens under my sternum. Not fear. Not exactly. More like muscle memory.

I've done this before, the apology tour, interviews where the questions are dressed up as curiosity but hit like judgment. Thanks to Alexia—and Marisol, for that matter—I know how to keep my voice steady, my face open, my answers clean.

What I hadn't planned on was going it alone. Defending myself—and Alexia—without Langston stepping in. Or at least standing beside me.

I rack through my catalog of Alexia PR-approved responses. "I think people like to tell stories when they're bored."

Cree hums, thoughtful. "Funny how those stories always follow you."

Oh, hell naw.

I literally bite my tongue to keep from cussing. Langston's lips press into a thin line.

"So you're telling us," Spencer continues, voice calm and annoyingly reasonable, "that there was nothing inappropriate?"

"I'm telling you people see what they want to see," I say, meeting his gaze and holding it.

To my relief, Spencer nods, almost as if he's taking my side. "Fame *can* complicate things."

"It can," I agree.

Cree smiles, not warmly, more like she appreciates the effort. "And yet," she says, "perception is everything."

The questions keep coming after that, polite and precise. What was said? What wasn't? Who initiated what? Each one wrapped in civility, sharp underneath.

Marisol's script scrolls through my head like cue cards.

Smile. Deflect. Never confirm. Never deny.

I fold my hands neatly in my lap and give them the version that's been rehearsed.

"Julian and I work closely," I say evenly. "We've spent long hours building something intense together. That doesn't make it an affair. It makes it theater." I add, softer, because silence is its own weapon in rooms like this. "There's a difference."

Langston's knee bounces once. Stops. His thumb drags slow along the rim of his glass like he's holding himself in place. He doesn't interrupt. Doesn't correct me. But when Cree presses again, his jaw flexes, subtle and tight, like he's swallowing something jagged.

I can't tell if he's giving me room to handle it or simply spacing out.

I answer the rest smooth, weeks of practice sliding into place. Public-facing, Alexia in control. It's only been like five minutes, but my palms are damp and my shoulders ache from holding myself together.

Langston says nothing.

Finally, Cree sets her flute aside, the sound small but decisive.

"Well," she says, glancing at Langston, "your brother's in his room. I'm sure you didn't come all this way not to see him."

Brother?

I look at Langston, confused.

I thought his brother was...

Langston stands without a word. No explanation. Just gestures for me to follow.

THE HALLWAY FEELS COLDER. QUIETER. LIKE SOUND DOESN'T belong here. Langston walks ahead of me, without looking back, not reaching for my hand.

"Okay. I get it. They're... a lot," I say. "But did you really have to introduce me as Alexia? I'm sure they would've come around to my personality eventually... Langston? Langston?"

He keeps walking.

Guess no talking's allowed on this leg of the tour.

I try not to read into it. Try not to let the silence bloom into something bigger than it is. But it's hard not to when we were just kissing on a plane, when he told me just a few hours ago that he didn't wanna lose me.

I thought we were past this part. Past the shutting down, past the little retreat when things get real.

But maybe "past" isn't a place you arrive. Maybe it's a door you keep having to choose, over and over. And right now, he's choosing a different one.

The walls are lined with framed photos. A boy with Langston's eyes. Same posture. Same devastating smile. The resemblance is unmistakable, even before I understand why I'm noticing it.

Inside the room, there's trophies. Programs. Awards. Photos frozen mid-performance, mid-laughter, mid-life. Moments people preserve when they're certain there will be more just like 'em.

Levi sits by a massive window, sunlight pooling around his wheelchair.

His body is there. Perfectly intact... but he ain't moving.

Langston steps forward and places a hand on his shoulder, his gaze fixed on the view outside as if they're sharing something unspoken. Something familiar.

Silence settles over the room. Thick. Expectant.

I wait. For an introduction. For context. For anything that tells me how I'm supposed to exist in this moment.

Nothing comes.

Clearing my throat, I step forward, forcing brightness into my voice. "Looks like someone needs a lesson in manners and hospitality." I extend my hand. "Nice to meet you. I'm Alexia."

For a second, I convince myself he just hasn't noticed me yet.

But Levi doesn't move or even blink. Just stares out the window, unbothered by my presence, unmoved by the outstretched hand between us.

My smile falters, and I look to Langston.

"He can't," he says quietly. "He had a bad brain injury. After the mugging. He's been like this ever since."

My hand flies to my mouth.

———

DINNER IS HELD IN A DINING ROOM SO GRAND IT FEELS staged.

A table long enough to seat a small orchestra stretches beneath a chandelier heavy with crystal. Place settings line the table in careful symmetry.

Three forks. Two knives. A spoon I don't recognize.

Servers line the walls, hands clasped behind their backs, appearing only when something needs refilling, or when they sense a pause that needs filling.

Which happens often.

I keep thinking about the empty space at the table, the one Levi should occupy. No wheelchair or acknowledgement. It's like he only exists upstairs, conveniently out of sight.

Langston doesn't look at anyone. Not even me.

Is this what he couldn't tell me? Is this what he brought me here to see?

The first course arrives, something delicate and expensive that smells incredible. My stomach growls loud enough that I'm positive at least one server hears it. But I sit straighter than I ever have in my life. I chew slowly. Graceful.

Alexia eats like this all the time. Alexia doesn't inhale food like it might disappear.

But after witnessing this whole family situation, I know Langston could use a lifeline right now. And I—*Yana*—need to be it.

Cree lifts her wineglass, watching Langston over the rim. "You look tired," she says.

Langston's jaw hardens. "I'm fine."

Spencer hums. "You always say that."

I glance between them, my fork hovering. The air is polite but sharp, like smiles that could bite if they wanted to.

"So, Alexia," Cree says softly, "how are you getting along with the cast and crew? The ones you haven't slept with, I mean."

Langston drops his fork. "*Mom—*"

Cree raises a hand without looking at him. "Broadway does have a reputation. I imagine it's... less controlled compared to film, don't you think?"

Langston stares at his plate, obedient, mouth shut.

You know, I used to look up to homegirl. That was five seconds ago.

"It's intense," I say, choosing to keep it classy. "But everyone's chasing the same opening night."

"My colleagues tell me those openings are no joke," Spencer says.

"Langston should know," adds Cree. "Perception is fragile. One night can change how a story is told forever."

It's like I've wandered on another stage. New cast. Different script.

Langston's fork scrapes against his plate.

"True," says Spencer, cutting into his food with precise, practiced movements. "That's the one people remember."

"Our Levi never understood that." Cree shakes her head, almost fondly. "But isn't that what big brothers are for?"

I feel it now, the subtle shift, like the room just tilted enough to throw us off balance.

This ain't about Alexia at all.

Cree dabs her lips with a napkin. "Levi was always the spontaneous one," she says. "His brother was supposed to be the careful one."

"And yet," Spencer adds quietly.

Langston pushes his chair back a fraction, then stops himself, and something cold slides down my spine.

It's almost like they planned this.

I set my fork down. Appetite gone.

"So," I say, my voice steady despite my pulse, "you're saying Langston should've stopped him?"

Both of his parents look at me like I've spoken out of turn.

Cree tilts her head. "We're saying brothers look out for each other."

Langston finally looks up, eyes dark. "That night wasn't my fault." The words sound practiced, but uncertain, like he's repeating something he was never allowed to believe.

"No one said it was," Spencer replies, lifting his glass.

But the silence that follows says otherwise. It stretches, deliberate and loaded. His parents sit back, composed and blameless, like they didn't just light the fuse and step away.

Someone needs to call this what it is, and it won't be them.

"Excuse me," I say, impatience edging into my voice, "Levi was a grown-ass man. What happened to him was tragic, but blaming Langston doesn't change that."

The room stills.

And I realize too late that I've stepped out of character.

In a panic, I look to Langston, but he doesn't look back. Doesn't defend himself. Doesn't even react.

Just great. I've taken the bait. Just like with Gracie. Just like with everyone else.

Cree takes a slow sip of her wine, never breaking eye contact with me. "You're very passionate," she says. "That's... admirable."

Spencer nods. "Youth tends to be."

They're not listening. They never were.

Langston stares at his plate, smaller somehow than when we sat down, like he learned long ago that speaking only makes it worse.

And suddenly I understand. These aren't grieving parents looking for peace. They're parents who decided a long time ago who was golden. And who wasn't.

———

LANGSTON'S BARELY SAID TWO WORDS SINCE DINNER, WHICH honestly doesn't seem out of the ordinary around here. This house runs on silence. On restraint. On conversations that never quite rise above a murmur. No slammed doors or raised voices bleeding through drywall. Just hallways that swallow sound whole. It feels less like a home and more like a landmark preserved for visitors. Sturdy. Polished. Presented.

The shower alone is bigger than any walk-in closet I've ever owned.

When I step out of the bathroom, steam trailing behind me, Langston's on the bed. He's propped against the pillows in a gray T-shirt and sweats, staring at a framed photo in his hands.

The room doesn't look like a boy ever slept here. No crooked trophies. No half-peeled band posters. No evidence of adolescence tucked into corners. Just dark wood furniture, a low leather bench at the foot of the mattress, a bookshelf arranged by height and color. Even the bedding is crisp and neutral, hotel-perfect. As if he was born with a five-year plan and no permission to cry.

The overhead lights are off. Just the bedside lamp casting a low amber glow. It hits the glass of the frame and throws a faint reflection across his face.

I pad over in borrowed cotton shorts and one of his old rehearsal tees, my natural curls finally free.

"What's that?" I ask, settling beside him.

He tilts the frame.

Two teenage boys. Same eyes. Same devastating grin. Backstage somewhere, velvet curtain pooling behind them. Levi in costume, stage makeup still bold under bright lights, arm slung over Langston's shoulder. Langston holding a trumpet over his head like he's just won something.

"My senior year," Langston says. "Spring musical."

I rest my chin lightly on his shoulder.

"Levi was the lead," he continues. "I was first chair."

There's a softness in his voice I don't hear often. Not pride. Not exactly. Something gentler. A memory he doesn't perform for anyone.

"Brilliant actor. Could dance circles around me. People couldn't get enough of his voice." A faint smile ghosts across his mouth. "All of us were certain he'd end up on the big screen, if not a recording studio first."

His thumb traces the edge of the frame.

"You make plans," he says quietly. "You think you know where you're headed. Then life edits the script."

I feel that.

It's not like this is where I expected to land. Answering to a name that isn't mine. Playing a role so convincingly I forget who's supposed to be standing here.

The image shifts in my mind. The wheelchair. The window. The way Levi didn't blink when I introduced myself. Didn't move. Didn't look.

Earlier, wandering the halls because the silence felt too heavy to sit inside, I'd paused outside his room. The door cracked just enough.

A nurse stood at his side, speaking softly as she lifted a spoon. Waiting. Then tipping it gently past lips that didn't open on their own. No applause or spotlight. Just patience.

I stepped back before I was noticed, something settling low and heavy beneath my ribs.

Upstairs, he exists.

Downstairs, there's an empty chair.

Langston sets the photo carefully on the nightstand. The mattress dips as he leans forward, elbows on his knees.

"I know you were blindsided," he says. "And I'm sorry."

I let the words sit. They soothe and sting at the same time.

"When my mom called," he continues, eyes fixed on the blanket, "she said, 'Bring Alexia.' Wanted to finally meet her."

He rubs his hands together slowly.

"I had every intention of correcting her when we arrived." His voice doesn't break. It just thins. "But when the door opened, I panicked."

The moment flashes through me. The quick hugs. The assessing smiles. The choreography of it all.

"And with everything that's happened, I didn't want to explain. I didn't want to justify. I didn't want to give them one more thing to... to dissect. Not tonight."

I think about the dining room.

The way his mother raised her hand, and he stopped mid-sentence without even realizing it. The way they agreed brothers look out for each other and meant something else entirely.

Langston leans back, staring at the ceiling.

"I didn't mean to put you in that position," he says. "I know you handled it. I just... I should've handled it too."

I nod, because I saw what they do to him. And I know what it feels like to choose silence just to survive the room.

Across from us, I can see my reflection in the dresser mirror. My curls fall damp against my neck, soft and unguarded. No razor-sharp bob. No flat-ironed polish.

There's a particular ache in wanting to speak and not being able to. In knowing exactly what you should say and feeling your throat close anyway.

I slide closer and wrap my arms around his waist. For once he doesn't stiffen, just exhales into me. Presses a kiss to my hair.

The house hums faintly around us. Air shifting through vents. Pipes settling. A door closes somewhere down the hall.

"I'm sorry," he says again. Softer.

And I let that be enough.

———

SOMETIME IN THE MIDDLE OF THE NIGHT, I WAKE LIKE I never fully slept at all. My mind won't quiet. And the mattress beside me is cool.

For a second, I lie still, disoriented by the dark and the unfamiliar ceiling above me. The house feels different at night. Not just silent. Listening.

"Langston?" I whisper.

I push up on one elbow. The bedside lamp is off. The hallway beyond the cracked door is dim, only a faint wash of light stretching across the polished floor.

Guess he couldn't sleep either.

The exchange at dinner was heavy. Grief is heavier.

I slip out of bed and head for the hall, bare feet quiet against hardwood. The house feels more chill now. Less curated.

The hallway stretches long and still. Framed accolades glint faintly under recessed lighting. Gold plaques. Smiling faces frozen in premieres and opening nights.

Proof of impact. Proof of legacy.

In this house, everyone's stuck somewhere.

I move slowly, not sure whether I'm searching for him or just trying to outrun the weight pressing at my ribs.

His apology helped. It didn't close anything.

There are still pieces of this story he's holding like they'll cut me if I touch them.

Marisol didn't speak like a woman planning a funeral. She spoke like a woman buying time. And that could only mean one thing.

Alexia isn't gone.

Not the way they keep pretending she is.

I follow the faint spill of light toward the back of the house and ease through the doors onto the patio. The night air hits cool against my skin, enough to wake every nerve.

"Alexia, please."

I stop.

Langston stands near the edge of the lawn, phone pressed to his ear, shoulders tight, head bowed slightly like he's trying to fold himself smaller than he is.

"Just call me back," he says quietly. "I need to know you're okay."

I cross my arms as I listen, the night wind cutting straight through me.

"I don't even need you to come back," he continues, and his voice cracks just enough to hurt. "Just... say something."

I step back in the shadows without thinking, my heart pounding in my throat. I don't want him to see me like this. Don't want him to know I heard any of it.

And suddenly, the fog lifts in the worst possible way.

Whatever happened to Alexia, it wasn't Langston's choice.

And he never stopped hoping he got a say.

23

After a restless night and a brutally quiet breakfast with Langston's parents, we left early. That alone should've told me everything.

For the past two days, Langston hasn't been himself. He stalks through the house like a ghost, barely acknowledging me. Loose sheets of music everywhere. Coffee cups abandoned mid-drink. His phone's been buzzing nonstop with meetings, revisions, deadlines—despite the Easter holiday.

He hasn't touched me all weekend. Not even in sleep. He comes to bed long after I've drifted off and leaves before the sun's up. When I wake, the space beside me is cold, like I imagined him.

And every quiet moment lets the same thoughts in.

Maybe he wants Alexia back. Maybe I was just a substitute. Maybe I was never enough.

Final rehearsals only make it worse. I'm at the keyboard, fingers steady, breath deep as I sing "Shine Through the Dark" riding the octave just like Langston taught me. And for a second, I almost believe I can outwork the stress.

But Julian raises his hand.

"Langston?" he says. "I'm getting déjà vu. I think it's time to cut Alexia's octave."

My fingers stumble. *What?*

Langston looks up from the pit, as stunned as me. "You're joking, right?"

"I'm not," Julian says calmly. "I hear the strain. Another week of this and she won't have a voice by opening night."

Langston straightens. "You think you know better than me what she's capable of?"

Julian doesn't blink. "Actually, I do."

A few snickers ripple through the room. It's subtle, but I feel it. The weight of last week's party, the rumors, the unfinished tension. Everybody pretending they're focused on music when they're really focused on the mess.

"I could try again," I offer quickly, trying to steady the moment. "I'm just a little rusty."

"Kinda like her mattress springs," Gracie quips from downstage.

Groans ripple through the auditorium. A couple of uncomfortable laughs follow. My stomach twists as heat crawls up my neck.

"Gracie, knock it off," Julian snaps. Then to me, gentler. "Let's try that riff from your first preview."

"That's crossing the line, Julian!" Langston explodes. "And you know it."

My pulse kicks hard. He's wound too tight, tenser than he even was over the weekend, like something already broke and no one noticed.

"Then again," says Langston, voice dropping low, "I don't know why I'd expect any better from you."

He said it softer, but still loud enough for Julian to hear.

"Would you get over your ego for one damn second and listen to me?" Julian fires back. "The octave needs to be cut."

"The octave is crucial to the *entire* setup!" Langston shouts. "Or do you not understand anything about character arcs at all?"

"I understand who's in charge here," Julian says flatly. "And who's not."

Silence crashes down on the room. Nothing but the hum of

the lights overhead and the weight of everyone pretending not to look directly at either of them.

Langston flips a music stand so hard it slams against the floor, metal ringing through the auditorium. He storms out without looking back.

Shit.

Kai stumbles center stage, hands on her head, staring at Julian, willing him to rewind the last five minutes.

Exhausted, Julian waves a hand. "Let's take a fifteen."

Kai nods, scrambling to recover. "You heard him, guys. We're taking a fifteen."

The auditorium exhales all at once. Chairs scrape. Music stands clatter. People start talking too loudly, too quickly, like noise will cover the fact that everybody just watched the ship tilt.

I take off after Langston.

He's already halfway down the hall, shoulders hunched, steps sharp. I follow him into the composer's studio, the door swinging shut behind us with a dull thud. He grips the piano like it's the only thing keeping him upright, knuckles tight, jaw locked.

I step closer and rest a hand on his back.

"This entire show is about to tank," he says, voice rough. "And it's going to be all his fault."

I choose my next breath carefully. Every instinct tells me to soothe, not challenge, 'cause one wrong step could send him splintering. I'm not sure if I'm afraid of losing him or watching him break right in front of me.

"He just... doesn't see my vision," he says, eyes raw and unfocused. "Doesn't he understand the emotional drive of the first act?"

He's not talking about Julian. He's talking about value. About needing it to matter enough that someone, somewhere, finally claps.

I slide my arms around him from behind, pressing my cheek

between his shoulder blades, holding him the way I imagine no one did for years.

"Listen," I say softly. "The show will be great either way. Always has been. Even when I wasn't singing the octave."

He straightens, shakes his head, and pulls away.

"You just don't get it... You don't..."

I wait, giving him space to finish the thought, to explain what I'm missing, why he keeps acting like I'm standing on the outside of his world instead of right here with him.

But he doesn't look at me. Just turns and leaves the room.

The door closes behind him, and the silence feels personal.

I swallow hard.

I don't know what it would take for him to hear me.

I step back into the hall and nearly collide with Gracie, who's chatting with Kai near the door.

"I'm sure things would be going a lot more smoothly," Gracie mutters, just loud enough, "if *some* of us could operate with more self-control."

I keep walking.

"I can see it now," she says louder, "'*Promising Broadway musical goes up in smoke due to salacious rumors and slutty behavior.*'"

I stop, turn, step right into her space. Death threats or not, if she wants blood, she better draw first.

"You got something you wanna say, Gracie?"

She looks me up and down, bold as hell. "I've got plenty to say."

My hands curl into fists at my sides. For a split second, I don't care who sees or what happens after. I don't care if my face, my real name, and my Social Security number end up splashed across *Page Six*. I am one misplaced breath away from committing a felony.

Kai rushes between us, arms flailing. "Ladies, ladies! Separate corners, please. We don't need any more confrontations today."

Fine. I walk away.

But the second Kai disappears down the hall, I spin on my

heels. I'm done swallowing things, done being polite, done being treated like a damn joke.

I find Gracie in one of the prop storage rooms, hunched over, blowing her nose. Of course, Regan's at her side.

"Fifteen years of lessons," Gracie sobs. "*Ten* vocal training. Danced ballet, lyrical, *and* tap. And still... it wasn't enough. It wasn't..." She dissolves into her tissue.

I roll my eyes. Then back into the hall, just outside the door.

It's just another act. I stay anyway.

"She's ruining everything!" Gracie cries to Regan. "This whole thing just meant so much to me. It was a dream to finally get that moment in the spotlight... And then to have it all ripped away, simply because... *she* came along? It isn't fair."

She almost said my name. But she knows if she reveals the truth she'll be out of a job.

The thought pops up once again:

Did she plan or hire someone to get rid of Alexia? Did it backfire when I showed up instead?

"You're right," Regan says quietly. "That is messed up."

Wait. What?

"Things were better before she came back," Regan continues. "Now fans talk about her mess more than the show. It's like people are just showing up for the behind-the-scenes drama. The whole thing's turned into a circus."

"Yeah," Gracie snaps. "With a clown leading the show. And what will that do to our résumés?"

I expect it from Gracie. But I didn't expect it from Regan. Not from someone I thought was my friend.

Gracie breaks down again, full body this time. "My... my dad was diagnosed with prostate cancer a year ago."

Regan gasps.

"And the medical bills are just... *killing* my family," Gracie sobs. "That lead role was supposed to pay enough that I could help. But now?"

I step back from the doorway as Regan pulls her into a hug.

Gracie couldn't exactly pay someone to get rid of Alexia. Even with her veiled threats, I'm not sure she could orchestrate anything. Sabotage takes calculation. She looks like she's barely holding herself together.

I feel for her. And I hate that I do.

I turn and head back toward rehearsal, carrying more than I went in with.

REHEARSAL RESUMES, BUT I'M NOT IN IT. MY FINGERS HIT THE keys a beat late. I open on the wrong verse of the duet with Noah, muscle memory betraying me.

The orchestra stutters, then fizzles out completely, sound dying in uneven fragments.

Silence drops hard.

Langston's staring at me from the pit, lips pressed thin, eyes sharp enough to cut.

I laugh, small and reflexive, but he's even less amused than usual.

"Not everything is some big joke, Lex," he calls up. "Dozens of people's careers are on the line here."

Every head turns. To Langston. Then me. Heat blooms beneath my skin all at once.

A few people shift in their seats. Someone coughs.

Something hotter settles low and stubborn behind my ribs.

"Now," Langston continues, voice cool, "are you going to pull it together, or should we call in your understudy?"

My jaw locks.

Downstage, Gracie smirks at Regan like she just won a point she didn't even have to play for.

That was personal. And he knows it.

"I'll be fine," I say, forcing the words through my teeth. Then quieter, "If you could stop being an asshole for five minutes."

Noah snorts.

A few people laugh. The orchestra rustles, uncomfortable but entertained.

Langston stares me down from the pit, eyes dark, as I realize maybe I didn't mutter that as softly as I thought.

Julian rubs his face. "Hey, Langston? Are we gonna get through this rehearsal today?"

"Maybe we could," Langston says, eyes still locked on me, "if... *Alexia* would stop treating each scene like a damn SNL script."

A couple groans ripple through the cast. Someone lets out a nervous snort. People glance at one another, caught between amusement and the growing sense that they should probably not be enjoying the drama encore.

"Maybe Alexia's just killing time," I snap. "Wouldn't wanna get bored and go looking for another bed."

The gasp is immediate. Loud. Collective. Every single person is staring at me now.

Both of us know boredom wouldn't be the reason. But they don't. Langston's glare cuts deeper.

I hate that I went there. I hate that he *pushed* me there. But after everything, he still refuses to treat me like her.

I'm still just a stand-in. A substitute. A placeholder for the woman he actually wants.

Julian lifts a hand and presses his fingers to his eyes. "Let's take another five."

———

Moments later, Julian points between our chairs, the universal sign for *I don't care who started it, you're both grounded.*

"You've got two minutes to hash this out," he says. "We've got work to do."

The door shuts behind him with a soft but final click.

The office feels smaller immediately. Soundproofed. Too

quiet. The second hand on the clock ticks loud. Langston's jaw jumps with it.

He breaks first. "You wait until final week of rehearsals to screw this up?"

"Oh, please." I stand so fast the chair legs scrape against the floor. "With a little practice, I would've gotten it right. The only one screwing anything up is you!"

He scoffs, standing too, hands braced at his waist like he's holding himself back. "You've gotta be kidding me."

"Am I?" My voice echoes harder than I expect. "You're the one stomping around here like somebody stole your damn lollipop. You're blowing up at Julian, you're blowing up at me, you're blowing up at the *crew*. This is the same shit you did to her, isn't it?"

He stills, eyes flashing. "You don't get to talk about her."

"And how are you gonna stop me, Langston? Hmm?" I step closer, heart hammering. "Go ahead and try to shut me up!"

He takes a step back like I've swung at him, looks at me, shakes his head. "You're unbelievable. You know that?" His voice stays sharp, but his face doesn't. Not completely.

"I could say the same about you."

His gaze drops to the floor. For half a second, he looks small. Wounded. I think about his parents, the way they sliced him apart with smiles. How when all was said and done the only one he wanted to talk to didn't answer his call. And I hate that I'm adding to that pain.

But he can't keep bleeding on everyone else and calling it art.

"Listen," I say, forcing my voice steadier. "I know you're dealing with a lot. But everybody's got shit, okay? You're not the only one."

He rolls his eyes. Says nothing.

I point toward the door, toward the stage beyond it. "Out there? On that stage? Nobody sees me. Nobody!" My throat closes just enough to piss me off. "I'm just another understudy. In the end, all accolades go to Alexia Hyrd."

He scoffs. "This isn't about you, okay?"

"Oh, you've made that *abundantly* clear."

"You can't just do whatever you want, Lex!"

The name stings like a slap.

His face changes as soon as the word leaves his mouth. And we both know he's got no reason to call me that. Nobody else is around.

"My name," I say quietly, throat burning, "is Yana."

"My point is," he says with a swallow, "you need to take this more seriously. You want to get the show pushed back and miss the cutoff for the Tonys? Have everything go up in smoke?"

Sure. Final week. We're all hanging by a thread. But when was the last time he checked on me? It's like his feelings are all that matter.

"Or do you mean *your* precious Tony?"

He just stares at me, something dark simmering behind his eyes.

All he cares about is his own stupid ambitions. And maybe Alexia. But definitely not me.

For once, I don't wait for permission. I leave first.

24

From now on, I'm all business. If everyone thinks I'm a clown, fine. I'll show them just how much of a diva I can be.

I nail the first preview back, every beat, every breath. It's not flashy. It's clean. Controlled.

I don't joke backstage. I don't chat at intermission. I don't linger after curtain call. I take my flowers with a nod and head off to study my tapes, and by the time Langston gets home, I'm already asleep, curled on my side, makeup barely wiped away.

The next day, I arrive early. I already know my notes. I don't wait for Julian to say them. No octave, and that's fine.

I anticipate changes before he opens his mouth. Adjust before anyone asks. I hit my marks with near-military precision. I stop asking if something works. I stop asking if I'm okay.

I am excellent.

As I watch more of her clips, I finally start to get it, feel myself slipping into her skin. Alexia's posture. Alexia's stillness. The way she takes up space without apologizing for it.

Lunch rolls around, and nobody follows me.

Usually someone does. Regan with a joke. Stella with a side-eye and a snack. Kai with a full recap of what just happened and three theories about why. Today, the room rearranges itself instead. People pivot. Water bottles disappear faster. Conversations dip half a notch when I pass.

Nothing dramatic. No confrontation. Just space. Me in the center of it.

Fine.

By the time we're reviewing blocking for the finale, my patience is thin.

Julian's stuck on Noah. Again. We've gone over this section a hundred times. The final cross, the timing of his turn, the way he's supposed to catch my eye before the downbeat, and still—

"Noah," Julian says, rubbing his temples. "You're late on the pivot. You're stepping into her light."

"I'm not late," Noah insists. "I'm just adjusting for her pace."

"My pace is fine," I snap, before Julian can answer.

Langston doesn't look at me. He's down in the pit, hunched over the score, scribbling, muttering. Locked in like the rest of us disappeared. I may as well not exist.

Julian sighs. "One more time from the pickup."

Noah runs it. Misses it. Again.

"What if," I say, planting my hands on my hips, "instead of crossing downstage, he holds for half a beat and lets the moment breathe?"

Julian looks up, considering, as Charlotte—my stepmother—chimes in from the wing.

"That would throw off the symmetry," she says. "The audience needs consistency."

"I wasn't asking you," I say, eyes still on Julian.

A ripple moves through the cast with scoffs and groans.

"Looks like the queen is back," Regan mutters downstage.

"Yeah," Charlotte adds. "She should try out for *Frozen.*"

I turn straight to her. "What's that supposed to mean?"

Before she can open her big, dumb mouth again, Julian claps his hands, loud.

"Okay. We're done. Take a fifteen."

"You heard him, guys," Kai echoes. "Fifteen."

I step offstage, heat buzzing under my skin.

———

LATER, I SIT ALONE IN THE MEZZANINE, PHONE GLOWING, scrolling through comments I promised myself I wouldn't read. My thumb hovers, itching to clap back, to remind everyone exactly who the hell I am.

That's when Stella sits beside me. She doesn't say hello. Just settles into the seat softly.

"See you've been taking notes from Alexia," she says.

I frown. "Meaning?"

"Meaning," she says, glancing at me sideways, "you've got enough sass to keep a cast of *Real Housewives* on edge. Check your tone with me."

I swallow. When Stella sharpens her voice like that, you listen.

"I'm not trying to be a bitch," I say carefully. "I just... I want them to respect me. Like they did her. Ya know?"

She studies me for a beat, long enough that I start wishing I'd kept my mouth shut.

"You think they respected her?"

The question sits there. I open my mouth. Close it.

"There's a reason someone wanted her gone," Stella says quietly.

The words hit wrong. Not cruel. Just final. Like a door I didn't realize was already closed.

She stands, brushing invisible lint from her pants. "Don't get it twisted," she says, not looking at me. "Power and isolation look real similar from the cheap seats."

Then she walks away, leaving the words sitting heavy between us.

She's not wrong. I know that. But knowing doesn't magically hand me a better option. If this doesn't make them take me seriously, I'm not sure they ever will.

———

I'M STILL TURNING IT OVER DURING PREVIEW WHEN STELLA, my fairy godmother—the building's watchful historian—knocks on Ella's door. Her presence comes off different today, less playful, more intentional.

"That audition tonight," she says gently. "You still wanna go?"

I answer as Ella, but it feels like me. "It doesn't matter."

"It matters to you," she says, brushing a hand over my knit cap. "I'll cover. If something goes sideways, I'll call."

I look at her like always, startled. Vulnerable. "You don't have to do that."

"I know," she says. "That's why I'm doing it."

She sits beside me on the bed.

"You deserve to be heard," she adds. "Not 'if' or later. Now."

The words hit me square in the chest, like she just named a want I've been pretending not to have.

———

AFTER THE PREVIEW, I'M BACK AT THE VANITY, PEELING myself out of Ella inch by inch. I scrub at my lashes with a cotton pad as a playlist of Alexia's top ten croons through my phone. Behind me, Langston's seated at the small table, pages spread out, pencil moving fast. He hasn't even changed out of his blazer.

I remind myself it's just pressure. Opening week. The weight of the show pressing down on him from every angle, on both of us.

But I miss the version of him that looks up mid-note like he's hearing me for the first time. The way he presses his forehead to mine when the world gets too loud. The way his hand finds my waist in the dark like he's making sure I'm still there. How he listens when I'm spiraling, really listens, like my words matter more than whatever's in front of him.

I don't want tonight to end like this. I don't want *us* to end like this.

I watch him from the mirror, the way his focus never lifts from the page, the pencil moving like it's the only thing keeping the world in place. Every mark precise. Every beat accounted for.

I don't care what anyone says...

He'd never treat Alexia like this.

The thought slips in uninvited and refuses to leave. Not because she was softer. Or kinder. But because she never looked unsure. Never waited to be chosen. *He* chased *her*. I heard it in his voice that night at his parents', the crack in it when he asked her to call back. To just tell him the truth. He wanted her voice. *Needed* it.

Me? I'm always adjusting mine.

What Stella said drifts back in, low and steady.

Power and isolation look real similar from the cheap seats.

You deserve to be heard. Not "if." Not later. Now.

I stare at my reflection, lashes half-gone, foundation breaking apart at the edges. I've been trying to earn something with precision. With distance. Control. But none of that makes him look up.

How long am I gonna keep borrowing someone else's voice?

I set the remover aside, catching his eyes in the mirror. Still smile the way I imagine Alexia would, lazy, confident.

"So," I say lightly. "You gonna tell me how amazing I was today, or you saving that for opening night?"

He doesn't look up.

"Your timing was tighter in the second act," he says. "Still rushing the pickup in measure forty-six."

My face stays pleasant. My chest doesn't.

Don't trip, girl. He just needs a little distraction.

Turning in my stool, I lean back against the counter and tilt my head. "You like the dress change? I saw you clock it."

"I clocked the lighting cue," he replies. "Costume needs to be half a beat faster."

"Wow. Okay." I push off the counter, heat crawling under my skin. "So... you don't see anything else?"

Finally, he looks at me. Calm. Distant.

"I see you doing the work."

That's it?

After everything, the early mornings, the silence, the discipline, the way I've folded myself smaller and sharper just to fit where he needs me.

"Are you still mad about last night?" I ask. "'Cause if you are, just say that."

He flips a page. "I'm not mad."

"I crossed a line more than once," I say, softer. "I know that. I shouldn't have said what I said."

The thought tastes bitter as soon as it leaves me. He trusted me with his dream. And I pissed all over it. Humiliated him in front of the cast and crew.

He shrugs, already back to his notes. "It's done."

Of course it is. Logged. Filed. Stored away like everything else I give him.

"Is that how this goes?" I ask. "I apologize and you just, what, check it off and move on?"

"I'm giving you notes," he says. "That's my job."

"And what about me?" I fire back. "Do you see me at all?"

He sighs, pinching the bridge of his nose. "Yana—"

"No," I cut in, heat flooding my chest. "What's it gonna take for you to actually see me? To treat me like an actual person?"

He stands, chair scraping back. "What are you talking about? Of course I see you."

"Oh yeah? Is that why you keep trying to curate me like a damn photo? *Calm down. Sing louder.* It's never enough for you."

His face tightens. "Why do you keep turning everything into a fight?"

"Maybe because you keep acting like *you're* the only one under pressure."

"And maybe that's because *I'm* the only one taking this seriously!" he shouts.

"I *am* taking it seriously! I've bent myself into knots trying to help your ass!"

He goes still. But I'm not done.

"It's no wonder Alexia wanted to get away from you!"

The words hit, and I don't soften them.

Because I am so tired of being the version he's still shaping instead of the one he can't live without. I don't wanna be the girl he refines. I wanna be the girl who rattles him. The one he reaches for without thinking. Not the one he reduces to timing and volume and posture.

Langston doesn't say anything. Just stares at me, stunned, like I've sucked the air out of his lungs.

Then there's a knock at the door.

And the two of us freeze. 'Cause both of us know just how thin these walls really are.

"Come in," Langston mutters.

The door opens just enough for Kai to slip inside. She doesn't meet either of our eyes.

"Julian wants to see you," she says softly. "Both of you."

Then she's gone.

WE STEP INTO THE HALL, THE DOOR CLOSING WITH A MUTED click behind us. The air out here feels thinner, like whatever we said inside the room is still settling into the walls.

We walk a few paces without touching. The distance between us isn't wide, but it's there.

Halfway down the hall, Langston slows.

When I turn back, he's already looking at me. There's something different in it now. Less guarded. Less composed.

"I'm sorry," he says.

It isn't dramatic. He doesn't dress it up. Just stands there and lets it exist.

"I've been carrying a lot," he adds quietly. "But that's mine. I shouldn't have let it spill onto you."

That hits deeper than I expect.

I nod once. "I know you're under pressure."

Opening week. Investors. His parents. The grief that shadows him, even when he pretends it doesn't.

He rubs the back of his neck, gaze lowering briefly before finding me again.

"I got stuck in director mode," he says. "And you weren't asking for that."

The clarity in it fills the space where the anger was.

I think about the voicemail. About him standing outside in the dark, asking another woman to just answer. About how small he looked in that moment.

"I'm sorry too," I say.

He blinks, inhaling slow.

"I think I was just... frustrated."

It sounds simple, but it isn't. 'Cause I'm hella frustrated.

Frustrated I'm always the last to hear.

Frustrated I'm giving everything and still competing with a ghost.

Frustrated I don't know where I stand when the music stops.

"I shouldn't have said what I said," I continue. "That wasn't fair."

He studies me for a long second, then steps closer. Reaching for my hand, he threads his fingers through mine. And my chest unclenches a notch.

"You're not her," he says quietly. "And you don't have to be."

The words move through me slowly.

They don't erase what I heard outside his parents' house. They don't untangle the grief he's still holding. But they do something else.

They choose me. Right here. Right now.

I squeeze his hand once, not trusting my voice to hold steady if I try to say more.

We start walking again, our steps falling into rhythm without discussion. The space between us narrows, even if the distance is still there.

When we step into Julian's office, the air changes immediately. He looks nauseous, shaken. Like bad news has already landed and settled. He doesn't bother with pleasantries.

"Kai brought something to my attention," he says, already unlocking his phone. "Another video just went viral."

My stomach drops so fast the floor feels unreliable.

The clip loads. Backstage. The lighting dim. The sound muffled. Me, leaning against a wall, laughing too loud, hands flying as I tell some half-finished story to someone just off camera.

Stella.

But you can't see her. Only me.

Sloppy. Unfiltered. A moment stripped of angles or optics or careful breathing, without the weight of Alexia Hyrd, Broadway lead. Where I was just... me.

The caption scrolls beneath it.

Something's wrong with Alexia.

My mouth goes dry. My pulse starts racing, loud in my ears. The comments flicker past in a blur, question marks, concern, people dissecting my smile, my laugh, my body language like it's evidence of something broken.

Stella's words echo in my mind again:

You think they respected her?

I watch myself on the screen, laughing, loose, unprotected.

The one moment I stopped pretending.

And the world noticed.

25

As always, the show must go on.

Twenty-four hours later, I sit alone in my dressing room—long after the applause has faded—the counter almost clear, mirror lights buzzing overhead. My makeup is half-gone, lashes discarded, costume heaped over the chair like it's as tired as I am. And I should be wrecked.

With all the quiet tension hovering in the air, the preview was intense. Emotional. The kind that settles in your bones and keeps humming after the curtain falls.

My voice should be the only thing on my mind. The lowered octave, the pacing, the notes Julian flagged. Instead, my thoughts drift backward as I swipe away the last of my foundation, catching my reflection mid-grin. Replaying last night like it might disappear if I don't hold onto it.

Langston finally reached for me in the dark, his arm sliding around my waist, pulling me back against him like it was the most natural thing in the world. Like his body had been searching for mine before he even realized it. His lips found the back of my neck, slow and warm.

"*I don't ever want you feeling alone in this,*" he whispered.

He stayed there, wrapped around me, his hand resting firm at my hip.

"*I've got you,*" he added, chest rising and falling against my back. "*Even when I get it wrong.*"

I didn't melt, roll over, or pretend the ache had vanished. But I did let myself lean into him.

Not because everything was fixed, but because he was trying. And effort means something when you've spent your life asking to be chosen.

The closeness felt fragile, like something newly mended that shouldn't be rushed. So we let it be that. Stayed in that narrow pocket of warmth until sleep finally pulled us under. For a few hours, everything was quiet. My heartbeat was steady.

But we're still not safe.

Whoever tried to hurt me is still out there. That doesn't disappear because we held each other in the dark.

And times like this, when I'm left on my own, the theater feels too quiet. They doubled security since the stage light fell. Extra guards at the stage door. Cameras everywhere. Still. I'm not sure how much all that will do to protect us from each other.

Where's my bodyguard when I need him?

I check my phone. Nothing.

The hallway outside my dressing room has emptied, laughter and footsteps absorbed into the bones of the building. I slip on my jacket, grab my bag, and step into the corridor.

Empty.

For a moment, that old ache creeps in.

Of course he left. Of course someone needed him more. But...

For half a second, my mind goes somewhere it shouldn't. These days, an empty hall doesn't just mean someone stepped out. Someone could be waiting. For me.

Then my phone buzzes.

Langston.

Meet me onstage.

That's it. No emoji. No explanation.

I exhale slowly and make my way toward the house.

When I push through the stage door, everything shifts.

The lights come up one by one. A soft wash of warm amber spills across the boards like honey. My keyboard, usually tucked into the second-floor apartment set, sits center stage instead, waiting. Then a single spotlight blooms from the house, trained low and steady.

The chandeliers glow at half-brightness, crystals catching and scattering light like a thousand quiet stars. The theater looks unreal, like a palace waiting for someone to claim it.

And there he is.

Langston. Hands clasped behind his back. Shoulders tight. Nervous as hell. He's not in rehearsal clothes. He's wearing a crisp white button-down, sleeves rolled, dress shoes polished to a shine.

I stop cold.

He dressed up for me.

"What is this?" I whisper, afraid my voice might break the spell as I approach.

He slowly steps aside.

Behind him sits a simple stool. On it, a small bakery box. And a slim velvet pouch. I recognize the logo immediately. My breath catches anyway.

"You said you wanted a real date," he says, rubbing the back of his neck. "I figured... this was our best option."

Glancing over his shoulder, he lifts a hand at the control booth.

"Thanks, Kai."

She waves back before taking off.

The lights stay warm. Intimate. Just us.

I move toward the stool slow, too anxious to rush it. I open the bakery box first.

Lemon blueberry.

My favorite cupcake. The forbidden one.

I laugh softly, already blinking too much. "You remembered," I say.

"Of course I did."

His expression is open. Unguarded. Like this matters just as much to him as it does to me.

I reach for the velvet pouch. Inside is a fountain pen, vintage, elegant, gold-capped. Heavier than I expect when I lift it.

"Every star signs their Playbill with something that feels right," he says quietly. "If you're going to sign hundreds of them, I thought you should do it with something beautiful."

The word *star* hits somewhere tender.

Me. Signing Playbills.

A future I've been squinting at finally comes into focus.

"Langston..." My voice wobbles.

Before I can say anything else, he moves to the keyboard. Sits. Presses his fingers to the keys. The melody is soft. Simple. Familiar in the way something feels when it's written with care. It's lovely.

"What's the name of that one?" I ask, warmth threading through my voice.

"It's called 'Yana,'" he says, not looking up.

My name. Not Ella's. Not Alexia's. *Mine.*

I laugh and cry at the same time, taking a bite of the cupcake even though my throat is tight. The frosting tastes like sugar and courage and the kinda joy I almost forgot I was allowed.

No one's ever done something like this for me before. Written me into the music. Said my name like it belongs somewhere permanent.

Yeah, he's definitely trying to get some tonight. Not that I'd be against it.

When the song ends, he stands and gently takes the cupcake from my hand, setting it aside.

"Dance with me."

I bust out laughing. "You don't dance."

A corner of his mouth lifts. "I do when I'm with you."

With the click of a remote, he takes my hand and guides me back to center stage. It's a recorded version of the orchestra playing the exact same song.

"When did you even—"

"*Shhh.*" He presses a finger to his lips, pulling me into his arms.

His hand settles at my waist, my fingers sliding behind his neck. The recorded orchestra hums through the speakers, just enough to make the empty theater feel alive. We sway, slow and close, like Cinderella and her prince.

"I know it's not perfect," he murmurs, forehead touching mine. "But I wanted to give you a taste."

He smiles soft, in the sweetest way, and it wrecks me.

"Just imagine," he says. "You. Me. Sardi's after the Tonys. I'm in my best tux. You're in that... jaw-dropping gown."

I cackle.

"And all eyes are on you," he continues, looking at me like I'm already there. "Jayana Gardner."

I swallow. Nod once. Not joking or pretending.

His smile fades just a little. He exhales, like he's been holding something back.

"I'm sorry," he says, voice thin. "I know I said it before but... I mean it."

I still for a beat, caught off guard by the way it feels hearing it again.

There's something stripped down in him now. The careful edges. The polish. All of it set aside.

He keeps his eyes on mine and lets the words stand on their own.

"I've been juggling fire, trying to win the applause of people who will likely never clap," he adds. "And you've been standing right here, reminding me I don't have to."

It settles somewhere deep.

Because while I've been reminding him—to breathe, to laugh, to loosen his damn grip—sometimes, still, I forget to remind myself.

I step closer, close enough to feel his breath shift.

"No," I assure him. "You don't."

He bobs his head, a quiet understanding moving across his

face. His mouth curves, small and unguarded, like he's finally laying down something he's been carrying for years.

His thumb brushes my side, gentle and slow. "Thank you. For being you." He hesitates, then adds, more quietly, "I see you. And one day soon... everyone else will too."

He leans in easy, no nerves in it at all.

And when he kisses me under the spotlight, the empty theater holding its breath, I believe him.

26

They cleared the Majestic lobby and dressed it up like a jewel box. Velvet ropes guiding foot traffic, branded backdrops gleaming. Soft lighting angled just right so nobody looks tired or like they're about to crack. Opening night energy hums everywhere. It slips under my skin and climbs my spine. Curtain goes up in a few hours, and the building feels like it knows.

Julian stands nearby, tie loosened, eyes bright in that way they get when adrenaline is doing the heavy lifting. He looks at me like he's biting back a whole speech, like the words are lined up behind his teeth and he's choosing restraint for once.

"You good?" he asks quietly.

I nod. "Yeah."

He smiles, brief and sincere, the kind that doesn't ask for reassurance back. "Whatever happens tonight... thank you. I mean that."

It's coded. We both know it.

Thank you for being Alexia when Alexia vanished.

Thank you for not asking too many questions.

Thank you for covering our asses.

"Let's go make some history," he adds.

I breathe in, steadying myself, while hair and makeup do their final checks around me. Powder brush sweeping my cheek. Lip gloss pressed and blotted. A stylist adjusts the neckline of my dress, tugging and smoothing like she's sealing me into place.

Maybe I'll watch Alexia's clips again. One more time wouldn't hurt.

I sneak a glance at my phone as Nia does one final check of my edges, then set it back in my lap.

No, Yana. You've got this.

Except my breath feels shallow, like something's already wrong and my body knows it before I do. My thumb hesitates for half a second before I open social media. That's all it takes.

The video is already at the top of my feed.

It's clear. Painfully clear. Receipts everywhere. Audition footage from years ago. Me in other shows. My real voice. My real laugh. My real name. Side by side comparisons, time stamps, screenshots, a conspiracy thread stitched together with surgical precision. And then the words that make my stomach drop straight through the floor.

Where is Alexia Hyrd?
And who is this??

Everything inside me goes hollow, like someone reached in and took the scaffolding. This can't be happening. This is a nightmare, the kind where you try to scream and nothing comes out. My hands start shaking so hard I have to tuck the phone against my thigh to keep anyone from noticing.

I scan the lobby until I find him.

Langston stands across the space, speaking with a producer, posture relaxed, jaw set in that calm, commanding way that always makes people listen. He looks unshakable. I cross the room fast, heart pounding so loud I swear someone's gonna hear it.

"Langston," I whisper, gripping his sleeve. "You need to see this. Now."

"We're on in five," he murmurs automatically.

"Please."

In all my anxiety, I can't be sure if I sound more like Alexia or myself, but something in my voice finally gets through. He excuses himself, then leans in when I lift my phone. I watch his face as the video plays, his expression stilling as something flickers across his gaze. He straightens, eyes scanning the lobby, assessing, calculating, most likely thinking three moves ahead.

"Hey," he says softly, pulling me close. "Don't panic."

"How can you say that?" My voice trembles. "This is undeniable."

"It doesn't have many views yet," he says carefully.

"*Yet*," I whisper.

His hands slide to my arms, grounding, warm.

"We'll deal with it after." He presses a kiss to my forehead, right at my hairline. "We're going to be alright. Believe that."

I nod because I want to, because I *need* to. Because believing him feels easier than imagining what happens if he's wrong.

The interviewer waves us over.

Showtime.

I square my shoulders and step into Alexia like armor.

The questions start easy. How does it feel to finally bring this show to Broadway? Julian answers first, talking about collaboration, timing, believing in the story. Langston jumps in, explaining how the music came first, how the score shaped the emotional spine of the show.

"And Alexia," the interviewer says, turning to me with a smile. "You're the heart of it all. What was it like stepping into this role?"

My pulse crowds my ears.

"Incredible," I say smoothly. "It's rare to find a character who feels so... seen."

I don't blink. Don't hesitate. I lock my smile in place and let muscle memory do the rest.

If I drop the mask now, there's nothing left underneath.

The interviewer grins. "Fans are buzzing about you and Langston possibly rekindling things. Any truth to that?"

Relief flickers through me. No Julian rumors. Thank God.

Langston laughs lightly. "People love a good story."

"Let's be real," the interviewer presses. "Isn't there something simply *magnetic* about Alexia?"

Langston bobs his head with a swallow.

"Tell us," the interviewer says, "what is it about her you find so... irresistible?"

It's perfect bait for ratings, for clicks and views. And without the slightest hesitation, Langston turns to me.

"She's always optimistic," he says, his gaze never leaving mine. "About the world. About people. She believes when most don't. And she works harder than anyone in the room, even when no one's watching."

Wait. Is he talking about Alexia... or me?

"She has this way of making people feel like they matter," he continues, mouth twitching. "And she pretends she doesn't know how special that is. That's hard to resist."

Each word lands and leaves a mark. He's talking about me. *Just me.*

Not the persona. Not the lie.

The interviewer chuckles. "Sounds like you've fallen hard."

I barely breathe. Langston's mouth curves into a smile I've barely seen him wear in public. It's private. Unfiltered. And just for me.

Is this happening? Is he about to say it?

'Cause if it's true, and if he does, I think—wildly, impossibly —that I might say it back.

"Langston Washington?" A man steps into frame, flashing a badge. "Julian Frazier? Jayana Gardner?"

My name cracks through the lobby and splits the air in two. Every sound around us drops out.

"Detective Morales with the NYPD," the man says, a couple officers in tow. "We need you to come with us for questioning."

Questioning?

"You've got to be kidding me," Julian says. "We open in three hours."

He releases an affronted huff, but no one else laughs.

"What's all this about?" Julian demands.

The detective meets my eyes as the cameras roll. "The disappearance of Alexia Hyrd."

TYPICALLY, IT WOULD TAKE A HURRICANE TO SHUT DOWN AN opening night on Broadway. But with the star, the MD, and the director being held at the precinct for questioning, this time the show could not go on.

The interrogation room is colder than it needs to be, the metal chair digging into my thighs. The table is scarred with old scratches, names carved by people who thought they'd be here forever too.

A redhead female detective sits across from me, posture loose, eyes piercing, like she's got all night and nowhere else to be.

"So let me get this straight," she says, flipping a page in her notebook. "You expect me to believe Alexia Hyrd just vanished. And you decided the most logical next step was to hop into her life?"

Marisol would have better answers than me. But she's also got contracts and lawyers and a job built around not telling the truth out loud. I'm not even sure what I'm allowed to say without detonating something I already can't afford to lose.

Besides, Gracie ain't the only one who signed an NDA.

"I didn't decide anything," I say, my voice sounding steadier than I feel. "I was asked to cover rehearsals. Then previews. Then—"

"Then you lied," she cuts in. "You impersonated a public figure. Signed contracts. Took interviews." Her gaze hardens. "Why?"

The room goes quiet. Even the buzzing light seems to hold

its breath. I look her dead in the eye. "Ain't you ever had a dream?"

Her mouth pulls taut in disappointment, like she expected better from me.

There's a knock at the door, and it swings open before she can answer. The detective who brought us in stands there, expression flat, beside a man in a trench coat and scarf, expensive and composed in a way that screams money. Legal money.

"You're going to be hearing from multiple lawyers," the man says, voice clipped. "Investors. Producers. Sponsors. You've delayed the opening of a *major* Broadway production. Thousands of patrons are already demanding refunds."

The words stack heavy and final.

Delayed. Opening. Major. Broadway.

I don't hear the rest. All I can think is that people are dressed up outside the Majestic, checking their watches, wondering why the doors aren't opening.

———

Langston looks like hell when they finally let us go. So does Julian. The precinct lighting has them both looking drained, like somebody pressed pause on them mid-breath and forgot to hit play again. Julian's mouth is set tight. Not mad. Just... weighed down.

When his car pulls up, he rests a hand on my shoulder. Firm. Quick.

"I'm sorry," he says quietly. "I never meant for this to fall on you."

I nod, because what else am I gonna do? Tell him it's fine? It ain't fine. But I know he means it.

He gets in the car and the door shuts between us.

The city doesn't care. Traffic keeps moving. Lights keep blinking. Somewhere, somebody's still celebrating opening night for something. But I feel exposed as we wait for our car. Like even the sidewalks know my name.

I turn to Langston.

His jacket hangs open. Collar loose. He looks older tonight. Not because of the precinct. Because of what tonight was supposed to be.

"Langston, I—"

I don't even know what I'm trying to say. I just know I don't wanna stand here like we're strangers after all that.

My hand drifts toward his. Our fingers brush just as the driver pulls up. Langston clears his throat and moves fast to open the door, stoic as he ushers me inside. Efficient. Contained. Like keeping things orderly will keep them from falling apart.

We slide into the backseat. The door closes. The city blurs past with twinkling lights.

He stares straight ahead for a long moment. His jaw flexes once. His hand rests on his thigh like he's holding himself still.

Opening night turned into questioning. Investors whispering. His name all over timelines before the curtain even had a chance to rise. He spent years building toward this moment. Tonight was supposed to be proof.

His shoulders shift.

I feel the hesitation before his arm comes around me.

He pulls me close, slower than usual, like he's making himself do it. His chin rests against my hair. His hold is firm. Steady. Like he's bracing us both.

"I'm sorry I let it come to this," he says.

That's different.

Not sorry we got caught. Not sorry for the headlines. Sorry he let it go this far. Like he saw the edge weeks ago and kept walking anyway.

I lean into him. I want him to say we're gonna be okay. I want him to say this doesn't undo everything we built. I want him to say we're still us. That tonight didn't turn me into a liability.

His breath shifts like he's about to speak. But he doesn't.

The silence between us isn't empty. It's crowded. With numbers. With headlines. With everything that hangs in the balance.

I know how much tonight meant to him. I know what daring to say "Tony" out loud cost him. I know how hard he's worked to get here. To push through, even when it felt like no one was on his side.

He's trying to stay here with me. I feel it in the way his hand presses into my shoulder, like he's grounding himself. In the way his thumb keeps moving against my arm, distracted, counting something only he can see.

But part of him is already somewhere else. Calculating. Measuring the damage.

And for the first time, I wonder where I fall in that equation.

———

THE SECOND WE ENTER THE APARTMENT HE POURS A SCOTCH.

"You want one?" he asks, already mid-pour.

"I'm good."

The amber liquid sloshes in the glass as he carries it to the piano. The room feels too quiet without the city noise beneath it. He presses his fingers to the keys and starts playing "Shine Through the Dark." Slower than usual. Stripped down. The notes stay low, close to the instrument.

Halfway through, the melody thins out. His hands settle. The last note fades and doesn't come back.

I move beside him, close enough to feel the heat off his shoulder.

"It's gonna work out," I say. I don't know how, but I've seen enough plot twists in my life to know the ending doesn't show up when you expect it to. "It always does."

He exhales, something between a laugh and surrender.

"If this pushes us past June, the nomination window closes," he says quietly. "And if that happens—"

The sentence dies before it can finish.

His fingers hover over the keys as his eyes drift shut.

"I hate that that's where my mind went," he says, voice low. "I'm sorry."

I study him. The way he's trying to outrun his own instincts. The way ambition still grabs him first, even when everything's burning.

He sets the glass aside.

"I saw her cracking," he says, after a moment. "Alexia. I thought pushing would focus her. Told myself *discipline fixes things*. At least, that's what I believed."

I feel something sink inside me. Because I've been pushing too.

Harder runs. Longer rehearsals. Studying everything I can get my hands on. Smiling wider. Standing taller. Making sure no one ever thinks I'm just filling in.

"I didn't realize she wasn't just tired," he continues. "She was disappearing."

The room tightens around us, and something in me shifts.

I know that feeling. The way you start shaping yourself into what everyone needs until there's barely anything left that's just yours.

"The night before she left," he says, "I found steroids in her makeup bag. Vocal ones. Not prescribed. She said she needed them to survive the schedule. Press. Recordings. Rehearsals. She wouldn't cancel anything. Wouldn't reschedule. Wouldn't let anyone see her struggle. And then..."

My mind jumps to the final rehearsal Stella told me about. The one where something went wrong and nobody wanted to talk about it.

I see it too clearly. Alexia center stage. Lights hot. Sound refusing to come. A room full of people pretending not to panic.

"During our final run-through, her voice collapsed," he says. "Not a crack. A collapse. I stopped the band. Julian panicked. She ran."

That's just what I did.

Chicago flashes through me, hot and fast. Sixteen. Stupid. Running because I thought love meant disappearing into someone else's plan.

Langston's hands knot together.

"When I confronted her about the steroids, she said she didn't want anyone thinking she was weak. Said she had to keep up. Said if she slowed down... they'd replace her."

Of course. That's been sitting in the back of my mind since day one. The quiet understanding that I stepped into a space that was never meant to stay mine. That if she came back, I'd slide right out of it.

"I was terrified," he says. "Terrified the show would fall apart. Terrified all of it would. And I wanted so badly for it to succeed."

He shakes his head, gazing out the bay window.

"I kept talking about the schedule. About tightening things up. More doctor visits. More breaks. Anything to get her through it."

He drags a hand over his face.

"She looked at me and said she couldn't believe she ever thought I loved her."

I stare at him, speechless.

All the times I asked, all the times he deflected. All the times he shut down instead of letting me in.

"When she disappeared, I thought maybe she just needed time," he says. "Julian agreed. Said reporting anything would spook investors. We told ourselves she'd cool off and come back."

He lifts his eyes to mine.

"I thought I was managing it," he says. "I didn't see how far gone she was until she was already gone."

Gone.

Not just missing from rehearsal. Gone from him. Gone from herself.

And through all of that, he never told me. Not when I agreed to step into her heels. Not when I signed my name to her contracts. Not when I stood under lights that weren't meant for me.

He keeps hiding things, shutting me out. Treating me like I'm just filling space.

"You let me step into this," I say, voice tight. "You let me walk around wearing her skin, taking her notes, fighting her battles, and you never once thought I deserved to know what I was walking into?"

"Yana, I didn't think—"

"No," I say, softer now. "You didn't trust me."

"That's not—" He stops. Breathes. "I thought I was protecting you."

I laugh once, sharp and tired.

"You don't protect someone by deciding what they can handle," I say. "You just take the choice away."

He flinches at that.

"I didn't want you carrying her ghosts," he says.

"But you were fine with me carrying her spotlight."

His mouth opens, then closes.

And in that quiet, something settles in me.

It's not that he doesn't care. It's that when things get hard, he closes ranks. He manages. He controls. He edits the story before anyone else can see the mess.

And I don't wanna be managed. I wanna stand by his side.

But the click of the door cuts me off. Soft. Careful. The kinda sound you make when you don't know if you're welcome.

I turn.

Alexia stands in the doorway.

Her hair is pulled back, not styled, her coat hanging open like she forgot to finish putting it on. She looks tired, unpolished. Real in a way she never was on social media or TV.

I've seen her everywhere for weeks. On billboards. My phone. In mirrors when I wasn't careful. But this is flesh and breath and weight. Alive.

She looks at Langston first. Then her eyes slide to me.

Like I'm a typo that doesn't belong.

27

I sink onto the sofa because my knees give out before I can stop them. A quiet betrayal of my body, like it knows something my heart is still catching up to.

Alexia stands across from me, coat draped over the arm of the chair like she doesn't mean to stay. Like she came to deliver something urgent and necessary and then disappear again.

For a second, I can't remember which of us is supposed to be real.

Up close, she really does look like me. Same height. Same build. Same face shape cameras love under good lighting. But the differences are everywhere once you know where to look. Her posture is tighter. Guarded. Years of being corrected in public have taught her how to hold herself like nothing can touch her. Her eyes don't wander like mine. They assess, then decide.

And her voice. It's softer than I expected. Careful, like every word has been weighed against the cost of saying it out loud.

Langston hasn't moved. He's standing near the piano, one hand braced against it like he needs the weight to stay upright. When he looks at her, awe and grief cross his face, like seeing a ghost that knows your name.

"You're back," he says finally. The words come out fractured.

"Yeah." Alexia's mouth tightens. "I am."

A hollow calm settles over me, like I've stepped outside

myself and I'm watching it happen. I swallow, slow, because if I don't, I might say something I can't take back.

She doesn't rush into explanation. She looks around the apartment first. The piano. The sofa. Me. Like she's evaluating what survived her absence.

"I didn't come to fight," she says quietly. "I came because... I'm tired of hiding."

I know that tired. That bone-deep tired that lingers long after the applause dies out. The kind that comes from holding your breath for months.

"Then tell me." Langston shifts, barely, like movement might undo him. "What happened?"

She exhales, already exhausted. "I saw a doctor the morning of our final rehearsal. Before everything went to hell."

Langston stiffens. His fingers flex against the piano. For just a second, his gaze flicks to me.

"He told me if I kept singing like I was," she continues, voice steady, "I was bound to hemorrhage my vocal cords. One more performance and I could lose my voice permanently."

Langston's face crumples, disbelief cracking through. "You could've told me. You didn't have to—"

"I know," she says. "But also... I left because I couldn't stand the idea of failing in public."

The air shifts. My chest pulls in on itself like it's bracing for impact.

"Marisol checked me into a private clinic," she says, softly. "Cleared the whole thing with my manager. Voice rehab. Anxiety treatment. No contact. No press."

Rehab. Anxiety treatment. Clean exits with good lighting.

"I should've told you," she adds, shrugging at Langston. "But I couldn't."

"Why?" Langston asks, his voice brittle and wounded.

She gives a small, humorless smile. "Because I built a version of myself that didn't quit."

She raises her chin a little, like she's proud of that fact.

"This version of myself that never cracked. Never canceled. And the second my voice gave out..." Her lips press into a thin line. "I saw it. The headlines. The pity. The replacement."

The word hums in the air again. *Replacement.*

I should feel relieved. It's not the answer I expected to hear but at least it's an answer.

Still, something sour settles in my belly.

I've been living her nightmare because she couldn't stand the optics?

Langston's eyes close, his jaw tightening hard enough to tick. "I told you I understood if you had to step down."

"Yeah, and you told Julian I wasn't ready," she snaps.

The words hang heavy. Unavoidable. His shoulders tense like something sharp just slid under his ribs.

"I heard you, Langston," she says, voice trembling with emotion. "That final rehearsal? I heard it all."

He absorbs it in silence.

"I was spiraling," she continues. "Press loved me. Fans loved me. But I didn't know if anyone loved the part of me that needed a day off."

Her eyes flick to him, searching.

"And I couldn't stand the idea of anyone seeing me weak."

I watch them and something clicks slow and cold inside me.

She didn't disappear because she was abused or in danger. She disappeared because she couldn't survive the humiliation of being human. Walked away from all that love and attention.

But attention ain't the same as being seen.

My hands curl into the couch cushion, thinking about it. The moment she broke. The moment she decided vanishing was safer than staying and failing in front of the world and him.

A muscle jumps near Langston's temple. "I left you *dozens* of messages."

"I know." She stares back without blinking. "I listened to every single one."

My stomach turns as I realize how easy it is to become scenery in a story that isn't fully mine.

Messages. Plural.

"I heard how wrecked you were in that last voicemail. And I wanted to fix it. Call and tell you I'd come back better. Untouchable." Her laugh is soft and exhausted. "Then I saw I'd been replaced."

Her gaze slides to me. The look alone is sharp enough to sting.

She straightens. "An understudy impersonating me. Wearing *my* voice. *My* mannerisms. *My* reputation."

Langston doesn't move. He doesn't reach for me or look up or even pretend to follow me with his eyes. He just stands there, weight sunk into himself, staring somewhere between the floor and whatever version of the past he's trapped inside.

"You thought you could just step into my life?" Alexia continues, moving toward me. "Do you have *any* idea what that did to me? Watching you pop up everywhere while I was trying to survive?"

I glance at Langston, but he gives me nothing.

He goes quiet the way he does when he's trying to hold the world together.

"You didn't exactly leave a squeaky-clean trail behind you," I say to her.

She squints but doesn't deny it. Each of us knows she can't.

"You think I asked for this?" I say, louder now. "I never planned to wear anyone's skin. I was hired. I did the work. Carried your show when *you* disappeared!"

Alexia scoffs. "You benefited from my collapse."

"That's not fair." I look to Langston, waiting for him to stick up for me.

But he stays silent.

He could say it wasn't my idea. He could say I mattered. He could look at me like I'm a person, not a complication. He doesn't. Just stands there, looking like he's searching for the right answer.

And I'm tired of being the question.

"I see," I whisper. Something in me finally gives way.

I push myself to my feet, legs trembling but stubborn enough to hold me upright. I turn toward the door, prepared to leave without another word.

Then a sound breaks the quiet.

The cockatiel chirps, a thin, crooked line of melody curling through the room.

"Shine through the Dark." Not Alexia's version. Mine. The notes are off, but the rhythm's familiar, just enough to crack my heart in two.

Langston sighs. "Yana—"

I hold up a hand. "Don't."

He ain't got a word to say when it matters.

My eyes burn, but I keep them dry. I won't unravel in this room. I take my jacket. My bag. The parts of me that still feel like mine. I leave without turning around. Because I know what it feels like to disappear inside someone else's panic.

I didn't come this far to be a damn punchline.

Behind me, silence settles into place like it owns the room. And for once, I refuse to wait for it to choose me.

I pick a hotel two blocks off Times Square because it looks anonymous, all glass and marble and people who mind their business if you look like you belong. I don't.

The clerk's eyes flick up the second I step to the counter. Then back down. Then up again, slower this time.

"Checking in," I say anyway, forcing my voice level. I slide my card across the counter and keep my gaze fixed on the little brass bell like it might save me.

He types. Clicks. Pauses.

"I'm sorry," he says, polite but stiff. "That card was declined."

I steady my hand on the counter, surprised it needs it. I pull out another card and hand it over with a shrug like this happens all the time.

"Try again."

More clicking. Longer pause.

"I'm afraid this one isn't going through either."

Shit.

I step back, phone already in hand, thumb flying. My bank app loads slow enough to feel cruel. When it finally opens, a bright red banner flashes across the screen.

ACCOUNT TEMPORARILY FROZEN

I stare at it, heart thudding.

Frozen.

Of course it is. All that money. *Thousands.* More than I've ever saved in my life. Gone.

The checks. The deposits. Every dollar I've been living on for weeks was technically hers. Alexia's. Not mine.

If I don't get a room tonight, I don't have a backup plan. I don't have a couch. I don't have anywhere to go.

I shove my real card across the counter, the one I barely ever use because there's never much on it. "Try that one," I say, sharper now.

He hesitates. "Ma'am, if the other cards—"

"Just try it."

My voice carries. I feel it the second it leaves my mouth.

A couple of heads turn. Someone whispers.

The clerk sighs and runs the card.

Declined.

Not enough for a room. Not enough for a night. Not enough to pretend I'm okay.

Behind the desk, the TV mounted above the lobby bar

flickers louder as a breaking news banner scrolls across the bottom of the screen.

ENTERTAINMENT TONIGHT • BROADWAY SHOCKER • WHERE IS ALEXIA HYRD? • IMPOSTER EXPOSED AHEAD OF OPENING NIGHT

My face fills the screen. Not Alexia's. Mine. Caught mouth open, mid-laugh, in some backstage clip. Raw, obnoxious, and unmistakably me.

"Isn't that her?" a woman says, pointing. The woman beside her throws a hand to her mouth.

The clerk stiffens, not even looking at me. I suppose I should be grateful.

I pull my hood up and yank my bag higher on my shoulder, turning away fast. The revolving doors whoosh open and cold air hits my face.

And just like that, I'm back at zero.

The city swallows me whole.

———

THE FOUNTAIN IN BRYANT PARK THROWS LIGHT INTO THE night like it's trying to be cheerful on purpose, water arcing and splashing, neon bleeding into every drop. Tourists cluster around it with phones raised, laughing, pretending this city doesn't eat people alive for sport.

I sit on the stone edge, arms wrapped tight around myself, phone vibrating in my hand again.

Langston.

His name lights up the screen like nothing happened. Like we're still standing in the same room.

I let it ring. Watch it pulse against my palm until the vibration fades.

Then he calls again.

I don't move.

A third time.

I flip the phone face down on the stone beside me and let it die out on its own.

If I answer, he'll make it make sense. And I don't want it to make sense.

The phone buzzes once. A text.

Against my better judgement, I check the message.

Your voicemail's full.

Then:

I should've said something.

Then:

Call me. Please.

But I won't.

I stare at the word *please* until it blurs. He wants to explain. He always does. But explaining ain't the same as choosing. He already did that.

If I answer now, he'll soften his voice. He'll say he panicked. Just like before. And I'll wanna believe him. I always wanna believe the version of a man who says he sees me.

But tonight, I watched him hesitate. I watched him look at her first. Watched him answer her first. Watched him calculate before defending me. And for a woman who's spent her entire life wondering whether she's chosen or just convenient, that feels like an answer.

My phone vibrates again.

Not Langston. Daddy.

I let it buzz once. Twice. Three times. But he won't be able to leave a voicemail. I wouldn't listen anyway. I don't need to.

I already know. He saw me. Everyone did. TMZ. Social media. The little ticker tape under my face telling the world I'm a fraud with a smile too big for her own ambition.

I press my palms to my eyes and breathe through the sting. I really thought I'd outrun this version of myself. The one who ends up right back here. No money. No home. No future that sticks. Circling the same drain over and over.

For a second, I'm sixteen again, sitting at the train station beside a man I thought would be my forever. Back when attention felt like oxygen. Back when being wanted felt like being known.

I trusted him. Trusted him enough to tell my parents I needed two grand for a class trip. Trusted him enough to believe when he said he had a plan for me. For *us*.

Then I woke up with nothing but my backpack under my head. Even my luggage was gone.

I told myself I'd never disappear inside someone else's dream again.

I tuck the phone away like it burned me.

Alexia said she built a version of herself that never cracked. I built a version that never stopped auditioning. Different costumes. Same stage.

"Yana?"

I stiffen, shoulders locking on impulse.

Of course. Prince Charming.

Noah stands a few feet away, holding a coffee cup like he's been walking with it a while, coat unbuttoned, hair loose around his shoulders. I half expect disgust. Or anger. Or that careful distance people use when they don't wanna catch whatever mess you're carrying.

I did more damage to him than anyone. To his career. To his name.

But instead, he looks... normal. Not panicked or pissed. Just tired.

"Feel like I should formally reintroduce myself," he says gently, like he's approaching a skittish animal.

"Funny," I say, forcing a smile. "You stalking fountains now?"

He nods toward the cup. "I live two blocks up. Think insomnia might win tonight." His gaze flicks to the trees lining the park, then back to me. "Show getting postponed didn't exactly help."

"Yep," I say, glancing at my hands in my lap. "All thanks to me."

He pauses, a charmed grin touching his lips. "Is that your real voice?"

I shrug and stare at the fountain, blinking against the sting.

He sits without asking. Close enough that his knee brushes mine when he shifts. I suppose I should be used to the proximity after swapping open-mouthed kisses for weeks on stage. My body recognizes his warmth before my pride does.

"I'm sorry," he says quietly. "As hard as you worked? There's no way all this didn't mean a lot to you."

I brace for sarcasm. Blame. But his expression doesn't change, like he truly saw me in it. All of it. And that's the dangerous part. When someone looks at you like that. Like they're not evaluating the role, just the person.

"You don't have to say that," I mutter.

"I do," he says. "Because people are acting like you woke up and chose chaos. And that's not what happened."

I snort. "You sure about that?"

He turns toward me fully, his thigh pressing into mine. "They needed you."

Needed me. I hate how much I want that to mean more than it does.

"The cast was scrambling. Julian was spiraling. Investors breathing down everyone's necks." He shrugs. "And you were... there. What passionate actor wouldn't jump at the opportunity?"

His eyes softly search my face.

I turn to the water, watching the spray catch the light.

"It wasn't supposed to be like this," I say. "I thought... I don't know. I thought I could handle it."

"You *did* handle it," he says quickly. "You carried the damn show."

I shake my head. "Until I didn't."

"Hey." He nudges my knee, lights twinkling in his eyes. "As fine as you are? You don't deserve what's happening to you." He says it soft, his face so close his breath tickles my chin.

And that's it. The one thing I didn't know how badly I needed to hear.

A beat passes, and his attention drifts to my mouth, the way it always does just before our finale kiss.

But... he wouldn't. Not now. Not after everything.

I turn away with a brittle laugh. "Tell that to my bank."

He frowns like he didn't quite hear me. "What?"

"My account's frozen," I say. "Because technically, I was being paid as Alexia."

"Langston won't help you out?"

"We're... kinda not speaking at the moment," I say with a sniff. "So yeah. No room. No backup plan."

Rock bottom. Again.

When I finally look back, Noah's studying me. Quiet. Sympathetic. Light caramel skin glowing under the city lights. Full lips parted like he's practiced this expression in the mirror.

His voice stays light, but his eyes don't. "Need a warm bed?"

———

His lips are against mine before the door shuts, him pressing me into it. His mouth is hot as it searches my jaw, my neck. Until the noise of the city fades and all that's left is breath and heat and the low hum of an old radiator somewhere down the hall. His apartment smells like cologne and old wood and something citrusy. Warm. Lived-in. The backdrop you'd expect for a famous bachelor.

His mouth finds mine like it's been waiting all night, like this is the part he understands best. I kiss him back because I don't wanna think. Because being wanted, even like this, feels better than being invisible. His hands tremble as they trail down my arms, settling at my waist with an urgency that feels less like desire and more like hunger.

"You have no idea how long I've wanted you like this," he murmurs.

Something in me goes rigid.

"You mean Alexia," I say quietly.

He chuckles against my skin. "You really think I didn't know?"

I pull back. "What?"

Noah exhales like I've asked a question that bores him. "Come on, Yana. I knew from day one."

The air shifts. Suddenly there's less room to breathe.

"She's conservative," he says, drifting closer again, arms sliding back around my waist. "You're laid back. She's complicated. And you're—"

"Simple," I say, finishing it for him.

The word lodges somewhere I can't ignore, like it's found a permanent address.

He laughs softly, low and indulgent, and returns to my collarbone. But he doesn't deny it.

Simple.

Adrien's voice flickers through my head, unwanted. I push it away.

I ain't gotta be the girl who waits to be chosen. I can choose for my damn self.

I need this. I deserve this. And maybe... maybe this is just who I am.

It's nothing like what I had with Langston. But I'm not sleeping on a park bench tonight.

Noah, however, is the type to talk. A lot.

He can't stop going on about all the naughty things he wants to do to me as he gropes all the places that once belonged to Langston, groaning at the thought of devouring everything that was off-limits.

We tumble onto his bed, kisses messy and unguarded. No audience, no marks to hit, no one calling cut.

I tell myself I've got a right to this. I don't know what Noah's angle is. Maybe he likes my curves as much as he liked hers. Maybe he's fine with settling for the next best thing. Either way, I stop trying to untangle it. All that matters is that the room is warm and I'm not alone.

"You weren't fooling anyone who was paying attention," he murmurs, kissing my shoulder.

I let out a soft, humorless scoff. "Is that supposed to make me feel better?"

"It's supposed to make you feel seen."

I stop and look at him.

Not wanted. Not needed. *Seen.*

Like he's already studied the script.

He cups my face, hands warm and steady. "You don't have to pretend here. You never did with me."

I think about the way he looked at me on day one. How he touched me, despite knowing the truth. How even tonight, he took the time to join me at the fountain, when so many simply kept walking.

My defenses crumble, and we kiss again, fast and hungry and desperate, like neither of us knows where else to put the night.

He's right. I'm sick of pretending. Pretending to be okay. Pretending to be someone else.

Noah's eyes burn with heat as his hand inches up my thigh, possessive, unwavering.

But the dude doesn't know when to shut up.

"I told Lexy the same."

I frown, pausing for a breath. "The same?"

He nods, gnawing his lip. "She was over Langston a long time ago. Just didn't know how to break it off without him short-circuiting before curtain." He leans down, returning to my neck.

But now I'm the one who wants to talk. "I thought she and Langston were in love?"

"Is that what he told you?" His chuckle vibrates against my

collarbone. "She couldn't stand that stiff. Probably why she ran into my arms... then Julian's."

Pieces click together, sharp and ugly. It's no wonder multiple people wanted her gone.

But Noah's voice darkens. "I'll have to thank her if I ever get a chance. Asshole deserves everything that's coming to him."

Thank her?

I pull away, sitting up on the pillows. "What do you—what do you mean?"

Noah props on an elbow, rubs a hand over his mouth as he looks me over.

"Two seasons ago when I was starring in *The Golden Prince,* he was brought in to give notes." Noah leans back against the headboard, staring at the ceiling like he's replaying it. "Cut my solo a week before previews. Said the show didn't need ego but restraint."

A muscle ticks in his jaw.

"Did it in front of the whole creative team." He looks back at me now, something sharp glinting in his eyes. "I was humiliated. Told myself if I ever shared a production with him again, I wouldn't let him walk away untouched."

Something curdles in my belly.

"So when I realized Lexy was bored... and willing... and pissed enough to make stupid decisions?" His smile turns thin. "I leaned in."

I wasn't the only one being used. All of them were using each other.

He moves back in, eyes dancing, but I keep my distance.

"So all that with Alexia was just you... trying to get revenge?"

"Well..." He tilts his head side to side. "It wasn't completely my idea. I wasn't the only one with a bone to pick."

My pulse spikes. "With Langston?"

"With Lexy," he clarifies. "But once we knew she was into me, the script sorta wrote itself."

We?

Thinking he's satisfied my curiosity, he leans in again. I slip out of bed.

"Hey, hey..." He pouts. "Listen, Alexia was playing games. Langston is an ass. The whole thing deserved to burn."

Maybe he is. Maybe he hurt me. But he didn't light a match and laugh.

"Who was helping you?" I demand.

He smiles slow and knowing. "Does it matter?"

It does. Everything feels wrong all at once.

"You exposed me," I whisper. "You tried to kill me!"

"No," he says too fast, standing. "None of that was my idea."

I back away, stomach churning. "You wanted to sabotage the show."

He lifts a careless shoulder. "Technically, you're right. But I wasn't the only one. She wanted chaos. I wanted revenge. The feeling was... mutual."

I stare at him. "Who?"

He smirks. "It was business, really. Once we finally got rid of Lexy, we knew it was downhill from there." He moves in, slipping his arms around me, smiling soft, almost fond. "You were... unexpected."

Unexpected.

The word twists low in my gut.

My skin crawls as Noah's eyes flick over me, dark and slow. "Why don't you let me thank you properly?"

The air feels thick. Dirty.

I step out of his reach. "So that's it? I was just... convenient?"

He frowns, finally sensing he miscalculated. "That's not what I meant."

"It is," I say, voice shaking now. "It always is."

I don't know who he's working with or what all this is about. But I want nothing to do with it. I grab my jacket.

"Yana, wait—"

I'm already gone. Out the door. Down the stairs. Back into the cold.

My phone keeps buzzing. But I don't pick up. I walk.
Because once again, I was never the story.
Just a plot device.

28

I head for the subway in hopes of getting some sleep. That's the plan, anyway. Ride the late-night trains back and forth until the hours blur, nod off in short, uncomfortable bursts that never settle into real rest. Just keep moving. I've done it before. My neck's already stiff just thinking about it.

No motel or couch. Just me and the city now.

Eighth Avenue slides past in gray and gold, idling trucks coughing exhaust, steam rising from a manhole like the city's exhaling something it's been holding too long. My boots scuff the pavement in uneven rhythm, and every step feels borrowed. Like I'm squatting in my own life.

I keep replaying everything, Noah's voice, Langston's hands, that stage light screaming toward my face.

I don't know what I'm supposed to do next. I don't even know who I'm supposed to be when the pretending stops.

My phone buzzes and I flinch like it burned me.

Laura. **We're here!**

I stop short. "Shit," I whisper, dragging a hand down my face. I completely forgot. Opening night tickets were impossible to get, so they said they'd drop in for night two instead.

Another text pops up.

Hotel's on West 45th. I'll send the address.

Hell's Kitchen. Of course it is.

The pin drops on my screen, glowing like a lifeline I didn't know I was allowed to have.

My cousin. The one person who knows the real me and still chooses me anyway.

I turn on my heel and start walking with purpose for the first time all night.

———

THE ELEVATOR SMELLS LIKE CHLORINE AND DEPARTMENT-STORE cologne, the kind that announces itself.

Laura sends another text as the doors open.

Room 1216. Come up.

Of course it's the twelfth floor. Of course my legs feel like they belong to someone who got hit by a bus.

I follow the hall signs past ice machines and muffled TV laughter, past one door where somebody's arguing in Spanish like rent is due tomorrow. I hear the crying before I reach 1216. High. Desperate. I hesitate. I am not exactly a calming presence. But I knock anyway.

Locks click. The door swings open. Laura's hair is shoved into a messy bun, her face shiny like she's been fighting for her life. She's got Kyng on her hip, brown skin warm and damp with effort, his little fists punching the air like he's trying to take down the entire city.

Roman's behind her, barefoot in sweats, making a bottle with the grim focus men only have when they're terrified of messing up. Even covered in formula with a burp cloth draped over his chiseled chest, the man is still offensively fine.

"Grab diapers," says Laura.

That's the greeting.

Not, *Oh my gosh you're alive.* Not, *What happened?*

I blink like an idiot. "Hey to you too."

"In the bag," she says, shifting Kyng from one hip to the

other, bouncing hard. "He just did a diaper situation that should be illegal."

Kyng lets out a scream that rattles the air.

Roman glances toward the hall like he's checking for witnesses. "He's been on one since Ohio," he says.

"Since the womb," Laura mutters.

I step inside and shut the door. The room is warm with that hotel air that never smells like outside. There's a stroller parked near the window, a pile of baby stuff on the chair, tiny socks on the desk like they came complimentary.

Laura moves across the space, pointing without looking. "Wipes too."

I find the bag on the bed, unzip it, and pass over diapers and wipes like I'm part of the pit crew.

Laura takes them with a tight nod. "Thank you."

That's the hug I get.

Roman twists the cap on the bottle and tests it on his wrist.

"Okay, sir," he tells Kyng, voice calm, "we're gonna eat. We're gonna chill. We're gonna stop acting like you pay bills."

Kyng answers with a shriek.

Laura disappears into the bathroom with him, still bouncing, still moving. Roman shakes the bottle like it's a science experiment, giving me a quick scan: the bob, designer dress, stiletto boots.

"You look rough," he says, which is something coming from him.

"Thank you," I say. "I was going for haunted."

He gives a small grunt that might be a laugh.

"Where are Maddie and Eli?" I ask.

"There's a game room downstairs," Laura calls from the bathroom. "Maddie's in charge."

Roman gives me a blunt look. "She's eleven."

"She's responsible," Laura snaps. "And she's got eyes."

Roman glowers as he tidies up some of the mess, the way men often do when they know they've already lost a debate.

"I'm actually glad Griffin postponed Jamaica," Laura adds. "The kids needed this."

"I didn't," Roman says under his breath.

I stand with my hands hanging useless at my sides, trying to figure out where to put all the panic I carried up the elevator. It's still in my chest, heavy and unsorted, like it doesn't trust the air in this room to hold it.

Laura returns with Kyng on her shoulder, patting his back. He's still fussing, his whole body taut like a tiny bowstring, outraged at life and gravity and the audacity of being tired. She passes him to Roman, then looks over like she's seeing me for the first time.

"Did you eat?"

My mouth opens. Nothing comes out fast enough.

She turns to the little counter near the TV where there's a bag and a couple plastic containers, digs around, and pulls out a small wrapped thing. "Here." She shoves it into my hands.

It's some kind of grain bowl. Brown rice or quinoa, chicken, greens, something that looks like it was grown by people who drink green juice for fun.

"Oh," I say, staring at it.

"Don't start. Eat."

I nod and sit at the desk. I suppose Langston's made worse.

Roman sits on the edge of the bed with the bottle, trying to angle it into Kyng's mouth. Kyng turns his head away like he's offended.

Laura drops into the chair by the window with a sigh.

"Let me tell you something," she says. "That drive was demonic. Kyng screamed for forty-five minutes straight. The hotel parking situation is a scam. The elevator took seven business days. And Roman snores like a lawn mower."

"I do not," Roman says.

"You do," Laura says. "And it's personal."

She's talking fast, complaining like it's oxygen, skirting around the thing sitting in my throat. The scandal. My face on the news. My name in strangers' mouths. Not asking how was opening night. Not questioning what's surely all over social media. Instead, she keeps her voice normal on purpose. Like if she talks to me the way she always does, I'll remember how to be a person instead of a headline.

My hands shake as I peel back the lid and take a bite. And it's not awful.

"Okay," I mutter, chewing. "This is annoyingly decent."

"See," she says, pointing at me. "Growth."

For half a second, Kyng latches, a small, fragile miracle, and the room leans in. Then he pops off with a scream sharp enough to break the moment in half, like the bottle betrayed him.

Roman stills, eyes flicking from the milk back to him. "Bro."

I swallow another bite. Hunger clocked out hours ago, but something eases anyway. Food settles in my stomach, like my body's finally willing to believe I'm allowed to stay upright.

Laura watches me a beat longer than she needs to. "Talk to me."

There it is. The acknowledgment. The awareness of my life imploding all over TMZ.

"I don't even know where to start."

Her eyes narrow, focused. "Start with what you're afraid of."

I give them the short, brutal version. The cameras rolling. Detectives flashing badges while the lobby watched. Hours at the precinct answering the same damn questions.

My throat goes dry as I lift a shoulder. "I'm scared I'm gonna get arrested."

Roman snorts, trying to get Kyng to take the bottle again. "Okay. But what did you actually do?"

I frown. "Excuse me?"

"What did you do that's illegal?"

"I impersonated a celebrity. Lived in her apartment. Took her money. I went on stage as her. My face was on the news. *My face.*"

Roman holds up a finger like he's counting. "You didn't steal money."

"Yes, I did."

"No," he says, steady. "You got paid for labor. You did a job. You didn't hack a bank."

I open my mouth, then close it.

He keeps going like he's building a case in court while a baby screams in his arms. "You didn't fake documents. You didn't cash her checks. You didn't lock someone in a basement."

Kyng wails, tiny fists swinging like he's about to file charges.

Roman nods at him. "Thank you. Exactly."

Laura covers her mouth with a laugh, worn out and helpless.

"That's not a crime," Roman says. "That's a mess."

Mess.

The word hits different than *fraud*. I hate that my chest loosens a little.

"Then why do *I* feel like the mess?" I ask.

"Because you're the one standing in it," says Laura.

"Messes feel worse when you're inside 'em. From the outside, it just looks human." Roman shifts Kyng against his shoulder, still fighting for his life.

The baby turns away hard, unleashing a scream like Roman offered him poison. Laura's chair scrapes back.

"Give him here."

Relief crosses Roman's face as he passes Kyng over, looking like sleep has been optional for years. Laura pulls the baby close and lets her body take over, shoulder to shoulder. But the baby keeps fussing, unconvinced.

Watching her handle it, watching her body move with this practiced strength, makes something in me crack.

Laura has survived.

I've watched her rebuild herself with bare hands, public heartbreak, private humiliation, reinvention that cost her more than she admits. She did it anyway. She still shows up with snacks and plans and a baby on her hip.

And I'm over here acting like one scandal is the end of the world. Which makes me wanna scream, because it feels like the end of *my* world.

"It might not have been my idea," I say, shaking my head, "but I signed up for this chaos. Settled for being a counterfeit when I knew it could blow up in my face. I was desperate."

"You were passionate," Roman says. "And passionate people go after their dreams, no matter the cost."

"There's not a person on this earth more passionate than you," Laura adds.

I let out a breath that's half laugh, half self-drag. "Yeah. Passionate and foolish."

All of them flash through my mind. Noah and Adrien. Bryant. Jarel. Same smirk. Same laugh.

"Buying the same damn lie every time."

Laura rests a hand on my shoulder, her concerned eyes searching mine.

"Yana, what's going on? Did something else happen?"

What hasn't happened?

The detectives. The shutdown. Alexia walking back in like she never left. Noah slithering up beside me like he'd been waiting for a cue. And the worst part, Langston's silence.

I shake my head, but my eyes burn anyway. "I'm just... tired."

Just like Alexia. But in a different way. Tired of being overlooked. Tired of being the joke.

"Tired of always being last."

"Last according to who?" Laura asks.

So I tell them. About Langston's loaded confession. About Alexia's return. That painful split-second he hesitated when she came at me. That pause.

Roman nods slow, processing. Laura's face tightens a little.

"And he didn't come after you?" she asks.

"He's been calling," I say. "But I don't wanna talk to him. It's enough. I'm always trying to hear everyone else out. But who's listening to me?"

Silence settles between us. Kyng keeps fussing like he's got commentary.

"But didn't you say he loosened up because of you?" Laura says gently. "That he opened up when it counted?"

For a second, I can't tell if I'm mad at her... or scared she's right.

I think about the way he looked at me when that interviewer asked whether he'd fallen. How he kissed me in the spotlight. Showed up for me backstage before that very first rehearsal. Invited me into the warmth of his home when I had nowhere else to go.

I nod.

"And from what I hear," Roman adds, "he's not the impulsive type. Some people fight loud. Some people think first."

I look at him. Roman's spent years choreographing egos in Hollywood. He knows what it means to pause instead of explode.

"Yeah, but that's not the point," I say. "I might cut up sometimes, but I'm not a child. I don't wanna keep having to earn my spot."

"Then don't," Laura says.

The simplicity almost pisses me off. Like, *Oh, okay, cool, I'll just uninstall insecurity real quick.*

But Stella's voice echoes anyway.

Take up the room.

Kyng's crying spikes again.

"He doesn't want this," Laura sighs, setting the bottle aside. "Roman, take him."

"Not me," Roman says, hands up. "He thinks I'm a villain."

Laura's shoulders drop as she looks at me, a tired smile tugging at her mouth.

"Give him to me," I say before I can second-guess it.

Roman's brows lift like he's surprised I volunteered for combat.

Kyng is warm when Laura places him in my arms, furious too,

his whole body vibrating with protest. At first, I'm all wrong angles and nerves. Then muscle memory kicks in. I pull him closer, adjust my hold, let instinct take over. Same way I used to when Maddie and Eli were little.

"Sir," I whisper, "you are being *extremely* dramatic."

His cry hiccups. Then this tiny sound slips out that isn't a cry.

It's a laugh. A full-out baby belly laugh.

Laura's mouth falls open. Roman stares like he just witnessed magic.

Kyng laughs again, softer, like he's proud of himself.

"Why did that work?" I stare down at him, stunned.

Laura wipes under one eye, smiling like she's trying not to cry. "Because you're you. You always have been."

Yeah. I guess so.

Kyng rests his cheek against me like he's decided the world might be survivable. Something in me loosens, just a little. A crack in the shame.

"I don't have anywhere to go," I say, flat, almost casual.

"You're sleeping here," Laura says without hesitation.

Roman's eyes go wide. "Babe—"

"Don't," she snaps. "It's not like we're booking her a room."

He lifts his hands. "We are at maximum capacity. Two kids and a very impatient baby."

"And we just saved money by driving here," she says. "Don't be silly, Roman."

Something muttered slips out of him that sounds like, *I am surrounded by chaos.*

It's settled. Laura's already moving, leading me toward the kids' adjoining suite. Two beds. A couch. She opens the closet, digs, and presses a pillow and blanket into my arms like it's a done deal.

"The kids can share," she says. "You take the other bed."

"I can take the couch."

She looks me over slow. "If you insist. It pulls out. You should be fine."

Fine.

A couch. A borrowed blanket. Somebody else's space.

Still, it beats disappearing.

———

LATER, WHEN THE BABY FINALLY QUIETS, MADDIE SHOWS ME the dance she's been practicing for recital, graceful as ever, and Eli insists on performing a magic trick that absolutely does not work until it finally does. Then I curl on the couch with the blanket tucked under my chin.

Laura and Roman move around next door in low voices, light spilling out when Laura peeks in.

"Love you, cuz," she whispers.

I feel it all the way through. "Love you too. Goodnight."

When the door clicks shut, I pull out my phone. No more texts or apologies. Just silence.

I stare at my reflection in the phone's black glass. Just me. Yana. A nobody again.

My thumb hovers over missed calls.

Daddy.

I hit call.

He picks up on the third ring, voice thick with sleep and worry. "Songbird," he says. "Where you been?"

My eyes burn. I press the phone to my ear like it's an anchor.

"I'm here," I whisper. "I'm still here."

And for the first time in a long time, that feels like a choice.

29

The hotel suite is still dark when I wake. Another gray morning that can't commit.

My body aches in dull, scattered places. I decided to try the pull-out mattress, but it's much too thin. The blanket's twisted around my legs like it never accepted me overnight.

Doesn't matter.

I'm here. I'm safe. I'm warm.

From the adjoining suite, Kyng starts up. Sharp, offended cries slicing through the thin hotel wall. Roman groans like a man bargaining with God. A drawer slides. Water runs. Then quiet. I can picture it, Roman pacing, the baby latching this time, the small miracle of something working when it didn't last night.

I roll onto my side and reach for my phone, still clinging to the tiniest morsel of hope. Instead of Langston's apology message, the headline's waiting for me like a trap.

ALEXIA HYRD RETURNS TO BROADWAY
OPENING SET FOR NEXT WEEK

Next week.
Not scrapped. Not delayed indefinitely. Just reassigned.
I read the article slowly, like if I don't rush, it might change.

Producers confirm Alexia Hyrd will resume the role of Ella following a brief hiatus. Rehearsals to resume immediately.

Resume.

Like a paused recording. Like I was never there at all.

I can feel the pinch behind my ribs, but I don't cry. The hurt is sharper than that. Cleaner.

Across the room, Maddie's sprawled sideways on one of the beds, one leg dangling off like gravity caught her mid-dream. Eli's in the other bed lying on his side, a soft halo of curly, afro-like hair partially flattened like sleep tried and failed to tame it. One with plans to become the next Houdini, the other to dance in the New York City Ballet. I know both of 'em will make it, so long as they don't give up.

My sigh is just loud enough to wake Eli. He shifts, blinking blearily, squints at me like he's still deciding whether I'm real.

"Mommy showed me you singing," he says, his 7-year-old voice thick with sleep. "She said this is your big one."

A soft, bitter chuckle escapes me. Until recently, I thought so too.

Eli rubs his eye with a fist, then smiles, proud like he's in on a secret. "Your destiny."

Destiny.

The word hits me square in the chest.

He doesn't know. He doesn't know anything changed. He just knows what he saw, what he felt, what made sense to him.

I think about the lights, the music swelling, the audience leaning in when I opened my mouth. I think about the way the stage felt under my feet, solid, demanding, alive.

I didn't imagine that.

"Yeah," I say quietly, more to myself than him.

Eli nods once and rolls back over, already drifting back to sleep.

From next door, Kyng lets out a small, content sound, milk-drunk and calm, and Roman murmurs something low and relieved. The world settles again.

Little Eli is right. I didn't borrow a dream. I showed up. I sang. Carried something that was falling apart and made it stand long enough for everyone else to breathe.

I used my voice.

I sit up slowly, phone heavy. I pull up Langston's message again.

I should've said something.

The carpet is cold when my feet hit the floor. I let its firmness ground me, then go in search of a toothbrush.

I know who I am. I know what I did.

And I refuse to let this get rewritten like it never happened.

———

THE AIR OUTSIDE THE THEATER TASTES LIKE EXHAUST AND OLD rain.

It's too early for this many cameras, too early for this many opinions. But the sidewalk is already stacked with bodies and lenses like they camped out overnight waiting to watch me lose.

Flash. Flash.

"Yana! Over here!"

"Jayana! Were you paid under a fake name?"

"Was Alexia locked up somewhere?"

Less than twelve hours ago, I was zipped into silk with a sculpted bob sharp enough to cut glass. Now my curls hang damp across my shoulders, still smelling faintly of Laura's coconut shampoo. Her sweater swallows my wrists. The jeans sit lower on my waist, but they'll do.

I keep my chin up and my pace steady. But my stomach is doing that slow, nauseous roll it does when I know I'm walking into a room that's already decided who I am. My borrowed boots hit the pavement in a tight rhythm.

Click. Click. Click.

A woman in a wool coat looks me up and down like I'm gum on her heel. A guy with a mic grins like he can't believe his luck.

"Do you feel guilty?"

"Are you going to apologize?"

I don't answer. If I speak, they'll cut the audio into whatever shape fits their story. Being Alexia taught me that. If I stay quiet, I'm easier to erase.

The security guard at the stage door steps forward before I even reach the awning. His eyes flick over my face, then past me. "Uh, no."

I stop. The flashes keep going behind me, a stuttering storm. The heat of the crowd at my back, my name getting chewed up into headlines.

"I work here," I say, voice even.

He lifts his hands, almost apologetic, but not enough to be kind. "Not without clearance."

A laugh pops from somewhere in the pack, and it slices right through my ribs. Like I'm a guest who overstayed her welcome. Like I didn't keep this entire production on life support with my throat and my spine.

I take my phone out with fingers that wanna shake and refuse to give them the satisfaction. My screen is a mess of notifications and tabloid banners. I ignore all of it and go straight to Julian.

You're not gonna let me in?

Three dots appear. Disappear. Reappear. Then his message hits.

One sec.

The guard's phone buzzes a moment later. He reads it, and his posture shifts like somebody yanked his leash.

"Go ahead," he mutters, finally stepping aside.

I move fast. Past the line I never thought I'd have to cross again, past the whispering mouths and sharp eyes, past the cameras still angling for one last shot of my defeat.

They don't get a say. Not anymore.

I pull open the back doors, and the sound drops off like a curtain falling.

The theater smells like dust, hairspray, coffee that's been sitting too long, and the faint metallic bite of stage paint.

Home.

For half a second, my chest loosens, like my body's hoping to stay for a while.

The stage at the front of the auditorium is lit, unforgiving and clear. Alexia's standing under the work lights like she never left, hair done, posture locked in, that celebrity calm wrapped around her like a coat.

Langston's standing next to her, their shoulders almost touching, and he's angled toward her in a way that feels private. Easy. Familiar.

When she looks up, he turns and sees me. Something shifts in his face. He takes a step toward the edge of the stage, then stops short.

What Noah said creeps in before I can shove it away:

She was over Langston a long time ago. Just didn't know how to break it off.

So why is he still by her side?

Then Eli's sleepy little voice flashes through me, bright and pure as sunlight.

Your destiny.

I swallow the questions fast. I can't focus on it now. I've got a point to make. I'm not here for him. I'm here for me.

The aisle feels longer than it ever has, like every step is a dare. Seats stretch out on either side of me in neat, endless rows, an empty that still feels crowded because Broadway theaters remember. They hold secrets. They hold judgment, and they don't forget who flinched.

Cast members are scattered in the house and near the front, some practicing, some chatting, others scrolling their phones. But the minute they clock me, the air changes.

There's a hush, not total but tight. People look away fast, like if they don't meet my eyes they don't have to pick a side. On stage, heads turn.

I'm sure Gracie's already annoyed with Alexia being back, but my arrival doesn't help. She stands with her heels planted, arms crossed, chin lifted like she's offended I'm breathing her air.

Alexia and Langston are still staring at me, a ghost in their happily ever after. And I force myself to shake the memories.

The keyboard. The Ferris wheel. The bird.

Julian's in the front row with Kai at his side, his notebook open, scarf slightly crooked, one leg bouncing like he's been running on fumes for weeks. He's mid-sentence calling notes up to the stage when he sees me, and the bounce stops.

I reach him fast, voice already climbing out of me. "Julian," I say. "I'm not gonna back down that easily. I've been working too hard and too long to just—"

He lifts a hand, stopping me short.

"I know," he says, glancing up at the stage. "But this isn't about me."

My breath thins as he nods toward the cast.

"You've gotta convince them."

The words feel like a shove and a gift at the same time. Because it's no different than it's always been. Even if Julian wants me here, I still have to survive the room.

Julian stands and claps once, hard enough to snap the air.

"Eyes up," he calls, and everyone who already hasn't freezes.

Langston's still watching me. And Alexia's watching him.

Julian rests a hand on my shoulder. "I want you all to hear her out."

"We can't afford to waste any more time," says Charlotte, rolling her eyes.

"We're gonna make time," Julian bites back, stepping into the aisle, voice carrying into the house like he means it. "Because if any one of you were standing where she is right now, you'd want the same."

Silence.

Then reluctant shifting. Regan exhales. Charlotte mutters under her breath. Just like Gracie, most of them are irritated but not brave enough to fight Julian on it. Kai gives a small reassuring nod, and everyone relents.

My heartbeat is so loud I can feel it behind my eyes as Julian nudges me into the light. I take a breath and force my voice to stay steady.

"I am not Alexia Hyrd," I say, meeting the original's eyes. "I'm Jayana Gardner. And whether you like how I got here or not, I'm here."

The words taste like metal and truth. My tongue wants to retreat because I can feel what they think I am: a lie, a stunt, a mistake that got too big and too public.

Stella stands at the edge of the stage, arms crossed but gaze unwavering. A warm, gentle grin on her face.

So I don't let my voice tremble. Not now.

"I've been broke, homeless, scared, alone, and I still showed up," I say. "Not because I was playing pretend. But because this dream is mine. Just as much as it is yours."

Members of the cast and crew stand back, stone-faced, like they haven't heard a word. But I'm not leaving until I've said my peace.

"I know what it looks like," I continue, letting the confession sit in the air. "I know some of you feel blindsided. Betrayed. Like you've been pulled into a story you didn't agree to be part of."

I let my gaze slide, daring Langston's eyes to meet mine.

"And I know how that feels."

My pulse pounds, but I keep going, because I can't be silent anymore.

"And I'm sorry," I say. "I'm sorry you weren't given the full picture. I'm sorry you were asked to trust me without being given the chance to decide if I was worth trusting."

I swallow, forcing the next part out clean.

"But I belong here."

The word *belong* cracks something open in my chest. 'Cause it's the one thing I've been afraid to claim out loud.

I've always wanted this room, this stage, this life. But wanting it and deserving it aren't the same thing. Not in their eyes. And up until now, maybe not even in mine.

"I didn't fall into this role," I say, voice steadying as I feel the theater listening. "I stepped into it when it was falling apart. Bled for this in ways you'll never see on a playbill. I held this show up when it was wobbling. Showed up when it would've been easier to disappear."

My gaze rests on Alexia, but she won't look at me now. I make myself look at each castmate, even if they won't look back. I make myself stand in the discomfort like it's a spotlight I earned.

"I'm no Alexia," I say, softer now, stronger for it. "But I can save this show. I *will* save this show. Hell, I already have."

The words hit the theater and echo back. Somebody starts to clap but stops.

Julian's face shifts and he stands straighter. "She's right," he says. "And all of us know it."

A few people stare at him like he just betrayed them, but I keep going because if I stop, I'll fold.

My eyes find Langston without permission. Because while this is about the show, I wanna make something clear.

"I've been a mess at times, I know," I say, holding his gaze. "Because I *did* fumble. Sometimes I goofed off at the wrong time. Fooled around when I was scared. But I get it now."

He inhales, and something in me settles.

"Talent isn't enough," I say, voice firm. "But when I focus, I sure as hell deliver. And if no one else will give me my flowers, I will. Because I owe that to myself."

Langston's throat bobs, but he says nothing. The silence after my last word is loud enough to hurt.

Gracie lets out a little laugh, almost casual but edged with something mean. "You've gotta be kidding me. Most of us worked our asses off to be here. This clown just showed up and expects applause."

A few people shift like they've been waiting for someone to say it first.

It stings. Not because she's wrong about the work. They did work. So did I. But because I know how this looks from the outside. Like I skipped the line. Like I slipped through a crack meant for someone else.

My hands curl at my sides. I've already claimed my name tonight. I'm not about to let her reduce it to a punchline one more time. I open my mouth to set her straight.

"Her name is Yana."

Langston's voice isn't loud. It doesn't need to be. The room stills anyway.

He doesn't look at Gracie. He looks at me.

"And she earned her spot here."

For a second, I'm caught in his gaze, the steadiness of it. The certainty.

Charlotte huffs, exhausted. "That's not what we're arguing. At least not me anyway. It's about what this does to the show. The press is already spinning it."

Kai leans forward slightly in her seat, hands clasped. "We can't ignore the fallout. This isn't just about rehearsal anymore."

There it is. The real concern. Not talent. Exposure. Risk.

I feel that old reflex spark. The one that says step back. Smooth it over. Make it easier for them. But I won't. Not anymore.

Langston speaks before I can.

"If the show can't survive the truth," he says evenly, "then we've got bigger problems than headlines."

He's standing center stage now, shoulders squared, gaze steady. I've seen him command a room before. I've seen him exacting and controlled in rehearsal. I haven't seen him like this in front of all of them. Not when it comes to me.

Why is he coming to my defense when the woman he's wanted all along is standing right there?

"She did the job," he continues, his gaze moving from Gracie to Charlotte to Kai sitting in the front row. "All of you saw it. Every night. Every rehearsal. Every note."

He lets that hang.

"We don't get to erase that because it's inconvenient."

Silence spreads slow this time. Charlotte's eyes drop first. Of course, Gracie rolls hers.

Stella shifts her weight and nods. "She did carry us," she says, soft but clear.

A stagehand near the back clears his throat. "We would've shut down."

"I saw her in rehearsal," Regan mutters after a beat. "She didn't quit. Not once."

It isn't applause. It's acknowledgment. And for the first time since I walked through those doors, I don't feel like I'm standing alone.

Then a harsher voice cuts through. "Let's not forget she was hooking up backstage while all this was going down."

The words slice across the house, sharp enough to redirect the entire room. Heads turn. I feel it before I see it, the way blame looks for somewhere soft to land.

Noah's hovering near the wings. I catch his eye and hold it. He knows exactly why. I'm done protecting anybody who plays in my face. If he doesn't open his mouth first, I will.

Luckily for him, he steps forward before I do.

"Listen," he calls to everyone. "This isn't on her."

The shift is immediate. Confusion ripples through the cast. Even I'm surprised by his boldness.

Noah swallows once.

"Yana told me to back off," he says. "She ended it... Alexia didn't."

Gasps break loose. Eyes bounce from Alexia to Noah to

Langston. He's the only one not looking around. Langston's gaze stays locked on Noah, steady and simmering.

"Why would you do that?" Langston asks.

"You cut my solo in *The Golden Prince*," says Noah, not backing down. "Made me look like an ass."

For a second I almost laugh. I thought my bruised ego was dramatic. I still can't believe he set this much on fire over a song.

Langston doesn't flinch. "I made a call for the show."

"You made a call that cost me!" Noah shouts across the stage. "You didn't even look back."

Alexia lets out a light scoff, brittle and disbelieving. "So you just slept with me to get back at Langston?"

Langston casts her a side glance. She takes a small step back without meaning to.

Noah lifts a shoulder at her like none of this weighs a thing. "You needed a distraction. I needed leverage. It wasn't complicated."

Mouths hang wider with every sentence.

"I just needed a break," Alexia says, nervously glancing round. "It was never about him!"

"You made that clear," says Noah, a sly gleam in his eye. "Again and again and again..."

The cast can't stop gasping, hands flying to mouths, heads swinging from stage left to stage right like they're watching a tennis match.

Julian raises a hand to stop them as if it's just another rehearsal. He blinks at Julian, baffled. "You knew who Yana was?"

Noah looks at me and nods. But his gaze keeps shifting between me and the front row, like he's calculating fallout in real time.

"That stuff that hit social... the affair with Julian, some of those viral videos..." His eyes shift again. "Kai was feeding it out. I helped amplify it. That part was on me."

A whisper breaks loose "What?"

The room explodes.

Kai doesn't move as she stares at Noah. Just sits still, like if she holds her posture long enough the accusation will miss.

"It was supposed to hit Alexia. Not her," says Noah, pulling his gaze from Kai back to me. "But Kai didn't know the truth about who she was. At least, at first."

My eyes draw shut as the memory clicks into place.

Raised voices. My dressing room. Kai's face when she stepped inside.

I turn to Kai, and my voice surprises me with how level it sounds. "You tried to kill me?"

"Not you." Her eyes flick to Alexia. "Her."

The house recoils. Whispers crash over each other, desperate to rearrange what they just heard. Alexia looks at Kai like the floor just shifted under her feet.

"You were trying to kill *me?*"

Kai lets out a small, humorless laugh.

"After Week Two? After you iced me out in front of the entire team like I was some intern you didn't recognize?" Her gaze never leaves Alexia. "You built your whole career off people like me, then acted like we didn't exist."

The room stills in a different way now. Quieter. I catch Gracie's eye up on stage. I understand that feeling more than I care to admit. I've wanted to swing on her a couple times myself. I just never let her drag me that far off my square. She looks away first.

"I handled your press. I spun your messes. Kept your name clean when you were unraveling behind closed doors." Kai's face scrunches tight, but her voice stays steady. "And the second you felt better, you treated me like I was disposable."

There it is again. *Disposable.* The word curdles in my gut.

Alexia's composure slips, just a fraction.

Kai stands slowly. "People like you float because people like me hold you up. You don't get to pretend we're nothing."

Chaos breaks loose. Voices layer over each other, hands

waving, bodies shifting. Langston moves without thinking, stepping in front of Alexia. She folds in behind him, smaller than I've ever seen her.

"Security!" Julian calls. He looks at Noah and Kai. "You're done. Both of you. Effective immediately."

Guards rush in from the back as if they've been waiting for a cue.

"And you'll be hearing from our lawyers," Langston adds, calm enough to quiet the room.

Kai's clipboard hits the floor with a hollow crack as the guards take her by the arms. She doesn't fight. Just stares at Alexia with a sharp little gleam in her eye. The kind that says this isn't finished, even if the room thinks it is.

I bet homegirl's grateful she disappeared when she did.

Still, watching Kai get dragged out like this twists something in me. Maybe if she'd said what she felt before it curdled into revenge, nothing would've gone this far.

They reach for Noah next. He doesn't resist either. Just looks at me instead.

"It wasn't fake," he says. "Not with you."

I frown. "That doesn't make it right."

He's still staring as they usher him out, but I won't watch him go.

And still, the mess remains.

Everyone turns to Alexia like the room has one final debt to collect.

She gathers herself the way she always does, chin steady, shoulders aligned.

"I left," she says. "No one took me. No one trapped me. I walked away."

A ripple moves through the cast.

"I wasn't ill... but I wasn't okay," she continues, voice even. "And I didn't handle that well. I thought if I pushed harder, performed harder, kept smiling through it, my body would fall in line."

Her gaze flicks briefly to Langston. Then to me. Only we know what that actually cost.

"I wasn't kidnapped or being manipulated," she says. "I made decisions. Some of them were reckless."

Reckless. Between the steroids. Noah. Julian. Felipe. That's a generous edit. Homegirl left a whole hurricane in my dressing room and dipped.

She takes a controlled breath.

"When Julian and Langston couldn't reach Yana last night, they didn't know what to do. Investors were nervous. The press was circling. I agreed to step in temporarily to stabilize things." She pauses. "Temporarily."

The word stretches, fragile and shimmering, like something suspended on a thread. For weeks, I've been bracing for the moment she'd take it back. The stage. The spotlight. Him. I've trained my body not to get too comfortable in borrowed spaces.

But *temporarily* doesn't feel like a countdown. It feels like a door cracking open. And for the first time, I let myself imagine walking through it without looking over my shoulder.

The cast listens now. No phones. No whispers.

"I wasn't here to reclaim anything," she says. "I was here because the show needed a body on stage while we figured out what to do. The same way she did for me."

Alexia's gaze meets mine.

"I asked her," says Langston stepping toward me. "When I couldn't reach you. I thought it was the only way to save what we'd built."

What *we'd* built.

The words hit somewhere tender I'm still pretending doesn't exist. I'm still mad. I should be. But hearing him say it like that, in front of everyone, does something dangerous to my resolve.

He isn't looking at the cast now. He's looking at me. *Only me.*

Maybe they're not back together after all?

Alexia nods once.

"But I've seen the footage," she says, turning to me fully. "I've read the reviews. And I've heard Langston."

Her throat moves as she swallows.

"You saved this show, Yana."

My throat burns as I digest the thought. Being seen after trying so hard not to be. Every member of the cast and crew's eyes are on me now.

"I'm not sorry I got help," Alexia says, her voice just above a whisper. She gives me a crooked grin. "But I am sorry for leaving all this on you."

Her gaze sweeps the cast.

"On all of you."

The cast and crew ripple with murmurs and shaking heads. But she raises a hand signaling she's not done.

"And I'm not interested in fighting for something I walked away from."

She and Langston exchange a look, the way artists do after the curtain falls. Measured. Respectful. A second too long to be casual but not long enough to be anything else. Whatever they were hangs between them for a beat. Then it fades.

A few heads lift. Stella exhales slow. Nothing dramatic, but final.

Langston doesn't move toward Alexia when she steps down from the stage. Doesn't reach for her or say a word. And for the first time since I heard him say her name, there's no conflict in his face.

Julian steps back beside me. "We vote. Right now. We're not doing this in whispers and side-eyes for another week."

People shift, uneasy. Gracie's arms are crossed so tight she looks close to snapping.

"All in favor of keeping Yana in the company and continuing with her in the role until opening?"

Hands rise. Not together. But steady. One. Two. Five. Ten. More. It isn't unanimous, but it's clear. My heart lifts when Langston raises his hand too.

Julian looks to Gracie, still unmoved.

"Noted." He claps once. "Good. Fifteen minutes. Then we get back to work."

The cast disperses in pockets of low conversation, the energy in the theater still buzzing. People move with purpose now. Rehearsal mode. Survival mode.

Show must go on.

I turn with them. *Work*. That's what I'm here for. If I stay moving, I don't have to feel anything cracking open under my ribs.

I don't look at Langston again. I can't. Not yet. Not while my pulse is still climbing and my name still feels different in this room. I take three steps toward the door.

"Yana! Wait!"

He says my name like he's afraid I won't answer.

I close my eyes for half a second before I turn. Because I won't run. I won't chase. But I know he'd want me to hear him out too.

He's already coming down the side steps, fast. As if the distance between us is unacceptable. He doesn't slow down till he reaches me. Stops close enough that if I lean forward, we'd collide.

"I'm sorry," he says, without taking a breath. "For everything that's happened. Last night, I thought if I reacted the wrong way, I'd make it worse. Hurt you. Hurt her. Hurt the show."

His voice tightens just slightly.

"I forgot that silence can hurt just as much."

I stand back and cross my arms. Because that's gutted me more than anything else. Not Alexia. Not the press. The quiet.

"I don't need you to manage disasters," I say carefully. "I need you to stand next to me when they happen."

He nods once like he couldn't agree more. "I thought if I stayed in control, no one else would get hurt," he says. "But I was wrong. You weren't asking me to control anything. You were asking me to choose."

I swallow. "And what if choosing costs you something?" I ask.

I don't say it. He knows what I mean. His reputation. The show. The Tonys.

He levels his gaze with mine.

"Then it costs me," he says, voice low. "What's the point of winning if you're not standing beside me?"

My heart stutters so hard it almost makes me angry. I've spent so much time bracing for the opposite. Bracing for the moment he'd look at me and see compromise. Risk. A place-holder until something shinier came back.

"I ain't no backup plan," I say. It comes out quieter than I expect. "I'm not the body you put onstage while you chase something bigger."

"You're not," he says, moving closer.

But I hold up a hand. "Let me finish."

I've done this enough times in my life. Withered mid-sentence. Relaxed to make others comfortable. Not today.

"I won't dissolve into your dream," I tell him. "I won't be convenient. I won't be manageable. If we do this, I'm standing beside you. Not behind you. Not on standby. Beside."

The space between us hums. His gaze grows soft with under-standing.

"From that first audition, I knew you were meant to be out front."

The warm certainty in his voice leaves me without a comeback.

For a second, I forget how to defend myself. I've spent so long fighting to prove that. It's a struggle to simply receive it.

"I don't know who I am without the work," he says slowly. "And that scares me."

I bob my head. Setting aside parts of your identity for someone else can be scary.

"But I know who I am with you." His eyes hold mine, and something old and ugly inside me loosens. The part that believes love is a competition. That I have to outperform someone to keep it. That if I stop dazzling, I'll be replaced.

But right now, he isn't looking past me. He isn't glancing toward the stage. He isn't measuring outcomes. He's here.

And I realize something terrifying and beautiful at the same time.

I already chose him. I chose him when I stood in that spotlight and didn't look away.

"And I'm sorry," he repeats. "For not being more transparent. For not opening up more. For thinking I could calculate my way through something that wasn't a calculation."

I hesitate for a second as his warm brown eyes search mine.

"For not speaking up when you needed me to."

My heart kicks hard. "I needed to speak up for myself."

He nods like that both hurts and heals.

"Then maybe I should too." His voice drops, steady and certain. "I'm in love with you, Jayana Gardner. No doubt about it."

Everything in me pauses. The fear. The fight. The guard. "You serious?"

That handsome smile graces his lips. "I've been serious since that first kiss."

I release a humored breath, full of healing and tears. "I'm in love with you too."

He leans in, and I meet his lips right in the center of the aisle, the stage still lit, the truth still hanging in the air.

His mouth moves against mine with a quiet urgency that steals the breath from my lungs. Weeks of restraint burn off in seconds. I feel it in the way his fingers flex at my back. In the way he pulls me closer instead of asking permission.

I kiss him back just as hard. Because I'm not being chosen out of convenience. I'm being chosen on purpose.

Somewhere, someone whistles. Julian claps once like we just nailed an eleven o'clock number.

When we finally break, my forehead rests against Langston's. I'm still shaking. But it isn't fear. It's possibility.

"Go to work," I tell him, smiling despite myself.

"Yes, ma'am." He squeezes my hand once before letting go.

And this time when I head for my dressing room, I don't feel like I'm borrowing anything. Not the spotlight. Not the role. Not the man.

This future is mine.

My destiny.

30

I t's opening night.

Outside the theater, the marquee burns bright enough to make the whole block look like a movie set. Spotlights rake across the sky in slow, indulgent sweeps like the night itself is dressed up for us. A velvet rope curves along the sidewalk, corralling a crowd that's buzzing and laughing and holding up phones, offering them to the gods.

Glitter. Flash. Anticipation.

I can picture it. Through the doors, past the gilded lobby where the air smells like perfume and champagne, donors and theater kids and tourists all jammed together under chandeliers, their voices bouncing off marble like excited birds. Ushers in crisp uniforms guiding people with practiced smiles. A few familiar faces hovering near the wall, pretending not to scan for investors. They're still uneasy.

I know because Julian's been vibrating all day, bones wound so tight I can hear it.

But they agreed to tonight.

One more shot.

Julian and Langston did what they do best: turned chaos into choreography. They sat in too many meetings, smiled too hard, spoke in numbers and buzzwords and confidence, telling the investors the truth dressed up in the right outfit.

Yana saved the show.

And then they made it impossible to deny.

Alexia and the cast even put together a video. Alexia in the center, eyes glossy, voice firm, the whole ensemble behind her like a wall.

We support her. We believe in her. We believe in the show.

I didn't see the investors clap. But I heard the shift in the building when the final decision came down, the way everyone stopped holding their breath and finally exhaled.

Now, backstage, the air is electric. It's hairspray and hot lights and the faint chemical tang of stage fog. It's the squeak of dance shoes and the snap of headset mics. Wardrobe racks rolling, actors weaving around each other in half-costume, and every person moving like they've got a purpose stitched to their spine. Someone laughs too loud. Someone else is already crying. The building feels alive, like the theater itself is breathing.

Up the hall, past the double doors, down a narrow stretch where the wallpaper is worn, a stagehand sprints past with a prop that looks fragile and priceless, a dresser following close like a mother hen, hissing, "Careful, careful!" And there's my dressing room.

My dressing room.

My name isn't on the door. Not yet. The name taped there is still hers. But the room knows me now.

My reflection stares back at me. Got the lashes. Got the contour. The mouth that looks like it knows how to own a room. Sure, I may look like her. But I'm not her.

The counter's cluttered with makeup brushes and bobby pins and a half-empty bottle of setting spray. The bulbs around the mirror throw a flattering glow that almost convinces me I'm not shaking.

And people keep opening the door. They pop in like I'm good luck. Like if they touch this moment, some of it will rub off.

"Break a leg," Regan says first, leaning in with that same swagger she has everywhere she stands. She's already in costume, radiant, ready to devour the stage. She holds up a hand, and we slap fives.

"Break both," I shoot back, and she grins. There's respect in her eyes now.

More faces come.

A dancer from the ensemble squeezes my shoulder. "You got this."

A dresser gives me a thumbs up. "You look gorgeous. Like, gorgeous."

"For real," says Mateo, Noah's understudy, stepping in dressed like Prince Santiago already belongs to him. He gives me a small, reverent smile. "You saved our jobs, you know."

I nod, because saying anything would absolutely make me cry, and that's not on the schedule tonight.

Mateo's been killing it in rehearsals and previews. Solid instincts. No ego. And most importantly? A closed-mouth kisser.

When they're gone, Gracie appears.

For a second, my stomach drops out of habit, like my body still remembers being hungry and wrestling her for mustard like we were in some low-budget survival show.

But Gracie doesn't have that lemon face today. She steps in slow, makeup sharp, hair polished and curled, costume perfect. She looks like the kinda woman who never loses. And still, she hesitates.

"Hey," she says, softer than I'm used to.

"Hey," I say, carefully.

She shifts her weight, eyes glance to the mirror, then to me. Her jaw works like she's chewing down pride.

"I'm not gonna lie," she says. "I didn't think you could pull this off."

I keep my face neutral. I'm not about to pretend we're besties. But I do wait.

Gracie exhales through her nose.

"And I still think I could've done it with the right adjustments. If Julian had..." She stops herself like she hears how that sounds tonight, like she realizes it isn't about her.

Then she nods once, decisive.

"But you did it. You pulled all this off. And I can respect that."

It settles inside me like a small, warm weight. Something earned.

I guess that'll do.

"Thanks," I say, and I mean it. Even if part of me wants to be petty.

Gracie's eyes flick to the mirror, then back to me. "Don't screw it up tonight."

She says it like an insult's the only way she knows how to bless someone.

"Break a leg." She turns to leave, pauses at the door, then adds, softer, "For real."

And then she's gone.

I stare after her like I just witnessed a miracle.

Stella comes in next, wrapped in a long charcoal cardigan, silver hair pinned low at her neck. Simply moving like she belongs in every room she enters.

My fairy godmother.

She steps behind me and rests a hand on my shoulder, steady, grounding. "Told you if you spoke up, they'd listen."

We share a warm smile that says everything we've survived to get here. Everything she's watched me fight through. Everything I didn't think I had in me.

"Thank you," I whisper.

Stella squeezes my shoulder once.

"Go be great," she says. Then she slips out like she was never here.

My phone buzzes on the table, breaking the silence. I reach for it without thinking, thumb hovering for a second like I'm afraid whatever's on the screen will make this all too real.

The message opens and my hand flies to my mouth.

A photo. Laura, Roman, Maddie, Eli, Mommy, Daddy, and my brother, all crowded together in the lobby under the chandelier, smiling big like this is a celebration and not a tightrope walk.

Daddy grins wide and proud in a way that makes my chest ache. My brother's got his arm around Mommy like he's holding her steady. And there's a text beneath it.

We're here. We love you. Break a leg!

They all came. Almost all of them. My brother's wife must be watching the baby.

I can't wait for everyone to meet Langston.

My eyes sting so fast I laugh, breathless. 'Cause I can't afford this kind of emotion. Not yet. But it blooms anyway, from the inside out. A warmth that spreads through my ribs like light. Like proof. Like God reaching down and saying, *Yes. This matters.*

I press my fingers to my lips, trying to keep the feelings contained, trying to keep the gratitude from exploding out of me. Tonight, they're out there, watching, believing.

The knock comes again, softer.

Langston.

I catch him in the mirror first, standing at the door like he's waiting for permission. Hands in his pockets. Suit perfect. Glasses catching the light.

And something's shifted in him. He's not tucking away his smile anymore. He's not pretending he's above this. He's somehow, surprisingly chill. Like the man's finally allowing himself to breathe.

Me? I'm a bundle of nerves in filthy overalls. I wring my hands in my lap, staring at him in the mirror instead of directly at his face. Like if I look straight at him, I might unravel.

"Ugh," I groan, bouncing my knee. "You'd think after all those previews, I'd be used to this jittery feeling by now."

I huff out a breath. I really don't wanna screw this up. Not tonight. Not after everything it took to get here.

Langston chuckles softly and pushes off the doorframe. He

strolls over like he's got all the time in the world, comes up behind me, and rests his hands on my shoulders. He starts to massage gently, thumbs working into the knots I didn't even realize I had. And the tension drains out of me like someone pulled a plug.

Mmmph. I could get used to this.

"No matter what happens tonight," he says quietly, voice low, "you're exactly where you were meant to be."

I meet his eyes in the mirror and smile. "Destiny."

He nods once. "Destiny."

Then he leans down and gives me a light kiss. Wouldn't dare ruin the masterpiece my face has going on. But he lets it linger a second longer than necessary. Like he's sealing a truth we've both finally stopped fighting.

"Thank you for saving this show," he murmurs against my lips. "For saving me."

My heart stumbles as he gently rests his forehead against mine, breath warm, grounding.

"Let's knock 'em dead, beautiful."

I cackle, cheeks flushing hot. "You really know how to calm a girl down."

He grins, full and unapologetic, then squeezes my shoulders one last time. He gives me a look that says, *You've got this,* and heads out the door.

I sit alone in my dressing room, staring at myself in the mirror. Hair done. Makeup flawless. Costume fitting just right. I'm breathless and terrified. But ready.

For a second, the world blurs, and I see her. The little girl sitting beside her daddy at the ice-skating rink, watching Princess Jasmine twirl on ice. The one who sang too loud, danced too hard, believed too much. The one who pressed her palms together and wished on stages she hadn't even seen yet.

She's here now. She made it.

I straighten my shoulders and meet my own gaze.

This is it.

———

THE REHEARSAL ROOM HUMS WHEN I STEP INSIDE. BODIES gathered close, that familiar mix of nerves and pride hanging in the air. Then someone spots me, and applause breaks out. Not polite or forced. Real. It swells and wraps around me like a hug.

"Okay, y'all. Stop!" I laugh, fanning my eyes as they water. "You gon' make me mess up my face!"

Everyone laughs, the sound bouncing off the mirrors, cutting through the tension like light. And just like that, it hits me again. This warmth. This belonging.

These people aren't just cast and crew anymore. They're *my* people. Even with the rumors. Even with the fractures. My family.

Long nights. Hard rehearsals. Too much fear and not enough sleep. Somehow, we came out on the other side still standing. I can't imagine being anywhere else.

Julian steps forward, hands at his waist, eyes bright beneath the brim of his cap.

"Alright," he says. "Before we get too emotional and I lose control of the room..."

More laughter.

"We've come a long way in a very short amount of time," he continues, voice settling into something steady and proud. "What we're about to do tonight didn't happen by accident. It happened because every single person in this room showed up. Again and again."

Langston nods beside him, arms folded, gaze sweeping the group.

"Regardless of what happens out there," Langston says, "we'd do it all over again."

"Well. Almost." Julian chuckles, slapping Langston on the back. "Maybe we could skip the scandals and death threats next time, huh?"

Langston's mouth quirks as laughter spreads, easing the last tight edges in the room.

Sometime last week, quietly and without an audience, Langston and Julian finally cleared the air. No theatrics. Just honesty. Apologies where they were owed. Boundaries where they were needed. By the time they stood from the table, the tension was gone, not erased but resolved. Since then, they've moved like a unit again. Focused, aligned, protecting the show and each other. Told me I can choose the octave or my riff. We'll see how I'm feeling tonight.

"But everything else? The work. The risk. The heart?" Julian taps his chest. "Worth it."

Someone reaches out. Then another. Arms loop around shoulders, hands grabbing backs, bodies pulling in close until we're one tight knot of sweat and nerves and love.

"Alright," Julian says, grinning. "You know how we do this."

He starts the chant low, rhythmic.

"One show."

We echo it back, voices layered.

"One heart."

Louder now.

"One family."

The words ripple through the circle, hands squeezing tighter, feet stomping in time. The rhythm builds, faster, fuller, until we explode in celebration. Laughter. Cheers. A few misty eyes.

I breathe it in.

This moment. This family.

***

The house is full tonight. I can feel it. The air backstage feels thicker, electric. Anticipation thumping like a steady heartbeat.

The audience hums beyond the curtain, restless and expectant. Some of them came to be moved. Some came to see if the rumors were true. Others probably hoping I'll crack so they can say they knew it all along.

I feel their eyes before they ever see me. The pressure to be flawless. Not just good. It presses against my ribs because, whether I like it or not, my past is still part of the story. This performance isn't just art. It's an answer. A final one. The sum of every sacrifice I made when no one was watching.

Years of study. Rejections that piled up so high I took my time opening emails. Motel rooms with flickering lamps and thin walls where I practiced scales under my breath. Late nights with Langston, my voice cracking, my pride bruised. Him pushing me again and again because he saw something in me that I was still afraid to claim.

The curtain breathes. The lights go up. Applause. The show begins.

Every moment leads here. Every lonely, stubborn, desperate moment.

My hands tremble at my sides. I press my palms together. Feel the soft thud of bass through the stage floor, the familiar pulse grounding me. My breath stutters, then catches. For one dangerous second, fear creeps in and whispers that I could still mess this up. That I could step out there and prove everyone right. That the dream was too big, too bold, too much for a girl like me.

If I fail now, it won't just be a bad night. It'll feel like confirmation.

Not just that I let Langston down. Or Julian. Or the cast and crew who wrapped me in their faith and dared me to rise. It'll feel like I let myself down.

If I step onstage now, I can't hide behind ambition or excuses or almosts. I can't pretend I'm still chasing the dream. I have to accept that I made it. That I'm here. That I deserve this life. This love. This applause.

"Ella... Ella!"

My stepmother's voice cuts through the dark, pulling me into place.

My cue. My moment.

I close my eyes for half a beat. Just long enough to thank the girl I was for not giving up.

Here goes nothing.

I step into the light.

EPILOGUE

The red carpet is a river tonight.

Flashbulbs pop like tiny fireworks, and the air tastes like perfume and nerves. Everything glitters. Everything moves. A sea of sequins and satin and smiles held just a little too tight. The kinda night people dream about when they're broke and telling themselves to keep going anyway.

And I'm here.

Not in the back. Not in the balcony. Not sneaking in on somebody's guest pass with my stomach hollow and my confidence taped together.

I'm here like I never had to borrow the invitation.

Langston's hand stays warm around mine as we step out of the limo. And even though he looks calm, I feel the truth in him. It's in the way his thumb rubs the side of my finger like he's keeping time. The way his shoulders are set, proud but braced, like he's ready for anything and still praying for one thing.

A photographer calls his name. Then mine.

"Jayana!" somebody shouts, and I almost flinch because my body still remembers when my name didn't mean a damn thing to nobody but the people who loved me. But I don't hide. I lift my chin. I give them the smile they came for.

I'm in a black sequined gown that catches the light. Hair laid. Skin glowing. Langston's in a tux that makes him look like he belongs behind glass. Just him. Handsome, composed, and dangerous in that quiet way.

We pause for photos, and I hear the whispers on the wind like they're part of the soundtrack.

That's her.

That's him.

That's the couple.

The couple.

I squeeze his hand once, and his gaze cuts to mine. He doesn't need to ask if I'm okay. He reads me like sheet music. But he asks anyway, because he knows I like to hear it.

"You good?" he murmurs.

"I'm good," I whisper back. "I'm just trying not to levitate."

His mouth twitches. "Don't levitate. They'll say it's a publicity stunt."

I snort. Then I catch myself.

No. Not catching myself.

I let the laugh live. I let it be heard. The cameras flash and gleam, catching every inch of my smile.

Inside, the theater is gold and velvet. It hums like live wire. A thousand people dressed like the night is a promise, and we're all about to find out if it keeps it.

A year of sold-out nights, standing ovations, and proving we belonged.

And finally, we're here.

We slide into our seats, and I take a second to let my eyes roam. I've been on stages. I've been in dressing rooms. I've been in places that smelled like sweat and hope and hairspray.

But this? This is the mountaintop.

And the thing about mountaintops is, the air is thin. You can feel yourself breathing. You can feel your heartbeat like it's your whole body.

Langston's leg bounces once, then stills. He catches himself, exhales slow. The camera glides past our row, and he turns his face into that calm mask he's mastered. Composer. Music Director. The man who never begs the world for anything.

But I know him.

I know the nights he didn't sleep. The nights he stared at the piano like it knew something he didn't. The nights he wanted to quit and didn't say it out loud because he didn't wanna disappoint himself.

I lean close, my lips near his ear. "You're allowed to want it," I whisper.

"Being here is enough," he says, like he's rehearsed it.

It isn't. I see it in the way he won't meet my eyes.

I smile anyway, close enough for him to feel it. He swallows.

"If it happens." He shrugs.

"It's gonna happen," I tell him, speaking prophecy into the room.

His hand finds mine again, and he holds on.

The show starts. The jokes land. The performances swell. Awards are handed out, claps rise and fall. People cry in their seats and pretend they aren't.

Ella: A Neo-Soul Musical is called early.

Best Choreography.

Best Costume Design.

Best Direction of a Musical.

Each time the name is spoken, my chest blooms with pride like it's my own bloodline being honored. Because in a way, it is.

That show almost died. It almost disappeared into the pile of what-ifs and almosts and could've beens. And now it's shining so bright it's hard to look at.

The host announces that the show will continue its Broadway run, and next season, a national tour will be announced. The audience cheers like they're cheering for a friend. Like they're cheering for survival.

Langston barely moves, but I feel the tremor in his hand. It's small. It's there.

Then the category comes.

Best Original Score.

And the air changes.

You can feel it in the way everybody leans forward. In the way the cameras sharpen their attention. In the way the nominees' smiles all look a little more fragile.

I breathe in. Out. In. My heart hammers my ribs like it needs to be free.

The presenter opens the envelope, and time holds its breath.

"And the Tony Award for *Best Original Score* goes to..."

My whole body stills.

"*Ella: A Neo-Soul Musical!* Music by Langston Washington!"

For half a second, the world goes silent. Because my brain can't process it.

Then the room erupts.

Applause. Cheers. The roar of a thousand people celebrating a dream that ain't come easy.

Langston's hand squeezes mine so hard it almost hurts. He turns to me and there's something on his face I've never seen before.

Relief. Raw, breaking relief.

His eyes shine as if he's trying not to cry and failing.

I laugh, breathless. "Go," I whisper. "Go get your award!"

He stands like he's being lifted. Like gravity isn't sure what to do with him anymore. He leans down and kisses me, quick, trembling and real. Then he walks to the stage. And the whole time he's walking, he keeps looking back at me like he's afraid he'll wake up.

I keep my eyes locked on his, holding the moment with him so it can't slip away.

"Wow," he says as he reaches the microphone, and the crowd laughs softly, giving him room to be human. "Okay. Um..."

He looks down at the award in his hands like it's heavy. Not in weight. In meaning.

"I've wanted this," he says, "for a long time. And for a while,

I thought wanting it made me selfish. Like dreaming that big was asking for something to take it away."

His gaze lifts and sweeps the room. And when it rests on me, it's like I'm the only person in the theater.

"But it turns out," he continues, voice thickening, "wanting it was just believing I had something worth giving."

My throat burns. Tears prickle hot and fast.

He shifts the award in his hands, clears his throat like he's trying to keep his composure.

"I need to thank Julian," he says, and there's a grin in his voice now. "Even though we've nearly killed each other about eight times. You're a madman. But you're my madman."

Laughter ripples through the room. Julian gives a soft, humored wave. I'm tempted to tell the people beside me I wrote that one. But this ain't my moment.

"I need to thank our amazing orchestra, cast, and crew," Langston continues, "for doing something impossible. For bringing heart, sweat, and brilliance into a story that demanded everything."

He pauses, and when he speaks again, his voice softens.

"And I need to thank the woman who saved our show."

I swallow. We didn't go over this part.

The room shifts as cameras turn on me. You can feel them lean toward the romance of it.

Langston looks right at me. No hiding or holding back.

"Jayana," he says, and my name in his mouth is a love song. "My fiancée."

The crowd reacts. A wave of delighted noise. The cameras swing toward me, and I can't even pretend to be cool. I flash my rock for all to see, like Beyoncé in her "Single Ladies" video.

Langston keeps going, eyes steady, voice breaking just a little.

"You were by my side," he says, "in one of the loneliest times of my life. When everything felt like it was falling apart. When I didn't believe in the music anymore. Like me, you knew what it cost to stay silent when everything in you wanted to scream."

His swallow is visible. His grip tightens on the award.

"And you showed up anyway," he says. "You sang anyway. You fought anyway. You didn't give up."

My chest aches. It's too much. It's everything.

"I'm standing here because of you," he says, voice low and sure. "I love you."

The room explodes again, but I barely hear it. Because my whole body is filled with one thing.

Being loved. For real. Out loud.

Later, after the press line and the handshakes and the noise, Langston's phone buzzes.

He pulls it out absentmindedly, like he's still floating. He glances down. Whatever he sees pulls him back to earth gently.

"What?" I whisper, searching his face.

He swallows hard, eyes flicking across the screen like he doesn't trust it. Then he turns the phone to me.

It's a text from his dad.

We're proud of you.

Langston laughs once, broken and disbelieving. He holds the phone to his chest like he's been waiting on that message longer than the award.

But both of us already know, he doesn't need it now.

He pulls me in tight, presses a kiss to my forehead. And I swear the whole room fades until it's just us.

———

LATER, AFTER THE CEREMONY, THE INTERVIEWS, THE CHAOS, we end up outside the theater where the city has turned into a glittering blur.

Fans cluster near the barricades, calling names, waving Playbills, holding up phones like they're trying to capture proof that tonight happened.

A girl, Keisha, fiddles with her sweater, eyes bright like she's holding her own dream as I sign her Playbill.

"I... I just... seeing you up there made me believe I could do this too."

My heart warms. Because that's the whole point, ain't it?

You can do it

I write with the fountain pen Langston gave me.

Don't let anybody tell you otherwise!

Then I sign my name. Not Alexia. Not Ella.

Jayana

The ink glides smooth, and it feels like closing a door and opening a new one at the same time.

"And I saw the trailer," Keisha blurts, like she's afraid she'll lose the nerve. "Your new film? I cannot wait to see it this fall. Me and my friends are going opening weekend. Like, we're dressing up."

I laugh, and it's full. Joyful. I don't rush past it.

Keisha gasps like I handed her gold as I pass the Playbill back. We take a selfie. We hug, quick and tight.

"This is a dream come true," she says, voice breaking.

Same for me.

I breathe a happy sigh as she rushes off. Then I turn and find the limo waiting at the curb, glossy and black, lights reflecting off its body like a polished obsidian mirror.

And there's Langston.

Leaning against the side like he's posing for a poster, relaxed. Eyes on me like the night doesn't exist unless I'm in it.

He straightens when I approach, looking me over slow, a quiet smile settling in as he opens the door.

"You ready?" he asks.

I glance back at the theater. The lights. The fans. The glittering city.

Then I look at him.

My fiancé. My composer. My love story written in real time.

"I'm ready," I say, and I mean it in every way.

Langston offers his hand, and I take it.

THE END

———

Want to see how Langston proposed?
Scan below to read the exclusive bonus chapter:

or visit:
dl.bookfunnel.com/s8gfj1ohwz

BOOK CLUB DISCUSSION GUIDE

GENERAL DISCUSSION QUESTIONS

1. What were your first impressions of Yana? How did your perception of her shift over the course of the story?

2. What were your first impressions of Langston? How did your perception of him shift over the course of the story?

3. How does the novel explore the tension between looking like you belong and believing you belong?

4. Langston challenges Yana both professionally and emotionally. How did their dynamic evolve from intimidation to intimacy?

5. Alexia's disappearance casts a long shadow over the production. How does that looming presence shape Yana's identity and choices?

6. The story includes moments of danger and vulnerability. How did those scenes impact your understanding of Yana's strength?

7. Both Yana and Langston use silence differently. How do those coping mechanisms protect them? How do they limit them?

8. At what point did you feel Yana began choosing herself rather than performing for approval?

IDENTITY & HEALING REFLECTION QUESTIONS

1. Have you ever felt like the understudy in your own life? What did that season teach you?
2. What parts of your identity have you had to reclaim after comparison, humiliation, or self-doubt?
3. How do you respond internally when you feel "almost enough" but not quite secure?
4. Have you ever used silence as a coping mechanism? Did it hinder or help?
5. What does belonging mean to you? Is it earned, granted, or claimed?

REFLECTIVE PROMPTS FOR DEEPER CONVERSATION

1. When was the last time you prepared for something no one else could see yet?
2. Have you ever stayed silent in a high-pressure environment when you should have spoken up? What held you back?
3. What is your version of deflection? Humor? Control? Withdrawal? Achievement?
4. What role does ambition play in your life? Does it energize you or intimidate you?
5. What dream are you still rehearsing for?

BONUS FUN

1. Dream Cast: Who would you cast as Yana and Langston in a screen adaptation?
2. Soundtrack Picks: What neo-soul songs belong on this musical's playlist?

3. Character Mirror: Which character's struggle felt closest to your own?
4. Post-Book Ritual: Do something bold this week that future-you would thank you for.

ACKNOWLEDGMENTS

Every book is a team effort, even when it begins alone at a keyboard.

First and always, to God. Thank You for the ability to create, for the endurance to finish what I start, and for grace in the seasons where the process felt heavier than the dream.

To my husband, Jaime. Thank you for holding it down while I chase stories. For the long talks, the late nights, and the steady love that makes the risk feel safe.

To Jonathan and Isabella, my greatest joys. Thank you for sharing Mommy with her characters and reminding me what really matters when the pages feel loud.

To Katharine. Thank you for protecting the heart of this story while pushing it deeper. Your notes sharpened Yana's voice, made Langston lovable, and strengthened the emotional spine of this book.

To Raquel. Thank you for your careful proofing eye. You catch the things I miss when I'm too close to the page. I'll forever be grateful for your encouragement, from before having an agent to choosing to do this thing on my own. You reminded me that true validation comes from within.

To Gowtham. Thank you for once again translating emotion into visual art. You get my vision, and you've helped me create a glamorous brand.

To my betas. Thank you for sitting with this story in its most vulnerable stages. For your honesty, insight, and care. You helped shape this book in ways others will never fully see, but I will always know.

To the rest of my readers, especially those who've been here since my debut. Thank you for trusting me with your time. Every message, every review, every quiet read matters more than you know.

And to the ones still chasing something that feels just out of reach... don't quit. You never know when destiny might pay a visit. Thank you for being here. 🖤

With all my heart,
Kimberly R. Vargas

ABOUT THE AUTHOR

PHOTOGRAPHY: LEO J. BROWN | LJB MEDIA

Kimberly R. Vargas is a contemporary romance and women's fiction author who writes emotionally layered love stories about ambition, healing, and women who refuse to disappear.

She's the creator of *The Next Chapter*, where she writes, reads, and champions indie Black romance, spotlighting bold storytellers and the readers who adore them. Her work centers women of color navigating love, identity, and high-stakes dreams in glamorous, high-pressure worlds.

When she's not drafting messy love stories or promoting indie romance, she can be found struggling to hit a Mariah Carey octave or dancing in her basement. She lives in Michigan with her husband, two children, and a very spoiled dog.

BEFORE YOU GO...

If this story moved you, the best way to support my work is to leave a review on **Amazon** or **Goodreads**.

AMAZON

GOODREADS

Your words help other readers discover the book and truly make a difference for independent authors like me.

Stay connected for bonus chapters, updates,
and indie romance recs at:
www.kimberlyrvargas.com

Come hang with me on IG, TikTok, and Threads:
@kvargasauthor

9 798999 519825